Dear Romance R[illegible]

This year Avon [illegible]
anniversary of "[illegible] [illegible]ars
of historical romances of the highest quality by
both new and established writers. Thanks to our terrific authors, our "ribbon books" are stronger and more exciting than ever before. And thanks to you, our loyal readers, our books continue to be a spectacular success!

"The Avon Romances" are just some of the fabulous novels in Avon Books' dazzling *Year of Romance,* bringing you month after month of top-notch romantic entertainment. How wonderful it is to escape for a few hours with romances by your favorite "leading ladies"—Shirlee Busbee, Karen Robards, and Johanna Lindsey. And how satisfying it is to discover in a new writer the talent that will make her a rising star.

Every month in 1988, Avon Books' *Year of Romance,* will be special because Avon Books believes that romance—the readers, the writers, and the books—deserves it!

Sweet Reading,

Susanne Jaffe
Editor-in-Chief

Ellen Edwards
Senior Editor

Other Books in
THE AVON ROMANCE Series

DARK DESIRES *by Nancy Moulton*
DREAMSONG *by Linda Ladd*
FORBIDDEN FIRES *by Elizabeth Turner*
INNOCENT FIRE *by Brenda Joyce*
MATTERS OF THE HEART *by Mayo Lucas*
PASSION STAR *by Mallory Burgess*
PRIMROSE *by Deborah Camp*

Coming Soon

HEART'S FOLLY *by Jane Feather*
TEMPTATION'S DARLING *by Joanna Jordan*

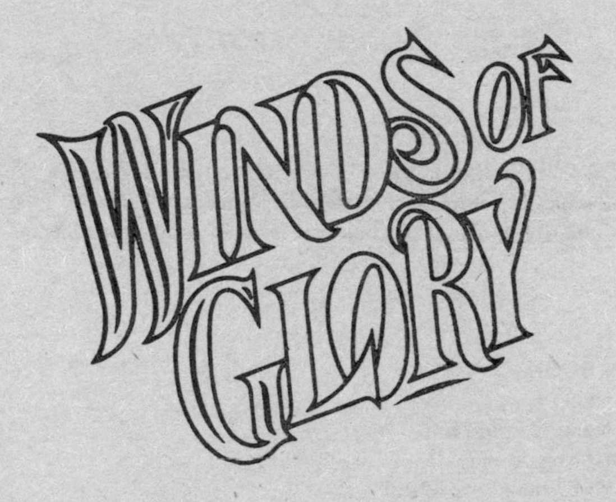

SUSAN WIGGS

AVON BOOKS NEW YORK

WINDS OF GLORY is an original publication of Avon Books. This work has never before appeared in book form. This work is a novel. Any similarity to actual persons or events is purely coincidental.

AVON BOOKS
A division of
The Hearst Corporation
105 Madison Avenue
New York, New York 10016

Published by arrangement with the author
Library of Congress Catalog Card Number: 88-91499
ISBN: 0-380-75482-7

First Avon Books Printing: August 1988

Printed in the U.S.A.

K-R 10 9 8 7 6 5 4 3 2 1

For Jim and Charlotte Wiggs,
with love

Acknowledgments

My thanks to:

The Preservation Society of Newport County,
Alberta Lloyd-Evans
and
Joyce Bell, Alice Borchardt, Arnette Lamb,
and Barbara Dawson Smith

Her modest looks the cottage might adorn,
Sweet as the primrose peeps beneath the thorn.
—Oliver Goldsmith

Prologue

Fort George, Rhode Island
9 December 1774

The musket ball entered Ashton Markham's body at an angle, ripping through the flesh of his left side and fortunately missing his vitals before lodging itself into the dry wooden planks of the ordnance house behind him.

As he was slammed against the side of the building and sank down into a snowdrift, Ashton found himself thinking—inasmuch as he was able to think—that the heat of the lead ball was the first warmth he'd felt in weeks. There was something oddly comforting in that, and in the soft winter silence that followed the single report. He heard his own breathing—ragged, labored—and saw a wisp of steam rising as his blood crept down into a cushion of new snow. He smelled the blood and the clean scent of the snow and the acrid burn of the powder that blackened the hole in his red woolen frock coat.

A strange whir began in Ashton's head as he looked away from his wounds and gazed out across the gentle, rounded snowscape of Goat Island, where as a lad he'd gone to the turtle races; they feted the winners and ate the losers.

Moonlight, white and shimmering, silvered the area surrounding the fort and carved deep shadows in the drifts. It was a scene of quiet beauty, one that, had he been free to do so, would have sent him galloping across the island on Corsair, his favorite mount. But Ashton hadn't been free to ride since the British army had claimed him with a shilling and a pledge four years earlier. And now, any movement at all was out of the question. He'd never felt so light, so groundless.

He blinked his eyes. The moon-dusted scene before him shimmered and quaked and lost form. In its place came other fragmented images, crowding into his mind. He saw his father and their cottage on the estate called Seastone, the huge stable of blooded horses they oversaw together, the summer races and autumn hunts. God, had life ever been so simple?

Ashton grimaced at the pulsating pain in his side. Life had been uncomplicated, even sweet, back then. Each day had slid effortlessly into the next. He trained horses, he raced, he won. Closing his eyes, he remembered the feel of a swift mount's sinews beneath him and the bite of the sea air on his face.

He hadn't thought about that other life in a long time. Not since the summons had come, calling him to serve in King George's army. He felt the corners of his mouth lift in a self-deprecating smile. He'd made a poor soldier, having no taste for endless drills, marching through Rhode Island's marshy wilderness executing pointless maneuvers. . . . But most of all Ashton had never been able to put his heart into subjugating the gathering storm of rebellion in the Colonies.

He tried to summon rage at the patriot who'd shot him, some unseen sniper lurking in the woods, trying to raid the ordnance house. But it was hard to feel anger when he felt as light and insubstantial as the snowflakes that winked and sparkled in the moonlight, dancing before his eyes until he had to close them against the brightness.

Above the vague whirring in his head Ashton heard a shout. Then another. And then footfalls thudding, cushioned by the snow. Dragging his leaden eyelids open, he saw torches bobbing across the compound. In seconds a circle of faces surrounded him.

"Markham? Markham!" That was Sergeant Mansfield, his cockney accent thickened by drink. "Hold that torch higher, private. Christ, he's been hit!"

Ashton felt himself being lifted onto a litter, heard exclamations of concern and angry oaths directed at the patriot sniper. He was borne away to the infirmary, only vaguely aware that a detachment of soldiers had been sent out to comb the woods.

A lantern hung overhead, and the surgeon, roused from his sleep, peeled Ashton's frock coat away. He hissed, drawing in his breath at what he saw.

" 'Tis bad," he muttered, grabbing a pile of linens. "Though not mortal." He lifted Ashton's head, offering a bottle of rum. "Hell of a way to get yourself discharged, Private Markham."

Discharged . . . Ashton felt himself begin to smile, and a warm feeling spread through him.

The patriot in the woods—God bless his rebel hide—had set him free.

Chapter 1

Newport, Rhode Island
May 1775

"Get your head inside the coach, miss," Carrie Markham said irritably. "You'll lose that bonnet I spent hours trimming."

Too excited for caution, Bethany Winslow ignored her maid's admonition and leaned farther out the window for her first glimpse of home in four years. Like the great rocks brooding upon the cliffs of Aquidneck Island, Seastone hadn't changed since she'd left for the Primrose Academy in New York at the age of fourteen.

The wide avenue leading up to the house was lined by budding larches laden with tiny cones and yellow with pollen. Box hedge, with its ever-present dry, pungent aroma, edged the massive stone house and wound through gardens graced by a springtime array of flowers. The huge gambrel-roofed building sat in quiet splendor amid a crowding abundance, a fullness of leaf, bud, and blossom.

"We're home, Carrie," Bethany said over her shoulder, hat ribbons and honey-gold hair flying in the wind. "Lord, but I've missed Seastone. I was happy enough in New York, but this is where I belong."

"Hmph." Carrie tossed her bright red ringlets and settled back on the bench across from her young mistress. "I much prefer New York. The gentlemen are so much more sophisticated there, and I didn't have Ashton and my father questioning my every move."

Bethany refrained from suggesting that perhaps Carrie

did need someone to watch over her. In New York the pretty young woman had managed to get herself into several romantic scrapes, some of them quite serious. But Bethany was too pleased at the moment to argue the virtues of New York and Newport with Carrie. She was home, and nothing could detract from her delight.

By the time the coach rolled up on the pebbled front drive, Bethany could barely contain herself. Ignoring another admonition from Carrie, she burst from the coach and hit the drive running. Her feet flew beneath her full yellow skirts as she mounted the wide stone staircase and opened the door to the foyer.

Familiar odors, the smells of home, wafted to her: the clean scent of verbena-polished woodwork, the aroma of fresh bread from the bake house, the faint tinge of the pomade her mother used on her absurdly lofty hairstyles. . . .

Bethany's tread on the parquet floor alerted Mrs. Hastings, the housekeeper, who had been fussing at a plant stand near the library door.

"Miss Bethany!" the woman exclaimed, straightening her mobcap and coming forward to enfold Bethany in her plump arms. "You're home at last! And look at you! Who would have thought our gawky colt who left Seastone four years ago could've become such a beauty. Turn around, child, and let me look at you!"

Smiling at the effusive greeting, Bethany complied, sketching a graceful turn. " 'Tis grand to see you again, Mrs. Hastings. Where is everyone?"

The housekeeper's grin sagged and she flushed, wiping her hands on her apron. "The library, miss. But—"

Bethany ran to the door, not of a mind to scold Mrs. Hastings for her life-long habit of nosiness. A loud metallic crash sounded from within and Bethany paused, hand closed over the polished brass knob. Her father's loud, cultured voice rose up in anger.

". . . never countenance this sort of dissention under my own roof!" Sinclair Winslow blustered. "By God, Harry, you're an Englishman, do you hear? I won't have you speaking treason against your king. I am shocked that you deem the rabble-rousers at Lexington Green worthy of your support.''

Harry's muttered reply was followed by the sound of a blow. Bethany's heart lurched at the noise of flesh cracking against flesh.

''This time you've gone too far, boy. Just look at your mother, barely able to raise her head for the shame of it. 'Twas bad enough, your taking up with that popish trash last month, parading her at our Junto reception like she was our equal. And now this—this talk of grievances against our king, waving Otis's scurvy pamphlet in my face—''

Bethany pushed the door open and stepped into the library, her hand at her bosom as if to still her pounding heart. Her eyes focused briefly on a hand-wrought iron fire back bearing the arms of King George III. The piece lay facedown in the grate. The people in the room fell silent as her troubled eyes swept the scene.

Lillian, her mother, sat in a Townsend armchair, wringing a dainty handkerchief and pressing it carefully to her powdered cheeks. Behind her stood William, Bethany's eldest brother, patting his mother's shoulder with one hand while swirling a cup of Jamaica water in the other. Harry and Sinclair were paired off in front of the great stone mantel, the father flushed and glowering, the son grim and defiant. The livid imprint of Sinclair's hand blossomed on Harry's cheek. Like an untimely shadow, dismay eclipsed Bethany's delight at coming home.

William, less handsome and more ambivalent than Bethany remembered, seemed to come to himself first. He rounded his mother's chair and approached Bethany, arms outstretched. Unsmiling, she went to him, smelling the rum on his breath. Then she kissed her parents, each in turn. They greeted her stiffly, still not recovered from the row.

Finally Bethany turned to her twin brother. From birth their spirits had been linked in an almost mystical way. They knew each other as thoroughly as a person knows his image in a looking glass. More often than not each was aware of the other's thoughts and feelings.

And Harry was in pain. Bethany stared into the depths

of his eyes—hazel flecked with tawny gold, like her own—and read a deep inner turmoil that caused her insides to twist in sympathy.

"What is it, Harry?" she asked softly, taking his hands.

"I'm sorry to spoil your homecoming like this, Bethany. I've been sent down from Rhode Island College."

"Among other things," Sinclair grumbled.

Harry directed a look of unconcealed loathing at the iron fire screen. "Aye," he said with soft defiance. "Among other things." He led Bethany to the library door. "Let's go out into the garden, where we can talk."

"Just a minute, you young whelp! We've not settled anything—"

"Yes we have, sir," Harry snapped, his eyes narrowing. "I think the conclusion of this discussion is clear. You'll not tolerate my views or the woman I love, and I'll not allow myself to be bullied by you. I shall leave. As soon as I've spoken with Bethany."

Dumbfounded, she stumbled along behind him. He didn't speak as he hurried down the narrow path to the summerhouse, passing a bench of straw beehives and, farther on, their mother's dovecotes. Bethany was holding her side by the time they reached the summerhouse. The small, decorative building sat upon a rise, overlooking the craggy shores of Aquidneck Island to the east and the spires of Newport to the south.

Bethany sat upon a bench, facing the restless waters of Narragansett Bay through an unglazed window. She glanced over at her brother and caught his frank perusal of her yellow lutestring gown with its dainty ruchings and lace.

"You've changed," he said, a shadow of his familiar gamin smile flickering across his face. "You used to be a skinny little hoyden with bare feet and burrs in her hair."

Bethany looked offended. "I?" she asked. "A hoyden?"

"Come now, don't tell me you've forgotten all our old escape routes from the schoolroom, the scores of places we used to hide from governesses and tutors. Admit it, Bethany, you were more at home riding the grassy fields of Aquidneck than in some stuffy parlor listening to the pianoforte or following the stilted steps of the dancing master.''

She grinned at the recollection of the prissy Sylvester Fine. ''Miss Abigail Primrose tamed me a little,'' she allowed. ''Although in her own way she made me wilder than ever.''

Harry raised an eyebrow. ''So the rumors are true, then. The needy gentlewoman recently over from England is not so proper after all.''

'' 'Precocious' is more the word for it. She had us reading Locke and Trenchard and excused us from lessons in needlework and deportment whenever possible.'' Bethany felt a wave of gratitude for her teacher. ''Polite accomplishments were never my forte. But you mustn't say anything, Harry. Miss Abigail depends on her academy's reputation. She'd be ruined if people knew she introduced her students to the radical dissenters like Gordon and Cato.''

Her brother looked suitably impressed. ''I'm glad you took your schooling there. You've too fine a mind to waste on petit point and parlor games, mincing empty words with society matrons.''

Complimented, Bethany took his hand. It was so like her own: slender, long-fingered, the oval nails well shaped. ''I think you'd best tell me what brought about the row.''

His smile faded. '' 'Twas more than a row, Bethany.'' He raked a hand through his hair. ''It all started last year when I brought Felicia home to meet Father and Mother.''

''You wrote me about Felicia. She sounds lovely.''

His expression softened and he looked a bit like the little boy he had once been, sweetness mingling nicely with mischievousness. ''She's more than lovely, Bethany. She's kind and bright and . . . she's everything to me. At first our parents were civil enough, thinking me too young to know my own mind, but they soon realized I'm serious about Felicia. I mean to marry her.'' He glowered down at the waves rising up to explode against the rocks far below. ''I wanted to give her everything she's lacked all her life, but it seems I'm to be cut off. Father's promised I won't have so much as a shilling once we're wed.''

''But, Harry—why?''

"She's Catholic, the daughter of a baker in Providence, and a few years older than I."

Bethany spent a pleasant moment considering the novel idea that her brother was in love. Then she turned her thoughts to the less pleasant situation with her parents. "What's this about your being sent down?"

"I burned a ship."

"You *what?*"

"There was a British ship, the *Antonia,* in the harbor. She was stationed there solely to harass American traders. One night my mates and I got to drinking a bit too much at the Old Sabin Inn and decided to rid the harbor of the *Antonia.* We rowed out and set her afire. The crew escaped unharmed, but the vessel was burned to the waterline."

"Dear God, Harry. How could you—"

He waved a hand to silence her. "Do you remember Sykes, my valet? Seems he found my boots and some clothing soaked with seawater and presented the evidence to the provost. I could have been tried for treason, but the college officials didn't want to create a scandal. So I was merely sent down. Needless to say, Sykes—the bloody traitor—isn't with me anymore."

"Oh, Harry—"

"Don't start in on me, Bethany. 'Twas a foolish thing I did. But I'm sick to death of British harassment. We're American, by God!" he swore vehemently.

"You talk of your countrymen—of *yourself*—as if they were the enemy."

"They could well be, if England continues this betrayal of her own colonies."

Bethany shook her head. Harry had always been impetuous and quick to anger; she could well imagine his involvement in the burning of the *Antonia.*

"My brother, the rebel," she said softly, and took his hand in hers.

"Aye. Does it shock you?"

"Not really. But it saddens me, Harry. I must agree with one thing Father said. You're an Englishman. No matter what you or Sam Adams or James Otis or any of the malcontents in Boston say, you are an Englishman."

"England's done me no favors. Bethany, you of all people should understand. Like you, I've grown up, I've changed. I have a mind of my own. Father can't accept that, nor will he consent to my marrying Felicia, so I must go."

"Harry—"

"There's no other solution, Bethany."

"But what will you do?"

"Marry Felicia, of course. We'll live in Bristol, where I've been offered a position with a man named Hodgekiss, who owns a shipping concern. I'll be keeping his books and such. Don't look at me so, Bethany; I shall be fine. And you must visit us once we're settled."

Together they stood and held each other briefly. Bethany swallowed to loosen the tightness in her throat. "I'll come; you know I will," she said softly, blinking tears from her eyes.

Harry lifted a strand of hair from her cheek, where the breeze had blown it. Tucking the deep golden lock behind her ear, he smiled. He had a sweet, wistful smile. In childhood Bethany had always been the bold one, the one to comfort Harry when trouble arose. Could he manage on his own? Perhaps so, for in the resolute depths of his gold-flecked eyes she saw the courage of his convictions.

Her tears spilled while she watched him go, his tall, slender form framed by Persian lilacs bending over the path. She heard him call to a servant to get his things together.

This was hardly the homecoming she'd envisioned while on the boat from New York. Instead of a happy reunion, she'd found her mother in tears, Harry and her father hurling angry words, William unsteady with drink. Enveloped by a feeling of loss, Bethany did what she'd always done when a shadow dropped over her life.

Lifting her skirts, she ran through the winding garden paths to the stables, a half mile distant.

Ashton Markham's currycomb scraped over the gleaming coat of a tall Thoroughbred. The stallion's midnight color was as rare as his fleetness on the racing green. As head stockman, Ashton could have left the task to one of the grooms, but he couldn't seem to do enough for this beast.

Corsair was the finest animal ever bred in the stables, the triumphant culmination of all the years Ashton and his father had been breeding horses for Sinclair Winslow. Every trait was carefully selected, from the clean, sharp lines of the large head and proudly arching neck to the elusive and highly valued quality known as heart. His fiery temperament perfectly matched Ashton's ambitions for him.

The currycomb moved restlessly under Ashton's hand, and suddenly his pleasure in the task was eclipsed by an overwhelming sense of futility. He was master of this horse in every way but the one that truly counted.

Corsair didn't belong to him.

All that Ashton did at Seastone was for Sinclair Winslow. Admittedly, the man paid him decently, but it grated on Ashton's pride to work for someone else. He wanted neither other men nor laws to tell him what to do.

Ashton was a man to whom the fates had been capricious. With the eye of an artist, he could detect beauty and promise in a horse, sometimes seeing those qualities while others were blind to them. Yet Ashton was poor, and such horses were dear. He had a gentleman's education and a scholar's mind. But aside from his father, he rarely conversed at length with anyone more erudite than a stable groom. And, hidden beneath the layers of a somewhat dispassionate and practical nature, Ashton had a heart that protested his lonely existence and a mind that cried out for companionship.

He was shackled to the Winslows by responsibility to his ailing father, not resentful of the burden but feeling its weight nonetheless. Roger Markham was seriously ill; Ashton had no choice but to carry on the work for him, despite an inability to understand his father's loyalty to Sinclair Winslow.

Thrusting aside the feeling of restlessness, Ashton turned his attention back to the stallion.

"You'll win every major race of the season, my friend," he said, setting a pail of mash before the horse. " 'Twas a lucky turn I was discharged in time to jockey you to vict—"

The wide double doors of the stables burst open, bright sunlight streaming into the corridor between the stalls.

Just as Ashton straightened, a yellow-and-lace-clad form hurled itself into his arms, sobs muffling against his chest.

Unthinking, Ashton brought his hand up to stroke the waves of thick, honey-colored hair. A subtle fragrance of jasmine wafted from the soft, shuddering form. A few seconds passed before he became aware of just who it was he held in his arms.

"*Bethany* . . . you're home! What's wrong, pet?"

But Bethany wasn't ready to speak. While she cried as though her heart were breaking, Ashton's memory stirred. He recalled her as a tall, skinny girl with features too large and vivid to be considered pretty. She'd been a precocious, sometimes bothersome child who was never quite proper enough to suit her demanding mother. Then, as now, she had run to him when she was troubled.

Years ago a broken toy or a stubborn pony reduced her to tears. Feeling the yielding softness of a woman's body now, Ashton suspected the trouble was something much more serious. Placing his fingers beneath her chin, he tilted her head upward and, stunned, found himself gazing at the most beautiful face he'd ever beheld.

High cheekbones, full lips, an adorable little nose, and huge amber eyes skirted by dark, curling lashes combined in unlikely but irresistible harmony. Bethany had truly blossomed.

Hiding his amazement, Ashton found a handkerchief in her sleeve and gently dried the tears from her cheeks.

"It's Harry," she said brokenly. Even her voice had changed: soft-pitched, low, and musical. "He and Father had a terrible row and he's leaving."

Ashton frowned. "I'd heard the servants' gossip, but I didn't realize the trouble had gone so far."

"Ashton, I don't want him to go. He plans to marry and labor as a clerk in Bristol. He's giving up everything, all for the sake of a woman and—and some foolish notion about fighting the British!"

He grinned. "I'm surprised at you, love. Most young ladies would find such a notion romantic."

"I simply don't understand. Ashton, is it possible for a person to love someone so much he'd turn his back on his family?"

"I can't answer that, Bethany. But it sounds like Harry already has." Ashton paused. He knew Harry. The youth was fiery and passionate, never one to let common sense interfere with his convictions. "I know you two are close and you'll miss him, pet, but let him go," he said. "His mind is made up."

She nodded. "I suppose I'm only being selfish." She caught her lower lip in her teeth as if to stave off more tears. Then she managed a weak smile. Once again Ashton was struck by her beauty. God, but she was a rare one. What was she now, eighteen? The transformation four years of absence had wrought was staggering.

Somewhat cynically he told himself he shouldn't be surprised. Bethany was a Winslow, after all, a member of one of the oldest families in Newport, as carefully bred as one of Sinclair's prize fillies. And, like one of the Thoroughbreds or smooth-stepping pacers in the nearby stalls, she was being groomed, trained, and exercised for a very specific purpose: to marry, and marry exceedingly well.

Some of that breeding showed as she dashed away the last of her tears and smoothed her shining hair back with an unconsciously graceful gesture.

"You must think me as impetuous as ever," she said with a self-deprecating smile. "Hurling myself at you as if I'd not been gone all of four years."

"I'd be offended if you behaved any other way, pet. I'd like to think our friendship hasn't changed." He eyed the fascinating new curves and swells of her body. "But you've changed a great deal."

"So Harry has told me." She looked puzzled. "But I don't feel any different." Brows knit quizzically, she tapped a delicate finger on her chin and glanced down at herself. "I've grown larger, perhaps," she ventured innocently.

"In the most intriguing places," he supplied with a grin, pulling her closer. The jasmine scent, dangerously enticing, nearly made his head swim.

A delightful blush stained her cheeks. "And smarter, in Miss Abigail's opinion."

"You were always smart, pet," he assured her, dropping a friendly kiss on her nose. "Most objectionably so."

"Well, I *am* more accomplished." Her chin tilted

proudly, and her topaz gaze had a startling impact on Ashton. "I've learned French and geometry and can argue philosophy with the scholars," she finished primly.

Ashton experienced an odd wave of depression. Admirable qualities, indeed, but how would they serve a young woman destined to become a rich man's parlor ornament?

Shrugging off the thought, he gave her a final reassuring squeeze before letting her go. "Welcome home, Bethany," he said.

She felt an odd stirring at the rich timbre of his voice, imbued by a distinct Kentish accent. Ashton Markham had always fascinated her. He'd been a serious youth, hardworking, although he had always managed to spare a moment for a little girl who, Bethany now admitted, must have been a singularly annoying child.

Ashton had bypassed all the gawky stages of adolescence, growing with maddening ease into this tall man with magnificent deep chestnut hair pulled carelessly into a queue at his nape. He had steady eyes, the blue of a wind-tossed sea, and rugged, sun-bronzed features alight with humor and a touching tenderness. Bethany wondered why she'd never noticed the endearing cleft in his chin or the contained strength of his large, squarish hands. Catching herself staring at him, she flushed.

"Thank you. 'Tis good to be home . . . I think."

"Is Carrie with you?"

"Of course. Oh, Ashton, do forgive me. I was so wrapped up in my own problems that I completely forgot you haven't seen your sister yet!"

"She'll keep," Ashton said dispassionately. Carrie, five years his junior, was a grasping young thing who thought the world began and ended with herself. At the moment she was probably disturbing their father's afternoon rest, wheedling halfpence out of him to buy a new ribbon or bauble in town. For the time being, Ashton was content to stay where he was, trying to get used to the idea that Bethany Winslow had become a woman of heart-stopping beauty.

"Who would've thought Miss Primrose would turn my gawky little filly into a consummate young lady?" he mused aloud.

"Gawky! Ashton Markham, I was never gawky."

He ambled over to a tack box and seated himself on it, stretching his long legs out before him and crossing his booted feet at the ankles. His gaze moved over her in amused appraisal. "Sure you were, love. Legs and feet always too long and too fast for the rest of you." His eyes warmed in frank admiration of her bosom and narrow waist. "But don't take offense, love. The rest of you seems to have caught up quite nicely."

Once again Bethany felt herself blush. It was odd and not entirely agreeable to feel uncomfortable around a person who had been her friend for years. But there was no denying the subtle tension that thrummed between them now. Studying the deep ocean blue of Ashton's smiling eyes, she realized they were no longer childhood playmates. She felt suddenly wistful, wishing there were some way to recapture the easy camaraderie they'd once shared.

"Corsair is looking fine and fit," she commented mildly, grasping at a neutral topic.

Ashton's face glowed with pride, and he gazed at the horse with almost fatherly fondness. "I'd lay a wager his qualities equal those of his great-grandsire, Byerly Turk." Ashton fitted two fingers into the corners of his mouth and whistled, a high, sharp note followed by a longer, lower tone. Corsair's ears pricked forward, and an impatient whinny shimmered from him.

Bethany felt a surge of admiration for the horse—and for the man who'd trained him. "I'm impressed," she said.

"That whistle's never failed me yet. The stallion comes to it every time, without hesitation."

"Have you raced him yet this season?"

Ashton shook his head and looked chagrined. "Corsair may be fine and fit, but I haven't been. I've only recently recovered from an . . . injury."

Guilt suffused her. "What a goose I am," she said. "I haven't even asked about you." She took his hand in hers, feeling a delicious inner ripple at the texture of his large, blunt fingers. "How were you injured, Ashton?"

He shrugged. "I was shot."

"Shot! Dear Lord, by whom?"

"By a patriot, in the ordnance raid on Fort George."

Anger flared within her. "The bloody patriots again. Who are these scoundrels?"

He grinned. "Oh, farmers and tradesmen. Preachers, men of letters. Your neighbors, pet."

"How can you smile about it?" she demanded. "You could have been killed!"

"I was dying a slow death in the army anyway," he said breezily.

A sudden fear seized her. "Ashton, you're not . . . like Harry, are you? You don't mean to fight the British?"

He shook his head. "I don't mean to fight anyone, Bethany. I don't believe in killing."

Relieved, she absently stroked his hand. It was true; Ashton had always been one to nurse a bird with a broken wing or set Harry's collected butterflies free before they died. The recollection made her want to stroke Ashton's tanned cheek and murmur something foolish to him.

"I'd best get back to my parents," she said softly, resisting the temptation.

Ashton nodded. "And I to my chores."

She went to the door, then turned back. "Will you ride with me sometime? Like we used to do?"

His eyes swept over her one last time. "Nothing is as it used to be. But yes, pet, I'll take you riding."

"Good Lord, but you've become stodgy for a young man of twenty-five, Ashton," Carrie Markham said in irritation. " 'Tis not as if I haven't earned a bit of fun after waiting on Bethany all day."

He glowered at his sister and picked up the supper utensils from the table, taking care not to wake his ailing father, who was napping in a chair, his breeders' journals strewn over his lap.

"Hector Northbridge is twice your age, Carrie, and crippled by gout. What interest could you possibly have in him?"

She laughed and stretched in her slow, catlike way. "Don't be naïve, Ashton. Why should Hector's age bother me when he gives me everything I want?" She brushed back her sleeve to reveal a bracelet of gold and garnets. "Pretty, isn't it, Ashton?" she inquired, dangling her hand before him.

Her brother turned away in irritation and began washing

up. He addressed his sister over his shoulder. "If you've no regard for your own reputation, at least think of Father. He didn't raise you to be a rich man's plaything."

Carrie sniffed and regarded her sleeping father with distaste. "What has he ever given me that I should behave for his sake?" She gestured around the small cottage. "A drafty hovel with a puncheon floor, the life of a servant."

"You've a good enough room in the big house and an easy job as Bethany's maid."

"No thanks to him," she retorted, jerking her head at Roger.

"He's done his best for us, Carrie."

She narrowed her eyes. "For you, perhaps, Ashton. He spent practically every shilling he earned sending you to Rhode Island College. You had a gentleman's education while I was made to wait on that worthless Winslow girl." She glanced again at Roger, her face pinched tight with resentment. "Fat lot of good your fancy education's done you. You're still mucking out Sinclair Winslow's stables."

Ashton clamped his jaw shut to stifle a retort. What Carrie said was damnably true, but he refused to give in to resentment. Until Roger's health improved, he was forced to remain at Seastone in another man's employ.

"Where are you going?" he demanded as Carrie moved toward the door.

She tossed her head proudly, spilling bright red curls down her back. She was a pretty woman, but her looks had a hard edge of bitterness and greed which lessened the effect of her lovely face and figure.

"I'm going into town. Any objections?"

"Chapin Piper has been wanting to welcome you back from New York."

"That settles it, then. I want to be well away from here when Chapin arrives. For God's sake, Ashton, the man's a printer's son—a pauper."

"I'd sooner see you stepping out with an honest pauper than being dandled on the knee of an elderly libertine."

Carrie sniffed. "Well, I'd appreciate it if you'd discourage Chapin from trying to see me in the future."

"I'm sure you won't need me for that, Carrie. You'll chase the man off most expediently by yourself."

* * *

By the end of her first week home, Bethany felt distinctly depressed. It was as if Harry Winslow had never existed. When she mentioned her brother to her parents, she was immediately cut off, the subject turned. And so she missed him privately, feeling as if some vital part of herself was lacking.

Although Harry wouldn't have been able to help Bethany escape her mother's dreary social gatherings, at least his presence would have made them bearable; he'd never stand for all the boring talk and overblown posturing. Today there would be no Harry to create a charming distraction while his sister loosed a mouse beneath the voluminous skirts of Viola Pierce, no impish lad chucking bombshell acorns into the parlor fire. . . . This afternoon Bethany had to brave the social niceties alone.

"There now, don't be puckering your brow like that," Carrie Markham said as Bethany scowled into her looking glass. The maid fetched a gold-worked muslin tea gown from the armoire. "No young man is going to notice you if you don't go down there with a smile on your face."

"That's just it, Carrie. I don't feel like smiling. It galls me that Mother parades me before every faintly eligible man in Newport."

" 'Tis only that Mistress Lillian cares about you enough to want you to marry well."

"I'm afraid my mother and I have very different ideas about what it is to marry well. Her only requirements are a fortune and decent social standing."

"What else is there?" Carrie asked, spreading her hands. "Me, I'd just settle for the money, never mind bloodlines."

Bethany turned while Carrie tied a tiffany sash about her slender waist. She recalled a conversation she'd had with Abigail Primrose in her last year at school. Miss Abigail's views on marriage were charmingly unconventional. The lady believed that the union should be founded on a deep, abiding love, regardless of fortune or breeding.

"Not I, Carrie," Bethany said pensively, staring out the window at a patch of foxglove in bloom, freckled pink and white. "I'd like to find some reason other than money and position to spend the rest of my life with a man."

"Nonsense," Carrie retorted, artfully twisting Bethany's shimmering waves and pinning them into side-coils. "You only say that because you've never done without."

Bethany shook her head; they'd had the argument before. Carrie was convinced that money was the key to all happiness. Perhaps it was, for Carrie. And perhaps she'd achieve her goal one day. She was pretty and bright and talkative; she handled men as skillfully as a jockey handled racehorses.

"Will you be needing me this afternoon?" Carrie asked as she tugged at a fold in the full gown.

Bethany shook her head. She gave Carrie her freedom whenever possible. The maid led a reckless life, consorting with whatever gentleman was willing to entertain her in style. In New York, only Miss Abigail's boundless tolerance had kept Carrie from being dismissed from Bethany's service for her escapades.

"You're free to go find your fortune, Carrie," she said with a wave of her hand. "I only wish I had as clear an idea of what *I* want."

Fixing a stiff smile on her face, Bethany descended to the foyer. As she stepped down the wide hardwood staircase, she marveled at the perfection of her mother's preparations. The woodwork gleamed from years of meticulous polishing; fresh flowers in pastel hues bloomed from costly vases of crystal and colored Sèvres porcelain. Every detail, from the freshly beaten Turkey carpets to the winking facets of the chandelier above the entranceway, had been arranged to impressive advantage.

Beneath the vaulted beams of the foyer, Lillian Winslow greeted her guests. Her formal smile never wavered, and her voice was rich with culture as she spoke empty words.

Although Bethany admired her mother's skill in orchestrating a social affair with such apparent ease, she couldn't help but feel a bit sorry for Lillian. The woman's life was consumed by doing things properly. Her every thought and action upheld the unwritten laws of propriety, from her daily appearance at precisely eleven—meticulously gowned and pomaded—until she retired with her coiffure wrapped, hands creamed and gloved.

Lillian offered her fingers to Hugo Pierce, holding her head slightly to one side, just so. Bethany wondered if her mother had ever done a spontaneous thing in her life.

"Miss Bethany!" She felt her hand gripped and raised to a pair of masculine lips.

"Hello, Mr. Cranwick," she murmured, extracting her fingers from his after pausing just long enough not to seem rude.

"My dear, I can't bear such formality. Please call me Keith."

"Of course. 'Tis good to see you again, Keith." Bethany struggled to keep a note of cynicism from her reply. It was amazing the effect a woman's few extra curves had on a man. Years ago, Keith Cranwick had been one of her chief tormentors, taking snide pleasure in informing her governess that she had sneaked out of church or that she'd glued Master Fine's shoes to the floor during dancing lessons. But Keith seemed to have forgotten those childish pranks. He fairly simpered as he admired her gown and the topaz teardrop at her throat. Bethany excused herself and went into the drawing room, which was jammed to the walls with Newport's perfumed and pomaded elite.

A dazzle of silks and satins moved about the room. The occasional flash of a scarlet coat and a burnished gorget betrayed the presence of British officers, who had recently joined the Quality. Bethany wasn't entirely certain she welcomed the newcomers.

At the punch bowl she spied Godfrey Malbone, monumentally wealthy and fantastically ugly. Concealing a smile, Bethany recalled a ditty Harry had invented: "All the money in the place, won't buy old Malbone a pretty face."

She lost count of the number of times she murmured polite, inane phrases to people she had absolutely no desire to know. Feeling like a puppet on someone else's string, she smiled woodenly at the Pierces and the Cranwicks, the Slocums and the Eastons.

Keith Cranwick maneuvered himself again to her side, looking every inch the dandy in his finery—ruffled shirt and cambric stock, embroidered ratteen coat, and green velvet knee breeches. His heavily powdered hair gave off an oppressive perfume which robbed Bethany of her appetite for the thick chowder, delicate pastries, and thinly sliced meats.

Afterward some of the ladies demonstrated their skill—or lack of it—at the pianoforte. Under her mother's look of smug approval, Bethany was paired off with several more partners. The polite gentlemen seemed to meld and fuse in her mind, their sameness of manner and dress rendering them indistinguishable from one another.

Thus the afternoon dragged on, the men finally going off to discuss the politics of the day, the women gossiping and chatting about fashion. Finding herself alone for a moment, Bethany compressed her voluminous skirts and slipped through the French doors to a raised verandah.

Exhaling her relief, she strolled slowly through the lilac arbor and sat down on a stone bench. She was immediately startled by a crashing in the box hedge below the verandah. A leaping ball of brown and white fur careened from the bushes.

"Gladstone!" she cried delightedly as the dog leaped to cover her surprised face with affectionate kisses and her skirts with sandy paw prints.

"Naughty dog, you've dug out of the kennels again," she scolded, laughing.

Gladstone regarded her with soulful brown eyes, the tip of his stubby tail quivering remorsefully. The spaniel had been Harry's Christmas gift to her seven years ago and was her special pet.

Hearing the music resume in the house, she reluctantly rose from the bench. "Come along, Gladstone," she said, patting her thigh. "I'd best put you away before you bother the guests. Somehow I don't think Mother's friends would appreciate being mauled by your sandy paws."

The dog followed her agreeably down three wide stone steps and along the garden path to the kennels. Promising an outing later, Bethany put him inside, latched the gate, and started back toward the house.

A waft of fresh spring air and the sweet trill of a finch in the lilacs made her hesitate. Her mind rebelled at the thought of spending more stifling hours in her mother's drawing room. Her heart yearned for something beyond the luxury and stability her usual suitors offered. Seized by a sudden irresistible impulse, she bypassed the verandah and ran down the path to the stables.

It was nearly time to light a lamp to chase away the dim shadows of the stables. The grooms had finished their chores for the day; Ashton stayed on to see that the horses were settled for the evening. It was a time to settle his mind, too, a respite from overseeing the endless chores of raising Sinclair's horses and worrying about his father and Carrie. Hearing a light step behind him, Ashton looked up. Suddenly he could think of no more unsettling sight in the world than Bethany Winslow.

He almost didn't recognize her in her full, rustling tea gown with its plunging neckline, her hair beautifully coiled. He still hadn't gotten used to the idea that Bethany was no longer the sunny, gangling child who had dogged his footsteps years ago. At the moment her stunning face was a study in impatience and supplication.

"Take me riding," she said. Without hesitation she pulled up the hem of her skirts and kicked off her high-heeled shoes. "I'm sure these groom's boots will suit me," she added, extracting a dusty pair from a chest. Pulling on them, she threw Ashton a questioning look.

"Well? Are we going riding or not?"

He grinned indulgently, shaking his head. "There now, have you ever known me to refuse you?"

She returned his smile, instantly contrite for her impatience. In minutes the two were trotting down the sandy lane to a broad field shimmering in the soft light of early evening. At first Bethany felt clumsy riding astride, her full gown bunched up in front of her. But soon the years of her absence rolled away and she dug her heels into the honey mare's flanks. With a joyful laugh, she felt the horse's muscles contract and extend beneath her in a wild gallop.

For the first time since arriving home, she felt a measure of the boundless happiness of childhood. She was doing what she loved most in the company of the only man at Seastone who didn't try to kiss her hand or tell her how charming she looked, all the while wondering what sort of portion her father would settle on her.

Ashton's grin as he passed her lit an ember of warmth in her heart. Unlike the gentlemen back at the house, who plucked handkerchiefs from their sleeves and pressed them to their ridiculously rouged and powdered faces, Ashton's good looks were natural. His rugged features were adorned by high coloring and masculinity alone; his mane of wavy chestnut hair would never stand for a covering of powdered wig. The dandies back in the drawing room were like stiff mannequins compared to the strength and vibrance that seemed to emanate from him.

He raised his arm and gestured toward the edge of the meadow. Bethany followed him down a path overgrown with gooseberry bushes.

"Where are we going?" she called.

"Just follow me." Ashton guided his horse between a great tumble of rocks. Periodically he glanced back to see if Bethany was negotiating the way. She sat Calliope with confidence, knowing the mare to be surefooted and responsive to a rider's commands. When they reached the bottom of the climb, she brushed a stray curl from her eyes and looked about her.

"Oh, Ashton . . ."

He leaped from his mount in a lithe motion and helped her down. "Like it?" His touch lingered like sunlight on the sand.

"It's grand, Ashton. I thought I knew every inch of this island, but I've never been here before." She ran down a ribbon of fine sable sand and whirled around, embracing the scene with outspread arms. Still more of her curls escaped their pins, but she didn't notice. She was captivated by the wild beauty all around her, the singing sea mists, the spray torn from the water by gusting windheads. The cove was flanked by cliffs on either side, fringed at the edges by wild roses in the first flush of delicate pink and deep scarlet blossoms. Waves rumbled up and caressed the sand with a hiss. The sky was painted amber and pink by a sweep of clouds spreading over the horizon.

Ashton took her hand and led her along the beach.

" 'Tis a fine place to come when the world starts chasing at your heels."

Troubled, Bethany glanced up at him. "Do I look as though the world is chasing at my heels?"

He smiled and stopped walking to face her. "Very much so, Miss Winslow." He rubbed his thumb gently over her brow. "You're far too young and pretty to be unhappy."

"I'm not unhappy," she countered, "but I miss Harry and I don't seem to fit in with my parents' friends at all."

He sent her a dubious look. He'd been thinking exactly the opposite. Bethany was as perfectly suited to her mother's elegant drawing room as the topaz teardrop she wore suited the color of her eyes. Despite what she said, she was the epitome of the well-bred young lady: lovely and graceful, her speech cultured, her manners impeccable.

"Come now, Miss Winslow," Ashton chided. "I'm not one to listen to servants' talk, but I've heard you already have half the swains of Aquidneck panting after you." When her glum look persisted, he swept the cocked hat from his head, pointed his toe, and dipped in an exaggerated bow.

"I beg you, my dear Miss Winslow, for the favor of one dance." His simpering lisp was a convincing parody of a parlor dandy's speech.

Bethany couldn't help smiling as she pretended to flutter a fan. "Certainly, Mr. Markham," she tittered, batting her eyes outrageously as she gave him her hand.

Humming off-key, Ashton led her through the steps of a minuet, playing the part of the besotted young gentleman to perfection. Bethany laughed and went along with the farce, grateful to feel the tension of the afternoon slip away.

But a new sort of tension arose between them as they moved over the mock ballroom. At first Bethany thought it was only the relief of having escaped her mother's dreary party, but soon she became aware of something else, a sensation she'd never felt before. Although Ashton's decorum would put even the most well-bred dandy to shame, she was stirred by his closeness, the warmth of his large, callused hand clasped around hers, the scent of the sea breeze in his hair.

She thought it odd to be aware of him in this new, unsettling way. In all the years she'd known him, she had never been so fascinated by the play of muscles in his shoulders, the compelling appeal of his smile, the deep, scintillating blue of his eyes.

But she was aware of those things now. And she was startled. When the mock dance ended, she immediately felt a vague loneliness for his touch.

"Better?" he inquired, flashing her a dazzling smile.

She lifted her eyes to meet his gaze. Although he'd been a man fully grown when she'd left, he seemed larger now: taller and broader, more imposing. She swallowed, then returned his smile.

"Much better, thank you. But then, you're far more agreeable company than the gentlemen I left back in the drawing room. They're only concerned about their fortunes—and mine, alas—and what color frock coat they'll commission from their tailors this season."

Ashton laughed. "Lucky fellows. We workaday chaps haven't the time to clutter our minds with such trivialities."

"I'm glad. I wouldn't be able to stand it if you were like that, Ashton."

Not for the first time, he caught himself admiring her beauty. Lord, but she was something to see. Tall and well proportioned, with a proud bearing and those incredible eyes blinking artlessly at him. She had a mouth as delectably ripe as a dew-moistened berry.

He tore his eyes away, pushing aside the tantalizing notion. It was unthinkable even to consider such a thing. Bethany Winslow, with all her ingenuous charm and natural beauty, was Sinclair Winslow's prize filly, probably just weeks away from being paired off with a Thoroughbred. Ashton cautioned himself to remember that in the future.

Nodding at a semicircle of rocks to the right, he said, "Good fishing over there."

"I didn't know you liked to fish." She frowned a little. "There's a lot I don't know about you. Tell me about yourself."

He raised an eyebrow. "That's an odd request, coming from you. You've known me all your life."

"We both grew up here at Seastone. And, Lord knows, I dogged your footsteps like a lost puppy. But you've never talked about yourself."

His smile was indulgent. He liked being with Bethany. Despite the years that had passed, she was still fresh and young and guileless. He sat down in the warm sand and patted the place beside him.

"Very well, love. But I assure you, no stars collided on the occasion of my birth. What would you like to hear?"

Bethany sank to the sand beside him, glowing with pleasure that he would take the time to talk to her. She traced a lazy flowerlike pattern in the sand with her finger.

"Tell me about your mother."

He caught his breath as a dim, sweet memory was suddenly stirred. In his mind's eye he saw himself as a frightened five-year-old boy, although he didn't quite understand that his mother was bleeding to death after giving birth to Carrie. He remembered standing at the bedside, leaning close to hear his mother's whisper. What was it she'd said to him?

"Ashton . . . ?" Bethany felt she'd blundered by mentioning his mother. "If you'd rather not speak of it—"

"I don't mind. I was just thinking of my mother's last words. She told me all the usual things, I suppose—to honor my father, be a good boy. . . . I believe the last thing she said was, 'You were born a bond servant's son, but never forget who you are.' "

"A bond servant's son?"

He shrugged. "She must have been confused, so close to death. My father wasn't a bond servant; he always worked for his wage." With a twinge of guilt he recalled Carrie's resentment about the fact that Roger spent those wages on Ashton's education rather than on her girlish whims. "I often wish he hadn't insisted on a proper education for me, but I suppose he believed it's what my mother would have wanted."

"Harry once wrote me that you were to graduate from Rhode Island College with honors."

"I felt the least I could do was be a decent student. But in the end it didn't matter; His Majesty's army summoned me before my schooling was done."

"Couldn't you have postponed your service? 'Tis what Father did for William—"

"Couldn't afford it."

"But that's not fair, Ashton. You were reading law—"

"In truth, the subject never appealed to me. If I'd pursued a career, I'd be sitting in some stale office right now, scratching a quill over someone's ledger books." He gave her a sideways look. "You must think it shocking, my not wanting to make a fortune as quickly as I can."

"Why would that shock me?"

"Isn't that how it's done in your world?"

"My world? What are you saying? You talk as though we come from different planets."

"So we might, in a way."

"I don't like the sound of that, Ashton."

" 'Tis the way of things. You, my dear, have been born and bred for a very specific purpose. At summer's end you'll doubtless have caught yourself one of Newport's most eligible men and be well on your way to society matronhood. You see, it's simple—"

Ashton stopped abruptly, to duck before the handful of sand that Bethany hurled at him hit its mark.

"Stuff and nonsense, Ashton," she retorted, threatening him with more sand. "Listen to yourself, talking as though my fate were sealed by some divine stamp."

He tried not to anger her further by chuckling as he brushed sand from his sleeve. "Perhaps it's true, love," he said.

"I don't accept that." Bethany leaped up and began pacing agitatedly down the beach. She didn't notice Ashton following close behind.

"Maybe I don't want to catch a husband or be a hostess at tea or commission a wardrobe from London," she railed, throwing her hands up. "Maybe I want—" She swung around and stopped abruptly, to find herself staring point-blank at Ashton. The evening sun had burnished his chestnut hair to an even richer hue. A soft breeze lifted a strand, blowing it against the tanned planes of his face.

"What, Bethany?" he asked, his voice soft and compelling. "What is it you want?"

She caught her breath. Lord, he was handsome; she felt she could drown in his blue eyes. A sudden, insistent urge possessed her; she longed to touch the tiny cleft in his chin, to run her finger, ever so lightly, over the upward curve of his lips.

"Ashton . . ." Her voice was a whisper on the evening breeze. Then with complete and total honesty she told him, "I think . . . that I want you to kiss me."

His smile broadened. For a dreadful moment Bethany thought he was going to mock her foolish request. But, mercifully, he didn't laugh. He bent briefly and plucked a white rose from the grassy fringes of the beach. With a slow, sensual movement he brought it to her lips, running it over them as he spoke.

"Have you ever been kissed before, Miss Winslow?"

She swallowed, feeling her knees grow weak as he continued to caress her with the flower. The rose left fever in its wake, shading her complexion a deep, warm pink. He must think her so absurd, so childish. She lowered her eyes and moved her head slowly from side to side.

Ashton tucked the rose behind her ear and placed his fingers beneath her chin, tilting her face upward.

"Then we'd best get on with your education, love," he murmured.

Bethany stiffened as if bracing herself. The blush staining her cheeks rose to even greater heights until she felt as though her whole face were in flames. She had an abrupt urge to flee, but Ashton, smiling down at her, his hands now firmly gripping her shoulders, kept her in a thrall of fascination.

That odd, unfamiliar smile still played over his features as he lowered his face to hers. He brushed her trembling lips with his mouth, lightly, as if aware of her hesitation. Her mind emptied of all thought. She marveled at the softness of his lips and wondered that so light a touch could create such an intense wave of emotion within her. Her eyelids fluttered shut as the pressure of his mouth deepened. Within her, something powerful and secret awakened, leaving her unsteady with awe. Her hands crept to the warm breadth of his chest. Incredibly, his heart seemed to be leaping as wildly as her own.

She wanted the moment to go on forever, to simply give herself up to the unfamiliar, surging sensations which swept over her like the waves rolling up to cover the sand. Ashton's nearness, the scent of his skin and hair, the movement of muscle and flesh beneath his cambric shirt-front, struck her with stunning pleasure.

She thought she knew this man she'd grown up with. But the tastes and smells and textures so uniquely his were completely new to her. Bethany, who had always listened with wry amusement as her schoolmates waxed endlessly about stolen kisses, suddenly learned with keen awareness that there was, indeed, something magical about a kiss.

It was all Ashton could do to drag his mouth from hers. But he did, using his entire will. At one time he'd believed nothing could be so harmless as kissing a maiden. Now he could think of nothing so powerful as the longing he felt for this woman.

He pulled away and gazed intently into her flushed face. She looked so sweet, so vulnerable. Her lips were swollen and moistened by his kiss. The taste of the cherry flip she'd drunk at her parents' party lingered on his mouth. Forbidden fruit, Ashton warned himself.

She searched his eyes and tried to read the conflict in their suddenly stormy depths.

"Ashton . . . ?"

"We'd best be getting back," he said. Bethany felt the warm stirrings inside her grow cold at the sharpness in his voice. She was a fool to think Ashton had been moved to kiss her by anything more than his own generous nature; he himself had often admitted he could refuse her nothing. His kiss, though it had stirred her to her very toes, had been to him merely the fulfillment of a request.

"I'm sorry," she said in a small voice. "I had no business asking you to kiss me."

He gave her a hard look, concealing his relief. Obviously Bethany required nothing more from him than to satisfy a young girl's curiosity. Well, he'd done it, far more thoroughly than he'd intended. And now it was time for them to go back to Seastone, to reenter their separate worlds.

Chapter 2

"Must you go this minute?" Ashton demanded, his voice tight and low with anger.

Carrie gave a careless laugh and preened before a small looking glass above the fireplace. Her bright ringlets bobbed and shimmered in the candlelight.

"Mr. Northbridge has invited me to a game of piquet, and I intend to win at least half a crown from him." She pulled a knitted shawl about her shoulders.

"Father seems . . . worse tonight," Ashton said.

Carrie tossed her ringlets. "Then send for Goody Haas. She'll cook up a draft of Venice treacle for him."

Ashton shook his head. "Her remedies do no good."

"Well, I shan't sit around and listen to him wheeze. Good night, Ashton. I'm taking the Indian pony. You mustn't wait up; I do so hate it when you check on me. . . ." She swept through the doorway and ran lightly down to the stables.

Ashton went as far as the threshold, snapping out her name with angry impatience. Then he slammed the door against the sound of her laughter.

"Let her go, son," said a raspy voice behind him.

Ashton wheeled and crossed the room to the bedside. "Father, I didn't realize you were awake." He cringed inwardly, wondering if Roger had overheard the discussion about his condition.

"Can I get you anything?"

Roger slowly shook his head. "Bring that stool over, son, so we can talk."

Ashton obeyed and, filled with an overwhelming sense

of helpless frustration, sat beside his father. Roger was but a pale shadow of the vital man he'd been—unbearably thin, his once handsome face now ashen and haunted by ominous hollows beneath his eyes. The stool scraped the puncheon floor as Ashton drew nearer to the bed.

"A game of piquet . . ." Roger said, his voice thickened by phlegm. "Who is this Northbridge fellow anyway?"

Ashton looked away, focusing on the smoking, spluttering betty lamp above the fireplace. "A friend."

Roger nodded. Perhaps he knew of his daughter's frequent trysts with various men; perhaps not. Either way, he was as incapable as Ashton of preventing her nightly—and nightlong—outings.

"She must be very much in demand, our Carrie," Roger mused. "Ah well, the girl seems happy enough." He tried to hide the regret in his eyes as he regarded his son. "Carrie should have had a mother to raise her properly."

"You've been both mother and father to her. To us both."

Roger's dry lips stretched into a smile. He was suddenly stricken by how much he would miss Ashton—his seriousness, his devotion, even the stubborn streak of pride that accounted for the way his son strode about Newport as if he owned the world. Roger's sigh escaped as a wheeze. There was so much to be said, so much more he should have taught the boy. Perhaps, too, it was time to confess he wasn't the wage earner Ashton had always thought him. But Roger discounted the admission. What would be served by telling Ashton he'd been Winslow's bondsman all these years?

An invisible weight pressed doggedly on his chest, and each breath he took required more of his fast-ebbing strength than the last.

"Time for some serious talk, son," he whispered. Seeing Ashton's eyes grow troubled, he held up a wavering hand. "There now, we needn't mince about the point. I've lived longer than I deserve. Long enough to see you grow into a responsible man—" A fit of coughing erupted from him. Ashton leaned forward and held his shoulders. Roger waved him back to his stool.

"What I regret most about dying," he said matter-of-factly, "is that I leave you with so little."

" 'Tis not true," Ashton protested, his blue eyes darkening with pain. "You've given me a fine life, an enviable education. Being your son is a privilege, sir."

Roger's hand rose again to silence him. He exhaled, and the breath rustled like dry leaves in his feeble chest. "I've often wondered if I did right in bringing you and your mother here all those years ago."

"You told me yourself the situation was intolerable for Catholics in England."

"Aye," Roger agreed. "Thank God, Newport is a free-thinking place. Roger Williams's descendants have never ejected anyone for nonconformity, eh? Sinclair Winslow—an Anglican—took me on to manage his stables. Like the shrewd businessman he is, he valued my ability with horses over the way I chose to worship."

" 'Tis as it should be," Ashton said. He noticed a wistful look on his father's face and knew that Roger was thinking of the old days, back in Kent. Roger Markham had not learned about horses by slogging through the stableyards there; he'd owned a modest country estate and had once ridden to the hounds on blooded hunters. But everything came crashing down around him with the arrival of Lord Sturgrove, fanatical in his hatred of Catholics. Roger could have retained his estate by renouncing his faith, but he'd chosen the more rocky path of devotion instead.

"You did the right thing. A brave thing, sir," Ashton said gently.

"Not so very brave," Roger objected, "tending another man's stock. Alas, your mother could never bring herself to do tasks beneath her; she was always so much the lady. . . . 'Tis no wonder she died bearing Carrie before our first year here was out."

Ashton looked at his hands, remembering. "Father, you were still young then. Why did you never take another wife?"

"Oh ho," Roger said with a wheezing laugh. "After one has ridden a Thoroughbred, one doesn't settle for a farm plug. Your mother's memory alone—and the fact that you're the very image of her—have sustained me these twenty years." The old eyes narrowed a little. "You're the one of marrying age now, son," he said faintly.

Ashton looked away. "I've naught to offer a wife," he replied, forcing a careless grin to conceal his bitterness.

"There is"—Roger wheezed—"one thing. Fetch the box with my rosary beads, son."

Ashton handed the beads to his father, wishing he could feel the comfort Roger seemed to find in the coral strand.

"There's something else in the box," Roger said. "Your mother's wedding ring."

Ashton extracted the small gold band: plain, and shiny still. His mother hadn't lived long enough to bruise the metal or wear it away.

"I'd wager," Roger said, "any number of girls would be proud to wear that. You've your mother's striking looks, my impeccable horse sense, and your very own brand of boundless self-assurance. You call that naught?"

"I've never known one's looks or attitude to put food on the table or clothe a body."

Roger lifted one corner of his mouth. "You speak with an American's practicality, son. Yes, exactly so; I wonder that I never noticed that before. . . ." The half smile disappeared, and a furrow deepened his brow. "What's to become of you Americans, Ashton? Civil war, or—"

" 'Tis no longer agitation, but armed rebellion. There's a proper army now—Continentals, they call them. General Washington is putting Boston under siege."

For a moment the dullness left Roger's eyes, replaced by keen probing. "You'll leave, won't you, Ashton?" he said.

"I'm here for as long as you need me."

"Ah, but we both know that won't be long."

"Father—"

"Never mind, just listen. Will you fight, Ashton?"

He looked incredulous. "I've proven my aversion to soldiering. Besides, I'm no Loyalist."

"A patriot, then?"

"Not that either. I'll leave the fighting to the rebels."

"Then where will you go, son?"

Ashton paused, pensively regarding the betty lamp,

which was down to its last drops of putrid tallow. Where, indeed? he wondered. Where did he fit in? He was educated; in addition to his schooling, Roger had taught him the manners of a polished—albeit penniless—gentleman.

He listened to the rush of the waves outside, and another sound came chasing on its heels: the imagined rhythm of hoofbeats and the roar of a crowd. He had heard those particular noises often, crossing the finish line on the finest and best-trained horseflesh in Narragansett.

"I believe," he said slowly, "I'll race horses. 'Tis a good bet the Quality in these parts wouldn't mind parting with some of their wealth if I can promise them what I've delivered to Sinclair Winslow."

The cornhusk mattress rustled beneath Roger. "Don't be hasty, son. At least stay the season here; wouldn't do to leave Mr. Winslow wanting a stockman. You could train Barnaby Ames to take your place. . . . And don't tell me you could walk away from Corsair."

Ashton hesitated. "I don't share your loyalty to Winslow, but it would be a shame to rob the stallion of a winning season. Very well, I'll stay. For a while."

The troubled look in the pale old eyes was replaced by a contentment so sweet that Ashton almost had to look away. Roger's dry lips cracked as he smiled.

"I can ask no more, son."

Ashton could see his father's strength ebbing. Over the past few days no fewer than three doctors had been to see him. The physicians and Goody Haas as well had not been able to offer any hope. The lung ailment was eating up Roger's strength with alarming speed and finality.

Ashton battled a terrible emptiness. Too full of raw emotion to speak, he gripped his father's hand, wishing that, by some magic, some of his strength could flow into Roger.

"Carrie . . ." Roger rasped, raising his head a little.

"She's not here, Father."

"No, of course she isn't." Roger lowered his head back onto the pillow. "Take care of her, son. Don't let her own foolishness get the better of her."

Ashton nodded.

"And do not judge her too harshly."

"I won't."

A strange, sweet smile crossed Roger's face. A single tear left the corner of one eye, but oddly, there was no trace of sadness about him. His wife's name issued on a sigh from between his parched lips.

Then, in a voice barely audible above the spluttering of the lamp and the distant swishing of the sea, Roger said, "I've done one good thing in my life, Ashton, God grant me that. I've raised a fine son."

The wick of the betty lamp guttered in its holder and the wavering flame died in the same instant that the light went out of Roger Markham's eyes.

In the garden a whippoorwill greeted the morning with three syllables, bright as liquid sunshine. But inside the shuttered cottage by the stables, all was dim and melancholy.

Unmindful of the uneven roughness of the puncheon floor, Bethany sank to her knees by the cot where Roger Markham's body lay. As tears flowed unheeded down her cheeks, she choked out a prayer for the gentle stableman she'd known all her life. She couldn't believe he was actually gone. He'd been so much a part of Seastone that, absurdly, she thought he'd endure like the stones and the trees and the changeless rhythm of the waves.

After a time she rose and placed a gentle kiss on Roger's stark, cool cheek. Summoning all her courage, she turned and faced Ashton. What did one say to a man who has just lost his father? No, not just a father. Roger had been so much more to Ashton. Friend, mentor, confidant, teacher. . . . Roger's love for his son had been so evident that, guiltily, Bethany remembered a time when she'd actually been jealous of them. But the jealousy hadn't lasted; that love was all Ashton had ever had.

"I'm sorry," she whispered brokenly, "so very sorry. . . . It won't seem the same without him." In the soft light of early morning she looked at Ashton's tense, haggard face and realized no words could comfort him. So she crossed the room swiftly and placed her arms around his neck, crying quietly as she reached up and stroked his hair and soothed his cheeks with her hands.

Taken aback by the unabashed tenderness of her gesture, Ashton looked away. "I'll be all right," he said hoarsely, as if trying to convince himself.

His stiff restraint frightened Bethany. He was riddled by a terrible grief he refused to show.

"You ache for him, Ashton," she whispered. "I can see it in your face. You must allow yourself to grieve; no good can come of holding back what you feel."

He shook his head, wishing she would stop touching him and looking at him with those drenched gold and hazel eyes. Even in his state of desolation some distant part of him was aware of her softness, the womanly curves of her body pressed against his. But he couldn't think of that now.

"You'll have to do the crying for me, Bethany," he said. "I can't remember how it's done."

"It doesn't work that way, Ashton." But despite her words, a fresh wave of sadness washed over her and tears coursed hotly down her face, soaking his shirtfront. "My weeping is selfish, much as I wish it weren't," she finished brokenly.

He gave her a final squeeze and, as he had so many times in the past, mopped her tears away. "You surprise me, love," he said gently, touched by her genuine emotion. "I never realized my father meant that much to you."

"But he did," she insisted. She looked wistfully at the crude fireplace at the far wall of the cottage. "How many times did I sit here, my head in his lap, listening to him talk? He had such a fine way of telling stories, I never minded when it rained and we couldn't ride. Your father was full of eccentricity and humor . . . and affection. How many times did I run to him for comfort when my pony suffered a lame leg or the colic? He was always there, willing to listen, even when my own father thought my problems too trifling to bother with."

Though sadness enveloped him, Ashton felt a surge of compassion for her. True, she had all the riches a girl could ask for, but aside from Harry, her family life had been emotionally barren.

"Father should have had a daughter like you to dote on," he said, his fine mouth curving into a sad smile.

She looked up. "But he had Carrie—" She broke off, looking around the cottage. "Where is she, anyway? I rang for her this morning before I knew what had happened—"

As if summoned by the query, Carrie Markham sailed into the cottage. Her pretty dimity gown was creased and sandy from riding, and her hair had a decidedly rumpled look. But she was smiling broadly, humming to herself as she swept off her shawl.

"Ah, what a glorious time I had, Ashton," she practically sang. "And profitable, too—" She broke off, noticing Bethany for the first time.

"What brings you here so early, miss?" she inquired mildly. "Oh my, you've been crying. Are you still troubled about your brother, or—"

"Carrie." Ashton's voice cut her off so sharply that she looked at him in surprise, catching her breath.

"Really, Ashton, 'tis not seemly for you to scold me in front of Miss Winslow." Carrie sent Bethany a conspiratorial look. "She, at least, has been generous enough to let me go about my business as I please."

Bethany looked away to hide the distaste she felt for her maid's escapades.

"He's dead, Carrie," Ashton said abruptly.

Carrie frowned, uncomprehending, then rushed to Roger's bed. She stopped a few feet short of him, staring, her back stiff. Bethany braced herself, expecting a show of grief. But Carrie merely stood and stared at the man who had been her father. A long, tense silence stretched over several moments.

Finally Carrie shrugged and turned around, her face expressionless, though pale. "God's will be done," she said, tossing her head. "Isn't that what we Catholics always say?" she added sarcastically. Then she left the cottage, striding purposefully toward the main house.

Bethany caught her lower lip with her teeth, watching Ashton with pain-filled eyes. She noted the white furrows of fury about his mouth and the way he stiffened, his fists clenching and unclenching. Tiny ice shards of rage glinted in his eyes.

"Ashton," she said hurriedly, fearing his anger, yet

forcing herself to face him. "Ashton, she didn't mean to sound so—so callous. This is a great shock to her. Later she'll grieve for him."

"No," he said. She saw his anger ebbing away, replaced by a poignant, world-weary look that caused her throat to ache in sympathy. "Carrie won't be bothered by his passing. He was nothing to her but a source of income. I expect she'll miss the money more than the man."

Once again Bethany rushed to him and wound her arms around his waist. How could he be so strong, so implacably calm, when he'd just lost his father? Without thinking she leaned up and kissed his cheek and then his eyes, as if to coax the healing tears from them.

But the tears didn't come. Instead a groan of agony was ripped from his throat as he caught her in a desperate embrace. Taking her face between his hands, he crushed his mouth down upon hers.

Unlike the time he had kissed her on the beach, there was no gentleness in his embrace. He held her in a grip of desperation, as if clinging to her to ward off the dreadful emptiness he felt. His mouth ground hotly down on hers, forcing her lips apart as his tongue sought the soft, untried recesses of her mouth.

Bethany felt a shocking explosion of sensation within her; even grief for Roger didn't overshadow a heated longing that caused her to quake and tremble. Not even Ashton's first kiss, its memory weeks old, could have prepared her for this desperate, sensual assault. In the kiss she felt his need even more strongly than her own. He needed her closeness, her compassion, and if he chose to take it in this way, then she would give it freely.

Relaxing against him, she invited the demanding caresses of his tongue and mouth, and moved her hands slowly over his back, trying to soothe the tightness in his muscles.

Yet Ashton's tension only increased under the tentative exploration of her hands. He released her abruptly. She watched the rapid rise and fall of his chest with fascination.

"I'm sorry," he rasped, looking angry at himself.

"Don't, Ashton. Don't apologize. 'Twas I who invited your embrace."

"I think you should go, Bethany."

"But, Ashton, you shouldn't be alone right now."

"Nor should I be with you. Something about you causes me to forget myself."

"Ashton—"

"Go, Bethany. I'll be fine."

She sent him a dubious glance, but he looked so hard and implacable that she dared not argue further. Stepping to the door, she turned. "I'll be back," she promised determinedly. "You cannot keep me from saying goodbye to your father at the burial."

Sinclair Winslow frowned when his daughter rushed into the dining room that evening. Bethany understood her father's expression. He disliked any disruption of his well-ordered life; punctuality was a virtue he prized.

"We've held supper an hour for you, Bethany," he said as William seated her. "What kept you?"

She didn't apologize. After the melancholy burial at the Common Burying Ground in Farewell Street, she and Ashton had talked idly for hours. She had cried again while he grieved in pained silence.

She said, "I was with Ashton Markham."

"Really, Bethany, 'twas not necessary for you to linger over the man," Lillian said, echoing her husband's disapproval. "We've already sent Ashton a basket of food."

Sinclair nodded vigorously. "I would have commissioned funeral rings, but the damned infernal Continental Congress included them in last year's boycott. I settled a generous bonus on Markham instead."

"And do you think that lessened Ashton's pain?" Bethany demanded hotly, her temper rising. "Do you think a few coins can comfort him? Ashton needed *me*, Mother. Not food, nor money, but me! He shouldn't be alone now."

Moderate as always, William said, "We all feel for the man, Bethany." He motioned for a footman to refill his wineglass.

"Then why don't you do something about it?"

"There now, Ashton will get over his father's death," Sinclair assured her. "He's a strong man. Lord knows, there'll be enough to keep him occupied now that the racing season is under way."

Bethany's anger dissipated to silence. Nothing she could say would cause her parents to feel a thing for Ashton. With a sick jolt of understanding she realized they didn't consider him worthy of their compassion. To them he was an employee, not allowed to have feelings but merely to be worked like a beast for their gain. Pressing her mouth into a firm line, Bethany vowed to be different. Never would she adopt their dispassionate attitude.

William noticed she hadn't touched her meal of roasted squab hen and spiced squash.

"Are you ill, Bethany? You've not eaten a thing."

"I haven't much of an appetite."

Lillian Winslow faced her daughter in agitation. "You mustn't be so morose, dear. You have been difficult ever since you returned from New York. Your fretfulness at the Malbones' ball last week was rather obvious."

Bethany was used to such criticism; her mother never failed to find fault with her. She shrugged. "I tried to be polite. I never once refused a dance."

"And you never once laughed or flirted or exchanged pleasantries with the guests," Lillian chided. "Really, my dear, you must learn to enjoy the company of your peers. You don't want gentlemen to find you dull."

"I don't think our Bethany has to worry about that," William said. "She could be daft as a dormouse and she'd still catch men's eyes." He grinned. " 'Tis my misfortune that the most comely lady in Newport happens to be my sister."

"William—" Bethany began. There was something objectionable about sitting around the elegant table receiving lavish compliments from her brother when Ashton was alone, sharing his supper with dim shadows and memories.

"Even Keith Cranwick, that cold fish, was remarking on the extraordinary color of those eyes," William continued.

"A girl's looks are important," Lillian agreed. "But, Bethany, you must make more of an effort to be sociable."

"I don't like your friends, Mother," she said cuttingly. Although usually respectful of her parents, she'd had an emotionally trying day and at the moment couldn't abide her mother's complaints about her behavior. "I don't like listening to Bach being mangled on the pianoforte by some lead-fingered ninny or being dragged around the dance floor by preening fops or pretending to be interested in endless discussions of who is wearing what at which ball this year." She stood up and flung her napkin onto the linen tablecloth. "I'd like nothing better than to be excused from all your dreary parties!"

But even as she fled to the haven of her room, Bethany realized it was hopeless. In time she would shed this black mood and once again be the dutiful daughter. Polite greetings and light, meaningless conversation would spring automatically to her lips and she would play the role expected of her. What was it Miss Abigail had once said? The more distasteful we find a task, the stronger we become in performing it.

Flinging herself on the bed, Bethany knew she would need a great deal of strength to be the person her parents wanted her to be.

A warm breeze redolent of summer stirred the fine grass of the Common Burying Ground. Bethany stood beside Ashton, gazing solemnly at the mound of earth that, for two weeks now, had covered the body of Roger Markham. Over Carrie's strident objections Ashton had spent most of Sinclair's bonus to commission a fine shale headstone from John Stevens's stonecutter's shop. Today the small monument had been placed where it would remain for all eternity.

The forceful, primitive melancholy of the carving arrested the eye and stirred the soul. Roger's name was inscribed beside that of his wife, with a verse from his favorite psalm chiseled beneath.

" 'Our soul waiteth for the Lord; he is our help and our shield,' " Bethany read softly. "He would have liked that,

Ashton." She bent and patted the earth beside the marker, where she'd planted cuttings of yellow primroses.

Ashton nodded. His pain had dulled during the fortnight since his father's death, although an empty, hollowed-out feeling persisted. He looked over at Bethany. Her eyes were moist, brimming with sincerity. She'd been with him nearly every day, braving even his blackest moods to draw him into conversation. Sometimes she merely sat and let him feel her closeness. He had an image of her leaning on the desk in the stable office, her chin cupped in her hands, watching him record an entry in a breeding book as if he were penning an epic poem. The image was immeasurably endearing.

"I've said it before, love," he remarked, surprised at the fondness he heard in his voice. "My father should have had a daughter like you."

"Oh, I wouldn't want to be your sister," she said, returning his smile, hoping the first stage of his helpless grief was coming to an end.

"And why not?" he asked.

Her cheeks reddened. "Brothers do not treat their sisters as—as you've treated me in the past."

Ashton's face hardened almost imperceptibly as the memory of kissing her came back to haunt him. " 'Tis best forgotten, Bethany," he said in a tight voice.

She turned an even darker shade of pink. But Ashton was her friend. She could say anything to him.

"I shall never forget." Long, curling lashes veiled her eyes. "I kept the rose you gave me that day on the beach. It's pressed in tissue in a volume of Anne Bradstreet's poems."

Ashton gave her a hard look, concealing a surge of desire. At first he'd been sure she'd forget her attraction to him. Now he realized he was wrong. She was as tenacious as she had been as a child, only her desires were more complicated and dangerous now. The soft, winsome way she was looking at him left no doubt as to what she was thinking.

"I'll walk you back home," he said abruptly, leading the way down the grassy hill. They strolled together through the wharf area of Newport. Sailors in tarry working garb or in gay shore togs of flapping trousers, crimson sashes, and eel-skin boots traded yarns and swigs of grog. Hucksters haggled over a few pence worth of calamanco. Gulls, attracted by the smell of fish and spilled rum, screeched their delight, adding to the frenzied sounds of the waterfront.

They left the bustling activity of the wharves behind and wandered homeward, hand in hand. When they reached the quiet, elegant estate, Bethany slowed her pace, reluctant to leave Ashton's company despite his despondent mood. She turned her attention to the gardens, which had blossomed into a summer fairy grove of color and scent. Tall Canterbury bells surrounded a plot of laburnums rich in streaming gold. Beneath a small, patriarchal grove of quince the summerhouse offered a quiet haven.

She moved up the path, motioning for Ashton to follow, and paused at a low bush of lad's love, plucking a sprig and inhaling its pungent aroma.

"Goody Haas once told me this is a love charm," she said lightly. "Guaranteed to make me irresistible if I tuck a sprig in each shoe."

Ashton grinned and shook his head. "You needn't worry about using love charms, Bethany. Doubtless any number of men already find you irresistible."

She nearly asked him if he was one of them, but she didn't dare. Ashton was too kind to tell her he wasn't attracted to her and too proper to tell her he was.

Seating herself on a bench in the summerhouse, she laid the bit of lad's love aside. Far below, the sea pounded its endless rhythm against the rocks. " 'Tis peaceful here," she declared.

"Aye," Ashton said. "Though I prefer buildings that have a more practical use."

"I've never thought of it that way," she said, sounding annoyed. "I think it's perfectly lovely."

His mouth compressed into a bitter line. The gulf between him and this charming, impossibly naive girl gaped wider. She was so accustomed to her life of softness and indulgence that she'd come to expect things like the ivy-draped summerhouse, never pausing to consider the expense involved. Ashton intended to be wealthy enough one day to build a dozen gazebos, but by that time Bethany would be safely married to a gentleman of her father's choosing.

Ashton felt an unpleasant start when he realized what he'd just been thinking. What Bethany did with her life was no business of his.

He drew his knee up to his chest and regarded her without expression. "I'll be leaving Newport soon," he said simply.

Bethany's jaw dropped. "You're leaving?"

His nod confirmed it. "Aye, pet. Now that Father's gone, there's little to keep me here."

He thought he detected a sparkle of unshed tears in her eyes, and regretted sounding so blunt.

"Seastone is your home," she said quickly. "You can't leave. You can't."

But he only shook his head and tried not to hear the desperation in her voice. "This is *your* home, love. 'Tis only my place of employment."

She gave him a look of stricken disbelief. Her eyes, large and luminous in the soft afternoon light, brimmed with disappointment. Ashton turned his head away, fighting an absurd sense of guilt. The girl looked hurt and desolate. Years ago he used to take her in his arms and tease her into laughter. But lately when he offered the comfort of his embrace, neither of them ended up laughing. Hardening his will, he told himself her reaction was a fleeting one, typical of a young girl's capricious heart. A week or two after he was gone Bethany would doubtless turn her attention to a more suitable gentleman.

"Where will you go?" she asked softly, her voice low and shaking.

"I haven't decided yet. I'll be following the racing circuit after the season here."

"But what about Carrie?"

"My sister has no need of me. She lives her life exactly as she sees fit and will undoubtedly be glad to see me go. I'll send her money when I can."

Bethany stared up at him with huge hazel eyes, their golden lights twinkling like bits of the sun's rays. Impulsively she took his hand.

"I don't want you to leave," she said fervently, and Ashton imagined he could feel the pain of her aching heart.

Heat leaped into his loins at the warm pressure of her hand on his. He filled his gaze with her beauty. Her hair was a long, loose cascade framing her face. Its color was extraordinary, like honey shot through with sunlight. A warm, ineffable scent of jasmine emanated from her. Her skin looked as smooth as cream, her lips full, begging him to taste their ripeness.

His hard-won resolve shattered when he saw her yearning. A groan of frustrated desire was wrenched from him as he pulled her swiftly to him and kissed her.

Bethany sighed sweetly in his strong embrace. Each time he held her, the bond between them strengthened; the silken cords of desire grew taut. As she fluttered her eyelashes against his tanned cheek, he heard her inhale as if drinking in his essence. Her hands began a compelling search over the muscles of his back.

His desire fueled by Bethany's mounting passion, Ashton wrapped her closer. Under the increased pressure of his mouth, her lips softened and parted. He slid his tongue past the tentative barrier of her teeth and heard a muted sound of longing in the back of her throat. She tasted of summer's sweetness, and her warm, yielding body molded itself to his with innocent yearning.

The heated, soul-searing embrace lasted for an endless moment until Ashton recaptured his resolve and reluctantly lifted his mouth from hers.

Bethany fell, trembling, against his broad chest, her heart leaping wildly. "Ashton, don't leave me," she breathed in an unsteady whisper. "I feel as if I've only just found you."

His voice was warm in her ear as he said gently, "I've gone too far already, Bethany. If you knew just what it is you do to me, you'd run screaming to the house in fear of your virtue. Let me go now, or I may not be able to bring myself to leave when the time comes."

"Then stay. Stay, so we can be together."

"That's just it, pet," he said more harshly, his Kentish accent becoming more pronounced. "Even if I were to remain at Seastone, we could never be together."

"Of course we could, Ashton—"

His eyes grew stormy and his grip bit into the soft flesh of her upper arms. "Is this what you want, Bethany?" he demanded, giving her a little shake. "A few stolen moments, groping in the garden like a pair of lovesick children?"

She shook her head slowly. With leaden sadness she stepped from the circle of his arms, conceding his point.

His sharp eyes scanned the garden for a moment, and a crooked, humorless grin crossed his face.

"What is it?" she asked.

"I was just thinking how dramatically my departure would be expedited if someone had seen us just now. Your father would arrange a regular rogue's march for me."

She tried to smile. Ashton wasn't afraid of anything, least of all her father's blustering.

Ashton stepped back, lengthening the distance between them. "I'd best see to my chores. Good day, love," he said abruptly, and retreated down the path toward the stables.

Bethany leaped from the figured brocade settee in the drawing room when her company announced that it was time to leave. She suffered the attention of her callers with cool politeness, not caring that people had begun to whisper behind her back that she was haughty and unapproachable.

Automatically she offered her hand to Keith Cranwick, her most frequent and least welcome caller. As he bent to press his lips to her hand, she looked away from the licentious gleam in his eye. Behind him, Mabel Pierce aimed a dagger-sharp look at Bethany. The fashionably pretty and socially ambitious girl considered Keith her private property and Bethany a trespasser.

Bethany's pasted-on smile wavered; someday she might tell Mabel just how groundless that jealousy was. Keith Cranwick held about the same appeal as a toothache.

Extracting her hand from Keith's, she gave it in turn to his companion. Unusually handsome, with dark hair and eyes, Captain Dorian Tanner was nothing like Keith. His features reminded her of a statue at twilight, full of secrets and shadows. Yet his uniform—a red coat faced with the dark blue of Hanover House—lent him a solid, trustworthy look. Dorian didn't actually kiss her hand, but bent over it with utmost decorum.

"Do come again," she invited, remembering her manners. "Perhaps another time I'll be more attentive while we're playing cards. I lost dreadfully today, didn't I?"

"There's no pleasure in besting you, Miss Bethany," Dorian said sincerely.

She held her smile in place as she stood at the door, waving as their coach rolled away and wondering when she'd spent a more boring afternoon.

That evening she went to the stables, clad in a sleek dove-gray split skirt and a matching jacket.

Barnaby Ames appeared, lifting his hat in greeting. "Always a pleasure to see you, miss. Shall I saddle Calliope?"

She opened her mouth to speak, but was interrupted by a rude snort from a nearby stall. Glancing over, she saw Corsair rearing his head and stamping his feet on the packed-earth floor. A smile spread slowly across her face. The stallion's restless mood perfectly matched her own.

"Saddle Corsair," she told Barnaby. "I think a more demanding mount would suit me better this evening."

Barnaby shuffled his feet. "Surely you can't mean to ride that infernal beast, Miss Bethany. The devil'd sooner toss you into a hedgerow as let you get the better of him."

"Nonsense, Barnaby; Corsair just needs a firm hand. Have you ever known me to fear a bit of horseflesh?" The stallion snorted again as if to defy her to make light of him.

The groom argued, but Bethany wouldn't be moved. Soon she was seated high on the black stallion's back in the stableyard, concentrating doggedly on controlling him. He snapped his head back and sidled to and fro, behaving with unconscionable skittishness. When Bethany tried to turn him toward the gate, the horse lifted his front hoofs and raked the air, whinnying argumentatively.

Suddenly the reins were snatched from Bethany's hands

and she found herself looking down into a pair of stormy blue eyes.

"What the hell do you think you're doing?" Ashton demanded, bringing the stallion in check.

Bethany tossed her head, as defiant as the horse moving protestingly beneath her. "What does it look like I'm doing, serving tea? I'm taking Corsair for a ride."

Ashton shook his head. "Sorry, pet, but I can't let you go."

"Who are you to forbid me to ride one of my father's own horses?" she asked, feeling suddenly and inexplicably petulant.

Ashton froze and grew completely rigid. "I'm in charge of the stables, and I won't allow you to ride Corsair." Like a deserter from a battlefield, Barnaby Ames retreated into the stables.

"I shall do as I please," she replied stubbornly.

"I see. The master's daughter expects complete obedience from a mere stable hand." Ashton's voice was bitter.

Bethany's hand flew to her mouth and she wished with all her heart she could snatch the words back. "Ashton," she said, "I didn't mean to sound that way. I—it's been a rather trying day and—"

"Oh, yes, I'm aware of how exhausting cards and backgammon can be," he remarked, idly stroking Corsair, who had settled down.

She looked away, refusing to let him see what his sarcasm did to her. "I intend to ride this horse," she said obstinately.

"Then I wouldn't dream of stopping you, *Miss* Bethany." As he spoke, he ducked into the tack room and emerged carrying a worn and dusty pillion. Before she knew what was happening, he had brought her to the ground and was securing the cushion behind the saddle.

"Ashton, what are you doing?"

"Taking you for a ride, love," he said amiably.

She drew herself up in indignation. "I've not ridden pillion since I was two years old."

He leaned down until they were nose to nose, the angry blue of his eyes clashing with the obstinate hazel of hers.

"You'll ride pillion with me," he said quietly, "or you won't ride Corsair at all."

Bethany tried hard to cling to her anger. She tried, and failed. For beneath his imperative words, uttered so close she could feel the heady essence of his breath, she recognized concern. Lovely warm feelings swept in and softened the edges of her temper. Holding his eyes with hers, she gave him her sweetest smile.

"Shall we go, Ashton?" she asked.

Moments later they were atop Corsair. The horse wheeled and pawed the air, and Bethany had to fling her arms around Ashton's waist to keep from falling off.

As they cantered down the lane and veered out across fields of waving poppies, bright Chinese red against the undulating gray-green grass, Bethany could feel Ashton's anger as acutely as she felt the awesome strength of the stallion's stride beneath her. She knew the ride would leave her sore for a week.

Ashton drove the horse to a full gallop, and Bethany could sense she was being tested. Beneath her, the pillion provided scant comfort. She gritted her teeth against each jolt to keep from crying out in pain as Corsair plunged across the fields.

Much later, miles later it seemed, Ashton relented and slowed the horse. Bethany moved gingerly in the saddle, squeezing her eyes shut against the pain in her thighs and backside. Ashton glanced at her over his shoulder.

"Enjoy your ride, Miss Bethany?" he inquired mildly.

"Damn you," was all she could say.

His amusement began as a vague trembling, felt by her arms around his middle. Then he gave full vent to his mirth, laughing richly and mercilessly.

Bethany began to smile in spite of herself. Wondering where her anger had gone, she said, " 'Tis not the first time I've humiliated myself on a horse."

"You always were a poor pupil," he chided, still chuckling. "Too impatient, never willing to consider caution. You still have a lot to learn, pet."

She nodded glumly. "Ashton, I'm sorry."

He patted her hand, knowing the apology had cost her a good bit of pride. Then he gave a light tug on the reins and they started homeward, taking the town route along Thames Street.

Although twilight gathered in purple splendor over the bay, Newport was astir. The wheels of commerce turned in the patterns of trade that had brought the seaport to great eminence in the Colonies. The merchants here achieved prosperity by ignoring the navigation laws and pursuing a policy of free trade, a policy the British officials had neglected for years.

There was plenty of money here, Ashton reflected. Glancing to his right, he saw tall ships, their billowing sails semifurled, wending in and out of piers looking for a likely spot to unload. Gimblets and rattinet were bartered right off the ships. The muted ochre and red houses of the shippers of Thames Street stood vigil over the busy scene.

"Ashton?" Bethany's soft query drew him from his reflection. "What are you thinking?"

"I was thinking about making a living, pet."

"You make a perfectly good living at Seastone."

His expression tightened. Bethany, who had never wanted for anything in her life, could hardly be expected to understand exactly how little he had. "I want more than a position as someone else's stockman."

"That was enough for your father," she insisted.

"But not for me. I made him a promise of sorts, just before he died. This is America, for God's sake, not England, where a man's station is determined the very moment he's born."

She folded her hands demurely about his waist as if in silent contemplation. Ashton wanted to explain to her how he felt, why he was driven to build upon what his father had left him. But before he could speak, he heard a male voice calling Bethany's name. Swiveling in the saddle, he saw a British officer striding up Thames Street. A decidedly unpleasant feeling snaked through Ashton as he slowed Corsair.

"Hello, Captain Tanner," Bethany said.

The Redcoat executed a precise bow. "Miss Bethany. Delightful to see you again."

"Captain Tanner, this is Ashton Markham," Bethany said. "We were just starting back to Seastone."

"I see," Tanner replied, his glance dismissing Ashton but focusing with open admiration on Bethany. "Good evening, then, miss."

With a nod as brief and curt as Tanner's glance had been, Ashton urged Corsair forward.

"A friend of yours?" he inquired over his shoulder.

"He's called once or twice," she supplied casually. "He has a faultless hand at piquet."

"I suppose," Ashton said, with unaccountable animosity, "Captain Tanner finds time to hone his skill in between harassing the citizens of Newport."

Bethany's laughter sailed like bright music to his ears. "Honestly, Ashton, you sound as resentful as Harry."

Maybe I am, he thought, and then put the notion away as they left the town behind them.

As Corsair galloped past flower-studded meadows, Ashton's thoughts turned to more pleasant subjects. He found himself contemplating the arms circling his girth so trustingly. Feeling the front of Bethany's body pressing at his back, he fought an alarming sensation of arousal, which sent heat stampeding to his loins.

He began to regret his promise to Sinclair Winslow to stay through the season, racing his horses and training Barnaby Ames as his replacement. The sooner he removed himself from Bethany's company, the sooner he'd escape the wild, forbidden hunger she created in him.

Without thinking, Bethany let her gaze wander to Ashton's thigh, which was smoothly encased in tight buckskin riding breeches. The leg looked long and strong, the muscles tensing against Corsair's black hide. As if mesmerized, she put out her hand and touched him. The sinews hardened even more under her light pressure.

Ashton cleared his throat. "Bethany, please . . ." She could not know what she was doing to him. Her very nearness was unsettling enough, but this little exploration was more than he could bear. "Didn't anyone ever warn you about teasing a man in that way?"

With a mortified exclamation, she mercifully took her hand away. In her innocence she hadn't considered his reaction. Ashton couldn't suppress a grin, knowing she must be blushing to the tips of her ears.

They rode the rest of the way in silence, Ashton feeling overwarm and restive, and Bethany a little foolish at her bold behavior. At the head of the avenue leading up to the house, a brown and white streak of fur hurled itself toward them. The spaniel circled Corsair, barking sharply and bowing his chest down in a playful attitude, the waggling stub of a tail high in the air.

"Gladstone loves this horse," Bethany said with a smile. "He's trotted at his heels ever since he was a pup."

"The friendship seems a little one-sided," Ashton said dryly, helping Bethany down when they reached the stables. "Corsair doesn't seem to like the little nipper playing about his feet."

"But Gladstone doesn't mind," Bethany said thoughtfully, then sighed. "I wish it could be that way with people. Few humans can show adoration so freely, asking nothing in return."

Ashton regarded her keenly for a moment, then shrugged and walked the horse into the stable. Frowning, she followed him. Sometimes he baffled her. He could be warm and teasing one moment, sinfully sensual the next, cold and indifferent after that. As she watched him performing the familiar routine of putting up the horse, she admitted he fascinated her. And frightened her a little.

Miss Primrose had always told her to face her fears squarely—to get to know them like old friends, for who could ever be afraid of an old friend?

Very well, Bethany thought, no more mincing about the point. She squared her shoulders and went to stand behind Ashton as he slung the saddle over the side of a stall. When he turned, she was standing so close she could feel the warmth of his body.

Not daring to hesitate, she wound her arms around his neck and pressed herself against him. Immediately the lovely, melting sensations she'd lately come to associate with Ashton washed over her.

He created a breathless yearning in her that she didn't quite understand. Full of questions, begging for answers, she tilted her head back and stared up at him. Passion and reason warred in his stormy blue eyes.

"God's blood, Bethany," he said gruffly, "what are you doing to me?"

"What does it look like I'm doing?" she teased, with more bravado than she felt. She continued to gaze bravely at him, a mute message of longing in her eyes.

He exhaled loudly. Muttering a curse, he wrapped his arms tightly around her.

His kiss was swift and impassioned, all-engulfing. He made no attempt at gentleness as his lips bruised hers. Bethany could only sigh her elation. Her body burned from head to toe and she felt her legs grow weak and wobbly.

Ashton's strong arms supported her. Lifting his mouth, he touched his lips to her eyes, her cheeks, the leaping pulse at her throat. She slid down to a soft bed of hay, pulling Ashton with her. The nickering of horses and the distant pounding of the surf mingled with her own inner throbbing, and suddenly she no longer felt weak.

Fire raced through her veins as she pressed even closer to Ashton, boldly covering his astonished face with kisses. She sampled the warm flesh of his neck, delighting in the taste of him. His loose white shirt gaped open, revealing a glistening chest with a fascinating patch of reddish hair and the tense, flat muscles of his midsection.

"Ashton . . ." She murmured his name against his mouth.

At the sound of her voice he relinquished her and sat up abruptly.

Bethany roused herself slowly, bewilderment shadowing her features. "What is it?" she asked hesitantly, not yet recovered from the searing heat of their embrace. She reached out to place her hand on his shoulder.

He pulled away and wiped his sleeve across his face as if to rid himself of the taste of her. "We cannot be doing this," he told her harshly.

"Why not?"

"By God, but you try a man. It isn't right; can't you see that?"

"You're always saying that," she countered, thrusting

her chin upward at a mutinous angle. "And yet, you always seem to forget."

He glanced away to conceal a tiny unbidden smile. She could not know how adorable she looked, her chin held so insolently, her mouth pursed in a tempting pout. "You'll learn, as you get older, that a young lady doesn't dally with her papa's employees. And she certainly doesn't enjoy it."

Bethany scooped up a handful of hay and tore savagely at the strands. "Since when can you tell me what I do and do not feel, Ashton Markham?" she demanded.

He forced his eyes from the inviting moistness of her lips. "We're worlds apart, love," he explained.

"Only because you make it so," she retorted, glowering resentfully in the face of his apparent coolness.

"You don't even know what you want, pet," he told her, calm and resigned.

"But I do! I want *you.* I want us to be together, like—like lovers."

He eyed her keenly. Perhaps, for all her naïveté, she did possess a bit of worldliness.

"If it's a lover you want, Miss Winslow," he snapped, "you'll have to look elsewhere. You'll have to find a more docile studhorse than I." He turned away and left the stables.

Bethany leaped up and ran after him. Her passion had been awakened, and the feeling raged like a tempest at sea. Windheads of desire buffeted her senses. "What about what just happened in there?" she demanded.

"You'll get over it," he said over his shoulder.

"I won't. I swear I won't." She kicked up puffs of dust in the stableyard as she walked beside him. "You're cruel," she accused.

He stopped in his tracks and grasped her shoulders roughly. Then, seeing her wince, he softened and traced a gentle finger along the line of her jaw. "It would be far more cruel for me to indulge your urges, love. It may not seem so today, but it's true."

She searched his face, noting every detail: the tiny lines beside his eyes, the endearing dimple in his chin, the firmness of his jawline, the utterly fascinating curve of his lower lip. . . .

As she stared, something curious happened to Ashton. She thought she could see a slight gale of disturbance in the stormy depths of his eyes. For the briefest of moments, he seemed to be mentally reaching out to her in a way so elemental that she shivered.

But he reined himself in so quickly that she was sure she'd imagined the look of longing. The flicker had lasted only an instant, a heartbeat. Yet it was enough to tell her that Ashton was far from indifferent to her.

Chapter 3

Bethany stood outside the fence of the training compound watching Ashton break a new horse to saddle. Not break, she corrected herself quickly; Ashton always thought of the process as a gentling, an instilling of mutual trust.

The fence she leaned on was an unmortared stone wall, laid as much to get the stones out of the way of the sandy track as to confine the stock. Heedless of the rough surface, she leaned on her elbows and cupped her chin in her hands.

The day was glorious, the air softly warm, the gentle breeze scented by sea and horse, bee balm and southernwood. Golden sunlight dappled the track; in her imagination one particularly bright shaft seemed to have singled Ashton out for illumination. His thick chestnut hair was alive with flames of light. The bleached muslin of his loose shirt glared to impossible brightness in the shadowless day. And those eyes, though so often stormy, were today twin gems of summer-sky clarity.

Bethany boosted herself up to the top of the fence, swinging her bare legs to the inside.

The rose-gray mare Ashton had just bridled caught sight of the movement and jerked her head imperiously.

Ashton flashed Bethany a grin. "Sorry, love, but it seems my lady friend here wishes a bit of privacy." The mare snorted as if to confirm his words.

Bethany was not offended, for she knew Ashton took his work seriously. She was as concerned for the welfare of the horse as he was with succeeding in his training. She climbed down from the fence and retreated to the discreet shade of a hackberry tree, where she was able to see the training compound without threatening the mare.

Ashton gave his full concentration to the task at hand. His every movement bespoke quiet strength and boundless self-assurance, as if the whole world existed as a forum for his skills. Watching him, Bethany shivered, feeling oddly chilled yet gloriously warm as well.

The rose-gray mare, aptly named Zoe for the sparks in her eyes, tossed her head in resentment of the training bit. Her flesh quivered beneath the saddle. Fascinated, Bethany observed as Ashton approached the horse, sidling gracefully toward her, murmuring soothing words that sounded like a lover's endearments.

When he reached for Zoe's bridle, the beast jerked away with a grunt, nostrils flaring. Ashton's teeth flashed whitely in the sunlight; he planted himself in front of her as if daring her to accept his challenge.

The mare shied back, hesitant, yet at the same time intrigued by Ashton. Inevitably her curious nose pushed toward him a little. Moments later she was nuzzling his hand, hungry for whatever enticement he held there.

Chuckling, Ashton yielded the bit of maple sugar and insinuated himself closer, reaching up to stroke the mare's neck and muzzle, his stream of low talk never ceasing. He whistled, too; he always whistled to the horses. Perhaps one day Zoe would be as responsive to the sound as Corsair was. Before long he had hung the reins evenly over the neck. Then he angled himself against the mare's side, still stroking, banishing her fears with insistent gentleness.

Zoe hesitated still, stiffening and flattening her ears distrustfully. Again Ashton put her at ease, whistled and fed her from his hand, then returned to her side.

In a movement so lithe and quick Bethany would have missed it had she blinked, Ashton was on the mare's back.

This sent Zoe into a panicked frenzy; she bucked and snorted, all four hoofs leaving the ground at once. Determinedly Ashton clung with his strong thighs, not at all nonplussed by the reaction. The mare was practiced in the art of ridding herself of riders; she sidled and ran headlong, changed direction without warning, charged to and fro, until Bethany feared that even Ashton would be thrown.

But he rode out the storm, actually seeming to enjoy the ordeal. His will matched the proud obstinance of the horse; he used his strength gently yet compellingly.

He conquered the mare.

Bethany wasn't certain exactly when the change occurred. One moment the mare was resisting Ashton with her every fiber; the next, she was being controlled by him, responding to his unyielding guidance at the reins and the pressure of his legs upon her sides.

He was not a domineering master, never one to press his advantage. Although in control, he allowed Zoe to gallop, to experience his guiding weight without learning to resent it.

Bethany's breath caught as she watched the soaring gallop, the beauty of the newly reined mare a perfect complement for Ashton's masterful riding.

Then he slowed the horse, drawing on the reins. He guided the mare to the center of the sandy track, where he brought her gradually to a halt.

The horse hung her head, looking replete rather than defeated. Ashton spoke softly to her as he gave her sides a reassuring squeeze with his thighs and then leaned forward, draping his arms over her neck, still whispering.

Bethany had nearly stopped breathing. Her insides quivered and warmed as she stared. She had a sense of having witnessed something much more complex and dramatic than the mere gentling of a beast. The challenge, hesitation, soaring consummation, and wistful afterglow had less to do with horse training than it had with the sudden clash and fusion of two proud spirits. . . .

Ashton dismounted and raised his face to the sun, revealing a profile so fine and purposeful that Bethany was seized by a sudden weakness. Swathed in golden light, he looked like a mythical prince. Yet his rough, squarish hands and the ruggedness of his features gave him an earthy quality that was more endearing than the cold perfection of a storybook hero. Ashton was a fantasy she could reach out and touch. She leaned against the hackberry tree, feeling the rapid rise and fall of her bosom against the whalebone stays.

I love him. Bethany's hand flew to her mouth as if she'd startled herself with the revelation. The notion, which had been fermenting in her mind for weeks, was not grounded in logical thought but rang with stunning clarity nonetheless.

"Oh, my God," she breathed aloud. "I do love him."

"Love who?" came a voice from behind her.

She swiveled around to see Carrie Markham standing there, mobcap askew as usual, holding a packet of calling cards. Invitations, no doubt, to a half dozen functions Bethany had absolutely no desire to attend.

"Love who, miss?" Carrie asked again, handing the cards to Bethany, who held them absently at her side. Carrie grinned broadly. "About time you made up your mind, miss; the season's half-over." The maid plucked a red-brown berry from the tree and rolled it thoughtfully between her fingers. "Let's see, could it be the handsome Keith Cranwick's finally found your favor? No; you've barely given him the time of day. . . ." Carrie tossed the hackberry over her shoulder, clearly enjoying the guessing game. She snapped her fingers. "I've got it! 'Tis the British officer, what's his name? Ah yes, Captain Tanner. And a good choice he is, miss. Probably has a fortune back in England. . . ."

Bethany barely heard her maid's prattle. Her mind refused to budge from the wonderful, absurd, terrifying, and utterly *correct* notion that she had fallen in love with Ashton Markham. Her gaze moved back to the fenced compound, settling caressingly on the object of her startled adoration as he exited the yard with the rose-gray mare in tow.

"What's the matter, miss? You look a bit dazed." She followed Bethany's rapt gaze. "Sweet God in heaven," Carrie almost shouted. " 'Tis Ashton!" She grasped Bethany by the shoulders. "Are you saying you're in love with my brother?"

"I . . ." Bethany looked down at her hands, which nervously clutched the invitations. The feeling was so new, she wanted to keep it close to her heart like a precious secret.

But Carrie wouldn't stand for her reticence. The canny maid had not mistaken the look of wonderment on Bethany's face.

"You do love him, don't you?" she demanded.

Bethany tried to form a denial, but she could only nod. "I only wonder that the realization was so long in coming."

Carrie's mouth formed a surprised O. Then a range of emotions flitted across her face: derision, amusement, irony . . . and finally, complete and utter satisfaction.

"Perfect," she said briskly. "Absolutely perfect."

Bethany blinked. "It is?"

"Of course, miss. Oh, I'll allow you're letting yourself in for trouble; your parents won't like this a bit. Ashton's penniless, but your portion'll take care of that nicely. Quite nicely indeed . . . for all of us." Carrie rubbed her hands on her apron. "Now . . . what to do next?"

Bethany moved toward the path to the stables.

"Where are you going, miss?"

"To see Ashton, of course."

Carrie planted herself in front of Bethany, barring her retreat. "Come now, you can't do that. You'll only blurt it out that you love him."

"That's exactly what I intend to do."

"Wait a minute. I know you're all atwitter over this, but think. What'll Ashton do if you march down to the stables and announce that you've fallen in love with him?"

"Why, he . . . he'll . . ." What, indeed? She could just imagine the smooth smile, the barely discernible twinge of annoyance in those blue eyes. She'd seen that look many times when Ashton wanted to put her off without hurting her.

"He'll tell you to forget him, to go get yourself a proper husband, the type of man your parents would want for you."

Bethany deflated, slumping against the stone fence. "You're right," she conceded. "That is precisely what your damned proud, fatalistic brother would say." She raised troubled eyes to Carrie. "What shall I do?"

Carrie flashed a triumphant smile. "For once you've asked my advice on something I truly excel at. 'Tis about time. I may not mend your smallclothes well or style your hair fashionably, but I can tell you how to handle a man. Even one as tiresome as my older brother." She took Bethany's hands as she led her to the house.

"You can't run headlong into Ashton's arms," she said, adopting the attitude of a general plotting battle strategy. "We both know what his reaction would be. There's no appeal for him in that. Men are thickheads; they often don't see the truth even when it stares them in the face. You must prove to Ashton that he wants you; force him to play the part of the pursuer. After all, who gets more enjoyment from the hunt—the hunter or the hapless fox?"

Bethany frowned. "Carrie, I was Miss Abigail's best student of geometry and logic, but I'm afraid I shall need a bit of remedial help in this matter."

Carrie nodded. "I thought as much. Now, the best way to show Ashton he wants you is to let him know exactly what it feels like *not* to have you."

"You're not making any sense—"

"Hush up and listen. Trust me, I know. Remember when we used to steal persimmons from the Pierces' orchard?"

"How could I forget? I almost lost a foot to one of the dogs the groundskeeper set on us."

"But we always went back for more, didn't we? We could have had our pick of Seastone's orchards, so why did we risk our necks stealing the Pierces' persimmons?"

Bethany considered for a moment, recalling the quivering anticipation of the childish plot, the artful thieving, the illicit deliciousness of warm, sweet juice running down her chin as she and Carrie giggled over their success.

" 'Stolen waters are sweet,' " she quoted, feeling a wicked grin steal across her face, " 'and the bread eaten in secret is pleasant.' "

Although Carrie didn't seem to recognize the verse from Proverbs, she clapped her hands. "Exactly so, miss. 'Twas not so much the fruit as the act of getting it. Now put yourself in mind of Ashton. Don't offer yourself to him on a gilt salver; make him *want* you."

"How, Carrie?"

The maid led the way into Bethany's room and closed the door. "Well, he can't very well 'steal' you like a persimmon unless he believes you belong to another."

"But I don't—"

Carrie held up her hand. "Maybe not, miss, but there's no harm in letting Ashton think you've given your attention to another man. Now, let's see . . . who could we set Ashton against?"

A discreet knock sounded at the door. Carrie opened it to admit a footman.

"A visitor to see Miss Bethany," he announced. "A Captain Dorian Tanner."

When Carrie turned to face Bethany, her face was lit by a scathingly calculating smile. " 'Tis a sign from above, miss," she remarked. "This opportunity has just been laid before your feet. Captain Tanner is besotted with you already; he's the perfect one to dangle before Ashton's nose." Carrie rushed forward to fuss at the folds of her mistress's gown.

But Bethany put her off. "I think I'll wear a riding habit. I'd like to take Captain Tanner for a ride."

Carrie looked suitably impressed. "You learn quickly, miss." Twenty minutes later the maid closed the door behind her exquisitely garbed and groomed mistress. She whirled, laughing, around the room.

"Play the part well, miss," she said to herself. "I shall dearly love becoming your sister . . . your *equal.*"

Bethany kept a jaunty smile on her face as she led Captain Tanner down to the stables. Although he was unpracticed in the art of flirtation, Dorian's attention and light conversation made her feel pretty and feminine . . . and oddly powerful.

"I'm looking forward to our ride, Miss Bethany," he said as he held the gate to the stableyard open for her. "It's been a long time since I've sat a decent bit of horseflesh."

She watched him as he closed the gate behind her, admiring the handsome fit of his scarlet uniform and his impeccably styled black hair. The officer had a face so perfect that Bethany had the sensation of looking at a statue: his straight brow, perfectly formed nose and chin, and sculpted mouth might have been rendered by an artist rather than by nature. Dorian Tanner was an interesting man; his speech was strangely precise, as if he was concentrating more on how he spoke and less on what he said.

"Are you fond of riding, Captain?" she asked.

"Most assuredly, Miss Bethany."

A wicked thought occurred to her, and her smile became more genuine. "And do you favor a spirited mount?"

He drew open the stable door, one perfect eyebrow cocked. "Is that a challenge, Miss Bethany?"

"We'll see, Captain," she said over her shoulder. She called for Barnaby Ames and had him saddle Calliope and Corsair. When the groom led the horses out to the sandy yard, Dorian Tanner's pleasant smile vanished. He gazed at Corsair raptly, his eyes searching the gleaming coat.

"He's completely black," Bethany assured him as she mounted Calliope. "Some of the stable hands swear he's got a soul to match."

"We'll see about that, old fellow," Dorian said, taking the reins from Barnaby.

Bethany heard the muted tread of a boot on the sandy yard. She turned in the saddle and was confronted by Ashton Markham's disquieting stare. The ferocity of his expression gave her pause, but she forced her smile to widen and jauntily tossed her head.

"Hello, Ashton. Captain Tanner and I were just going for a ride. I thought I might take him to that lovely private cove you showed me."

She saw him stiffen. His hands clenched around the breeding log he was holding until his knuckles whitened. Oh, Carrie, she thought, what have you talked me into now?

"Haven't you learned your lesson about Corsair?" he asked tightly. "The beast's not used to anyone but me."

"Then obviously," Tanner drawled, "the poor fellow's never had a proper master."

Bethany held her breath. Tantalize, Carrie had said, not infuriate. But it was out of her hands now. Dorian Tanner knew nothing of her game, yet he obviously knew plenty about masculine rivalry.

To Ashton's credit, he didn't rise to the barb, but stepped back in a conciliatory attitude. "Have at him, Captain. But he'll give you his worst, make no mistake."

With a dismissive shrug Dorian confidently swung up onto the horse. Corsair began his ornery antics, but Dorian brought the reins up harshly.

Bethany saw Ashton wince at the jerk of the bit in Corsair's sensitive mouth.

Dorian's smile glittered. He tipped his hat, looking every inch the well-bred cavalier.

With a lordly hand on the reins, he turned the horse and pressed his heels into his sides. Corsair charged from the yard down the lane, leaving dust and the Redcoat's hat in his wake. Then Dorian wheeled the mount and started back, this time bringing both legs to one side, lowering himself until his boots brushed the ground. The impetus lent his feet wings; his legs came up and swung to the other side. The motion was repeated twice and then Dorian landed back in the saddle. Bethany watched, dumbfounded and impressed by the symphony of symmetry and motion and color of the steed and its red-coated rider.

"Carnival tricks," Ashton muttered. "Could your captain have learned *that* while riding to the hounds?"

"My," said Bethany, "you do seem to hate it that another man can handle your stallion, Ashton."

"I hate it even more that you'd taunt me about it, pet."

I will not apologize, Bethany vowed. Pressing her lips together, she turned away. In a full gallop, Dorian swooped down and retrieved his fallen hat, nodding at Bethany before setting it on his head.

"Shall we go, miss?" he asked nonchalantly.

Bethany chanced a gamin smile at Ashton. He stood immobile, his eyes boring through her as he watched her show Captain Tanner the way to the cove.

On a splendid August day Ashton stared morosely into his tankard of ale at the White Horse Tavern in Marlborough Street. Earlier he'd won a quarter-mile race at Cheltham's Green, earning a small silver plate and a decent-sized purse and, as always, the praise of Newport's elite. Yet he felt no flush of victory, no sharp satisfaction at having bested a dozen of the ablest jockeys in Narragansett country.

Something was seriously amiss in his life.

It was not just the fact that his father was dead and Carrie was behaving more outrageously every day. Nor was it his own eagerness to get away; at month's end he'd be leaving to take possession of the bit of Aquidneck beachfront he'd been granted on his discharge from the army.

Still, something was wrong.

He scowled at his ale, reluctant to admit the source of his discontent. Yet, try as he might, he could not dispel the images that wove into his consciousness like some insidious illness of the mind.

He continued to stare into his cup but didn't see the bubbles rising laconically to the surface to cling and then disperse. He barely noticed a thin, tartly grinning wench who sidled up and, surmising his mood, retreated to a more friendly corner of the taproom.

Ashton saw, and silently cursed, Miss Bethany Winslow, hurling himself into his arms for comfort like a hurt child, laughing as they held a mock ball on the beach, inviting his kisses with a budding sensuality that promised to blossom into passionate abandon. . . . But he hadn't seen that endearing side of Bethany in a long time.

He shifted restively on his stool, growing angrier by the minute. He should have taken Bethany's sweet offering weeks ago, and to hell with propriety. Instead he'd nobly denied himself her charms. And for what?

So she could throw herself at the dashing and prepossessing Captain Dorian Tanner. For six weeks the two had been inseparable, tiring the horses Ashton cared for so diligently, spending long, lazy hours indulging in the very delights Ashton had forbidden himself.

So much for the idea that women preferred well-behaved gentlemen. Tanner played up his elegant manners, but Ashton was bothered by an odd avidity in the man's eyes and the frankly carnal way the Redcoat regarded Bethany when he thought no one was watching.

Ashton took a long draw on his ale, despising himself for caring that Bethany's fast-awakening desires were now being sampled by another.

'Tis what you knew would happen, he told himself darkly. So why does it needle you, my friend?

The appearance of a newcomer in the tavern spared him from having to answer that question.

Captain Dorian Tanner—swaggering, scarlet-clad, infinitely confident—cast disdainful eyes at the patrons. The White Horse was known as a patriot haunt, where seditious pamphlets were discussed and toasts were raised not to King George but to the other of that name, General Washington, who, that summer, had been directing the rebel siege of Boston.

At first Ashton ignored the intrusion; then Tanner's voice carried to his ears.

"Ah, 'tis Goodman Finley Piper," Tanner remarked, fixing a black-eyed glare on a middle-aged man in rumpled and ink-stained shirtsleeves. "How goes it, Mr. Piper? I heard your printing press was working late last night."

Piper looked across the table at his son, a gangling youth called Chapin, but said nothing.

Ashton had known Finley and Chapin Piper all his life. The father was an extraordinarily ordinary man, a rickle of sticks assembled as if his Maker had done the job in haste. Yet the widower was shrewd and well educated in a way that made his ordinariness seem less noticeable. Chapin was a few years younger than Ashton. Lantern-jawed, his throat all cords, he said little but always seemed to have something—usually Carrie Markham—on his mind. The Pipers adopted an attitude of quiet insolence as they regarded the Redcoat.

Frowning at the printer's lack of reaction, Tanner strolled over to the table and leaned his sword against Finley's side at a meaningful angle.

"What's the matter, sir?" Tanner asked smoothly. "Have you something to hide?"

"Nothing at all, sir," Finley replied, looking suddenly very unlike the simple tradesman he was. As Ashton watched, he straightened his shoulders, tipped his chin, and flexed his large, competent-looking hands. "There's no law says a man can't labor after hours."

"True enough!" Tanner exclaimed. "But I'm intrigued, Mr. Piper. You worked until dawn, yet I wasn't able to find a single copy of your product."

Finley allowed himself only the smallest of smiles. "My publications have become exceedingly popular of late, sir," he said politely. But his expression turned abruptly to one of consternation when Tanner pressed his knuckles into the rough surface of the table and leaned forward in a menacing attitude.

"Mr. Piper," he said, enunciating very clearly and quietly, "your seditious writings are but rumor today." Tanner moved so close that his nose nearly touched Finley's. The printer didn't flinch as the officer added, "But I shall prove your treason; if not tomorrow, then the next day, or the next . . . and God help you when I do."

Ashton's stool scraped savagely on the floor as he got to his feet and went to Tanner's side. "You wouldn't want folks to accuse His Majesty's officers of harassment, would you, Captain?" he asked mildly. "A spotless reputation is so vital in these unsettled times."

Tanner looked momentarily unnerved, having caught Ashton's slightly threatening tone. Then he laughed. "Of course. Good of you to point it out, Markham, although I'm surprised a common laborer like you is aware of the political situation." With an exaggerated gesture he drew a watch from his waistcoat and made a great show of checking the time. "I must be going anyway. Miss Winslow is expecting me."

He noted Ashton's look with a fierce grin. "Poor sod," he ventured, shaking his head. "Your eyes catch fire at the very mention of her name."

Ashton's hands clenched into fists. He was as furious at himself for having reacted to the taunt as he was at Tanner for delivering it.

Only the slight pressure of Finley Piper's hand on his arm stopped him from driving his fist into Tanner's perfect face. He set his jaw hard against his temper and forced himself to remain still as the officer swaggered out into Marlborough Street.

" 'Tis best you let him go, my friend," Finley murmured, pushing a fresh tankard of ale into Ashton's hand. "It wouldn't do to come to blows over a trifle when the future will offer us ample opportunity to fight for a much more meaningful cause."

"Not 'us,' Finley," Ashton said sharply, feeling a sudden distaste for battle-hungry agitators like Piper. "Leave me out of your fraternity. Such issues belong to those who are willing to kill and die for them. I don't happen to be that sort of man."

"But you will be, my friend," Finley vowed. "I already see the anger in you; 'tis only a matter of time before the commitment nudges you in our direction."

Ashton shook his head, but when Chapin raised another toast to General Washington, he was surprised to see his mug lifted high in salute.

Bethany devoured Harry's letter, the first she'd received since he'd gone off to Bristol. Her brother's missive was optimistic; he and Felicia were abysmally poor but deliriously happy, expecting a child in the spring. Harry invited Bethany to visit and ended with a postscript: "I entrust the enclosed letter to you, to be delivered with every discretion to Ashton Markham."

She picked up the folded and sealed enclosure and turned it over in her hands. Why was Harry writing to Ashton? And why did he want this letter delivered with "every discretion"? Shrugging, she placed the note in her pocket and walked down to the stables. At the very least the letter was an excuse to see Ashton.

Since she and Carrie had embarked upon their campaign to get him to notice her by pretending to enjoy the attentions of Dorian Tanner, she had seen far too little of Ashton. At times she questioned Carrie's tactics, although every so often she caught an unmistakable glimmer in Ashton's eyes that told her the ruse was not lost on him.

Bolstered by the thought that her plan was working, she found Ashton in the small office in a corner of the stables. She paused behind his chair, feeling a rush of sensation at the sight of him. His head was bowed in concentration over a calf-bound breeding journal. Roger Markham's handwriting covered the top part of the page; halfway down, the handwriting changed to Ashton's. The son had taken up where the father had left off.

Ashton wore his father's spectacles, which gave him a look of pensive intelligence. His shoulders were inexplicably taut; Bethany experienced a sudden urge to touch him there, to knead the tension away with her hands.

For weeks she'd been in the company of Dorian Tanner and was the envy of every young woman in Newport. Yet Dorian's classic handsomeness and smooth manners held little appeal for her. Each time she looked at that flawless face she found herself longing to gaze upon another, upon Ashton Markham's rough features, to feel the earthy bluntness of his hands and to enjoy his completely unaffected personality. The flaws added up to a whole that was infinitely more human and approachable than Dorian Tanner's bloodless perfection.

Swallowing a surge of longing, she took Harry's letter from her pocket.

"Ashton."

He looked up sharply. Behind the spectacles his eyes narrowed.

"Another outing, love?" he asked harshly. "Will your captain take time out from harassing the townspeople to abuse Corsair again?"

She winced at the anger in his voice. "He doesn't mistreat the horse, Ashton. You know I would never let him."

"Then how do you explain the oyster shell I found in the beast's front hoof yesterday?"

She stepped back a little. "I didn't know about that, Ashton, truly." Defensively, she added, "I apologize; perhaps we were too preoccupied to notice."

He came to his feet, tearing the spectacles from his face and flinging them on the table. "So the good captain preoccupies you, does he, Miss Bethany?" He stepped very close to her, so close she could smell the scent of saddle soap and horse that clung to him, so close she could feel the warmth of his breath on her face and see small, cold shards of anger in his eyes.

"I . . . we didn't . . ." She felt hot color rise.

Ashton chuckled humorlessly, flicking his hand insolently over her cheek. "Doesn't take much to fluster you, does it, pet?" he asked.

Her eyes flashed defiance. "A lady is always flustered by rudeness," she snapped. His hand moved from her cheek to her hair, his fingers weaving into her curls. "Let go of me, Ashton; I didn't come here to—"

He drew the angry protest from her lips by covering her mouth with his in a wickedly insinuating kiss.

Bethany struggled against his chest. For weeks she had longed for his embrace, but not in this way. She wanted gentleness rather than anger, desire rather than demand. But, she reflected with sudden insight, her behavior lately hardly invited gentleness and desire.

She felt dizzy and somehow violated when at last Ashton relented and released her from his ruthless embrace. Tears stung her eyes as she gazed up at him.

"Why did you do that?" she asked.

"You used to enjoy it, love."

Slowly she shook her head. "I used to enjoy your friendship, Ashton. Your approval. Without that your kisses mean nothing."

Flinging Harry's letter onto the desk, she fled.

A soft morning breeze, imbued with the scent of spicy honeysuckle and marybud gone to seed, dried the tears from her face. And with the tears went her feeling of having been violated by Ashton. Because suddenly, with startling certainty, she realized what had happened in the stable office.

Ashton had just given vent to jealousy.

Her mood was high the next day when she entered the library, summoned there by her father. Sinclair sat behind his massive block-front Goddard desk, smoking a clay pipe and looking over a small stack of correspondence.

He regarded his daughter with a satisfied smile. "Lovely," he said, eyeing her tawny gold outfit. "Not many women look so well in those starkly tailored riding habits, but you've precisely the height and slimness for it."

"Thank you, Father. I thought to ride before breakfast."

"You'll have time. What I have to say won't take long. Your mother and I are sailing to Little Rest with William, and we won't be back until tomorrow. Your brother's decided to enlist in the king's horse corps, and I've a bit of trading to do."

"William will be . . . a British soldier?"

"Aye, if he manages to stay sober enough to sit a horse. His damned commission cost me a small fortune."

Bethany felt her face go white. Harry had sided with the rebels and William with the British. They'd grown up brothers; they could well die enemies.

But her father seemed unconcerned about his sons. Smiling across the desk at her, he said, "I want you to think about something while we're away." He tamped his pipe on the cork ball of an ash-salver and set it aside.

"Captain Dorian Tanner has offered for you."

Bethany stepped back, dumbfounded. "No. . . ."

Sinclair's brows drew together. "Why so surprised, my dear? I daresay you've given him plenty of encouragement."

"Yes, but that was because . . . because . . ." She let her voice trail off. Her father would neither approve of nor understand her reasons for entertaining Dorian. "He's been pleasant enough company," she conceded hastily, "but I've no intention of marrying him, Father."

"But you will, my dear girl. In two months. Tanner has gone off on a tour of duty; he's promised to keep an eye on William, as a matter of fact. I've assured the captain that he'd find you most agreeable when he returns."

She curled her gloved hands into small fists at her sides. "You should not have presumed to know my mind."

"In the end your sympathies matter not at all," he informed her coldly. "I need you safely married, and I need grandsons. Both your brothers are lost to me, William to his drinking and carousing, and Harry to his lowborn bride and infernal sedition."

"I do not feel obligated to provide you with an heir."

"Naturally that is not my only reason," he explained calmly. "Bethany, the country is being torn apart, even though we may not feel it here at Seastone. The rebels in Boston and Virginia have drawn the sword against our king; I need to know you'll be safe if the conflict ever reaches Newport. Dorian Tanner is a good man, a committed soldier. Alas, I've been able to find out little enough about his family, but I'm sure he'll clear that up when he returns from his tour of duty. You should be pleased to have attracted his notice; he can offer you security."

"I will not have him," Bethany vowed, trembling as her hand found the doorknob.

"You will," Sinclair returned. He gave her a genial smile. "Go have that ride, my dear, and sort it all out. You'll see I've chosen wisely for you."

She ran from the library to the haven she'd sought since childhood: the stables and Ashton Markham's soothing arms.

Chapter 4

The deck of the sea-battered ferry lurched beneath Ashton as more passengers boarded from the small quay at Bristol Ferry. The August day had grown dark, the air heavy with rain as yet unshed. Ashton gripped the rail of the shallop and looked out across Narragansett Bay, puzzling over the letter Bethany had delivered the day before.

Harry Winslow was in some sort of trouble; that much Ashton had surmised from the cryptic message. Something about documents to be delivered in secret and a singularly canny British sympathizer who must not, at any cost, observe the exchange. . . . Ashton muttered a curse, calling Harry every kind of fool for involving himself in a conflict that could only mean danger.

"Why me?" Ashton said softly through gritted teeth. Harry knew how he felt about the civil war, knew he determinedly favored neither side. Yet here he was, furious at the responsibility he felt toward the impetuous young man.

It had always been that way with Ashton and the privileged Winslow offspring. All three of them had spent their lives sparing nothing for prudence and responsibility. What should have been intelligent judgment in William had been smothered by his fondness for women and drink; Ashton had spent more than one sleepless night dissuading him from dueling over a lady, or getting him out of a gambling scrape. Young Harry was little better, although his ideals were somewhat more admirable than his brother's. Not that Harry was wicked, but forethought never preceded his actions. As a child he'd been wont to climb trees he could not descend, to make promises he could not keep. The task of rescuing the lad had always fallen to Ashton. And then there was Bethany. . . .

She was the best and worst of Harry and William combined: smarter than William, braver than Harry, and more spirited than both. In all fairness, the child she'd been had presented no special problems for Ashton. But the woman she had become did create a dilemma.

Lately she'd haunted his sleep and deviled his days, all large sparkling eyes and impossibly golden hair. Thank God, Ashton reflected, the girl seemed to have no notion of her effect on him. If she knew what her little flirtation with Dorian Tanner did to him, she'd be positively giddy with feminine power.

A gull wheeled overhead, hanging suspended in the moist air before winging southward. Ashton watched the bird, envying it its freedom, and tried to tear his thoughts from Bethany. But, unbidden, an idea took hold of his mind.

I miss her.

He scowled and nearly stumbled against a wooden grating as the ferry lurched again. He did miss her, damn the girl. He missed the easy rides and conversation and the way she always used to need him, the way she ran to him to share a small triumph or a great disappointment.

A shout interrupted his thoughts. The ferrymaster had been about to cast off for Bristol when a slim, gold-clad figure leaped up the entry-plank. Ashton barely had time to react before he found his arms around Bethany and his shirtfront already damp with her tears.

"Ashton," she sobbed, "I needed you this morning and you weren't there. I only found you because Barnaby said you'd asked about the ferry schedule to Bristol." Her eyes darted at the passengers on the boat and she lowered her voice. "I—I nearly winded Calliope getting here. But the ferrymaster's son promised to walk her for me." Her gloved hands twisted into the fabric of her riding habit. The edge of hysteria in her voice told Ashton her worries were not entirely for the horse.

Emotions too numerous and fleeting to identify eddied through him: annoyance, elation, confusion, amusement.

He squeezed her hand and set her away from him, offering a handkerchief from his pocket. As he watched her mop her tears, the weeks seemed to roll away and he forgot his bitterness.

"There, love," he said, "what's troubling you?"

His tone of voice caused a new flood of tears to erupt, this one more torrential than the first. While he wondered how the girl could look so lovely even while weeping buckets, Bethany tried to choke out an explanation.

"Ashton, I've gotten myself in—in such t-terrible trouble. My father s-said Dorian and I must—must—"

He laid his fingers on her lips. "Hush now, love. Calm down a little and you can tell me about it later."

She quieted and leaned against him. Ashton stroked her hair self-consciously, aware that at least half a dozen passengers had sidled closer, as if curious about the singularly lovely young woman who was pouring her heart out against his chest. He experienced a sudden pang of fierce protectiveness. Taking Bethany's arm, he led her toward the canvas-sheltered bow of the ferry, away from the prying eyes and the mist of rain that had begun to fall. The ferry cut away from the quay with a shudder.

Bethany gasped and stumbled, clutching her midsection. Her face went pale, and the color that returned was far from healthy; a curious shade of gray-green appeared on her trembling lips.

Ashton gave her hand a squeeze. "What?" he asked, lifting an eyebrow. "An islander who has no sea legs?"

Her smile was thin and rueful. "I don't understand it. The voyage from New York was most pleasant." She hiccuped a little and swallowed hard.

Ashton helped her to a lashed-down bench beneath the fulling jib on its taut forestays. Crouching beside her, he said, "At this rate we'll make port at Bristol in less than an hour. I gather this is an impromptu voyage?"

Bethany nodded. "No one will worry. My parents and William have gone to Little Rest on the mainland." Her tear-drenched eyes grew troubled as she added, "William has joined the king's horse corps and has gone on a tour of duty with Dorian Tanner."

Ashton's jaw tightened. So that was the cause of her

distress. Bethany's suitor had left her, so she came running to him. He turned sharply away.

"William has my sympathy," he said tautly. But you don't, pet, he added to himself. You don't.

Unaware of Ashton's thoughts, Bethany gazed out at Hog Island. "In a way I'm glad I came," she said. "I've been trying all summer to get away to see Harry." She moved her hands absently against her midsection as if to still her discomfort. "But what about you, Ashton? Are you going to see Harry, too?"

He nodded and turned his eyes northward. The ferry was closing in fast on the port.

"Why?" she asked. Then she placed her hand on his arm. "It was the letter I brought you yesterday, wasn't it? I meant to stay and see what it was about, but you . . . we . . ." The sudden flush of pink in her cheeks contrasted with the pallor around her lips.

Ashton patted her hand, amazed at the speed with which his resentment fled. For the first time in his life he apologized to a woman for kissing her. Bethany's dewy-eyed countenance made it easy. "I was a bit out of sorts," he admitted dryly. "Sorry, love."

"Why were you out of sorts, Ashton?"

He looked away, fastening his eyes on the blue and ochre facades lining the port of Bristol. "Weren't you just asking about your brother?" he reminded her.

He thought she would press him to give voice to something he wouldn't even admit to himself, but she relented, gripping the bench as the ferry rode a particularly rough swell.

"Tell me, then," she said tautly. "Anything to take my mind off how dreadful I feel. Is Harry in trouble?"

He shrugged. "He may need someone to temper his rebel fervor a little."

"Yes," she agreed. "Yes, *please*. I simply don't understand why Harry is so sympathetic to the rebels. He was raised a proper Englishman."

"I see," Ashton said, nodding. "And proper Englishmen keep their mouths shut when Lord North's hands rifle their pockets."

She glanced at him sharply. "Ashton, listen to yourself. Don't tell me *you* agree with that rabid Sam Adams."

He grinned. "Never fear, love. I prefer my own authority to that of the patriots or the British."

"I am a Loyalist," she proclaimed. It was to be a prim announcement, but another swell caused her eyes to widen with acute discomfort.

"Perhaps you'll do your brother more good than I," Ashton said. He was about to inquire again about why she had sought him out, but she looked so miserable that he was reluctant to bring up the subject. He held his silence—and her nervous, clammy hand—until they made port.

As they walked away from the rain-drenched wharves, Bethany sent Ashton a grateful look; his mere presence had helped her weather her seasickness on the short voyage. The brisk walk to Hope Street revived her feeling of well-being, and now she was eager to see her brother.

She hid her surprise when a tall, thin Negro man opened the door of Number 10 Hope Street in a quiet section of Bristol.

"I'm Bethany Winslow," she said hastily, dipping her head. "And this is Ashton Markham." The Negro searched their faces, his eyes narrowed distrustfully.

"Who is it, Justice?" called a male voice from somewhere behind the narrow stairs of the modest town house.

Bethany burst past the solid wall of Justice's chest, calling her brother's name. In moments she was enfolded in Harry's arms. While Harry and Ashton exchanged a handshake, she studied her twin.

He looked different now, in ways that gave her pause. His clothes were somewhat shabby, although clean; the elbows of his frock coat had been mended by a meticulous hand. He was thinner, too, yet Bethany recognized his usual restless energy. His face lacked color; she reminded herself that Harry no longer took invigorating rides. At the moment his brow was furrowed in concern.

But beneath the look of worry and want, Harry's hazel eyes held a new, unfamiliar light. Despite his impoverished circumstances, Bethany was struck by the realization that her brother was now a deeply happy man.

Before long, she learned precisely why. Felicia Winslow served a modest tea on chipped and mismatched china in the tiny parlor. The woman's manner was briskly friendly; with delight Bethany discovered Felicia had none of the affectations of the overprivileged and overbred ladies of the Newport elite. Like Harry, she didn't seem to mind the lack of worldly possessions at all. She was attractive in an earthy way, with soft brown hair and fine, clear eyes of a startling green. Her smile was genuine, wide and big-toothed. The frank devotion with which she regarded Harry made Bethany warm to her at once. Felicia, Bethany decided, would act as an anchor to Harry's restlessness.

"This tea is most unusual," she remarked, after they'd caught up on the two months that had passed since Harry's departure.

Felicia and Harry exchanged a conspiratorial look and Felicia emitted a friendly chuckle.

"Dreadful, isn't it?" she said cheerfully. " 'Tis a decoction of raspberry and lemongrass. A poor substitute for the China brew, but we make shift with it."

"I wasn't aware tea was so dear," Bethany commented, setting her cup aside.

Ashton laughed aloud, shaking his head. Bethany glared at him and began to sense her companions had launched a conspiracy against her, a private joke she didn't understand. As she framed an angry retort, Ashton placed his hand on her arm.

"We're not laughing at you, pet," he said mildly. "You've no reason to concern yourself with the politics of tea. Harry and Felicia make their own brew to protest Parliament's tax on imported tea."

Now Bethany understood. Until today, the fact that outlaws in Boston and Norfolk had taken to dumping East India tea overboard had only been a bit of news for people in Newport's salons to shake their heads over. Now, in this drab town house where her brother lived, she realized that those outlaws had support.

"I find it perfectly ridiculous that English tea isn't served in an English household," she told Harry mutinously.

He smiled warmly rather than taking offense. "An *American* household, my dear."

"How can you say that, Harry?"

"I've lost my taste for English tea," he stated. "I've lost my taste for all things English when it comes to that. The tighter Parliament grips us, the more determinedly we shall struggle to be free."

"I *am* free," Bethany insisted. "Free to do whatever I please." She blinked, realizing what she'd just said. If her father had his way, she'd give up her freedom to Captain Dorian Tanner in two months. But she didn't want to discuss the dilemma with Harry; he seemed too wrapped up in his own affairs as it was. Ashton was a far more sympathetic listener, but the discussion about Dorian would have to wait for a more private moment.

Harry patted her hand. "Let's not quibble over loyalties. If England has your support, then perhaps there's hope for the empire yet."

Bethany thought it an odd thing to say, but she forgot the disagreement as the conversation turned to other subjects and the afternoon slipped away. She forgot her initial worry about Harry; now she knew her brother was utterly content with his gentle, adoring bride. He was even able to joke about his work at Hodgekiss's, proudly displaying his ink-stained sleeve as proof of his toil.

She smiled at Harry and Felicia, feeling faintly wistful about the intimacy they shared: the fond glances passing between them, the occasional pat of affection.

"You're everything Harry said you would be," she told her sister-in-law.

"So are you," Felicia replied. "Harry speaks of you often. But he forgot to mention how beautiful you are."

Bethany's blush was genuine.

"I suppose Harry would consider it vain to mention his sister's looks," Ashton suggested, "since they resemble each other so closely."

"That must be the reason," Felicia said with a laugh. "Truly, Bethany, only now that I've met you do I feel I know Harry. I've just made the acquaintance of my husband's other half."

"You're his other half now," Bethany replied humbly,

not at all disturbed by the change. "I've never seen Harry so happy."

They turned at the sound of a footstep in the doorway. Justice stood there and flicked his dark, somber eyes at the passageway to the rear of the house. Harry and Ashton excused themselves and left the parlor.

"Where are they going?" Bethany asked Felicia.

"I believe Harry has some business he wants to discuss with Ashton."

"Rebel business," Bethany snapped.

Felicia looked disappointed. "Can we not leave off this subject, Bethany? I'd rather hear about what Harry was like as a child." Her eyes twinkled. "And I'd love to talk about the baby we'll be having in the spring."

The prospect of a new niece or nephew cheered Bethany, and she was suddenly glad she'd come to Bristol.

"Bethany's appearance surprised me," Harry murmured to Ashton as they made their way to the tiny dooryard behind the house. Evening was approaching softly on the heels of the rainy afternoon.

"Your sister knows little about why I came," Ashton replied, sitting on the stoop beside Justice, whose eyes never stopped moving watchfully about the yard.

" 'Tis just as well," Harry said. "I'm afraid I've gotten in a little thick."

Justice spoke for the first time. "A little," he echoed in a basso voice. "It's a wonder you're not swingin' from the gallows, mon." The melodious notes of the West Indies rang in his speech.

"What's happened?" Ashton asked.

"We've found a source of gunpowder for the patriots. This is a crucial time for us; we must keep the movement alive as militias are formed throughout the Colonies. Thanks to your training, Ashton, I happen to excel at riding express and have been entrusted with some highly sensitive material. We've got a chance to get our hands on some of the finest explosives known to man. It comes straight from the laboratory of Antoine Lavoisier."

Ashton frowned. "A Frenchman? Sounds unlikely, my

friend. Why would France want to supply a band of American rebels?''

''This has nothing to do with governments,'' Harry insisted, his eyes dancing.

''Aye,'' Justice said with a grin. ''What can governments do if a private company happens to sell warlike supplies to the Americans?''

''They call themselves Hortalez et Cie,'' Harry explained. ''We'll have their powder by winter if our negotiations succeed.'' He plucked a scarlet poppy from a small bed near the steps and gazed at it glumly as he spoke. ''Things went smoothly for a time. I've slipped the British lines around Boston more times than I care to count.'' He drew in his breath and flung the poppy away.

''But . . . ?'' Ashton prompted, already aware that something had gone wrong.

''But he was caught,'' Justice said mournfully.

Harry nodded. ''By the cleverest infernal spy as ever swore allegiance to King George. The documents are safe, thank God, because Justice slipped away with them, but my face was seen. So far, no one's come banging on the door to arrest me; perhaps my name is still unknown.''

''How does this spy operate?'' Ashton inquired, wishing he were anywhere but in this drab little yard, about to be pressed into a damnable favor he had absolutely no desire to give.

''That's precisely the thing,'' Harry said. ''We simply don't know. I was so certain all was well. We made an exchange a week ago Sunday in Brunswick Church, all according to plan. I'm sure not a soul noticed; people were all agog because Miss Abigail Primrose was up from New York. She was Bethany's teacher, remember? Anyway, the entire operation went off without a snag.''

''Until that night,'' Justice supplied.

Harry nodded again. ''I shall miss the courier work,'' he admitted. ''Now I'll have to enlist to fight.''

Ashton scowled. ''That's nonsense, lad. You're no soldier.''

''Neither are any of the farmers and tradesmen and parsons who took on the Redcoats at Lexington and Concord. Neither were the Boston merchants who fought on the hill where Mr. Breed and Mr. Bunker used to graze their cattle."

"What about your wife?" Ashton asked in annoyance. "And the babe that's coming in the spring?"

"Felicia feels as strongly as I," Harry countered. "We want our child to grow up unencumbered by the yoke of English oppression."

Ashton bristled at the familiar show of Winslow bravado. Perhaps because of his upbringing—so privileged, so insulated—Harry believed himself invincible, and always counted on someone to be there to pick up the pieces when he made a mistake. But he was no longer a youth embarking on a sophomoric prank; he no longer had his father's influence to buy him out of trouble.

Seemingly unaware of Ashton's thoughts, Harry leaned forward, an avid look on his face. "You'd best go back in, Ashton. Justice and I will prepare the packet for you to transport to Newport, but 'tis best you know nothing of its origin."

Ashton scowled. "I've not said I'll do it."

"But you must. There's very little danger—"

"I'm not afraid of the danger. I simply don't want to get involved."

"You won't be, not really," Harry insisted. "All you need do is deliver it to Finley Piper at the White Horse."

Ashton stood up with the slightest of nods. It was far from the first time he'd given in to a Winslow's whim, and with acute self-disgust he knew it would not be the last.

Bethany was alone in the parlor, nibbling on a piece of toast and moving her hand pensively over a worn quilt on the settee. She looked up when Ashton entered. Even in the dimness she could see a war being waged in his eyes.

"Where's Harry?" she asked.

"He'll be in shortly. Felicia?"

"She went to the market for a last-minute item."

They sat together on the wooden settle, watching the shadows on the whitewashed wall across from them. Bethany picked up the teapot and filled a cup with lukewarm brew. "Tea?" she asked.

Ashton took it from her. Some of the agitation seemed to slip from his eyes as he raised the cup to his lips.

"Thank you," he said, then laughed.

"What is it?"

" 'Tis such a homely little scene," he remarked. "Anyone might mistake us for man and wife."

Bethany nearly choked on the bit of toast she was chewing. All at once she remembered why she had followed Ashton to the Bristol Ferry. Surely he'd think of a way to make her father change his mind about forcing her to marry Dorian Tanner.

"Ashton," she began, "there is something I must tell you. You're the only one who can help. Dorian—"

"Dorian again, is it?" he asked. A tic of irritation leaped at his temple. "Why don't you ask him for help?"

"I cannot! You see, he is the cause of—"

The front door crashed open and six British soldiers burst in, bayonets held ready. The officer, a sergeant, nodded briefly to Bethany.

"Sorry, Mrs. Winslow," he said curtly. "Duty, you see." Then the sergeant fastened his eyes on Ashton. "Harry Winslow," he intoned formally, "in the name of King George, I arrest you."

Bethany was on her feet immediately. "But he's not—" She fell silent when Ashton's hand bit into her wrist.

"What crime have I committed?" he demanded. Briefly, his eyes flicked to the passageway leading to the back of the house. Bethany nearly choked when she realized Ashton had willingly assumed Harry's identity.

" 'Tis not my place to explain, sir," the sergeant replied, "but we rarely arrest men we don't intend to hang."

Bethany clutched Ashton's arm as he went calmly to the door with the officer. "You can't do this," she cried urgently. "You mustn't let them take you."

But already Ashton had stepped outside with the Redcoats, who flanked him front and back and on either side. As the soldiers prepared to march, he turned back and looked at Bethany, who sagged against the door frame.

"A last word with my wife, sergeant?" he smoothly requested. The officer nodded, cautioning him to be brief.

Moments later Bethany was in his arms, biting her lips

against sobs of confusion and frustration. ''Ashton,'' she whispered, ''Ashton, this is all a terrible mistake.''

''Of course it is, pet,'' he replied.

''Then let's just tell them you're not Harry.''

''So they can arrest your brother instead?''

She gave a little squeak of alarm. Ashton spoke quickly. ''Have Felicia get word to him. He's not to show his face in Bristol until this blows over.''

''But you may be killed!'' she whispered desperately.

He shrugged. ''I won't put your brother before the hangman.''

''Ashton—''

He silenced her with a hand on her mouth. ''Come now, love, let me go. Give me a kiss like the good little wife you are.''

There was nothing reassuring about Ashton's kiss. It was desperate, hopeless, unbearably hard with passion and fear. And then he moved away, stepping amid the soldiers to be marched off to another man's trial.

Chapter 5

The swirling sea mists of evening lent an aura of nightmarish unreality to the scene in front of Harry's house. The setting sun, filtered by shifting clouds, limned the impassive faces of the soldiers and the determined firmness of Ashton's profile.

This isn't happening, Bethany told herself, battling the panic that spiraled up her spine.

Yet the sergeant's barked order and the subsequent rhythmic tramping of soldiers' boots snatched away the dreamlike quality of the scene, lending it fearsome reality.

"Where are you taking him?" Bethany asked, her voice shrill with alarm.

"The jail in Court Street, ma'am. He'll be brought before Colonel Darby Chason in the morning."

Bethany bit hard into the back of her hand to stifle a protest as the contingent disappeared down the street.

Felicia found her in this stricken stance when she returned from the market with a basket over her arm. "Bethany?" she asked softly.

Bethany swallowed, gathering together the frayed shreds of her composure. "Where's Harry?" she asked quickly.

"He'll be back shortly. Bethany, what—"

"Ashton has been arrested."

"What's he done?" Harry asked. He and Justice had entered from the back. Harry clutched a hemp-bound package under his arm.

Anger stabbed at Bethany as she regarded the bloom of exhilaration in her brother's cheeks. This was all just a game to him, another adventure.

"Ashton has just saved you from the hangman, Harry. 'Twas you they came to arrest, and Ashton didn't tell them otherwise."

Annoyance rather than consternation veiled Harry's face. His eyes dropped to the packet he held. "What now?" he asked Justice in a low voice.

"Your friend did a brave thing, mon," Justice replied. "He must know the importance of the cause."

"Ashton's only 'cause' is saving your foolish neck," Bethany told Harry. "You'll have to leave Bristol without delay. 'Tis only a matter of time before Colonel Chason finds out he has the wrong man."

Harry glanced down at his packet, cradling it like a rare treasure. "Damn," he said, half to himself. "How the hell are we going to get these to Newport now?"

"I'll try," Justice offered.

Harry shook his head vigorously. "And risk ending up on the auction block?" He raked a hand through his hair, pulling strands from its queue. "Maybe Ashton—"

"I'm sure he has no interest in your documents now," Bethany said bitterly. "You're wasting time, Harry. I shall see to Ashton. 'Tis the British army holding him; he's an English citizen."

"The Redcoats are not to be trusted," Harry warned.

"Have you a better solution?" she snapped.

His shoulders sagged a little. "Still getting me out of scrapes, aren't you?"

She'd softened to that boyish, appealing look many times in the past, but not now. "I can only wait until court sits in the morning. By then you must be well away from Bristol."

Harry handed his packet to Justice. "Do what you can. And look after Felicia while I'm gone." Justice nodded and receded back down the narrow passageway.

A short time later Harry was on his way to Providence, where Felicia's father would shelter him until it was safe to return.

Pale and shaken, Felicia set to the routine chores of fixing supper. She laid a meal of stew and bread on the table. Bethany nibbled at a corner of bread but declined the stew, having no room for food in the dreadfully twisting hollows of her stomach. Felicia ate with good appetite, blushing as she reached for a second helping.

"You must think me unfeeling to be eating like this after what just happened," she said.

Bethany forced a smile. "Eat, please do. You've the babe to think of."

Felicia attacked her meal again. Bethany marveled at the slimness her sister-in-law maintained despite her appetite; not the slightest swelling betrayed pregnancy on her willowy body.

"Why would the British want to arrest Harry?" Bethany asked.

Felicia wiped her mouth on her napkin and kept her eyes fastened on the oiled linen table covering. "My husband's loyalties are a threat to them."

"But men are not arrested simply because of political disagreements."

Felicia looked up. "Where have you been these past years, Bethany? Do you not know what has been happening? The British have begun to fear the patriots. Men have been dragged from their homes on the flimsiest of charges—"

Bethany brought her fist down on the table. "For God's sake, Felicia, an innocent man is being held for something Harry has done. I would know what that is." Felicia's eyes lowered like shutters, and Bethany's anger rose. "You can trust me with the truth. I may not agree with Harry's politics, but I'd never betray my own brother."

Felicia nodded, looking relieved. "Of course. Forgive me for even hesitating. Harry's been . . . active in the rebellion. Riding express and . . . procuring information about the British defense."

Bethany's face sank to her cupped hands. "A spy, then," she said dully. "Harry is a spy. Oh Lord, 'tis worse than I thought."

" 'Tis no sin," Felicia declared. "He has to follow his convictions. You of all people should understand that about your brother."

"Yes," Bethany said. "Harry will do what he must, no matter what the cost." No matter, she added silently, that Ashton is being held for crimes he hadn't committed. No matter that Felicia had been left alone in Bristol. "What will you do?" she asked.

"I must stay here. If I go to Providence, Colonel Chason's men are sure to follow me. Harry will find a way back to me."

"I don't like to think of you here alone."

"Justice will see to my needs. He's very loyal to Harry. He's also a skilled carpenter. You should have seen this house before Justice set to work on it. The man was . . . in dire circumstances when he arrived in Bristol."

"Justice is from a slaver, isn't he?" Bethany said with sudden insight. Felicia dropped her eyes. Bethany gave leave of the matter, seeing the answer in her sister-in-law's evasiveness. Damn Harry. Riding courier, spying, and harboring fugitive slaves. Yet the last of the three crimes met with her unabashed approval and exonerated him from the first two. Harry had a decided talent for endearing himself at the precise moment when he should be chastised.

Restlessly Bethany's thought moved to Ashton. Where was he now—in manacles somewhere in the jail, wondering how on earth he had landed himself in such an unenviable position, and how he could get out of it?

Frowning, she absently traced circles on the tablecloth with a nervous finger. Tomorrow this Colonel Chason would realize his mistake and release Ashton. But Harry was still in danger. Glancing at Felicia, Bethany felt an inkling of hope. Surely Chason was not so heartless as to take the life of a man whose wife was expecting a baby.

Feeling somewhat encouraged, she decided that, should Colonel Chason ever get his hands on Harry, the baby would provide ample cause for mercy. She went to bed that night in the house on Hope Street assuring herself that the nightmare would be over, for Ashton at least, when she presented herself before Colonel Chason in the morning.

Yet she awoke at dawn, her heart pounding from some unremembered dream. Her first conscious thought was, what if Chason was not the fair officer she expected him to be? What if he managed to find Ashton guilty? Unlike

Harry, Ashton didn't have the sentimental shield of a pregnant wife.

But Chason didn't know that. As she pulled on her rumpled riding habit, a grim smile tightened her lips.

Ashton sat stiffly on the hard wooden bench where he'd attempted to sleep the previous night. His elbows were on his knees, fingers steepled together in front of his face. The combined annoyances of a half dozen matters had robbed him of sleep and given him ample time to think. And to grow dangerously angry.

Harry Winslow was prominent in his black thoughts. The pup had no business riding express for the patriots, endangering his own life, and jeopardizing the future of his wife and child as well. Damn, was he even worth what Ashton had done on his account?

Yet Harry wasn't the only object of Ashton's temper. His thoughts swung to Bethany, who, after flirting for several weeks with Dorian Tanner, had suddenly come running to tell him of some as yet undisclosed trouble. He was beginning to feel like a human handkerchief for the girl, for God's sake. What was it she'd been trying to tell him just before Sergeant Watson had crashed into Harry's house?

Whatever outrage Dorian had committed had sent Bethany riding at breakneck speed to pour her heart out to Ashton. He was almost glad she'd not had the chance to saddle him with her worries. He'd shouldered enough of other people's problems.

Scowling into his hands, Ashton turned his mind to his latest and most immediate annoyance: the British militia. Granted the Redcoats believed him to be Harry Winslow, guilty of high treason, but they treated him more like a condemned man than a prisoner awaiting trial. He'd been given lukewarm beer and days-old bread to eat, this abominable bench to sleep on, and not enough water even to wash his hands.

Sergeant Watson opened the door with his shoulder. "Up with you. Court's about to sit."

The guards flanked Ashton, snapping their heels smartly at Watson's commands. The corridors of the building were thick with soldiers. Ashton paid them little heed until he heard a man speaking with a familiar cockney accent.

"Jesus," said Sergeant Mansfield, peering curiously at him.

Ashton would have been grateful to stop and explain his situation to the man who had been his superior at Fort George, but Watson's men hurried him through the corridor. He could only spread his arms helplessly as a bayonet nudged him into a receiving chamber appointed with a long table in front, benches along the back.

On the far wall was an overlarge and overflattering portrait of King George III in his coronation robes. A more accurate picture, Ashton decided cynically, would depict a fat man with pop eyes. For years King George had been a dim abstraction three thousand miles away, but if his army continued this harassment, the monarch would soon become a very real abomination.

The British officers at the table supported enough brass on their uniforms to sink a whaler. The men were groomed and wigged far too grandly, Ashton thought, for the task of finding a man guilty of treason. In the middle sat the presiding officer, Colonel Darby Chason. Ashton stood before this man, meeting his gaze directly.

Darby Chason appeared the consummate officer, sitting ramrod stiff in a thronelike wooden chair. He had a hawk nose and keen eyes, one of them enlarged by a gilt-edged monocle, and lips so severely thin that they appeared almost nonexistent. There was anger in that imperious face and a glint of cynicism in the magnified monocled eye.

Chason studied Ashton for long moments, as if testing his prisoner's ability to withstand the pressure of his scrutiny. Then he neatened a stack of papers in front of him and nodded at the bailiff.

Before the bailiff could open his mouth, there was a scuffling sound at the door. It swung open and Bethany Winslow pushed inside, staring down the guards as if defying them to attempt removing her.

Ashton couldn't help but admire her aplomb, her regal bearing as she crossed to the long table. Today her beauty was endearingly flawed; he noticed smudges of fatigue beneath her large eyes and a decided lack of color in her cheeks. He was not surprised she had come alone; Harry was either too wise or too selfish to appear.

He couldn't deny his gladness at her arrival. As she faced the Redcoats, she reminded him of a slightly rumpled flower. Ashton's pleasure slipped away when he noticed a defiant gleam in her topaz eyes. He realized she fully intended to complicate an already troublesome situation.

"Get her out," he growled, jerking his head.

Bethany planted herself beside him, tossing her head. "I've a vested interest in the outcome of this proceeding."

Sergeant Watson stepped forward and whispered something to Colonel Chason, who nodded. "You may take a seat by the door, Mrs. Winslow," he said finally. Then, as a concession to Ashton's obvious displeasure, he added, "You will be removed at the slightest outburst, ma'am."

Bethany settled herself on the bench. Ashton fixed a hard stare on her, trying to tell her wordlessly that she'd jeopardize Harry's life if she insisted on speaking up. She met his eyes placidly, her face immobile, her resolve as firm as her upturned chin.

"Shall we proceed?" Colonel Chason questioned.

The bailiff clapped his heels together and the court scribe dipped his quill.

"State your name," the bailiff intoned.

Ashton almost smiled at the irony of it. "Just who do you think you've arrested?"

" 'Tis accepted procedure," the bailiff said, non plussed by Ashton's easy and cynical manner.

"Ah yes, we must behave acceptably at all costs."

Colonel Chason cleared his throat and shook his head in annoyance, raising a waft of heavy-scented pomatum that caused the lieutenant beside him to cough. "Let us get on with this, Mr. Winslow. You've been arrested for high treason. What say you to the charge?"

"I'd say, sir, that the fact that I've been arrested is undeniably true."

Chason shifted his monocle from one eye to the other. "Have you any political opinions, Mr. Winslow?"

Ashton grinned and hooked a thumb into the waist of his breeches. "None whatsoever, sir."

"Yet you've just admitted to treason."

"No, sir. I admitted to being arrested for treason."

The officer scowled. "Are you a patriot, Mr. Winslow?"

"I am a horseman, sir."

"I think you are being quite deliberately evasive."

Ashton gave a short laugh. "What's this? A soldier who *thinks?*"

The monocle dropped from Chason's astonished eye. The scribe's quill scratched furiously.

"Would you insult an agent of your king, Mr. Winslow?" the colonel demanded.

"Would you rather I insult King George himself?" Ashton returned. " 'Tis no difficult task, that. The monarch you so loyally serve is a soft-brained madman who would milk the Colonies dry to fill his privy purse, whose ministries are headed by ill-informed mediocrities."

Chason shook his head. "God, what has England bred in her Colonies?"

"A generation of men and women who think for themselves," Ashton shot back.

"A generation of outlaws," Chason snarled.

Ashton shrugged. "Just keep Lord North's hands out of our pockets and we'll be obedient servants."

The colonel's hand clapped down on the table. "Have you no principles, sir?"

"Oh, aye," Ashton assured him. "But it just so happens my principles are at variance with the policies of His Majesty's government."

"That is treason in itself!" Colonel Chason shouted, his lips receding completely into his face.

"Is it now?" Ashton queried calmly.

"Are you aware that you've committed a hanging offense?"

"Aye, sir. More than one in your august judgment."

Chason blinked very slowly. Almost reluctantly he replied, "Then there is nothing more to be said, no need for witnesses." The monocled eye raked over Ashton. "There is but one way to save yourself from hanging."

Ashton smiled. "I am—dare I say it?—dying to know what that way is, sir."

"This court would show you mercy if you were to . . . cooperate."

"Cooperate?" The word felt bitter on Ashton's tongue. "You mean name names, places, that sort of thing?"

"Yes. Spare yourself, man. The lives of a few radicals aren't worth hanging for."

"Who am I to decide that, Colonel?"

They stared at each other for a long, tense moment. "So," Chason said, "you'll tell us nothing?"

"No." Ashton had never meant anything more sincerely in his life.

"I'm afraid there's nothing more I can do," Chason said. The other officers nodded. The gavel descended onto the table. "By the authority of His Majesty King George the Third, I sentence you, Harry Winslow, to hang at noon on this day, the eighteenth of August in the year of our Lord seventeen hundred and seventy-five."

Ashton heard a soft gasp behind him. He was as surprised as Bethany by the sentence, delivered even before the charges had been debated and borne witness to. He wondered how far he should push the officer before revealing the misunderstanding.

"About the hanging, sir," he said slowly. "Must it be so . . . expedient?"

"I've little time to spare granting last requests to wastrels like you. Besides, were we to keep you in custody, you'd likely meet a slow, tormented death aboard one of the prison ships."

Ashton considered that, then grinned. While in the army, he'd heard dreadful tales of the conditions on prison ships. Keeping his grin in place, he bowed to the colonel with mock formality. "I defer to your better judgment in this, sir. Hanging is far more merciful."

He nearly laughed aloud at the expressions on the assembled officers' faces. "There now, gentlemen," he added consolingly, "there's nothing at all to choosing a way to die. 'Tis choosing a way to live that presents a puzzle. A puzzle you have so kindly spared me from having to solve."

"You are either very brave or very foolish, sir," Colonel Chason said. He waved an agitated hand at the guards. "Take him away. Prepare to carry out the sentence."

Bethany was on her feet immediately. *"No!"* Her ragged, horrified objection filled the silent room. She rushed across to Colonel Chason, looking like an impossibly lovely tawny-gold angel. "This man is innocent!"

Chason shook his head, scattering more powder. "His actions over the course of the summer have been noted by my informants. His speech today only proves his utter impenitence." Again Chason nodded at the guards. "Carry on," he snapped.

Bethany placed herself in front of Ashton. The sergeant took her by the arm. "Mrs. Winslow—"

"I am *not* Mrs. Winslow, you infernal fool! I am *Miss* Bethany Winslow, and this man you intend to murder is not my brother Harry!"

A murmur went up from the assembly as the door opened to admit several more Redcoats. Ashton expelled his breath as he recognized the officer who had just entered the room. The ruse would soon be over.

The man presented himself to Colonel Chason with a smart salute. "What is it, Sergeant Mansfield?"

"Permission to speak, sir."

"No one else has done me the courtesy of asking," Colonel Chason replied dryly. "You may speak."

"I saw this man being brought up from the jail and thought to point out to you that Ashton Markham performed four years of loyal service under my command. He was wounded in the line of duty at Fort George nine months ago."

"Who the devil is Ashton Markham?"

"Why, the prisoner, sir!"

The buzz in the room swelled to a low roar. The bailiff pounded madly with his staff and shouted for silence.

Colonel Chason leaped to his feet. His monocle swung, unheeded, against the front of his scarlet coat. "Sergeant Watson, what is the meaning of this?"

The sergeant reddened to the tips of his ears. "Blimey if I know, sir. I was only carrying out orders."

The colonel held himself stiffly. "Take your men and find Harry Winslow straightaway," he ordered.

The sergeant scurried from the chamber, and Colonel Chason switched his agitated gaze to Ashton, who was trying to conceal a look of amusement.

"You've an insolent and infuriating manner, Mr. Markham," the colonel said. He turned and addressed Mansfield. "The punishment still stands."

Bethany stepped in front of Ashton, her face deathly pale. "But he's done nothing, sir."

The colonel opened and shut his mouth three times in quick succession. "Miss Winslow—or whoever you are—this man has committed treason and slander in this very room. For that he must hang; 'tis a matter of political necessity."

"Mr. Markham was tried without benefit of counsel or witnesses. He—"

Ashton touched her shoulder, no longer amused but too astounded at Chason's high-handedness to fully appreciate the severity of the sentence he'd been dealt. " 'Tis all quite legal, I'm afraid, love."

She whipped around fiercely, her eyes snapping with fury. "Will you just let them hang you, then? Without any protest at all?"

His anger matched hers as he was suddenly stricken by a keen sense of his own mortality. "I don't see as I've been given any choice."

Colonel Chason barked an order and the men formed up in readiness to escort the prisoner from the chamber.

"Wait!" Bethany shouted, standing in the doorway and gripping its frame as if to fix herself there for all eternity. Ashton studied her searchingly. He could almost hear the whir and click of her mind as she rapidly calculated. What was she up to now?

Without looking at Ashton, she calmly addressed the colonel. "Sir, in the name of decency you cannot allow Ashton Markham to hang."

"And why not, pray?"

She moistened her lips and drew a deep, shuddering breath. "I didn't want to bring up an indelicate subject, sir, but I see that I must. I need Ashton Markham, and he's of little use to me dead."

Ashton couldn't help the smile that curved his lips. Although misguided and certainly futile, the arrogance Bethany showed the British officer ignited a flame of tenderness within him.

"My dear," Chason said patronizingly, "this man has spoken treason before this court of military law."

"Still," Bethany said, an odd, strained look on her face, "I cannot believe our sovereign's army is completely heartless."

Chason groped for his monocle and raised it to his eye. "What's that? Are you a Loyalist, then, miss?"

"To my very soul," Bethany returned primly.

"Ah. Then perhaps you can solve this mix by telling me your brother Harry's whereabouts."

She regarded him steadily. "I do not know where Harry is."

Ashton was impressed by her finesse in lying. Chason obviously believed her, for he questioned her no further.

"Colonel Chason," Bethany said, "I respectfully ask that you release this man."

"I'm sorry, miss," the colonel said with new sincerity, "but I cannot. The ruling can only be overturned in the case of some mitigating circumstance."

"There is one," she said faintly. Ashton glanced at her sharply. She looked almost as pallid as she had on the ferry yesterday.

"What's that?" the colonel said. "Speak up, girl."

She cleared her throat, and Ashton discerned a light sheen of moistness on her brow. "Colonel Chason," she said more loudly, "there *is* a 'mitigating circumstance.' " Her chin tilted up at a determined angle. "Ashton Markham has compromised my honor, sir, and gotten me with child. If he is hanged, I'll be forced to bear the babe in shame and rear it in poverty."

Ashton's breath left him with a great whoosh. Bethany's words stunned him more than the death sentence he'd just been dealt. And hurt him more than the rough hemp of a noose biting into the flesh of his neck.

As the assembly murmured and exclaimed among themselves, a great rage took hold of Ashton and squeezed, hard. Suddenly things came together to form a picture with dreadful clarity. So this was why Bethany had sought him out so frantically yesterday, why she had been so ill on the voyage to Bristol. Dorian Tanner had gotten his bastard on her and refused to marry her. *The most awful thing has happened*. . . . The words she'd choked tearfully against his chest on the ferry, evoking tenderness, now swam through his mind and evoked nothing resembling tenderness at all.

The revelation seethed and swelled in Ashton's mind. He didn't hear Colonel Chason until Sergeant Mansfield nudged him in the ribs.

"I asked, Mr. Markham," the colonel repeated, "if you did, indeed, compromise Miss Winslow."

"I've no doubt the young lady has been compromised," Ashton answered.

"Were you aware that she is—er—enceinte?"

Ashton looked at Bethany. Their eyes met and clashed. Then she looked away, shuddering as if chilled by his icy stare.

"I am now," he said.

Colonel Chason waved his hand at the scribe, who had been scratching away with his quill. "That will do, Walker. This entire affair is distasteful enough; no need to make it a matter of public record." He turned back to Ashton. "What do you propose to do, Mr. Markham?"

"I seem to recall I've been sentenced to hang, sir."

Colonel Chason cleared his throat. "Yes, well, I think not. Instead you will marry this poor girl. Perhaps the responsibilities of a wife and child will make you think twice about spouting sedition and insulting the king's men. I may even dare hope the lady will teach you some measure of loyalty." He addressed Sergeant Mansfield, who looked vastly relieved. "Is the magistrate in this morning?"

"Aye, sir, just down the hall."

Chason gave a satisfied nod. "Fetch him without delay." The monocle came up to magnify the eye that focused on Ashton. "Count yourself lucky for Miss Winslow's intervention, sir. And if you hope to seek an annulment or desert the young lady, think again. My informants will be watching you. If I learn you've not done right by Miss Winslow, you will hang immediately."

Bethany gasped, then pressed her lips together, clutching the doorway for support. Ashton tried to keep the terrible rage from his voice when he said, ''Really, Colonel Chason, I don't think—''

The colonel smiled, slowly and diabolically. ''Why is it, Mr. Markham, that you are less reluctant to meet the gallows than your bride? Perhaps, as they say, you deem matrimony with Miss Winslow a fate worse than death.''

Ashton set his jaw hard and looked longingly out the window, where a picket detachment had begun constructing a gallows. Then he raked Bethany with a gaze so furious that she winced visibly.

''Exactly so, sir,'' he said.

The wedding, such as it was, consisted of a hasty signing of papers and another stern warning from Colonel Chason.

Ashton felt only hollowness where his heart used to be. In the space of one hour, two entities had conspired to rob him of his freedom: the British army and Bethany Winslow Markham.

Chapter 6

Ashton took the length of Court Street with strides so long that Bethany had to run to catch up. He didn't look back at her; he didn't say a word. Her mind reeled with the impact of what she'd just done; she, too, was speechless. Later there would be much to say—she dreaded to think just how much—but such was not for the ears of the seamen and soldiers and women who hurried through the busy street.

The entire morning had been a series of absurdities that would have struck Bethany as farcical had it not been so terribly real. And final.

She couldn't blame Ashton for being angry at having been forced to marry her. Yet the alternative was hanging! Couldn't he see that she'd only lied to save his neck?

He stopped at one of the wharves and had a word with the ferrymaster, then turned to her.

"Wait here," he ordered. "I'll be back shortly."

"Where are you going?"

A scowl would have been more encouraging than the cold smile he gave her. "To find Justice Richmond. I seem to recall he and Harry had a delivery they wanted me to make." Without pausing for an answer, he pivoted on his boot heel and strode away.

Bethany watched his retreat, unaware that she had lifted her knuckles to her mouth and was savaging her flesh with nervous teeth.

"Oh, Lord," she murmured, "what have I done?"

"What, indeed, Miss Bethany Winslow?" came a clipped voice behind her. Bethany turned to see Miss Abigail Primrose, who had appeared on the dock, her tiny kid-clad foot tapping with studied precision on the wooden planks.

"We are not a flytrap," Miss Abigail intoned crisply. "Close your mouth, miss!"

Responding automatically to her teacher's familiar imperative, Bethany snapped her mouth shut. Then she said, "I'm sorry, Miss Abigail. You surprised me."

The lady waved a small, immaculately gloved hand. "I am on holiday from New York. The academy has been turned into barracks for His Majesty's soldiers." With eyes the color of gunmetal Miss Abigail took in Bethany's poorly done hair and rumpled riding habit.

"I never thought it important to dwell on grooming and dress in my teaching," she said severely, "but perhaps I should consider introducing those topics into the curriculum. Bethany? Child, have you heard a word I've said?"

Bethany drew a shaky breath, tasting the bitterness of brine in the air. "No, ma'am," she admitted. "I—er—"

"What's this?" Miss Abigail said, raising her tiny chin high above her stiff white collar. "My best student of elocution is at a loss for words?" She paused, leaning forward to peer more closely at Bethany. Her voice softened. "Tears, miss?" Suddenly Miss Abigail's body became supple and mobile beneath its starched exterior. She stretched out her narrow arms. "Come here, child. You've not forgotten I am your friend as well as your teacher."

Bethany stumbled forward, drawn by Miss Abigail's gentleness. Although the lady was considerably smaller than Bethany, she had a firm embrace and a generosity of heart that made her seem much larger.

"There," she soothed, her familiar scent of barley water enveloping Bethany, "you may as well get over your tears straightaway, for I shan't release you until you do."

Bethany nodded against the corded silk of her shoulder and stepped back. "I'm sorry, Miss Abigail."

"Stop apologizing, child. 'Tis an explanation I want. What is troubling you?"

Bethany lowered herself to an upended barrel. As Miss Abigail's penetrating gray stare appraised her, the fog lifted from Bethany's mind. She scarcely knew where to begin.

But Miss Abigail was waiting. The crisp breeze didn't dare stir a single ebony hair on that erectly held head.

"I'm married," Bethany confessed.

Miss Abigail rarely showed surprise, but she allowed one carefully plucked eyebrow to lift. "I see. Was that your husband who just walked away from you?"

Bethany nodded. "His name is Ashton Markham."

"He's inordinately handsome."

Bethany's eyes widened at the idea that Miss Abigail Primrose would notice—and appreciate—a man's looks. "Yes," she agreed. "Yes, he is that."

"Yet I sense a certain . . . commonness about him."

"There is nothing common about Ashton Markham," Bethany said quickly. "If he looks somewhat . . . unkempt, 'tis because he spent last night in the custody of Colonel Darby Chason."

Miss Abigail's other pruned eyebrow joined its partner high on her forehead. She seated herself beside Bethany and folded her gloved hands primly on her knee. "It appears we've much to discuss, child," she murmured.

The entire incredible, absurd story poured from Bethany then, beginning with her fascination with Ashton upon returning to Seastone and her plot to use Dorian to make him jealous, and ending with the wrongful arrest and travesty of a trial.

"He was sentenced to hang, Miss Abigail," Bethany said. "So I simply blurted out that he—he'd gotten me with child."

"And has he?" Miss Abigail's voice sounded higher than normal.

"Of course not," Bethany assured her quickly. "I'm as chaste as I was when I left the academy." She looked down at her hands and added, "Unfortunately, most of Bristol now thinks otherwise. The idea had been lurking in my head, I suppose, because Harry's wife is expecting. I remember being surprised that she looked so slim and fit."

Something akin to admiration glimmered in Miss Abigail's shining eyes. Birdlike, she cocked her head to one side. "You always had a lively imagination," she commented. "And a quick wit. A bit too quick, I fear, for your own good."

A wan smile haunted Bethany's lips as she regarded her teacher. No one but Miss Abigail would accept her story so matter-of-factly. Her timely arrival on the dock had been a godsend.

A gloved hand smoothed back Bethany's wind-tangled hair in a gesture more maternal than any Lillian Winslow had ever bestowed. Bethany studied her teacher for a moment, seeing her in a new light. Why had she never noticed how remarkably pretty Miss Abigail was, with her raven hair and china-doll face? Her tiny figure was compact, as well proportioned as a Bartholomew fashion baby. With a start, Bethany realized her teacher was probably not much older than thirty.

"Thank you for listening," she said. "I needed a friend just now. Miss Abigail, why is Ashton so angry? He barely spoke to me after we left the jail."

"You saved his neck, child, but at the price of his pride."

"I don't know what you mean."

"His pride, child. Men are fools when it comes to such things. In one morning you've managed to wrest control of his life from his own hands. From the way you described Mr. Markham, I'd say that's no small price."

"But he'd have died!"

"It sounds as if the man condemned himself. Yet he did so of his own free will."

"And the marriage was willed by me," Bethany added dully.

"Exactly."

"What shall I do, Miss Abigail?"

The tiny kid-clad foot began tapping again. "Your parents are sure to object, and Mr. Markham is furious at you. But you say you love him, Bethany. Hold on to that. Be a good wife to him, even though he resents you. Tread lightly on the man's pride; it's been deeply wounded."

"Damn Harry," Bethany murmured, half to herself. Seeing Miss Abigail's questioning look, she added, "If it weren't for him, I wouldn't be in this fix. At least he's safe in Providence—"

"Your brother's gone to Providence?"

Bethany nodded. "To his wife's father's." Briefly she wondered why her teacher seemed so interested in Harry.

Miss Abigail glanced back at the street and stood, resting her hand firmly on Bethany's arm. "Your husband is coming," she said quickly, her other hand moving to eradicate a single wrinkle in her corded silk skirt. "Please try not to botch the introductions, child."

But botch them Bethany did, stammering as she presented Ashton to her teacher. "My hus—" she faltered, then began again. "Miss Abigail, this is Ashton Markham."

He bowed slightly, the parcel under his arm rustling with the movement.

"Your wife was always a favorite of mine," Miss Abigail said firmly, as if daring him to contradict her. "She is a young lady of considerable intelligence and heart."

"I agree with you about her intelligence," Ashton said smoothly, looking down to meet that gunmetal stare. "About the heart . . . I am not so sure."

"Then you'd best be about getting to know the girl," Miss Abigail said imperatively.

He cast a cool glance at Bethany, who shivered under the assault of his too blue eyes. "I daresay I know her abundantly well, Miss Primrose. Good day." He captured Bethany's arm and turned smartly.

"I'll write," she said over her shoulder.

Miss Abigail Primrose lifted a white-gloved hand in farewell, and her thin lips formed an encouraging smile. But Bethany didn't feel encouraged; Ashton was pulling her along the dock to the ferry, and the bite of his grip promised something far less agreeable than a honeymoon.

By the time the stabler at Bristol Ferry brought the horses around, Bethany's nerves were wound taut with tension. Ashton had completely ignored her during the short voyage across the bay, in favor of a lively discussion with a Quaker man on the merits of the hackamore over the bit. Bethany mounted and watched as Ashton did likewise. He twisted in the saddle to secure his package with a leather strap.

As Bethany's eyes were drawn to the hemp-strung parcel, she suddenly remembered where she'd seen it before, remembered Harry passing it to Justice, murmuring, "Do what you can with this."

There was no mistaking the significance of Harry's papers. Windheads of fear and disappointment added to the emotional hurricane that had raged in her all morning. She looked up; her gaze locked with Ashton's. Lord, why had she never noticed how utterly cold those eyes were?

"Oh, no," she said softly, braving his icy stare. "Oh, Ashton, you cannot get involved with the rebels."

He laughed humorlessly; the bitterness in his voice stung her like a lash. "Involved?" he queried. "I believe I have just proven myself one of them."

"But you must not—"

" 'Must not,' Bethany? How quickly you take to wifely imperatives." He nudged Corsair with his heels and led the way to Newport.

Bethany brought Calliope in step with the stallion. "Please, Ashton," she called over the sound of cantering hoofs, " 'tis only that I fear for you."

"You're just smothering me with your favor this morning, aren't you," he sneered.

"Don't be this way," she pleaded, feeling her throat constrict with the ache of unshed tears. "Please don't be so angry. I—I'm sorry you were given no choice about marrying me, but I didn't know what else to do."

"I believe you knew exactly what you were doing," he returned harshly. "Still, I suppose I should sink to my knees in gratitude. You did, after all, snatch me from death's door so I may spend the rest of my life in matrimonial bliss with you."

She recoiled inwardly, lanced by his sarcasm. The girlish fantasies she'd indulged all summer suddenly took on a nightmarish quality. Miss Abigail had once warned her about wanting something too much; achieving a dream often led to disillusionment. Here she was married to the man she loved, but nothing had happened the way she'd imagined it. There had been no tender proposal on bended knee, no church bells and well-wishers, no grand ceremony to end in a loving kiss.

There was only the heaviness of sorrow over what she'd done, and Ashton's bitterness over the fate she'd forced on him. Still, Bethany clung to the idea that she had saved his life. She glanced at him, trying not to flinch under his sharp glare.

"Am I to feel guilty, then, for having induced Colonel Chason to spare your life?"

His lips twisted into a sarcastic smile. "You've never been one to feel guilty, my love."

For the first time in his life Ashton entered the Winslow mansion through the front door, snatching Mrs. Hastings's composure as he strode across the vestibule, Bethany following with small, hurried steps. Graceful mahogany newels and balusters flew by in a blur as he crossed to the library door and pulled it open with a jerk. He stepped into a room that smelled of leather and tobacco and the less tangible but quite noticeable tinge of money.

Sinclair Winslow raised startled eyes from his copy of the *Newport Gazette*. "Ah, there you are, Markham," he said briskly, placing his knuckles on the surface of his Goddard desk. "I've been wanting to see you about a horse trade I made in Little Rest yesterday."

Ashton took a moment to study the man who, save for a four-year hiatus in the British Army, had been his employer all his life. Sinclair Winslow was shrewd, severe, arrogant, and so brimming with blue blood that he found it hard to contend with ordinary people. A sapphire stud of considerable size winked from his cambric stock.

"Send for your wife, Mr. Winslow," Ashton said. "I must speak to both of you." He looked back at the door. Before Mrs. Hastings could duck guiltily away, he repeated his request to her. The housekeeper hurried off to find Mrs. Winslow.

Moments later Lillian appeared, touching a pampered hand to her faintly puckered brow.

"Please sit down, Mrs. Winslow," Ashton said gently. His voice hardened perceptibly as he added, "Bethany and I have something to tell you."

Lillian arranged herself in the Townsend chair by the

fireplace. Ashton moved to the sideboard and poured a generous dram of brandy for Sinclair and a crystal goblet of Madeira for Lillian. The Winslows were apparently too shocked by his overly familiar actions to protest. He handed them the drinks, his brow as dark as a thundercloud.

"Bethany and I were married this morning."

Lillian's mouth formed a silent O.

"What!" Sinclair exploded.

"You heard me. Bethany and I are man and wife."

Sinclair's brandy disappeared in a single gulp. "By God, this is an outrage, you greedy upstart! I'll have you flogged within an inch of your life!"

"Father, please," Bethany said.

He turned the full force of his glare on her. "And you, young lady—how dare you defy me in this way? I told you only yesterday that matters had been satisfactorily settled with Captain Tanner."

God, Ashton thought. Was Winslow actually pleased Tanner had ruined his daughter?

"To your satisfaction, Father, not mine," Bethany retorted.

"And this"—Sinclair waved an agitated hand at Ashton—"*this* is satisfactory to you?"

" 'Tis done," Bethany replied quietly, keeping her eyes averted from Ashton.

"Oh, Bethany," Lillian wailed, fanning herself with her hand, "think of your reputation."

"That is exactly what she was thinking of," Ashton commented dryly, unmoved by Sinclair's temper.

"I will not allow this," Sinclair blustered. The sapphire stud winked as he loosened his stock. His neck was flushed an angry red. "We'll arrange for an annulment at once."

"No!" Bethany cried, remembering Colonel Chason's promise of dire consequences should they not remain married.

Lillian wept softly into her manicured hands as Sinclair absently accepted more brandy from Ashton. His murderous gaze climbed to the younger man's face. "How much?" he asked sharply.

"Sir?"

"Don't play ignorant with me, Markham. 'Tis clear you wed Bethany to get your hands on her portion. I'll pay you double that—whatever price you name—if you'll consent right now to an annulment."

Bethany blinked at Sinclair. What a dry stick her father was. Such a man of facts and figures would never be moved by human emotions.

She saw Sinclair stiffen as Ashton's eyes stabbed him with furious resentment. " 'Tis all shillings and pence with you, isn't it?" he asked harshly.

"I suspect a man like you is vulnerable to my brand of persuasion."

"Not at all, sir. I will not take so much as a single copper from you."

"Do you realize how much money I'm willing to part with, Mr. Markham?"

"Keep it," Ashton growled. "Every bloody penny of it."

"You drive a keen bargain, Markham."

"I drive no bargain at all. Believe me, money was the last thing on my mind when I married your daughter."

Sinclair rose from the massive desk, taking the length of the library with angry strides. "Just how do you intend to support Bethany?"

"As I've supported myself all my life. By the sweat of my back. Her pampered life will be a thing of the past, of course, but she didn't pause to consider that this morning."

"I can't bear it," Lillian wailed into her hands. "My daughter, living in a servant's cottage—"

"Bethany may stay here," Ashton snapped. "In her own room with my sister dancing attendance on her. But not for long, I'm afraid, Mrs. Winslow. I've decided to peddle my horseman's skills elsewhere. We'll be leaving soon."

Sinclair wheeled about. "What's this?" he demanded.

"I shall be leaving your employ," Ashton repeated, enunciating very clearly.

"But you cannot! What about the races, the breeding program—"

Ashton's laughter cut a dry, humorless swath through

the tension-thick air. "Have I not mortified you enough by marrying Bethany? Would you still keep me around to pander to your horse trade?"

"I am a businessman before all else," Sinclair said. "I've never made light of my admiration for your skill with horses."

"I see. I'm good enough to raise your horses but not to marry your daughter."

"Quite so. You cannot leave. I'll become a laughingstock if my horses cease to win. Damn, but I was wrong to think you'd inherited your father's loyalty. . . ." Sinclair broke off abruptly and snapped his fingers. He rushed to a Smibert portrait of one of his horses and moved it aside to reveal a wall cache. From this he extracted a document, yellowed and crisp with age, and handed it to Ashton with a tight smile. "As a matter of fact, Roger did leave you something. A legacy, if you will. You won't be going anywhere for a long time, Markham."

"What is this?" Ashton asked. He fished his spectacles from his pocket.

"An old debt," Sinclair said. "One I'd forgotten until you gave me a most unpleasant reminder today."

Ashton's eyes scanned the page, narrowing behind the spectacles. His jaw grew tighter and tighter as he read. Dread seized Bethany as she strained to read the document.

Sinclair chuckled humorlessly. "Seems your father never told you he'd indentured himself to me, Mr. Markham. Fool that he was, he accepted a wage instead of serving out his seven years. Had some infernal idea about getting you a gentleman's education."

"What has this to do with me?" Ashton asked tautly.

"Read on. There's a clause in the agreement stating that if Roger failed to serve out his bondage, the obligation would fall to his firstborn son." Ashton found the clause. The edges of the paper crumpled helplessly in his hard grip. Bethany's gasp shuddered through the air.

"You're mine," Sinclair announced. "You belong to *me*, body and soul, and you'll breed and train my horses exclusively for the next seven years."

Ashton let the document slip from his fingers. It wafted

gently to the floor and settled in front of Sinclair's silver-buckled shoes.

"I demand my portion!" Bethany burst out. "I intend to buy Ashton's indenture from you."

Ashton tore off his spectacles and turned on her, stiff-lipped with rage. "I am already your husband," he snarled. "Would you call me slave as well?"

"No! Ashton, I didn't mean—"

On feet made swift with fury, Ashton left the house. Her heart in her mouth, Bethany heard the clatter of Corsair's hoofs on the stone drive as Ashton drove him to Newport.

She faced her father with wide, horrified eyes. "How could you?" she whispered. "How *dare* you?"

"I have done nothing amiss," Sinclair said. "I am merely invoking the terms of Roger Markham's indenture. Terms he readily agreed to."

"Because he trusted you! He never would have wanted his son to be a bond servant!"

Sinclair extracted a wad of tobacco from his leather-clad humidor and tamped it into his clay pipe. "I'm sure Roger never expected his son to do so foolish a thing as to marry above himself."

"Why, Bethany?" Lillian asked suddenly. "Why did you marry him?"

Bethany turned to the French window and allowed a sigh to shudder from her lips. Nothing would be served by spilling the entire twisted tale to her parents. They would only be hurt to learn Harry was a fugitive from justice. And they would never understand the lie she had told to induce Colonel Chason to revoke Ashton's sentence.

"You had everything," Lillian persisted. "Every advantage we could give you."

Bethany smiled bitterly out the window. "Not quite everything," she contradicted. "You've spent a small fortune on my education and clothes, but when did you ever give me the love I needed? How young was I—three, four?—when I learned not to muss your gown by crawling into your lap? By the time I was five I discovered there was more companionship to be found in the stables than at your knee!"

"Bethany, I do not see what this has to do with what you have done. You could have had any man you chose. Captain Tanner has offered for you—"

"I *chose* Ashton Markham," Bethany said firmly. Foolishly, perhaps, and impetuously, but she *had* chosen him, long before this morning. She moved toward the door.

"Where are you going?" Sinclair demanded.

"To pack some things. I shall be out of the house in an hour."

"Bethany," Lillian said faintly, "surely you don't mean to live in that—that hovel by the stables."

"I mean to live with my husband." She fixed a stare on her father. "Thanks to you, that 'hovel' is to be my home for the next seven years." She walked out and closed the door.

Only when she was safely outside the library did Bethany realize how badly she was shaking. Behind her she could hear the muffled sounds of her mother's sobs.

Regret came on tiptoe, seizing her by surprise. Never had she deliberately hurt her parents. They'd done nothing to deserve such a shock. Her hand found the brass door handle. Perhaps she should speak to them again, try to explain. . . .

"Let her go," her father was saying. "She'll come running back as soon as she gets a taste of what little Markham has to offer her."

"I cannot bear the shame," Lillian wailed. "I shall not be able to face my friends! And Governor Wanton's reception is next week. . . ."

Bethany's hand dropped from the door handle and she walked listlessly away. Her mother's greatest concern was social disgrace, not the fact that Bethany might have just made the most desperate mistake of her life.

"This isn't how we'd planned it at all," Carrie Markham said as she selected an assortment of smallclothes from a lowboy chest and tossed them onto the bed. "Are you sure your father won't settle your portion on you?"

"Even if he did, Ashton wouldn't accept it."

"Then he's a fool," Carrie snapped.

"He's a proud man." Bethany shuddered to think how many times that pride had been trodden upon in the space of one day.

"Stupid of me," Carrie said, half to herself. "I should have thought of your parents. While you wooed Ashton, we should have been preparing your father and mother for this moment." She jerked the walnut armoire open, fingering the silks and velvets of ballgowns and formal dresses.

"Leave those," Bethany said with a dismissive wave of her hand. "I shan't be needing them." Ruefully she shook her head. She owned perhaps two dresses that wouldn't look completely out of place in Ashton's cottage. Yet she knew she wouldn't miss her ridiculously extensive wardrobe.

"What about me?" Carrie's voice was strident.

"You shall have to stay on here in some other capacity."

"As what? A slut in the scullery?"

"Mother's maid is getting on in years. Perhaps you can take Edith's place."

"But I can't possibly please Mistress Lillian. I'd need four hands just to do her hair."

Feeling tugged in all directions, Bethany wished Carrie would stop complaining. Ashton's resentment, her father's duplicity, her mother's wailing . . . and now Carrie's self-pity and unconcealed disappointment at not having a portion of the new wealth she'd expected all gathered into a wave that threatened to overwhelm her.

Her heart was heavier than the tightly packed valise she carried down to the cottage by the stables. She wondered why she'd never noticed the great distance between her father's house and the stable compound, or the sharpness of contrast between the gambrel-roofed mansion and the stone-end cottage with its split-maple shingles.

She stopped before the door and set down her valise to stare at the place that, because of her father's treachery, would be her home for the next seven years. Currant bushes, gray with years and sea air, brushed the whitewashed walls, sheltering a late-summer array of sweet

William and snowy phlox. Aggressive thick stems of portulaca framed the door.

Bethany stared for a long moment at the entrance. She found herself comparing it to the door to her father's house, its panels polished to reflect the caller, its jewel-like side panes and fanlight shining above, its heavy brass knob and knocker speaking with quiet eloquence of the wealth and privilege contained within.

The door to Bethany's new home was different. Its vertical planks were roughly hewn from knot-infested pine slathered with whitewash and held together by a handful of iron tacks. The hinges whined a rusty creak as she pushed the door open and stepped inside, to be greeted by a hollow ring of bleak emptiness.

Finley Piper didn't smile as he enveloped Ashton's package in the folds of his frock coat, but there was an unmistakable glimmer of satisfaction in his pale eyes as he looked across the corner table in the White Horse. His son, Chapin, lank-haired, his bony knees bumping the underside of the table, displayed less reserve as he lifted his mug of beer and grinned at Ashton.

"Well done," he said. "Your countrymen are in your debt."

Ashton pulled long at his beer, raising an eyebrow over the rim of the tankard. "My countrymen?"

Finley dipped a thick, ink-stained finger into his collar and drew out a small silver amulet suspended on a length of black ribbon. Ashton recognized the insignia of the Liberty Tree and looked away.

"We need men like you," Finley said compellingly, "to keep our tree alive."

"I'd say your tree needs pruning," Ashton replied. "Just how are you involved with the patriots, Finley?"

Finley and Chapin exchanged looks. "I'm a member of the Committee of Safety. We're concerned with communication, sabotage, espionage." He patted his coat. "And now this. We achieve by stealth what we cannot get by free will." His eyes probed Ashton. "What brings you into our fold?"

He smiled ruefully into his mug. "If I told you, you'd

never believe me. Suffice it to say I've recently been given a taste of British military justice and found the experience decidedly lacking in fairness."

Chapin nodded vehemently and leaned forward. "Can we count you as a friend, then?"

Ashton surveyed father and son for a moment. They were good men, simple men, Finley a widower who reminded Ashton of his own father, Chapin a young man eager for action. Catching Ashton's perusal, Finley said, "Chapin and I are men of the printing trade, extraordinary only in that we live in extraordinary times. The one remarkable thing about us is that we've been pushed to the limits of our tolerance by the high-handedness of the British ministry."

"We've no wish to be heroes," Chapin added, looking suddenly very unlike the lantern-jawed hobbledehoy he'd seemed on first impression. His eyes, brown and alight with commitment, now regarded Ashton with knifelike keenness. "But I would lay down my life for the cause of liberty."

A vague chill crept up Ashton's spine and stole across his scalp. Many a bell-voiced patriot had brayed out similar words in town meetings in the Brick Market, but never had he heard them spoken with such artless conviction. Amazing. Only weeks ago Chapin's loftiest goal had been to attract Carrie Markham's attention.

"You're a bit young to be taking on the British Army," Ashton said mildly.

" 'Tis we who must live in the world we make for ourselves," Chapin explained. " 'Tis we who must take a hand in its shaping."

Finley rose from the table. "I take it you'd not be averse to other . . . assignations?"

Ashton steepled his fingertips and his gaze rose to the older man. "I'll not kill or injure anyone for any reason."

"Quite so," Finley said agreeably. He leaned forward and lowered his voice. "All summer long we've been deviled by a spy. Too smart to be regular army; too discreet to be an ordinary Tory. I'd dearly love to speak to you about this devil. Are you still working for Sinclair Winslow?"

"Aye." Ashton almost choked on the admission. "And will do so for the next seven years."

"Winslow is loyal to England."

"Rabidly so," Ashton concurred.

"Raises horses, doesn't he?"

"He buys them, I raise them."

Finley rubbed a finger over his chin. "Hm. The Continental Army could use some good horses."

"They're not mine to give," Ashton said. "Besides, the horses aren't battle-trained."

"We shall have to take great care to conceal our purpose." Finley pushed Ashton's nearly full mug toward him. "Drink it to the dregs," he said jovially.

Ashton raised the mug slightly and sipped. "My friend," he said darkly, "I can already taste the dregs."

He lingered to drain two more mugs before stepping out into the fast-gathering twilight.

As he rode home, his mind filled with the one thing his thoughts had been fleeing from all day.

Bethany. His wife.

Bitterness mingled with the taste of stale beer in his mouth. The laughing, guileless companion he'd once trusted as a friend seemed like a dream now. Beneath that impossibly wide-eyed gaze and childlike demeanor he'd suddenly discovered a cunning and guile that defied imagination. She'd given her innocence blithely to Dorian Tanner and maneuvered Ashton into salvaging her reputation. Granted, his neck had been spared because of her treachery, but at what cost!

Ashton hoped Bethany had sense enough to stay in her father's house tonight. He didn't want to be responsible for what he'd do if he found her.

Bethany sat gazing down at her knuckles, which had been struck raw by the flint and steel she'd used to set a spark to a bit of scorched linen from the tinder box. Pride had kept her from begging a panful of glowing coals from her father's kitchen, and she took a certain grim satisfaction in having coaxed a fire in the hearth by her own hand.

She turned those hands over, studying the unfamiliar array of blisters at the base of her fingers. The bucket, stone, and chain of the stable well-sweep had placed the blisters there, chafing the untried flesh of her hands as she drew water and brought it to the cottage. In one afternoon she'd discovered her complete ignorance of the steps in performing the simplest of domestic chores.

Gladstone, whom she'd fetched from the kennels to keep her company, lazed on a rag rug by the hearth, oblivious to her turmoil. She stooped to ruffle the spaniel's ears, then looked around the cottage.

The fire snapped impatiently in the grate as she tried to accustom herself to the idea that this was now her home. For the next seven years she would tread this rough puncheon floor and gaze out the tiny glass panes of two windows. She, who had never brought so much as a crumb to table, would learn to prepare meals and clean up afterward. Hands that had never known the harshness of lye soap would now become rough from washing. A body that had for eighteen years been pampered and fussed over by others would now know the aches and twinges of having worked.

Bethany didn't need to invent chores with which to busy herself while she waited for Ashton to return from wherever he'd gone to spend his anger and disappointment. She stowed her belongings in the Duncan chest at the foot of the bed. The watery soup she'd concocted from beans and turnips and a few shreds of salt meat from the tiny larder was dismally bland, yet it tasted of her success in having prepared her first meal.

Now that night had crept over the two-roomed cottage, she was restless. She added a log to the fire and, with prickling trepidation, laid her white lawn nightshift on the rope-framed bed.

She had often envisioned her wedding night, an image suffused with half-formed ideas of coupling, ideas garnered from Carrie's prattle and the secretive giggles of the girls at school. Yet never in those vague imaginings had she considered that her new husband would avoid her. Where was Ashton?

Apprehension seized her as she recalled Harry's package. If Ashton was caught with the secret documents, he might never come back. She might never have the chance to prove to him that she'd done the right thing by lying to Colonel Chason.

Her fingers were cold as she unbuttoned the riding habit she'd worn for two days and let it drop to the floor. Quickly she pulled on the nightshift, shivering as she drew the combs from her heavy, waving locks. She sent a rueful smile at the riding habit, which lay in a heap on the floor. Gladstone got up and meandered over, sniffing disinterestedly at the pile.

"It's not going to get up and walk to the chest by itself," she said to the dog. For some minutes she worked at folding the garment. Carrie always made it look so easy, yet Bethany couldn't seem to smooth the sleeves and skirt at all. In the end she wadded up the riding habit and added it to the chest.

The August night was warm, softly breezy, redolent of late-summer flowers and the nightingale's song. Yet Bethany couldn't help the shiver that trembled through her as she slipped between the coarse muslin sheets of the bed and felt the unfamiliar and oddly comforting rustle of cornhusks beneath her. Gladstone settled on the floor at her side.

Trailing a blistered hand over the dog's silky head, she closed her eyes tightly. Yet still a pair of scalding tears escaped and slid down her temples into hair that hadn't been brushed by anyone but Carrie for as long as she could remember.

A pair of hands bit into her shoulders and pulled her roughly to a sitting position, drawing her from a warm cocoon of sleep. She found herself staring into the darkened hollows of Ashton's eyes.

"What are you doing here?" he demanded, his breath warm and smelling of malt. His fingers curled deeper into her soft flesh.

Bethany winced. "You're hurting me."

The grip slackened immediately, but his voice remained harsh. "I'd not be doing so if you'd had the good sense to stay in your own room."

Her chin climbed a notch. "I live here now, Ashton."

"Don't be absurd. You no more belong here than a hot-house rose belongs in a weed patch."

She kept her eyes steady despite the pressure of his fingers and the bitterness of his voice. "I belong with my husband," she vowed softly, "wherever that may be."

He released her so suddenly that she dropped back onto the pillow. "I think not," he snapped, and rose.

"Where are you going?"

"To the stables."

She leaped from the bed, earning a splinter from the puncheons. Wincing, she placed herself in front of him. Her lower lip threatened to tremble, but she chewed it into stillness.

"Stay, Ashton," she said. "Please."

She heard him hiss as he sucked in his breath. "Why?" he asked sharply.

"Because you can't avoid me. What we did today is irrevocable."

"You may have shackled me in law," he returned, "but not in fact."

She touched him, laying her hand alongside that hard, angry, handsome face, and felt it tighten beneath her warm palm. "I do not wish to shackle you, Ashton," she whispered. "I love you."

He flinched. "As a sailor in peril of drowning loves any port in a storm."

The sting of his comment knifed white-hot through her, lodging in her heart. "I speak the truth," she insisted. "I do love you, and have ever since I returned to Seastone. Before that, too, but not as I do now."

"Ah, yes," he snapped. "That would account for your flirtation with Captain Tanner."

She looked down, fastening her eyes on the faintly glowing fire in the grate. "Dorian is nothing to me. 'Tis you I want, Ashton."

He grasped her chin in his fingers and forced her to meet his eyes. "Why can't you look at me when you say that?"

She blinked and swallowed. The firelight gave his features a hard, forbidding look. His stare both challenged and chilled her.

"I want you," she forced herself to say, "in every way a woman can want a man. I want you so much I ache inside."

The smile that twisted his lips was cold. His hand snaked into her hair with an ungentle tug. "Aye, my love," he said. " 'Tis a way, I'm sure, with which you are intimately familiar."

Chapter 7

Ashton watched her throat work silently as she swallowed again. ''I know you're angry,'' she whispered, ''but 'tis not in my power to release you from either the marriage or my father's indenture.''

''I should forgive you because you cannot undo what you've done?''

''Perhaps 'tis too soon to expect forgiveness.''

''Then what do you expect from me?''

''I . . . 'tis our wedding night, Ashton.''

The log flared with a hiss, illuminating her eyes. She looked as innocent as a kitten and he almost softened . . . until he remembered that she had claws. Of course she wanted him to lie with her. Perhaps, in her foolishness, she thought to convince him that the babe Tanner had saddled her with was actually his.

''So you want me in your bed, do you?'' he asked.

Her gaze fled from his. ''Yes.'' The admission came on a nervous sigh.

His hand twined more insidiously into the heavy silk of her hair. ''I didn't hear you, my love.''

Her eyes sought his again. ''Yes,'' she repeated in a steadier voice. ''I want you in my bed, Ashton.''

He disentangled his hand from her hair and tugged ungently at the ribbon at her throat. The lawn shift gaped wide, revealing a smooth, blushing expanse of bosom that sent rivulets of desire gliding through him. Her flesh was dewy, and a maddening scent emanated from her, the warm tinge of sleep mingling with her jasmine perfume. His own exigency ignited anger as well as desire.

"You'll not find me gentle," he warned, and he impaled her with a challenging stare.

"You'll not find me fearful," she countered, and her chin rose defiantly.

Ashton hesitated as two impulses warred within him. Reason dictated that he had every right to toss her roughly on the bed and show her the fate she'd tempted in forcing him to marry her. The other was to succumb to the powerful magic of her eyes, to enjoy the enchanting offering of her scented flesh, to eradicate her memory of Dorian Tanner by driving her to mindless passion.

As he fitted one arm about her slim frame and the other behind her knees, Ashton wasn't certain which impulse would win out. When he lifted her to his chest and felt her curl trustingly against him, he found himself seized by an absurd tenderness that made sport of his anger. After he'd placed her on the bed and lowered himself beside her, the urge to bury himself thoughtlessly in her began to seep away. When he dropped his gaze to the luminescence of her eyes and the moist fullness of her mouth, he suddenly knew anger would have no part in the love he intended to make to her.

Even as he cursed the tenderness welling within him, Ashton bent his head and took her lips with a raging thirst. Beneath his mouth, hers slackened. Under still more pressure, her lips parted. His tongue grazed her teeth and probed the yielding softness beyond. The taste of her was warm, welcoming, too impossibly delicious.

"Dear God," he murmured as he felt her body shudder to life beneath his questing hands, "what is wrong with me that I find you so sweet? How is it that I still want you after you've shackled me to you?"

"Perhaps . . ." Her tongue darted out as if to sample the taste he'd left on her lips. "Perhaps you'll find we've not committed such a terrible mistake."

His hands became hard and demanding on her pliant frame. "By all rights I should show you the error you've made." Inexplicably, his harsh touch became a soft caress over her lovely contours. "Yet instead, for some strange reason, I want to show you where the stars are conceived."

Her response was a sigh and a tiny smile that held no hint of the guile he knew she possessed. Her hands crept, tentative and searching, around his neck, and she offered him her lips again. He drew her next sigh into his mouth and gloried in the dulcet cushion of her body even as he cursed the weakness that made him want her so. When the heat in his loins ignited to unmanageable warmth, he drew back, studying her lovely face, so radiant in the burnished firelight. A look of heartaching wonder shone in her eyes as she gazed up at him. Her hand moved from his neck to his face, and he was startled by its rough texture.

Gently he removed her hand and held it before him, his brows descending as he took in the array of blisters. He questioned her with a look.

She answered him with a smile. "I've been drawing water."

He felt a prickle of surprise. "You?"

"Aye. I suppose my hands will soon become accustomed to the work."

He laid her blistered palm in his, noting the raw and broken skin of her knuckles. "And this?" he queried.

"Striking flint for the fire. I'm afraid it took several dozen attempts."

Something quivered deep inside him as an image formed in his mind of Bethany performing chores so far removed from her nature and upbringing.

"You'll never be happy with me," he told her roughly, tracing the marred flesh of her hand with a finger.

"My happiness does not depend on the way I live," she countered softly. "It lies with you, Ashton."

Anger bristled disquietingly within him. "Have you not already saddled me with enough responsibilities? Must you insist that it is in my power to make you happy or unhappy?"

"I do not insist. I merely state a fact."

His lips drew upward in a rueful smile. "I see. Tell me, then, Mrs. Markham, what you would have me do to ensure your contentment."

A blush crept to her cheeks, and her lashes swept downward. "It makes me happy to hear you call me that," she admitted. "And to feel you . . . touch me."

Anger deserted him as she faced him with a sweet-sad smile. He brought her hand to his lips and kissed it, giving each finger the feathery attention of his mouth before kissing the blistered palm. He folded her fingers into a fist as if to keep the kiss within.

"My touch?" he queried, watching the blush spreading downward into the gaping neckline of her shift. " 'Tis little enough to ask."

" 'Tis all I ask."

The fire in his loins screamed out for him to have done with inane conversation and meaningless love games and spend his mind-sapping lust without delay. But he hesitated. For reasons he refused to scrutinize, he wanted her ready, in body as well as in spirit. He steeled himself against the need that ran rampant through his veins.

He drew her to her feet. Inexplicably he found himself on his knees before her, his face pressed to her thighs, his hands caressing the delicate flesh at the back of her knees. Coming slowly to his feet, he lowered her shift. The fabric glided over Bethany's breasts before pooling at her waist.

Ashton stepped back and caught his breath, studying her like an artist admiring the work of a superior craftsman. Her breasts were two perfect swells of flesh adorned by crests of an enticing dusky rose hue. She shivered and brought her hands up to cover herself.

He shook his head. "You shrink like a virgin," he told her harshly, drawing her hands away.

"I—I've never—"

"Did your captain never look upon you?" Ashton demanded. "Did he never pleasure himself with the sight of your breasts?"

"Of course not! He—Dorian merely—"

Ashton laid his fingers on her lips. "Speak no more of him. You're an artful actress, Bethany. Perhaps we could play this as if it were the first time." He drank from her lips and mumbled against them. "Your first kiss . . ."

"But—"

He silenced her again with his mouth and moved his hands over her breasts. "Shall we pretend, pet, that I am the first to touch you here," he continued, and one hand disappeared beneath the shift. "And here . . ." As he caressed her trembling body, he could almost believe he *was* the first. Her responses were so fresh, so unguarded. She seemed clean, unsullied, despite what he knew of her. God, he wanted to forget that, beneath his very hand, the evidence of Dorian Tanner's predominance grew in her still flat belly.

He paused to peel off his shirt and drop it on the floor. He felt her eyes on him, a shy caress from beneath a thick skirting of dark honey lashes. When she lifted her eyes to his, he saw astonishment on her face.

"You act as if you'd never looked upon a man before."

Her gaze moved slowly, caressingly, over his shoulders and down to the patch of burnished chestnut hair on his chest. "I have not," was her soft admission.

Ashton stood and shed the rest of his clothing. Either she lied with incredible virtuosity or Dorian Tanner knew nothing of making love to a woman. Bethany studiously kept her eyes on his face as he lowered himself beside her.

"You are free to look on me, Mrs. Markham," he invited.

"I—" She swallowed hard. Her blush was furious now.

"You said I'd not find you fearful."

She lifted her chin and eyed him boldly from head to toe. She fingered the scar in his left side. Her touch felt hotter than the musket ball that had put the scar there. Her hand trailed upward, finding places Ashton had never realized were so damnably sensitive.

"You seem . . . well made," she whispered unsteadily.

For some reason Ashton found her assessment absurdly pleasing. He circled her waist with his hands, loosening the shift until it drifted to the floor. Then he untied the ribbon at the top of her pantalettes. These he lowered slowly, his desire mounting as the thin fabric descended.

"And you," he said roughly, "are nearly perfect." He glanced for a moment at her midsection, which would soon swell with a child not of his making. "Nearly," he repeated, and saw her flinch at the anger of his tone. "I think," he added quickly, "that we both settled for something less than perfection in this marriage."

She caught her lower lip with her teeth, and her eyes filled. Ashton brushed at a tear; it seemed to scald his finger.

"I want no weeping girl in my bed," he told her gruffly. Then he relented, kissing her. "We've talked much tonight and said little. I think perhaps the time for conversation is past." He laid her on the bed. His kiss deepened and his hand played downward, paying court to her unresisting body.

Then his mouth left hers to follow the path his hand had taken. A pulse leaped in her pale throat, its rhythm matching the racing of his own heart. She tasted of feminine dew and flowers, a combination far more heady than the spirits he'd quaffed at the White Horse. His tongue licked her blushing breast, evoking a small whimper of wanting. He took the crest into his mouth, nearly bursting with desire when his teeth and tongue encircled the pouting pleasure point.

Beneath his ever-lowering hand Bethany quivered; Ashton sensed her desire in the faint lifting of her hips. He indulged in teasing then, barely brushing her flesh, sharpening her appetite with gossamer touches. When the movement of her hips became more pronounced, he slid his hand downward, to touch and caress the soft female flesh of her.

She stiffened and tried to pull away. "Ashton!"

He raised his head and gave her a questioning look.

"Not . . ." Her voice trailed off as his hand filled itself with her.

". . . there," she finished weakly, but her passion-drenched eyes told him otherwise.

"Especially there," he assured her, and lowered his mouth to her other breast. She relaxed with a sigh of capitulation.

Ashton found her utter trust in him inordinately exciting. The joy he took in pleasuring her was as compelling as the most intimate caress she could have bestowed on him. When he felt her rapture crest and spill beneath his hand, he experienced her shudder as if it were his own. And as if it were completely new for both of them.

Bethany's eyes glowed with wonder as she recovered

from his touch and raised herself to press a kiss on his shoulder.

"Ashton. Ashton, is there not something I should do to . . . ?" She let her voice trail off. God, he thought, had she really taught herself to blush at will? Did she know how beautiful those spots of color looked in her cheeks?

"To what, Bethany?" he asked, his fingers leaving her ready moistness to trail upward over her midsection.

"To—to please you?"

Lord, he thought, how had Tanner managed to plant his seed in her without teaching her anything?

"I shall leave it to you to discover that, pet," he told her, dropping a kiss on her nose.

"Oh," she murmured. Then, shyly, her hands and lips found him, moving with gathering confidence over his shoulders and neck, his chest and then his hips. Those hands worked magic on a body that had long since grown cynical of artful wenches and tavern bawds; Bethany touched him as he'd never been touched before. When one hand brushed him intimately, he nearly cried out at the searing sensation that ravaged him.

His desire for her breached the wall of bitter resentment he'd spent hours erecting, driving him mindless with wanting. She was alternately brazen and bold, shy and shrinking as her hands and mouth explored and tasted him, drinking from his lips and flesh until boundless urgency hammered at his resistance.

"Bethany . . ." he grated.

She paused and lifted her eyes to his. "Have I done something wrong?"

He tried to smile through the fog of desire enveloping him. "I daresay you've not made a single false move, love," hc admitted.

"But you look as if you're . . . in pain."

"Aye, painful it is to want you so badly."

"Then . . . ?"

He answered her with a swift movement of his body, bracing himself above her to look intently into her lovely, confused face. "Then," he replied, "we stop these games."

Her arms wound about his neck. The look of astonishment on her face raised a small glimmer of hope in him. Could it be that he was mistaken about Tanner, that the Redcoat hadn't taken her innocence after all?

His every muscle strained as he poised over her, waiting, wanting to know, yet dreading to find her sullied by another.

"Ashton?" she whispered. She shifted her thigh; the satin-smooth limb brushed him in a way that banished all hesitation. He moved inexorably downward.

"Raise your hips to me, pet," he instructed. The glimmer of hope flared brighter; how could she not know how to position herself to receive a man?

Sweetly she complied and he lowered himself to her in one great caressing movement, praying he'd encounter the evidence of her innocence.

But her flesh didn't resist him; her body welcomed him.

Surrounded by the moist silk of her, he found he no longer cared. With long, slow strokes he reveled in her warmth and filled her with the passion that, he now admitted, had hammered away at him for weeks.

Her breathy cries reached his ears and he knew it was good for her, that he'd answered her need. She was all dewy satin and feminine softness and seemed—incredibly—surprised to feel the rhythm of his lovemaking.

Through a burgeoning rush of desire, Ashton felt he was touching her in places she'd never been touched before, pleasing her in ways no man had ever pleased her.

Because she told him so in a soft, soft whisper that reached his ear like an intimate caress. Her hands spoke her pleasure, too, feathering across his shoulders and sliding down his sides, then rising again to thread into his hair. While he moved above her, she blossomed beneath, taking deep, startled breaths. Her scent was all the perfumes of a summer garden, wave upon wave of heady, sensuous sweetness.

Nothing in Ashton's past experience could have prepared him for the intensity of her response as she spiraled to ecstasy beneath him. When she whispered that she loved him, he came so close to believing her that his passion crested and he joined her in the dark, sweeping pleasure of utter completion.

He left her with slow reluctance and settled at her side, shifting to find room on the narrow bed.

" 'Tis rather close," Bethany said.

"You've a roomy four-poster in the big house," he replied. "I can afford no better."

"I don't mind," she said quickly. She settled her tousled head into the crook of his neck and warmed his flesh with a sigh. Ashton found himself wishing she weren't so agreeable, so infernally accommodating. Even the jasmine scent of her hair was enough to ignite his passion anew. A muttered oath, directed at his own weakness, escaped him.

He felt her stiffen and she lifted troubled eyes to search his face. "Ashton," she said, "did I not behave . . . correctly? If I've failed you in some way—"

His fingers crept to her lips, silencing her. "Hush, love." How could she not know what she did to him? "In the space of one day you've saved me from the hangman, married me against my will, and goaded your father into making me a bond servant." His fingers left her lips and wandered leisurely downward. "But tonight . . . ah, tonight, pet, you've made me forget all that." He punctuated his statement with a teasing touch to her thigh and felt her quicken in response.

"I—I have?" she wondered.

"Aye, love. Most exquisitely."

She was more bold after that, full of newfound confidence and insatiable youth. As Ashton came to her a second time, he reflected that, although Dorian Tanner had taken her, he hadn't taken the best of her.

The first of Bethany's faculties to come to life the next morning was not her reason. Nothing so coherent as thought disturbed the quiet shifting of her mind; she was aware only of the warm cradle of Ashton's arms, the unfamiliar and fascinating scent of his body, the hardness of his sinews as, in a luxurious stretch, she ran her feet up and down his legs.

Feeling him stir, she raised her eyelids. Her gaze slid over the dawn-lit expanse of his chest, the muscles rising and falling in a rhythm of deep slumber. His hand lay on her shoulder, slack-fingered and tan against her paler flesh.

Memories returned, memories of what that great blunt-fingered hand had done to her last night, teaching her things about herself she'd never known, igniting feelings of a power she'd never imagined. Ashton's lovemaking had left a sweet ache within her that stirred again now, and the ache became a nest of need. Fingers hungry to explore crept from beneath the covers and trailed up the length of his torso, encountering firm plains and ridges shaped by hard muscle, a texture so compelling that she caught her breath.

Ashton stirred beneath her touch and she raised herself on an elbow in time to see his eyelids lift.

She smiled. His hand moved beneath her chin.

"Could you parcel out and sell that smile, pet," he told her in a sleep-rough voice, "you'd be a wealthy woman."

"I *am* a wealthy woman." She shifted closer still.

A tremor passed through him. "I can't dispute that you're a woman . . . lately." The statement was punctuated by a kiss that seemed to envelope all of her, awakening urgent clamorings and an unabashed greed for fulfillment. She returned his caress with hands that knew, despite her inexperience, how to touch him. His body sprang to life with a speed that filled her with a heady sense of sensual power.

A sigh seeped from her lips as he soothed her ache with the heat of his desire. She wondered if her soft cries could be heard in the stable compound outside. And then she ceased to think at all.

Afterward she wanted to bask for hours in his embrace. But the kiss he dropped upon her lips before sliding from the bed was distracted, as if his mind had wandered to other things.

"Stay with me," she begged, her body already lonely for his touch. " 'Tis not yet full light—"

He pulled on his breeches and threw an unreadable look over his shoulder. "A workingman has no time to lie abed, Bethany."

The statement fell hard on her ears, hammering home the notion that she was married to a man who lacked the leisure to rise when he would. Blushing, she hastened into her nightshift.

Ashton sluiced water from the basin over his face and neck, furrowing droplets through his hair before tying the chestnut locks in place with a leather thong. Bethany watched furtively as he drew a clean shirt over his head, his muscles rippling with the movement. He eased into stockings and boots, then drew a woven hemp belt around his waist.

His routine act of washing and dressing looked, to her, like an intricate and fascinating dance. Glancing at her, he seemed amused by her expression.

"You're staring, Mrs. Markham."

Color stung her cheeks. "This is all terribly new to me."

His mouth grew hard above the endearing cleft in his chin. "You'll soon find marriage tiresome enough."

"You're determined to make me regret what I did in Bristol," she shot back in sudden annoyance. "But I will not, Ashton. I mean to be a good wife to you."

His lip curled, but not into a smile. "You do, eh? Very well, then. I've a long day's work ahead of me. I should like to start it with breakfast."

She caught a challenging gleam in his eye and squared her shoulders, marching past him to the kitchen. Feeling his eyes on her, she set the kettle she'd filled the day before onto its crane in the hearth and bent to add fuel and stir the fire to life. Ashes rose and smudged the pristine sleeve of her shift; still more tickled her nostrils, and she stifled a sneeze. Her nerves tingled as she went to the larder and stood peering into gloomy shadows, finding herself at a loss.

Ashton laughed harshly at her look of confusion. "Are you surprised," he asked, "to discover that breakfast isn't a meal that suddenly appears on a silver tray at your bedside?"

A chilly tremor scuttled through her at his taunt. Finding her voice, she said, "I'm surprised by only one thing, Ashton. How is it that last night you were so . . . considerate of me, yet this morning you seek to hurt me?"

His throat worked as he swallowed. Eyes narrowing, he

said, "Some aspects of marriage are pleasant, but all is not kisses and sighs in the dark. There's a lot more to living together than the marriage bed."

She veiled her hurt with lowered lashes. "I'm determined to be a good wife to you. But I shall need your help."

He took in his breath with a hiss. "I've little time to train you in housewifery." Taking his cocked hat from a hook, he jammed it on his head and went to the door. "Don't bother with breakfast this morning."

He left with the cool breeze of dawn, taking Gladstone with him. Bethany stood at the doorway, listening to the thud of his boots on the path and watching as his broad form was swallowed up by gray light.

She leaned against the frame, her nostrils filled with the morning scents of bay and ribbon-grass, her heart filled with the pain of loving Ashton, and not knowing where to begin proving her faith to him.

But begin she did, sparing not a moment for worry or regret. The kitchen clock at the manor house was marking the hour of six when she appeared, hair flying and apron askew. Dudley, the cook, twitched his mustache in surprise at her appearance. Two maids peered curiously from the pantry, whispering behind their hands.

"Miss Bethany?" Dudley asked. "What's your pleasure this morning?"

"I'd like you to teach me to cook, Dudley."

The mustache worked agitatedly in the cook's sharp, thin face. Bethany forced a smile. " 'Tis no jest," she said quickly. Her eyes flicked to the whispering maids. "My capacity here has changed, Dudley. I have to learn my way about a kitchen."

"I hardly know where to begin, Miss—"

"It's Mrs. Markham now. Surely the gossip has reached the kitchen, Dudley." Her smile took on genuine amusement at his amazed expression. "Actually, you ought to start calling me Bethany; I'm afraid there can be no formality between us now. And then you may teach me to prepare supper for my husband."

And so Bethany, who had once contemplated Euclid's

axioms, now contemplated a lump of bread dough. A mind once occupied with Berkeley's idealist philosophies was now absorbed in the proper way to dress a chicken for roasting.

Her studies had never exhausted her like Dudley's tutelage. That afternoon when she made her way back to the cottage and set about preparing her first meal, she didn't allow herself to consider failure.

Ashton hesitated on the path to the cottage, frowning at the unexpected aroma of roasting chicken that wafted from the window. His stomach, whining aloud for want of food, quickened his step as he entered the dooryard. Gladstone waited, ears perked and tail quivering, on the newly swept stoop.

He pulled the door open and the dog darted inside. Ashton's stomach stilled. Dumbfounded, he contemplated the scene before him. Years of clutter had been cleared from the keeping room. A quilt concealed the scars and gouges in the wooden settle; the mantel was free of dust, its few ornaments polished to a reflective shine. Mary-bud and sweet William primroses graced a corner shelf. The rag rugs had been beaten, the floor swept, and the betty lamps wiped clean of soot.

Ashton took in the changes with a single glance. Then his eyes were drawn to the kitchen. In contrast to the spotless keeping room, the area was a place of unrelieved chaos. Every surface, from sideboard to floor, was dusted with flour and cornmeal. His amazed eyes moved to the hearth, where every pot he owned seethed and spluttered, then to the table, which was piled high with utensils. A crock of molasses oozed dark stickiness over the table and down one leg, pooling in the flour coating the floor.

Ashton's gaze jolted to Bethany, chopping onions at the sideboard. She wielded the knife clumsily, reducing the onion to several uneven chunks. Her hair hung, carelessly tied, down her narrow back. Every so often a flour-coated hand came up, whitening the honey-gold strands about her face as she brushed them aside.

Ashton cleared his throat. Bethany pivoted, knife

pointed outward. He swallowed mirth at the unlikely sight of her startled, flour-smudged face.

"Hello, pet," he said, a sudden warmth suffusing his voice. "I see you've been busy."

"Aye," she replied, setting the knife aside and wiping her hands on an impossibly soiled apron. "Supper is nearly ready." She whipped into action again, scooping up the onions and hurrying to the hearth. Before Ashton could give warning, she seized the lid of a pot, then yelped as the lid fell from her burned hand and clattered to the floor. The onions dropped into the fire and her seared fingers flew to her mouth.

"Do you," she said around her fingers, "mind your chicken without onions?"

"Don't give it a thought, pet."

She sent him a grateful look. "Then shall we eat?"

Ashton washed his hands, brushed flour from the bench, and sat down. Bethany lowered herself opposite him, her brow furrowing at the molasses crock.

"I haven't set a very good table, have I?"

"Never mind."

She looked blank for a moment, then shook her head in self-disgust. "Here I am sitting like an idiot, waiting for someone to serve me." She climbed to her feet again. This time she remembered to cloak her hands with a linen towel before lifting the iron roasting pan. She set the meal on the table with a smile aglow with pride.

"I did it all myself," she boasted. "Save plucking the bird with my own hand." With equal pride she produced a pot of Indian pudding and went to the brick oven, removing a loaf of bread.

At least Ashton thought it was a loaf of bread. His eyebrows rose as her face fell. The loaf was hoecake-flat, charred on one side and pasty raw on the other.

"I don't understand it," she said. "I did everything Dudley told me—"

"Never mind," Ashton said quickly, his stomach clamoring now. "We'll do without."

But his stomach quickly shrank in revulsion when he sampled the chicken. Like the bread, it was half-raw. Bethany's aggressive seasoning of sea salt and white pepper caused his mouth to scream for a draft to chase away the evil taste.

He braced his hands on the table, about to bolt for the cider keg at the sideboard, when she smiled expectantly at him.

"Well?" she asked.

His knuckles paled as he gripped the table. The morsel of near-raw chicken mingled with the sting of salt and the burn of pepper in his mouth. She was looking at him so eagerly. She'd worked so hard. . . .

Summoning the armor of a palate made hardy by four years of poor soldier's fare, Ashton swallowed. His eyes stewed in tears with the pain of having ingested the volatile substance.

"Ashton . . . ?" Bethany leaned forward, her fork poised daintily, her round eyes bright.

He found his voice in the burned, stung, and tortured recesses of his mouth. " 'Tis . . . highly seasoned," he remarked, wishing his voice didn't sound so raspy and broken.

"It is," she said, and the smile that blossomed on her lips suddenly made the torture all worthwhile. "But perhaps I should have sprinkled it around a bit; it all seems to be concentrated on your portion."

Ashton tried to be nonchalant as he moved to the sideboard and drew a mug of cider from the keg there. Soothed by the cool drink, he tried not to look too suspicious as he took another bite of chicken.

Bethany, he saw, barely sampled her food, so intent was she on watching him. He braved the Indian pudding, finding the molasses-spiced corn mush as heavy as chalk ballast, but digestible after he drowned it with cream. Somehow the food on his plate disappeared and he swiped in relief at his mouth with a napkin. He couldn't help but smile at Bethany when he'd finished.

Her eyes swam with tears. "How can you look so pleased with me, Ashton," she asked brokenly, "when I've nearly poisoned you?"

Tenderness curled deep within him—unbidden, unwelcome, but so much a part of his feelings for her that he couldn't help himself. "My smile has little to do with the fare," he admitted gently, "but everything to do with your efforts." His hand crept across the flour-dusted table and closed over hers. Her fingers clung tightly.

"Why is it," she wondered, "that you are kindest to me when I least deserve it?"

His smile broadened and lingered about his mouth. "Let me help you clear up," he suggested, avoiding her question as he began picking up soiled pans and utensils. Gladstone's less-discerning appetite made short work of the chicken.

Ashton left Bethany elbow-deep in wash water and went behind the house to bring in the small wooden tub from its hook. Setting it before the hearth, he filled it with water from the red cedar bucket by the door. Bethany swiveled around, eyeing him questioningly.

"I think we could both do with a bath," he explained. "I've the grit and sweat of a day in the stables. . . ." He snared a dewy droplet of perspiration from her brow with his thumb. "And you, love, have not had a moment's relaxation all day, from the looks of you." He caught her watching him as he warmed the bath with a kettleful of boiling water. A mocking grin tugged at the corners of his mouth. "Aye, this is how one draws a bath when one lacks servants to do so."

She finished in the kitchen and stood looking curiously at the small wooden tub, the steam rising from it misting her face. "I know so little about being a wife," she admitted.

He came and stood before her, searching deep for the anger she deserved, finding instead that he plumbed a well of tenderness and understanding. Could he really blame her for what she'd done? She was young, alone, rejected by the man who had replaced her innocence with the scourge of an illegitimate child, a notion frightening enough to make a young girl go to desperate—and forgivable—lengths.

His hand crept behind her waist and he plucked at her apron strings. "I am no lady's maid," he told her quietly, "but I, too, am willing to learn." She gasped and shivered as his fingers climbed from her waist to her nape, leaving a row of unfastened buttons in their wake.

By God, but her beauty stirred him. Ashton dealt uncomfortably with the hungry ache in his loins as he finished divesting her of her clothing and held her hand at a dainty angle to steady her as she stepped into the tub.

Shyly she drew her knees up to accommodate the tub's smallness. Ashton found himself wishing the tub were large enough for the two of them, that his hands could join the warm sluicing water that trickled in a liquid caress over her shoulders, arms, breasts, and thighs, which trembled beneath his stare as if he'd actually touched her.

Bethany was maiden-shy as she bathed. He had to remind himself that she was far from the innocent child she seemed. Not so very far, though. He busied himself with sweeping the kitchen as she washed her hair and rinsed its dark honey length, her back curving like a willow bough as she bent to dip the strands into the water.

She finished bathing and wrapped a linen towel around her slim form. Only with concentrated effort did Ashton keep himself from following her wet trail into the bedroom.

He hurried through his own bath. Desire flared high as a droplet of water trickled into his mouth and he imagined it tasted of Bethany. By the time he hastened to the bedroom, as ready as he'd never been ready before, he nearly shook with wanting her.

He approached the bed, his eyes moving over the delicate slimness and enticing fullness of her prone form. The flames of hunger leaped higher. He lowered himself beside her, his mouth exploring a soft temple, his hand rising to the undercurve of her lawn-clad breast.

She sighed and curled near. It was not a sigh of desire but one of deep, exhausted sleep. Ashton's smile was rueful as he gritted his teeth and stilled the clamoring in his loins, battling his hunger until at last he joined his wife in sleep.

But later, much later, when Bethany stirred and turned to him, she was a bounty of tireless warmth and generous femininity.

Chapter 8

Bethany had been married six weeks and her monthly time had not visited her yet. She lay staring in terror and wonder at the rough-beamed ceiling over the bed, alternately smiling and shivering at the thought that she was pregnant.

She was not at all surprised. In the fourth week of marriage she'd become aware of an inexplicable breathlessness, a tenderness of breast and thigh that put suspicion in her head. In the fifth week queasiness began visiting her on tiptoe each morning. And now this. The bleeding she could have marked a calender by had not come.

No, not a single surprise in that, Bethany decided as she came gingerly to her feet and awakened her face and neck with water from the basin. Although the days of their marriage were riddled by hard work, tension, and Ashton's moodiness, the nights were swathed in splendor. Lovemaking, frequent and intense, had become their refuge from Ashton's bitterness, her parents' disapproval, and her own uneasiness at having forced Ashton into marriage.

By day there were petty annoyances and uncertainties; by night there was mindless passion and fulfillment of needs they dared not speak of. Mornings were tense with apprehension about what the day would bring; evenings were soft with anticipation of emotional comfort and physical release. Ashton had said on their wedding night that their union was less than perfect, and that was true. But the compatibility they found in the creaky rope-framed bed banished, if only temporarily, their other problems.

Bethany dressed in a cotton gown, running her hands

over her still slim waist. The bodice hugged a bosom that was, perhaps, slightly fuller, although the change could be due to the fact that she had discarded her corsets and stays, finding them a hindrance as she worked in the kitchen.

She dressed, fed a ravenous appetite on the cornbread and bacon Ashton had fried for his breakfast, and promptly lost her meal into the basin. Her stomach felt wretched; her heart soared. She ran down the path to find Ashton.

Instead she was intercepted by Dorian Tanner, coming from the opposite direction, splendid in his scarlet uniform, tight-lipped with anger. For the first time since she'd known him, he gripped her with a touch that hurt.

"I returned home from my tour of duty thinking to find a fiancée," he growled at her. "Instead I find you the bride of another man."

Bethany fixed a glare on the manicured fingers that curled into the flesh of her wrist. "Let me go, Dorian."

"Not until I have an explanation. We were inseparable for weeks, Bethany."

She cast her eyes downward, dismayed by a riddling of guilt. "I'm sorry I misled you, Dorian. I never meant for you to read a deeper meaning into our friendship."

"How could I not?" he demanded harshly. "You forswore other gentlemen—"

"Aye," she admitted. "But my heart was always in another's keeping." Her lashes brushed her cheeks. Never had she considered that Dorian's feelings would be hurt. She'd been so intent on flaunting him before Ashton that she hadn't considered the possibility that Dorian would come to care for her. Her hand climbed to his cheek, lying lightly upon that too perfect face. She stared into eyes that looked not hurt, but nakedly angry and frustrated. "Forgive me, Dorian," she murmured. "I've been so selfish."

"I'll forgive you, my dear," he told her, "if you will forgive this." An insinuating hand wrapped her against him and his sculpted lips insulted hers with a punishing kiss. Bethany gave a frightened squeak of protest and arched back, fighting with no hope of besting his unyielding strength. He tasted of bayberry perfume, heavy and sweet, a scent that tickled her already churning stomach until it threatened to erupt a second time.

The soft thud of a footstep parted them as if two great hands had torn them apart. Bethany stumbled back, aghast to see Ashton mounting the path, Gladstone trotting at his heels. His gaze impaled first Dorian, then her, driving needles of ice into her heart.

"When you're through with my wife," his voice lashed, "I'd like a word with her." Then he was gone, leaving a wake of shivery cold behind him despite the warmth of the autumn day. Gladstone left to examine a chipmunk hole at the base of a southernwood tree.

Bethany gave Dorian no chance to speak. She knew he'd seen the same dangerous rage in Ashton's eyes, and he made no protest when she fled after her husband, nearly stumbling in her haste. She reached him in the dooryard in front of the cottage. When she called his name, he spun, and she found herself facing a cold wall of anger.

"I want you to go back to your parents." He spoke very, very quietly. "I'll not have you entertaining your lover here."

Bethany's breath left her as if a blow had landed in her midsection. "He is not my lover," she stated, wishing her voice were steadier.

"Would you call me a liar after what I just saw?"

"Ashton, that was not what it seemed. Dorian and I had a . . . misunderstanding and he grew angry."

His laugh sliced the air. "Ah, yes, I could see his wrath in the way he kissed you."

"I—he was deeply hurt that I'd married you. Believe me, Ashton, I had no idea he felt that way about me—"

A curtain of fury dropped over his face. "Or you would have waited, is that it? Aye, 'twas an unfortunate mistake you made, my dear, for he would have made a far better husband than I."

"I won't be seeing him again. I promise."

"Your promises mean nothing to me."

Her throat and eyes ached with unshed tears. "And I, Ashton? Do I mean nothing to you?"

His eyes narrowed to cold blue slits. "On the contrary, love, you mean a great deal to me. You mean seven years in bondage to your father. You mean an impediment to what I'd hoped to do with my life. You mean not one, but two extra mouths to feed, and neither of them of my making."

She felt all color slide from her cheeks. *"What?"*

"Pretending again, Bethany?" he demanded harshly. "You know well and good what I mean."

She shook her head. Her hand trailed to her belly. "No, I . . . How did you know about the baby?"

"By God, do you think me blind and deaf? You followed me to Bristol, ill with pregnancy and clamoring to unburden yourself to me. You announced before the military court that you were with child!"

She stumbled back, clutching at the vine-covered pickets of the fence. Her mouth worked; no sound save a small sob of protest came out. At last she understood Ashton's anger, not so much at the idea of marrying her as at his belief that she'd been pregnant at his trial. Pregnant with another man's child.

Hope flared within her. Once she explained to him, he was sure to forgive her. And his forgiveness would mark a fresh beginning for them.

She caught his gaze and held it, moving her head slowly from side to side. "Ashton, listen to me. I was not pregnant at your trial. 'Twas a lie I invented to induce Colonel Chason to set you free. He wouldn't waver until I told him of a mitigating circumstance. I was certain you didn't believe the falsehood, or I'd have explained long ago."

Something flickered in his eyes. Not a softening, not a weakening, but a vague lessening of distrust. The hope blossoming within her chest unfurled its petals further.

But his eyes narrowed again. "If what you say is true," he challenged, "then how is it you didn't come to your marriage bed a virgin?"

Her mouth dropped open. "You presume to tell me I was not a virgin?"

"I tell you only what I felt. You weren't intact the first night we lay together."

She felt the heat of color rise in her cheeks and could no longer meet the frank accusation in his eyes. "I know very little of such things. If I was not . . . what you expected on our wedding night, it wasn't because I'd . . .

been with someone else.'' She dragged her eyes back up to his.

Again that flicker, that waver in his cold blue depths. But it was gone even more quickly than the first. ''There are some things,'' he informed her, ''that you cannot falsify.''

Anger reared up from the stew of emotions that held Bethany in a relentless grip. ''You presume to know much of women,'' she said. ''And you presume it is a necessary thing for a woman to come to her husband a virgin. What if I made the same requirement, Ashton? What if I thought less of you because you were not a virgin on our wedding night?''

'' 'Tis hardly the same for a man,'' he muttered.

''And why not? Can a woman not have the gratification of knowing she was the first, the only? Or is that a fantasy reserved for men only?''

He looked sharply away. ''I never pondered such questions when I was a ready youth.''

She studied his profile and all anger drained from her. ''I've turned your prejudice back on you, haven't I, Ashton? But I'm not so petty that I would even care, or hold it against you.'' She chanced a step closer and placed her hand on his sweat-slick forearm. ''I was a virgin on our wedding night, despite what you say. If I'd known you thought otherwise, I'd have told you then. I was not pregnant at your trial . . .'' She drew a deep, steadying breath. ''But I am now.''

He flinched away from her. ''How many lies have you told me, Bethany? How many more will you put before me with your limpid doe-eyed stare and your soft voice?'' A sigh shuddered from him. ''You claim the child is mine. Very well, claim it if you like. I trust only time to give me the truth. If you birth a child in less than nine months from our wedding day, I'll know you played me for a fool.''

She swallowed hard. ''Nine months is a long time to wait for your trust, Ashton. A long time for me to ponder your insulting accusations. Suppose I do carry the baby to May. What then?''

His eyes returned to her, no longer angry, but lacking in trust. "Then I hope you'll humble me properly."

A tang of winter sharpened the December air as Ashton crossed Marlborough Street, heading toward the White Horse Tavern. Newport was different, the change having been brought about as much by the winds of rebellion as by the winds of winter. The town had closed in on itself, windows and doors shuttered against the Redcoats who strode with surly contempt among the wharves and billeted themselves in the citizens' houses. Captain James Wallace of the HMS *Rose* had earned the title of scourge of Narragansett Bay. Only friends of the Crown remained unmolested by his fleet.

Ashton didn't like the situation, but he hoped Newport would weather the invasion. He almost felt guilty that his life had, thus far, been so untouched by the rebellion.

His work went on at the stables as usual. His marriage to Bethany followed an uneven course of peaks and valleys, the unborn child a constant thorn between them. As if by mutual agreement, they spoke little of the babe. But sometimes, when he saw Bethany rest her hands on the gentle swell of her middle, bitterness and confusion stabbed at him. She was so steadfast in her contention that Tanner had nothing to do with her pregnancy.

Yet solid, logical contradictions stared Ashton in the face. Her body had not been virginal on their wedding night. She was pregnant far too soon for him to be absolutely certain that he, and not Tanner, was the father. The timing of her confinement would tell all.

Still, there were times when she touched him so intimately that he felt she had branded his soul. Times like that almost made him forget his distrust. Almost.

The wind scuttled a torn broadside across the street in front of him, and he caught a fragment of the message the printed scrap of paper bore: "To Arms! Rise, all ye lovers of freedom, ye patriot sons . . ." Shaking his head, Ashton set his foot upon the broadside and walked on. Finley Piper's press had spat sedition all through the autumn of 1775, flirting with the royal officials' patience, courting reprisal from wealthy Tories. Ashton tried to temper the printer's zeal, but to no avail. Finley would not keep quiet about the precepts he held dear, no matter the cost.

That Finley had requested today's meeting with such urgency boded ill. Ashton entered the tavern on a cold gust of wind that swirled his greatcoat about his knees. A few of the patrons looked up, gave him a cursory glance, and went back to their idling.

The arrival of British ships had given birth to a great slowdown of commerce. Newport's silent partner—the Atlantic—had been completely silenced now by Wallace's menace. There were no sailors to slake, no ships to unload, no tea to brew, no rum to distill, no accounts to copy, no barrels to build . . . At Madame Juniper's brothel, the girls had resorted to taking in laundry.

Ashton spied Finley and his ever-present son, Chapin, and joined them at their table. The alewife provided a noggin of mulled wine, warmly spiced and steaming.

"Your broadsides are not to be avoided," Ashton said. "They blow about the streets like carrion birds."

Finley grinned. "No stopping us, eh? I wonder when you'll take refuge beneath the branches of the Liberty Tree."

"Refuge? 'Tis like running into a raging inferno to warm myself against the cold."

"But surely you've a patriot's heart," Chapin remarked.

"I've a common man's distaste for the high-handedness of the British ministry, and a coward's fear of the bloodshed in Watertown and Norfolk."

"You? A coward?" Finley laughed and shook his head. "I seem to recall a story about a Newport man putting his head in a noose to protect another. Hardly a cowardly act, my friend."

"How did you find out about that?"

"There's no such thing as a quiet act of heroism, Ashton. The news was all over the colony by summer's end."

Lines appeared between Ashton's brows. Despite the tales, doubtless embellished by exaggeration, he knew better than to consider himself a hero. No hero would allow himself to be saved by a woman's lies. Self-disgust furled within him.

"We've something to discuss with you." Finley was

suddenly serious and businesslike. "It concerns your wife's brother."

"Harry Winslow?"

"Aye. He's been found. And arrested."

Ashton clenched his fists in frustration. All he'd done on Harry's account had come to naught. "But how?" he demanded. "No more than four people knew of his whereabouts, and none of us would have divulged—"

"I don't know how it happened. I suspect the same British sympathizer who tried to foil our commerce with Hortalez et Cie."

"Damn," Ashton muttered. "So the lad's doomed after all."

"Not necessarily," Chapin cautioned. "Curiously enough, the informant has a heart. He betrayed Winslow's whereabouts only after an assurance that the young man wouldn't be put to death."

Finley nodded. "There's a good chance we can gain his release by means of a prisoner exchange."

Ashton smiled ruefully. Harry Winslow seemed to have an angel of mercy riding upon his shoulders.

"Problem is," Finley continued, "we don't hold a prisoner the Redcoats want badly enough to release Winslow."

Sudden comprehension added a bitter tang to the wine Ashton sipped. "And you want me to procure one."

"Aye. Find him, capture him, and take him to Butt's Hill Fort for the exchange."

"I'm no kidnapper," Ashton said darkly.

"But you're discreet, swift, and cunning. Totally unknown to the British, and you've access to the fastest horses on the eastern seaboard. Few in Newport claim those qualities."

"Just who is it you would have me abduct?"

Finley wrapped an ink-stained hand around the base of his mug and spoke into its rim. "Captain Dorian Tanner."

Ashton couldn't help flinching at the mention of the name that had plagued him like a nightmare for months. Each time he looked at Bethany, softly lovely with the child that grew within her, he was reminded of the likelihood that her beautifully rounded form swelled with the fruit of Tanner's loins.

Nor could Ashton help the sudden surge of satisfaction at the notion that, should he accept Finley's errand, Dorian Tanner would be a prisoner of the patriots he'd harassed all year.

"What am I to do?" he asked, disgusted by his own thoughts and by the idea that, once again, Harry Winslow's well-being had been placed in his reluctant hands. "Shall I knock the captain senseless and truss him up like a spring turkey?"

"Actually, that's not far from what we had in mind," Chapin said, grinning.

"You'll have to move tomorrow night," Finley added. "We've found out that Tanner will be celebrating Christmas Eve with the ladies of Madame Juniper's. The sooner we place him in the hands of Winslow's captors, the better."

"How will you inform the Redcoats that, indeed, we hold one of their own?"

"That'll take time. Another day, at least."

"And what am I to do with the prisoner during that time?"

"We were hoping you'd provide a solution to that, Ashton."

Bethany quickly composed her face when she heard Ashton lift the latch and enter the cottage. The tiny bunting she was embroidering for the baby lay neglected in her quilt-covered lap, several stitches knotted by her nervous hands. The hearth fire flared as wind gusted in the open door. Gladstone whined a greeting.

"You should have gone to bed," Ashton remarked, removing his greatcoat. The sharpness of cold sea air mingled with his scent. The wind had placed color high in his cheeks, accentuating the rugged bones of his face.

"It's late, Ashton," she said softly. "Where have you been?"

"You needn't concern yourself with my whereabouts."

She glanced away, but her chin rose. For four months she'd endured his distrust, his disbelief that the child she carried was his. She'd grown accustomed to the hurt, but not so accustomed that she didn't feel it anymore.

"Am I not permitted to worry about my husband?"

He leaned his forearm on the mantelpiece and studied the gray stones of the chimney, stones that had once been black with soot but were now clean due to Bethany's meticulous whisking. She saw a tightness in his shoulders and a slight droop to his head as he said, "Aye, Bethany. Worry if you will, but spare me your questions."

She shivered, and not from the cold. Always Ashton hid the better part of himself from her, as if afraid of what would happen if he returned her feelings.

She rose from the chair and went to him, running her hands up the back of a woolsey shirt defined by the taut sinews beneath, sinews that tensed beneath her touch.

"Talk to me, Ashton," she said softly. "Don't wall yourself off from me. I'm your wife."

He turned and froze her with his stare. "A marriage should be forged by trust, wrought by love. We were thrust together by happenstance."

"But I love you, Ashton. I do."

"You love a girl's fantasies, some image you've built up and carried around with you." He encompassed the keeping room with a sweeping gesture. "Is this what you wanted?" he demanded. "Seven years as a bondsman's wife in a house so small you can barely turn around? Being snubbed by people who used to welcome you in their drawing rooms? Has it made you happy?"

Tears sparkled on her lashes. "I don't care where I live or whose soiree I've been excluded from. I just want your trust."

"You commend your heart into my keeping and expect me to know what to do with it."

"You know," she insisted. "I've felt it." Her hand reached for him, encountering the warmth and hardness of a chest that rose and fell too quickly. "I've felt it each time you forget yourself and smile at me. I've felt it when you draw water for my bath or spare me from doing the laundry on cold days. I've felt it when you hold me in your arms at night and make love to me."

At first the softening of his face was so slight that she

thought she'd imagined it, and turned away. He brought her back to him with a hand on her shoulder, and then she knew; she knew some of what she'd said had breached his indifference and touched him in the place he guarded so jealously. There was no bitterness in his eyes as he wrapped her against him, winnowing his fingers into her hair and clasping her cheek to the inviting expanse of his chest.

"Aye, Bethany," he said roughly. "You do touch me with your big hazel eyes and your sweet, sweet smile. There have been moments these past months that I've found ease with you."

Bethany shivered and hugged her brown wool cloak around her, shielding herself from the biting December wind. The windows of Peleg Thurston's shop were fogged and frosted, the display within rather dusty and haphazard, but her eyes fastened hungrily on one object, which drew her attention like a beacon.

"Lordy, an' will you look at that!" exclaimed a voice beside her.

The woman's rouged and powdered face and the garish gown peeping from beneath a threadbare cloak marked her as one of the "fancy women" from Madame Juniper's. She sent Bethany a wide, brazen smile and pointed at the window. "Them ostrich feathers must be a full yard high. Lordy, but wouldn't I like to have 'em for a bit of extra plumage."

"They're . . . rather striking."

The woman laughed in a voice made rough by drink. "Not exactly to your likin', eh? So what're you lookin' at here?"

Bethany indicated a small calf-bound volume, its pages edged in gold leaf.

The woman shrugged. "I ain't much for readin'."

"The pages are blank. It's a journal."

"Ah, for writin' down your thoughts an' such."

Bethany nodded, feeling more comfortable talking to this painted stranger than she ever had with any of her high-born friends. "I thought to give it to my husband for Christmas."

"Well now, that's just fine, missus. That man o' yours must be somethin' special; wouldn't mind getting my hands on one like that myself."

Bethany smiled. Ashton hardly had to pay for what she adored giving him, night after night.

"I'm off then," the woman said, wrapping a frayed scarf around her frizzy red hair. " 'Tis nigh time for work; I've a big night ahead o' me. Merry Christmas, missus, an' many happy returns o' the day!"

Bethany lowered her head into the wind and plunged gratefully into the warmth of Peleg Thurston's. She dropped back her hood to inhale the warm fragrance of spices and coffee.

"Well, well," tinkled a crystal-hard voice. " 'Tis our own Bethany."

Bethany's hackles were already up by the time she turned to see Mabel Pierce and Keith Cranwick standing near the big central stove. Her friends from the past had deserted her last August, so swiftly they might never have existed. Her marriage had been fodder for the gossip mongers; now that her pregnancy was evident, she was aware of much finger counting and speculation as to why she had, so suddenly, married far beneath herself.

An angry retort leaped to her lips, but she reeled it in. Nothing disinfects like sunshine, Miss Abigail used to tell her, and so she forced herself to smile.

"Hello, Mabel, Keith," she said brightly. "Monstrous cold, is it not?"

"Indeed it is," Mabel replied, tossing her ringlets over the fur-lined collar of her cloak. "If I had a smidgen of sense, I'd have stayed home today, but I simply had to do some shopping before your parents' reception tonight." Her hand fluttered to Keith's sleeve. "Mr. Cranwick was kind enough to accompany me. I do find shopping so tedious." She fingered a frieze of green and scarlet, then nodded meaningfully at her maid, a skinny slave girl who staggered beneath the bulk of a half dozen parcels.

"I'm sure the chore is very hard on you," Bethany murmured.

Keith's smile glittered. "Will you be at the reception

tonight? Your former teacher, Miss Abigail Primrose, is over from Bristol for the season, I hear."

Bethany eyed the journal, which the proprietor had already removed from the window. Mr. Thurston had seen her coming and was well aware that she'd longed to buy the journal for weeks. Ashton will love it, she told herself with a private smile. Aloud she said, "I'm sure I'll see Miss Abigail while she's in Newport, but not at the reception. Ashton and I will be celebrating quietly at home, Keith."

"A pity," he said smoothly. "I simply cannot imagine you living in that crude cottage with a stable hand."

At last her smile wavered. "If you'll excuse me, Keith, I've come to buy my husband his Christmas present."

She caught Keith's remark about how her manners had suffered along with her reputation but ignored the gibe as Mr. Thurston wrapped the journal in a neat parcel and accepted her small purse of coins, painstakingly hoarded over the weeks. She turned to see Keith and Mabel still looking at her. Mabel was murmuring something behind her kid-gloved hand. Both their faces held such smug pity that her temper finally flared.

"Excuse me," she said. "I'm sorry I can't stay around to entertain you any longer."

"Bethany," Keith said patronizingly, "we're concerned about you. 'Tis a crime you're married to an unwashed commoner, and a rebel to boot."

She chewed her lip. Ashton had had nothing to do with the patriots since the day they'd married. "Why do you say he's a patriot?" she asked.

"I've seen him hanging about the White Horse Tavern."

"Ashton is free to go where he will to relax over a tankard of ale."

"More than ale is served at the White Horse. A man can get a generous helping of sedition there as well. I saw Markham slip into the taproom not an hour ago, as a matter of fact."

"You needn't inform me of my husband's whereabouts, Keith."

Mabel said, "Bethany dear, we're your friends. We don't want to see you shamed by such a man."

"Nor do I need your concern, Mabel," she snapped, and brushed past them. She paused only to borrow Mr. Thurston's quill and pen a message on her manila-wrapped package; *Merry Christmas, my dearest love.*

Stepping onto the street, she drew up her hood and started toward the little pony-driven trap she'd brought into town. The wind had gathered strength, pushing a bank of heavy clouds over the harbor, turning the bay waters into a frothy tempest the color of raw iron. Flurries of snow swirled through the air, filling the cracks in the brick street and stinging Bethany's face. The bell of Trinity Church tolled, its rich sound reverberating through the snow-laden twilight.

Possessed of a sudden impatience to be home, Bethany climbed to the hard bench of the trap and chucked the pony into a slow walk. The meeting with Keith and Mabel had left a bitter taste in her mouth, and she couldn't seem to get away fast enough.

Snowflakes swirled in a vigorous, wind-tossed dance as she drove up Marlborough Street. Red brick and pastel-painted buildings wavered uncertainly through an ever-thickening curtain of whiteness. In the distance a figure appeared, emerging from the White Horse Tavern in a whirl of dark wool. A queue of chestnut hair hung over the collar of the greatcoat, sending a stab of pleasure through Bethany as she recognized her husband.

She called his name, but the wind stopped her voice short and curled it back to her. Heedless and seemingly distracted, Ashton hurried off in the opposite direction. Bethany urged the pony after him, but the animal refused to quicken its pace beyond a reluctant plod. Anxious and frustrated, she kept her eyes fastened on Ashton as he swiftly passed Vernon's silverworks and the Brick Market and slowed when he reached a tall, narrow town house with a pink facade and a welcoming glow in its front windows. Madame Juniper's!

Bethany suddenly went cold. She hauled on the reins, bringing the trap to a stop as dead as her heart had suddenly become. Even as her mind screamed a denial, she stared, knifed by dread, as Ashton cast a swift look right and left and went inside the brothel.

Comprehension crashed through her mind, sliding icy fingers like the December wind through her heart. So this was where he had been last night, and Lord knew how many other nights. What was it, revenge or lust, that sent him to the arms of Madame Juniper's ready courtesans?

Bethany couldn't cry, for no tears were hot enough to warm the ice that froze her heart. She couldn't curse Ashton, for she knew no words foul enough to describe the shattering disillusionment that roiled within her.

"Why?" she whispered brokenly, and the wind picked up her voice and swirled it away. Why did Ashton seek the skilled but impersonal arms of a whore when Bethany's willing love awaited him at home? Did he find her so repellent that he needed the solace of another woman? Did he think her so tarnished that one of the painted birds at Madame Juniper's looked more savory to him?

An image pushed its way into her mind, an image of Ashton enfolded in the plump white arms of a woman like the redhead who'd admired the ostrich feathers in Thurston's window. Revulsion welled in her throat as she turned the pony northward and plodded to the place she no longer wanted to call home.

Snow crunched beneath Ashton's boots as he stepped up the path toward the cottage. It had been snowing ceaselessly since late afternoon. The box hedge and yew trees lining the path were vague, drifting shapes.

At least the wind had settled, Ashton told himself. Captain Dorian Tanner, locked in a distant salt lick shed in the eastern meadows, had ample clothing and covers to avoid freezing to death. Although no sound disturbed the snow-cushioned silence of the cottage dooryard, the Redcoat's bellows of rage and fear still belled through Ashton's mind.

The abduction had gone smoothly: A sack of gold slipped into Madame Juniper's hands, another to the shapely octoroon who entertained Tanner, and the hapless captain had fallen like a ripe apple into Ashton's hands. Unsteady with rum punch and blinded by the sudden dark when the courtesan had doused her lamp, the Redcoat was an easy mark.

Tanner hadn't awakened from the blow Ashton had laid to the vulnerable spot below and behind his ear until they'd reached the stout rubble-built shed.

Ashton told himself he was entitled to feel a certain grim satisfaction that the lordly Captain Tanner had become a prisoner of the rebellion. But all he felt was grim. Things would be tense until tomorrow night, when he'd transport his furious and unkempt prisoner to Butt's Hill Fort.

Blowing out a sigh that froze in the air before his face, he quietly lifted the latch and stepped into the cottage.

Something was different and he couldn't quite mark it. All was in place; the keeping room was snug and warmed by fireglow. Sprigs of holly and yew surrounded bayberry candles on the mantelpiece; the scents of the candles and greenery lingered in the air, adding a bit of holiday cheer. All the small comforts and homey niceties Bethany had brought to this house were in place: the bright quilts on the settle, the basket of pinecones at the hearth, the sprays of drying herbs on the sideboard. . . .

An inexplicable shiver of apprehension gripped Ashton as he stepped into the keeping room. Spying a small parcel on a settle, he went to inspect it.

Merry Christmas, my dearest love was written on the manila parchment in Bethany's neat, apothecarylike script.

"Sweet God in heaven," he murmured as the wrapping unfurled. "I've forgotten Christmas."

He looked at the gift: a handsome journal. He nearly released it, burned by a feeling of shame. How perceptive of Bethany to give him a journal. And how pointed a statement. He spoke little to her; perhaps she'd guessed he might like to record his thoughts and dreams on paper. How had she known?

His mouth thinned into a grim smile. How, indeed? A foolish question. Bethany had an uncanny gift for anticipating his every need, his smallest desire, sometimes even procuring what he wanted before he was aware he wanted it.

He slipped the journal into his pocket, full of warmth at her generosity, full of regret at his own thoughtlessness.

Hard-pressed to select a gift for Bethany, who had once had servants dancing attendance on her and more clothes and jewels than a half dozen ordinary girls, Ashton had planned on giving her his mother's wedding ring. But Harry's emergency had driven all thoughts of keeping Christmas from his head. Until now. He wondered if she would accept the gift, if she would appreciate its significance. She asked for little, yet she craved the impossible.

She did want something from him, Ashton realized with an uncomfortable twisting of his gut. She wanted him to believe against all opposing certainty that she'd been a virgin on her wedding night, that the child swelling her middle—far too greatly for a four-month babe—was his. She wanted his faith in her, his trust.

She wanted his love.

He moved restlessly to the hearth and laid a pine log on the embers, hearing the hiss of the sap, smelling resin. The feeling that something was out of kilter nagged at him once again.

And then realization came to him. Never had he entered the cottage to this misleading silence, this false peace. Gladstone, ever ready with his big, clumsy paws and wet tongue, was nowhere in sight. No matter how late it was, Ashton could always be sure of a low whine of greeting or the thumping of the spaniel's tail on the puncheon floor.

With a hand gone suddenly cold, he pushed the bedroom door open and peered unseeing into the gloom. He listened. And heard nothing, not Gladstone's whine, not Bethany's soft breathing, not the rustling of the cornhusk mattress.

Panic leaped high in his throat as he swung the door wide to let the glow of the hearth fire fall in an elongated triangle across the rom. The light told him what he already knew, what he'd been dreading since the moment he'd stepped into the cottage.

Bethany was gone.

Chapter 9

The wind numbed his ears and snow dusted his hat and shoulders as he ran through the mile-long maze of paths to the main house. Let her be there, he thought over and over again until the words were like a tattoo of pleading. Let her be there. Let her be safe.

Other thoughts crowded into his mind as he progressed toward the house. In the past four months he'd suggested dozens of times that she return to her parents, to live the life she was accustomed to and remain his wife in name only. He had suggested the idea in anger over the bitter futility of his situation, in concern when he saw Bethany struggle with some unfamiliar task, in annoyance when he saw how unsuited she was as a bondsman's wife.

But she'd never wavered in her determination to be a wife to him in the fullest sense of the word. With stubbornness and fierce pride she declared that her place was with him.

So why now? Why, after all the months of enduring his silence and distrust, the bursts of temper that outnumbered the bursts of passion, would she at last succumb to his suggestion?

Winter-bare willows loomed over the path; naked branches clacked in the wind like dry bones. Why, indeed? Ashton thought with a surge of self-loathing. The answer to that was obvious.

It was Christmas Eve and he hadn't come home to her. Guilt writhed through him as a picture formed in his mind of Bethany waiting for him so she could place her gift in his hands. No matter that his task was to save her brother;

she couldn't know that. All she knew was that it was Christmas Eve and he hadn't come.

He sprinted across snow-blanketed gardens to the manor house. The ballroom windows glowed golden. Music tinkled in the snow-wrapped silence. He could hear the laughter of footmen and drivers who waited in the carriage house and guest stables. The Winslows always celebrated Christmas in grand style, opening their home to scores of visitors who drank and danced until the wee hours.

Ashton stepped up to the verandah. The French doors, rimmed by frost, framed a flurry of color and motion. He looked past a pinwheel of gold-shot gowns and scarlet uniforms, through a sea of powdered hair and black-patched faces, and his eyes found, with relief and dismay, a bright head of honey-gold hair framing a pale oval face and two impossibly large eyes.

She wore a dress he'd never seen before, curiously old-fashioned and maddeningly becoming. The gown was of some shimmering dusky rose fabric, high in the neck and falling loosely below her full breasts to cloak her swelling middle. A black velvet ribbon circled her throat, centered by a scrimshaw brooch that rode upon her flesh like a work of art. Bathed in candlelight and framed by the frost-clad windows, Bethany looked as beautiful as a goddess.

Nearby, a cluster of women cast scandalized looks at her and whispered behind their hands, no doubt speculating as to why, after having married a commoner, she was in their elegant fold once again.

Ashton's heart ached for her when he saw the way she was smiling. It was a haunted smile, too bright around the mouth and not bright enough about the eyes.

He recognized the two people with whom she was talking. One was that birdlike teacher he'd met briefly in Bristol, the one who, despite her small stature and prim mien, looked likely to eat him alive if he harmed Bethany. Miss Abigail Primrose was on the arm of a monocled officer in a braided wig—Colonel Darby Chason.

Ashton wondered what Bethany had told the colonel about their marriage. Had she fed the man's male pride by declaring that he'd done the right thing in forcing them to marry, or was she confessing that she was desperately unhappy?

Ashton didn't know which, because he still didn't know his wife. He knew her routine, the way her newly capable hands kneaded bread dough or wielded a birch broom. He knew her warm responses and sighs of passion when he made love to her, the way she awakened each morning like a flower unfurling its petals to the sun. But, to his profound regret, he realized he didn't know what his beautiful, intelligent wife thought from day to day.

He was certain of only one thing. It was Christmas Eve and Bethany had left him.

On Christmas day Bethany sat in the summerhouse with winter all around her, the gardens stark and barren and the sea below the cliffs shifting, gray as a headstone. Wind slid icy fingers through the open windows, seeming to reach in and curl around her heart. Her hand cupped the burgeoning swell of her middle.

There was only this one warm spot within her, where even the bitter wind couldn't reach. She'd been visited this morning by her child. For the first time she'd felt a quickening as she lay alone in the beautiful pink and white room of her girlhood. The sensation had begun as a vague fluttering, then the stirring became more apparent.

Ashton Markham had taken her heart and torn it asunder. He'd taken her faith and trust and the wealth of energy she'd expended in pleasing him. He'd taken her very soul and turned it bitter with his betrayal.

The babe fluttered again.

But he hadn't taken this from her. No matter what he did, he could not spoil her love for this child.

She wrapped her brown cloak more tightly about her. The wind caught her sigh, and the air chilled it to icy vapors.

"Young lady," said a curt female voice behind her, "just why are you mooning about on Christmas day?"

Bethany snapped to attention on hearing her teacher's query. "Good morning, Miss Abigail," she said. "Many happy returns of the day."

Miss Abigail negotiated the snow-clad steps of the summerhouse with dainty precision. Her hair was covered by a voluminous rabbit-lined hood, and the cold had placed spots of color high in her fine-skinned cheeks. A hint of redness even dared show itself on the tip of her tiny nose, looking incongruous in an otherwise elegant face.

Miss Abigail perched like a chickadee on the seat Bethany had brushed off for her and fixed a keen stare on her former pupil.

"So. You've not answered my question. You evaded me last night as well. How is it you arrived, quite late, quite unattached, and quite . . . enceinte, at your parents' party?"

Bethany looked away, reluctant to share her troubles even with Miss Abigail. "I . . . 'tis Harry," she said quickly. Even her radical brother was a less painful topic than Ashton. "I've not heard from him in some weeks, and I'm beginning to fear something went wrong in Providence."

"Don't worry about Harry," Miss Abigail said. "He's fine . . . er, I'm sure you'll soon find he's quite well."

Had Bethany been less despondent about Ashton, she might have given more thought to Miss Abigail's statement; she might have wondered how her teacher could sound so sure. But, deeply troubled by something more immediate, she merely sighed and leaned back against the side of the summerhouse.

Eyeing her thoughtfully, Miss Abigail said, "You're not telling me everything, Bethany."

"Must I ever unburden myself to you, Miss Abigail?"

"Indeed, you must. By the way, the gown you wore last night was stunning. 'Tis a shame your husband wasn't present to enjoy it."

Bethany winced.

Miss Abigail nodded sagely. "I thought as much. What sort of rift drove you back to your family?"

"I . . . we . . . I can't talk about it. Ashton betrayed me and I had to get away."

"I must remember to thank your husband for allowing you and me to meet again at the reception," Miss Abigail said wryly. Again those shrewd eyes probed. "Colonel Chason certainly asked you a lot of questions."

"He wanted to make sure Ashton had done right by me."

"And you told him he had."

"Of course. Colonel Chason has promised to hang Ashton if his orders are violated."

"I see. And you don't want your husband to hang."

"What he's done . . . is not a hanging offense."

"Yet you're offended."

"Aye."

"And in pain."

"Aye." The admission was dragged from her on a sob. Then Miss Abigail's arms were around her, small yet strong, narrow yet wiry. Perfectly tailored merino-clad shoulders received Bethany's tears until her sobbing dissolved to bitter hiccups.

"Will you go back to him?" Miss Abigail gently inquired.

"He never wanted me in the first place. Now I don't know if I want to be with him."

"But you're not certain."

"No. I'm not certain of anything, Miss Abigail."

"Neither is your husband."

Bethany regarded her quizzically until Miss Abigail pointed over the balustrade of the summerhouse, indicating a snowy ribbon of sand below the cliffs. A figure stood on the beach, very still, hands secreted in his pockets, facing out to sea. Waves played hide-and-seek between jagged ice-capped rocks, and curlews braved the wind in the gray sky overhead, their sharp cries cutting through the song of the wind and the roar of the dark sea.

"That *is* Ashton, is it not?" Miss Abigail inquired.

The wind lifted a rich chestnut strand of hair and curled it skyward. Bethany nodded. "Yes. Yes, 'tis him."

He made a lonely picture, standing pensively, surrounded by wind and water. His shoulders seemed somehow heavy.

"He appears troubled," Miss Abigail commented.

Bethany shivered. "Perhaps," she murmured. But why? Was he regretting that he'd spent Christmas Eve at a brothel rather than home with his wife? Or was he only sorry that Bethany had found out, as he must have realized by now?

"I must go," Miss Abigail announced. "Colonel Chason has offered to escort me to Little Rest. I'll be spending the remainder of my holiday with the Bryce family." She gave Bethany a quick hug and moved to the steps. "Talk to him, child. Whatever it is between you two must be discussed. Nothing will be served by feeding your hurt with silence."

"But I can't—"

" 'Can't,' Bethany? Do you not recall that I banished that word from your vocabulary at the academy? You *can* overcome your problems with your husband. You will."

"Yes, ma'am," she replied softly. She watched Miss Abigail leave, her dainty steps sure as she picked her way through the bare fingers of the Persian lilacs framing the path. The lady looked back and sent Bethany an encouraging smile. Bethany returned the gesture halfheartedly. Then she turned her sorrow-heavy gaze back to Ashton.

The wind bit at Ashton's face, but he didn't turn from it. His mind seethed with worries more discomforting than the winter cold. Tonight, Finley had told him. Tonight, under cover of cold and dark, he would undertake to deliver Captain Tanner to the small fort ten miles to the north. And that, he hoped, would be the last time he'd have to concern himself with Harry Winslow.

The problem with Bethany was not so easily resolved. Problem? Ashton wondered with a rueful smile. She'd done exactly what he'd been wanting her to do for the past four months. She'd returned to her parents, to the luxury and security he could not give her.

'Tis exactly what you wanted, he told himself angrily. *So why do you dwell on it?*

It was the manner in which she'd complied that bothered him. It was because, in order to get her to obey, he'd had to hurt her. She must remain in protective ignorance of his patriot activities at any cost. Would he have to explain about last night?

Perhaps his gift would soothe her pain. The thin band of rose gold would look good on her finger.

The idea of giving Bethany a wedding ring gave him

pause. In so doing, he'd be giving credence to the fact that, however reluctantly, he recognized her as his wife. At one time he could have been sure of her delight; now he didn't know whether or not she'd accept his gift.

At last Ashton turned from his contemplation of the cold, shifting bay waters. He glanced up, his gaze moving between a great cleft in the rocks. At the top stood the summerhouse. A sudden warm feeling seeped through him. He remembered kissing Bethany as they sat in the summerhouse once, long ago, when kisses were easy to give.

As he watched, a figure appeared at the balustrade. Bethany. She looked curiously small in her brown cloak, her face a pale oval too distant to read the expression.

On feet made swift by sudden urgency, Ashton climbed the rocks to his wife.

Bethany stifled an urge to flee as she watched him approach. Remembering Miss Abigail's insistence that she face her problems rather than run from them, Bethany stayed where she was.

Ashton scaled the last steep crag and, placing his hand on the railing, vaulted over the balustrade in a single lithe movement.

His hair, wind-tossed and in a state of appealing disarray, framed a face made ruddy by cold. His eyes were too blue, too searching, and for once not cold at all. But he wasn't smiling.

"Hello, pet," he said. He reached into his pocket and produced a small velvet bag. "Merry Christmas to you, love."

She backed against the balustrade. "No, Ashton," she said. "I . . . couldn't accept a gift from you, not now."

"Wear the ring, pet. Please." Before she could object again, he'd slipped the ring on her finger.

She stared down at the new, cold presence on her hand and said, "Thank you." She cringed inwardly. How absurdly formal they were both being. Did all married couples face major disasters with such impersonal formality?

"Bethany." His voice, low and grating, reached for her. She dragged her eyes to his. "Bethany, I'm sorry."

"You're sorry," she echoed hollowly. "Is that all? No explanation?"

"There is one, pet."

"Such as . . . ?" Please don't lie to me, she prayed silently. I couldn't stand it if you lied to me. Silence stretched between them, punctuated by the roar of the sea and the mournful whine of the curlews. Suddenly she cast her reticence to the winter wind and faced him squarely.

"Shall I spare you the trouble of inventing excuses, Ashton? I know perfectly well where you were last night, and exactly what you were doing. I was in town buying your journal and I saw you."

Real alarm leaped to his eyes, more damning than any denial. "Bethany," he said, "I had no choice."

"No choice?" she demanded. "I suppose I truly am naive about men, then. Exactly what imperative compelled you to seek the company of one of Madame Juniper's whores?"

Emotions skittered across his features: confusion, surprise, annoyance . . . and finally relief. "Is that what you thought I was doing?"

"I am not so thickheaded that I don't know what goes on at a brothel."

"But . . ." He snapped his mouth shut and narrowed his eyes.

"Ashton, *why?* Why did you seek the arms of a stranger when I never denied you—"

"Don't carry on like this, pet," he said quickly. "I never . . . Bethany? Bethany, don't cry."

"I understand at last, Ashton. For months I've been denying that our marriage is a sham. You told me from the start that we don't belong together. Time and time again you've tried to drive me away with your cold, silent indifference. But I ignored the signs of your discontent, even when they were staring me in the face." She choked back a sob. "You must be grateful I've finally fallen back to earth."

He ached to gather her into his arms and soothe away the hurt etched on her face. It's not what you think, he longed to say. Never would I desire a stranger when I have your willing warmth.

But he kept his mouth pressed into an implacable line. The belief that he'd spent Christmas Eve with a courtesan broke her heart. But far more damage would be done if he succumbed to the clamoring instinct to explain everything to Bethany, to soothe her pain by admitting he'd only gone to the brothel to secure a prisoner to exchange for her brother.

He'd committed an act punishable by death if he was caught. If Bethany knew about his activities, he'd be placing her in danger as well. It wasn't fair to burden her with knowledge that could make her fall prey to a British inquiry.

"Bethany," he said, feeling the fat tear that slipped down her cheek as if it were his own, "I never meant to hurt you." His eyes moved to the distant manor house, starkly grand in its setting of pristine white. "I understand why you returned to your home, but I'll miss you. I'll miss you every minute of every day."

Anger drove away the hurt in her eyes; a violent swipe of her hand dried her tears. "But not at night, Ashton," she accused. "You have other women to fill those needs."

Bethany stared at her reflection in the gilt-framed looking glass on her dressing table. The flesh beneath her eyes was swollen and dull red, but her eyes were dry now. She had no more tears to spare for Ashton Markham.

A figure came into view in the looking glass. The bright red hair and blue eyes of Carrie Markham had once been a familiar sight; now Bethany felt surprise at seeing her former maid.

"I've come to help you dress for supper," Carrie announced, crossing the room. "Lord, but I'm glad you're back, miss. Your mother can't make up her mind about anything. Has me running in circles trying to gather things for her toilette every morning. I still don't know pomatum from cerise, rouge from carmine. Sometimes I think the Lord made women imperfect just to confuse me with all those cosmetic remedies."

"I really don't need any help, Carrie. I've learned a lot about doing for myself lately."

"Thanks to that mule-witted brother of mine," Carrie

grumbled. "Honestly, the man's seven kinds of a fool. Only Ashton would manage to get himself in such a fix, marrying quality and finding himself a bondsman the same day. I just wonder that it took you so long to tire of playing house with him and come back where you belong."

"I don't belong here," Bethany mused. "Nor do I belong with Ashton." But she didn't object when Carrie took out a loosely cut *robe à l'anglaise*. It was one of the few garments she owned that would accommodate her growing figure.

As Carrie fastened the loop catch at the back neckline, Bethany said, "I'm going for a walk. A very long, solitary walk."

"Oh no, miss, you mustn't go out in the cold. Think of the babe—"

"Goody Haas says moderate exercise does no harm at all. Don't look so dubious, Carrie. Tell my mother I'm not feeling well and not to expect me at supper."

Half an hour later, dressed warmly against the cold, Bethany walked away from the manor, away from the family that pitied and misunderstood her, away from the husband who had betrayed her. Evening was stealing softly over the island. The westering sun glowed pink and amber over soft waves of snow, cushioning the sounds of her footsteps.

With feet clad in riding boots, she stepped high through drifts and clambered over a rubble-built stone fence, making for the broad eastern meadows. All was silence and solitude; she felt at home in the bleak surroundings. The wind had gentled to a chilly breeze, stirring up tiny tempests of powdery snow.

She had taken this walk to escape, to relieve herself of the bothersome thoughts that nagged her. But instead of relieving her, the scenery made her even more wistful. All around her were stabbing reminders of happy times long past. To her left was the stock pond, frozen over as it did each year.

Memories crept out of a corner of her mind—memories of the blithe girl she'd once been. She recalled tagging after Ashton, begging him to wait for her, the laces of her ice skates dragging. She remembered how he had taken her about the waist and guided her until she could skate on her own. Harry always whooshed past, far more interested in speed than in form; inevitably he ended up in a snowdrift, laughing. William always played the gallant, trying to impress the girls with his smooth style on the ice.

Those days of innocence were so long past that they might have been a dream. Now Harry was a rebel and a fugitive, unwelcome in his family, unable to support the wife and child he'd taken in defiance of his father's wishes. William's reports from the army post in Connecticut hinted that he'd not changed his habits of drinking, gambling, and entertaining the ladies. And Bethany was the unwanted wife of a man shackled in bondage to her father, big with a child he would not claim.

Never in their youth could they have anticipated that rebellion would tear the family apart. Never had Bethany realized she could hurt so deeply. Her eyes made a restless survey of the surroundings.

Straight ahead, some yards distant, was the salt lick shed where she and Harry had often hidden from overbearing nurses and exacting tutors. To her right was the trail to the cove Ashton had showed her, where she'd first felt the magic of his kiss.

The wind moaned across the meadow. Bethany stopped, frowning. The wind wasn't blowing hard enough to raise an eerie sound like that. She heard the noise again and realized it was not the wind at all. A pair of stable cats embarking on their evening prowl, perhaps? No; the sound held a distinctly human quality. And it was coming from somewhere in front of her, perhaps in the salt lick shed.

Apprehension tingled down her spine. She glanced skyward, noting that the pink and amber sunset had melted into the deep, secret purples and indigos of twilight. A few stars winked like cold white eyes in the sky. It would be dark soon. She should go back.

But she heard the moaning again and thought she detected a note of pleading. Gathering up the hem of her cloak, she plunged through the snow toward the shed. The moaning grew louder and was punctuated by inelegant curses, sounding curiously like the speech of one of the cockney sailors who haunted Long Wharf. Then curses gave way to disjointed prayers for mercy.

"Hello!" Bethany called, her voice weak and shaky with apprehension. "Hello!" she called again, more loudly.

"Who goes there?" The voice became clipped and alert. Cautiously she approached the salt lick shed, surprised to see a latch on the door made of new wood, fitted snugly into the wooden handle. The door was locked from the outside.

She pressed her lips to a crack in the wood, wondering who in heaven was being held in this crude prison, and why. "Who . . . who are you?" she inquired.

"Bethany?" The whisper was hoarse, incredulous, full of gratitude. "Open the door, Bethany."

She stumbled back. The voice that had been uttering cockney curses now became Dorian Tanner's familiar, precise speech.

"Dorian?" she asked. "Dorian, what are you doing here?"

"Let me out, Bethany. I shall try to explain before I freeze to death."

Her fingers were cold and clumsy as she dislodged the wooden latch from the door handle. The latch fell and the door swung open on its wooden hinges.

A disheveled and shivering Dorian Tanner tumbled from the shed.

"Where the devil am I?" he wondered.

"Why—at Seastone. Dorian, what happened?"

"I was set upon by rebel scum," he said angrily, stamping his booted feet to warm himself. He grew still and measured her with drink-reddened eyes. "Bread and brandy were my only fare," he grumbled. Then his look became grateful. "Thank God you happened by."

Suddenly she found herself straining against his weight. At first she thought the ordeal had weakened him so much that he had swooned, but then she felt his hands plunge into the warm folds of her cloak.

"'Twas ungodly cold in there," he murmured. "So cold . . . and you're so warm, Bethany."

His kiss was wet and brandy-sweet. Bethany's compassion for him fled as she struggled to free herself from his unwanted embrace. But she was pinned between his warmth-hungry body and the shed, and could not escape.

Breathless from struggling and from the shock of discovering the officer in such an unlikely place, she couldn't give warning as, suddenly, a shadow loomed behind Dorian, broad and black against the deepening twilight. An arm rose high and then descended with blinding swiftness.

She heard a dull thud like a muffled musket shot and watched, aghast, as Dorian moaned and slid to the ground.

Chapter 10

Bethany shrank against the building, squeezing her eyes shut in anticipation of a second blow. But all she felt was the stinging lash of Ashton's harsh chuckle. "Don't think I'm not tempted, pet," he told her grimly. "But I won't hit you."

Her eyes flew open and widened in horror. "Ashton!"

"If I'd known you were so frantic to find your lover," he bit out, "I wouldn't have detained you at the summer-house this morning." His gaze settled disparagingly on the ring he'd placed on her finger. Turning away, he lifted Dorian, staggering momentarily beneath the weight. He barely looked at Bethany as he crossed the meadow, his strides swift despite his burden. He dumped the captain into the bed of a cart.

Bethany ran up behind him, her mind a stew of confusion, anger, and disappointment. "What was Dorian doing locked in that shed?"

"Swilling brandy, by the smell of him."

"That is not an answer," she retorted. But she didn't wait for one before firing off another question. "Where are you taking him?"

Ashton slid a cold glance at her. "You need not wonder about that." To her horror, he bound Dorian's wrists and wound a length of torn wool over his mouth before covering him with a tattersall blanket.

"But Dorian's a British officer. His superiors must be notified—"

Ashton drove his icy stare at her. "You'd do that, wouldn't you?"

She was allowed no time to respond. Her speech dissipated into a squeak of surprise when she felt Ashton position himself behind her. Hands like iron vises lifted her up and plopped her unceremoniously into the cart. Before she could react, he leaped in beside her and hauled on the reins. The horse surged into a smart canter. In minutes they were on a dark and lonely road, heading northward with all the speed Ashton could coax from the gelding.

"I can't risk leaving you behind," he said between teeth clenched in anger. "You're too much the avid Tory to be trusted."

Bethany felt dizzy with all the new and scathing things she had discovered about her husband in the past twenty-four hours. Once, she'd thought him decent; now she knew him to be a libertine who rejected his wife in favor of a courtesan. She'd thought him wise to moderate his political views; now she realized he was thick with the rebels. She'd believed him to be honest and aboveboard; yet he was abducting a British officer. Rage rendered her speechless; she was bitter beyond words, beyond tears.

The miles flew past, twilight sinking into night, cold and cavernously dark. Frozen bogs and marshes that yielded bayberries and wildflowers in the warmer months were now stark and draped in winter white. The moon crept skyward, sending long fingers of pale light over the blanketed meadows with their small clusters of mulberry trees.

At length Bethany forced herself to look at Ashton. He stared straight ahead, his square jaw grim, his eyes narrowed against the oncoming stream of cold wind.

"Why have you done this to Dorian?" she asked.

"It certainly wasn't to procure him for a convenient lovers' tryst."

"I came upon him by accident," she insisted. "Was I to pretend I didn't hear his cries?"

"No," he admitted. "But you seemed to be enjoying his gratitude."

Bethany felt something inside her crumple. It had taken her weeks to overcome Ashton's fury at finding her in Dorian's arms that first time, back in September. Now he'd found them together again. Each time she was innocent, having fallen prey to Dorian's ardor. But Ashton would never believe that.

Yet he was the guilty one now, she thought with a renewed surge of anger.

"You're mistaken about Dorian and me," she said tautly, "but I was not, was I, when I saw you go into Madame Juniper's?"

He sent her a sharp glance, and she thought for an incredulous moment that he would deny it. But he only looked over the gelding's bobbing rump and said nothing.

They veered eastward, climbing the gentle slope of Butt's Hill, where a crude fort had been erected. Palisades of pine jutted upward, creating a jagged silhouette against the night sky, a dark monument to the rising tide of rebellion. And the fort was so close to home, so very close.

They came to a halt in the shadows. A gust of wind came scurrying up from the fields, sighing coldly. The gelding laid its ears back and turned a baleful eye backward; Bethany saw its nostrils flare and emit puffs of vapor. Ashton dropped to the ground with a soft thud.

Out of the corner of her eye she noticed a ripple of movement. For the first time, she realized they were surrounded by men. Apprehension crawled up her spine.

Keeping the tattersall blanket over Dorian's head, Ashton set the Redcoat on his feet. Dorian moaned and swayed. Ashton shoved him forward. The secretive movements of the surrounding men stilled as Redcoat and rebel approached the fort. The movements started again when Ashton and Dorian disappeared inside.

Bethany's teeth savaged her lower lip as she waited. The fabric of her cloak crumpled within her nervously twisting hands as interminable moments passed. Finally, when her composure was in shreds, she saw two figures walking down from the fort. She recognized Ashton's long, purposeful stride. The other man was tall and thin, moving with a vigorous step. They reached the cart and alighted.

Bethany drew back with a gasp. Ashton was driving away from the fort before she found her voice.

"Harry?"

His arm slipped around her in comradely fashion. "Aye, 'tis your brother, back among his own again."

He looked different. Thinner, his clothes shabbier. The lines made by his grin were deeper, and there was a world-weary dullness in his eyes that was new to Bethany. "What is this all about, Harry?"

"Didn't Ashton tell you? No, he wouldn't boast. The British found me in Providence." He scowled into the dark. "Came right to me, they did. Somehow our secret got out." He brightened. "But they decided not to hang me after all; they agreed to a prisoner exchange."

Realization dawned with a leaden thud in Bethany's heart. "Dorian Tanner," she said dully.

"Aye. Guess it took the good captain down a peg or two when Ashton snatched him from the arms of one of Madame Juniper's girls on Christmas Eve!"

Bethany expelled a shaky breath and looked at Ashton. He sat stiffly, his face expressionless. Suddenly all the scathing revelations she'd had about him dispersed like snow flurries in the wind, leaving a wake of shame and regret.

She moved closer to him; he drew away. She swallowed and cleared her throat. "I was wrong, Ashton. I'm sorry."

"You made a logical assumption. I can't fault you for that." But he spoke coldly and would not meet her gaze.

They took her brother to Bristol Ferry. Smiling jauntily, he embraced his sister before dropping to the ground. "There now," he said, oblivious of the fact that he'd been the cause of a major rift between her and Ashton. " 'Tis all over now. In a few hours time I'll be with my wife again."

Bethany didn't return his smile. "It *is* over, isn't it, Harry? I mean, you won't risk being involved with the rebels again."

He reached for her hand and squeezed it. "I can't make that promise, Bethany."

She extracted her fingers from his. "Then at least promise you'll have a care for yourself, Harry. And Felicia and the baby as well."

"That I will," he vowed. Then he frowned. "I'd like to get my hands on the bloody informant who gave me away to the British. . . ." He sent an inquiring glance at Ashton. "Will Tanner be a problem?"

Ashton shook his head. "He knows virtually nothing, not even that Bethany witnessed the exchange."

Reassured, Harry disappeared into the night, whistling as he ambled down to the ferry.

Bethany wouldn't have thought it possible to sleep in her troubled state of mind, but as Ashton turned the cart southward and made for Newport, she felt a great lassitude seep through her limbs, brought on by the confusion of the night's events and her pregnancy, augmented by the rhythm of the horse's hoofs and the warmth of Ashton beside her.

Her eyelids drooped; she dragged them open again. But they drooped again and she stopped fighting sleep. Dimly she was aware of the firm comfort of Ashton's shoulder beneath her head. Her last thought was a hopeful one.

He didn't pull away from her.

Ashton dressed hurriedly in the predawn chill of the cottage, his skin prickling and teeth chattering. The water in the pitcher had a skin of ice on it that he had to break with his knuckles before enduring the torture of washing.

Once he was dressed for the day, he looked back at the bed where Bethany slept beneath a mound of quilts, only the honey-gold silk of her hair and one hand and cheek visible.

He felt a familiar and unwelcome lurch at the sight of that hand. She'd come to this marriage untried in the ways of keeping house, her hands as soft and tender as the skin of her flawless cheek. Her cheek was flawless still, but her hand had become rough and chilblained with the day-to-day chores. She never complained about the work; each new task she mastered became a source of childlike pride.

Lately she'd taken to visiting Goody Haas, the midwife, exchanging women's talk and recipes. Bethany had proven herself an able tutor in that house, helping Goody's passel of grandnieces and grandnephews with their lessons.

She could be happy, Ashton thought. She could be happy if he'd give her what she wanted. His trust. His love.

A scowl dropped over his face as he turned away. He

wanted to trust her, but she'd lied to him about her innocence. He wanted—yes, he admitted it—he wanted to love her, but twice he'd found her in Tanner's arms.

Troubled, he didn't leave for the stables immediately. Almost without thinking, he stoked the fire and filled the kettle so she would have a warm cottage and warm water when she awoke. Catching himself in the midst of a thoughtful act, he scowled again.

It was little enough to do for her, he told himself. She did work hard for his comfort, mastering the cooking of johnnycakes and chowder, washing his clothes and keeping his house. He returned to the bedroom to pour warm water into the pitcher. Bethany was sitting up in bed, regarding him solemnly.

"I fell asleep before I had a chance to thank you . . . for getting Harry free."

"I'm used to getting your brother out of scrapes," he told her, then grew angry at his own gruffness.

Suddenly Bethany looked terribly fragile to him. Her eyes were wide and pleading; her lower lip trembled with a vulnerability that stabbed at him. Ashton tore his gaze from her, unable to tolerate the idea that she had made him wholly responsible for her happiness—and her lack of it.

"Why didn't you tell me?" she asked. "Why did you let me believe you went to Madame Juniper's for . . ." Her voice trailed off and she looked away, flustered and lovely.

"I didn't want you involved. You're a Loyalist, remember?"

"Aye," she admitted. "But I'm Harry's sister first. I wouldn't have stood in your way."

"What I did was dangerous, Bethany. If something had gone wrong, you'd have been implicated."

"I see. I'm sorry for the things I said in the summerhouse yesterday. I'm sorry I left you."

"Are you?" he asked sharply. "You seemed to be enjoying yourself at your parents' reception." Her frown told him he shouldn't have admitted he'd gone looking for her that night. Her sudden winsome smile told him she'd guessed at his frantic feeling of loss.

"It was dreadful," she said sincerely. "Only the fact that Miss Primrose was there made the reception bearable." She climbed from the bed and approached him, placing a sleep-warm hand on his sleeve. "I'm back now, Ashton. I realize nothing can be solved by running away."

He tried to put aside a feeling of relief, just as he tried to put aside the fact that he'd missed her—missed the heady scent of jasmine that clung to her, the warmth of her body sweetly pressed against his. But, like the wide hazel eyes studying him, the feeling wouldn't leave him alone. His arms went around her, hauling her close.

"You're not one to run away, are you, pet?" he murmured against her hair.

"No, Ashton. I'm home. And home is here, right here in your arms."

He felt a stir against him, a fluttering upon his middle. He stiffened and pulled back, filled with sudden alarm.

"What was that?"

There was soft mystery in the smile that tugged at her lips. "Did you feel it, too?" Her hand crept upward, lying in the hollow between his shoulder and neck. " 'Twas our baby, Ashton."

Emotions jumbled through him: wonder, excitement, suspicion, resentment. A familiar nagging question pushed into his mind. Was the tiny life that stirred so delicately against him of his making?

He wanted to be sure. And he wasn't.

But did it really matter?

He brought his hands up, cradling Bethany's face while his thumbs brushed tiny circles through the silky hair at her temples. Aye, he admitted to himself. It *did* matter. Not that he would resent an innocent babe, but if he found out Bethany had willfully lied to him, he wasn't sure he could forgive her. Aye, *that* was the part that mattered.

"Ashton?" Her breath was soft and sweet on his face. "Ashton, please forgive me. I should have trusted you, even when all I saw and all you said condemned you."

He sucked in his breath with surprise. Had she read his thoughts? Was her quiet apology a soft reproof against his own inability to put aside his prejudices?

She raised herself on tiptoe and found the corner of his

mouth with her questing lips. He groaned with frustration and desire. As he received her kiss, he found himself envying her the ability to trust, to put her faith in him with the same ease she now put, with bold and scorching sensuality, her hands and tongue into a motion that made him forget all his questions.

A fragile, tenuous peace settled over the cottage through the month of January. Outside, all was bleakness: white-gray skies and snow growing stale and crusty on the moors and meadows, the lonely cries of curlews and kestrels as they braved the wind in search of herrings and quahogs. But within, the abode was snug and golden with the hearth fire and the smells of Bethany's baking, at which she had begun to excel.

The horses required less attention during this quiet waiting season. Often Ashton was present, insulating Bethany against the cold, against the barbs of her former friends, against the onslaught of her parents, who sent frequent missives requesting her at tea, pointedly omitting Ashton from the invitations.

He liked to sit in his father's old armchair, spectacles perched on his nose, keeping his journal while the ever-present Gladstone lounged nearby.

The rebellion, it seemed, had decided to wait out the season as well. Things were at a deadlock in the arc of siege around Boston; the British still held that city, but the rebels hemmed them in and snapped at them like feisty terriers. General Washington's Eight Months Army had used up their commissions, yet many remained to fight, and still more trickled in from all over the Colonies. Farmers traded their rakes for entrenching tools to help dig in the assault. Jacob Dupuy, who had been Ashton's schoolmaster some twenty years earlier, gave up his chalk for a musket. Even prissy Sylvester Fine, the dancing master, had joined a regiment. These men were untrained as soldiers, yet they believed deeply in the cause that underlay the call to arms.

News filtered to Newport of a fat bookseller named Henry Knox, who was said to be bringing Fort Ticonderoga's heavy artillery to Boston. Few thought Knox would manage in the dead of winter to cover three hundred miles of roadless wilderness and killing ridges. But the unlikely had happened in this rebellion. Had not General Richard Montgomery pushed up into Canada and occupied Montreal in November?

Ashton never seemed surprised at the news that appeared in the *Newport Gazette;* Bethany suspected his cronies at the White Horse, many of them members of the Committee of Safety, advised him of events well before the news saw print.

There was a new wag-on-the-wall clock in the cottage from Miss Abigail Primrose, the only person to mark Bethany's marriage with a gift. One cold day, Bethany checked the hour as she looked over a tattered Cocker's Arithmetick, which she intended to present to the Haas children on her next visit. It was five o'clock. Ashton would be up from the stables soon, hungry for the warmth of the kitchen and for a taste of her buttery oyster stew.

Her brow wrinkled at the sound of a knock; she was expecting no one but her husband. Setting the book aside, she lifted the thumb latch.

She stepped back, moving her eyes down and then upward again, from polished jackboots topped by white gaiters to the handsome, impatient face of Dorian Tanner.

He seemed to sense her reluctance to invite him in, so he merely insinuated himself into the keeping room and closed the door.

"You know why I'm here," he stated simply, carefully lifting his cocked hat from his wig.

"Dorian . . ." She darted a quick look at the door.

"Afraid your husband might find us together . . . again? I say, he seems a rather jealous sort. Then I'll be brief. I want you to tell me who my abductor was."

She managed to send him a wide-eyed, guileless look. "I don't know, Dorian."

"You do," he insisted. "You were there, Bethany."

"I saw nothing." Her voice was angry now.

"Abetting the rebels is a serious crime, my dear."

"But ignorance is not. Dorian, I swear to you I know nothing of what happened." It was easy to lie when the truth was so damning to Ashton.

"You must have seen something," he snapped out in frustration.

She looked down at her hands. "It all happened so fast . . . I was startled and ran off. It was too dark to see anything."

He captured those nervous hands in his own. "How you've changed, Bethany," he murmured. "I wonder if you know how you blundered in flouting my favor for that of a bondsman. Instead of toiling over a kitchen hearth, you'd be gracing Newport's finest salons on my arm."

She extracted her hands from his, furious at his arrogance. "I'll never regret what I've done," she told him firmly. Dorian was so enamored of wealth and social position that he simply didn't understand her feelings for Ashton. She swung the door open, but Dorian didn't move.

"Bethany!"

She froze, seeing Ashton coming up the path.

"Hello, pet," he called. "Barnaby said we had a visitor." He entered the cottage, smiling. His face was ruddy, and the fresh smell of outdoors clung to his greatcoat.

The smile became a scowl when he saw Dorian. His nod was curt.

"Dorian was just leaving," Bethany explained hastily.

The Redcoat had spent a moment in silent assessment of Ashton. Apparently—and wisely—he chose not to brave Ashton's greater size and temper, for he placed his hat on his head.

"This business is far from over," he told Bethany. "I'll have the truth from you one day." The door slammed behind him.

"He was asking me about the abduction," Bethany said.

Ashton turned away, removing his hat and greatcoat and hanging them on pegs beside the door with unusual meticulousness. Always he arrived with a smile and a kiss for her. Always.

But not this time. Bethany swallowed. "I told him nothing, Ashton. He thinks I ran from the scene the moment he was knocked unconscious."

Without looking at her, Ashton said, "I thought you were the consummate Loyalist."

"My first loyalty is to you."

She watched his shoulders relax slightly. When he turned back to face her, he was smiling.

Bethany's eyes softened as she looked out the cottage window into the dooryard, now crowded with springtime abundance. Her hands worked idly over a batch of early peas in a half-full piggin, her attention caught by the scene outside.

Ashton had finished his chores for the day and was playing with Gladstone, flinging a well-chewed crook of driftwood for the dog to fetch. His low murmurs of approval and the spaniel's whines of excitement mingled with the buzzing of catbirds and the steady hum of bees.

Winter had lingered through March, but mid-April had given way to the new season. Bethany was only too happy to bid the cold and dark farewell, to shed her woolen shawl and scratchy stockings for voluminous dresses of cotton and linsey.

Goody Haas arrived, startling Bethany. The plump, apple-cheeked midwife was never wont to announce her presence by knocking. She moved into the kitchen, rattling as she walked. Bethany couldn't help smiling. Goody Haas's many-pocketed apron contained a mystifying assortment of herbs and remedies, metal fleams for bleeding, and the strange wooden devices of folk healing.

"Peas look mighty fine," Goody said. She spoke around the iron-maple burl pipe perpetually clamped between her teeth. Her small, bright eyes roved in frank assessment over Bethany. "Ye look fine, too, girl. How're ye feelin'?"

"Very well," she said. She hung the cedar piggin on a nail above the sideboard and began fixing tea. Although Goody sat at the table, her face impassive, Bethany could feel the woman's approval as she warmed the teapot with a small amount of water from the kettle before infusing the vessel with a fragrant mixture of lemon balm and chamomile.

"Ye've come a long way, girl," Goody said as Bethany set the pot on the table to steep. "An' I don't just mean the babe."

Bethany grinned self-deprecatingly. "Aye. Eight months ago I couldn't even boil water."

"Ye been takin' the Venice treacle I left ye?"

"Every day." She tried not to grimace as she remembered the foul taste of the concoction. She added a dollop of honey to her tea; Goody Haas added a dollop of something stronger to her own cup from the flask she kept in her apron pocket.

" 'S done ye a world o' good," the midwife said. "Yer cheeks're bloomin' an' the babe's already a healthy size." She chuckled and drew on her pipe, sending blue-gray smoke to the rafters. "Wouldn't be surprised if the child came early."

Bethany nearly choked on her sip of tea. "No!" she protested, clutching her cup to still the trembling of her hands. "The babe is not due for five more weeks."

A horny, brown-splotched hand reached across the table, settling comfortingly on Bethany's arm. "There now, don't get yourself all in a snit. Such has happened before."

"But it can't happen to me."

Goody leaned back and puffed thoughtfully. "Ah, I see the way things are. Ye've been married but eight months, eh, an' to a man who used t' oil yer harness. Worried about the month counters, eh?"

"N . . . no." Bethany studied the knotty pine of the tabletop. In truth, she wasn't. The parlor gossips and whispering biddies in church bothered her not at all. There was only one person whose opinion mattered. Ashton.

She knew he was counting the months as assiduously as any fence-post gossip, but he had a much greater stake in the outcome. If the baby was born too soon, he'd still doubt her.

"Then what's hectorin' ye?" Goody asked, fixing Bethany with a probing but kindly stare.

Bethany looked away. Involuntarily her eyes found the window, where Ashton was still tossing the piece of driftwood for Gladstone.

"There 'tis, then," Goody said briskly. " 'S him you're worried about."

Bethany felt her cheeks flame with color as she slowly nodded a mute admission.

"Were ye with another before him, then?" The dark eyes never wavered, nor did they accuse.

"No," Bethany said quickly. "But . . . Ashton thinks . . ." Her voice trailed off and her cheeks grew hotter.

"Lordy, girl, 'tis Goody Haas ye're talkin' to, not the parson's wife. Ye can tell me what's got ye all afluster."

"Ashton doesn't believe I came to our marriage a virgin." Her voice was a shamed whisper. "But I was, Goody, I swear it." She dropped her eyes. "I know little of such things, but there was no . . . difficulty, no pain on our wedding night."

"Hmph. Ye think the Lord made all women the same?" Goody retorted. "Why should a big, healthy girl like you, who's spent her life ridin' astride, be afflicted with a maiden's pain?"

"I never thought of it like that," Bethany mused. She brightened. "Ashton will have no more doubts once the baby is born. In five weeks." She stood and moved restlessly about the kitchen, aware that the midwife's keen eyes followed her.

"I dunno," Goody said. "Babe seems to've dropped some."

Bethany clutched protectively at her midsection.

"Aye. Things're bound t' be muddy."

No, Bethany protested silently. No, please. "Goody," she said, "how can I make sure the baby comes at the proper time?" In truth, her arms ached to hold the baby as soon as possible, but not at the cost of losing Ashton's trust.

"My advice t' you, girl, is t' take things real easy for a spell. No heavy work, no long walks." Goody extracted the pipe from her mouth, holding the smooth bowl and jabbing the stem at Bethany. "Most of all, no gettin' into a pother over anything. Steer an even course, girl. Ain't nothin' like gettin' the humors into a stew t' trigger early labor."

Chapter 11

A sheaf of broadsides, smelling of fresh ink, dropped in front of the kid-clad feet of Miss Abigail Primrose as she and Bethany negotiated the busy walk along Thames Street.

"Excuse me," murmured a masculine voice. A gray-haired, middle-aged man, hatless and coatless, stooped to retrieve the papers.

Miss Abigail fixed him with her most severe gray stare. "Sir, you've soiled the hem of my gown."

The look that had made Bethany squirm many times at school only made Finley Piper grin a bit sheepishly. "Well now, I'd brush it off for you, ma'am, but . . ." He held out a big ink-smeared hand in explanation.

Miss Abigail's eyes flicked over the broadsides. Her nostrils thinned in disapproval as she took in the headlines.

"Never mind, sir," she told him with quiet, controlled annoyance. "My gown is not so soiled as people's minds will be by your seditious broadsides."

He sank into an exaggerated bow, toe pointed. "Pardon me, your ladyship," he mocked. "I'd no idea I had the pleasure of staining a highborn Tory."

He bypassed her with a casual, ambling gait. Bethany wondered if Miss Abigail had ever been treated so. Apparently not. The starched front of her dress rose and fell rapidly, and twin smudges of color appeared in her flawless cheeks.

"Who *was* that dreadful man?" she demanded.

Bethany bit the insides of her cheeks in an effort not to

smile. "Mr. Finley Piper," she explained. "A printer by trade."

"And a rebel by design, I gather."

Bethany took Miss Primrose's arm and propelled her along the walk, anxious to dispel her teacher's anger. "Let's have our tea at Haskel House, Miss Abigail. I'm delighted to see you back in Newport again."

"I may be here for some time," Miss Abigail replied. " 'Tis comforting to know Admiral Howe's fleet is bound for New York, but all that digging the rebels have been doing about Long Island and Manhattan has me worried. They seem to be putting in for a long stay."

They were seated at a table set with Houplan crystal and Wedgwood jasperware. A single white rosebud arched from a finger-slim vase, quivering slightly as a servant came to pour. Only the finest East India tea was purveyed at Haskel House. A murmur of female conversation lowered to a whisper as Bethany and Miss Abigail sipped their tea.

Bethany was aware that she was the object of much gossip. She ignored the stares of Mabel Pierce and Mrs. Joseph Wanton and pretended not to hear the scandalized whispers of Julia Cranwick and Mercy Thompson.

Miss Abigail did not ignore the ladies in the salon. She systematically sought out each pair of eyes, holding them with a rock-hard, unwavering stare until the curious tearoom denizens were forced to look away in chagrin.

"Most unmannerly," she pronounced, and made short work of a comfit from a Vernon silver plate. "Perhaps I shall not find Newport society so agreeable after all."

"You must admit," Bethany said, "they've good reason to stare." She glanced with rueful fondness at her enormous belly, which touched the table's edge some inches ahead of the rest of her.

"I've always thought confinement of expectant mothers quite a lot of poppycock," Miss Abigail said. " 'Tis not as if you need be quarantined for some disease. There is no person so aglow with loveliness as a woman awaiting her first child. How much longer, Bethany?"

"Four weeks." *And not a day less.*

"Things are . . . better between you and your husband?"

"Better, yes."

"But not how you want them to be."

"Perhaps I want too much, Miss Abigail. Perhaps what I want doesn't exist."

"More poppycock."

Bethany found both humor and encouragement in Miss Abigail's stern fondness. "I'll make things good between us," she vowed.

"The child won't solve everything, Bethany," Miss Abigail cautioned. "Your differences over the political situation may divide you still."

Bethany regarded her teacher in alarm. "Ashton's never done anything out of rebellion. There have been . . . circumstances that have required him to act in concert with the patriots."

"I see. I hope your brother has learned his lesson."

"My . . . Miss Abigail, how did you know about Harry?"

The lady's hand was too quick as she reached for another comfit. Her teacup spilled, amber liquid soaking into the crisp white linen of the tablecloth. With an expression of concentrated annoyance she daubed at the tablecloth with her napkin. "Yes, well, things do get around," she muttered. "I heard, for example, that you became an aunt last month."

"Aye. Felicia had a little girl; they named her Margaret. Harry told me in a letter that Felicia's confinement was difficult . . . and she probably shouldn't have any more children."

"Forgive me, but your brother is a young fool. He should know better than to say such things to an expectant mother."

Bethany wondered how Miss Abigail knew so much about Harry, but there was no time for further questions. The sounds of shouting and running feet broke the quiet of the elegant tearoom. She and Miss Abigail exchanged glances, then hurried to the door.

A mob of angry, fist-shaking men surged down Thames Street, cursing and singing songs of defiance. In the middle of the mob, straddling a length of pine, was the terrified Mr. George Tweedy, a royal customs official. Wig askew, face pale with agony, he bobbed helplessly over the shoulders of the surging rabble. Bethany saw resentment on the men's faces. In better times such men would be away at sea; now they were restless, looking for someone to blame, and easily manipulated by sly leaders.

The leader of this mob was a man Bethany knew as Bug Willy. Sometimes a sailor, more often a wharfside idler, he had a reputation for inciting violence and an unfortunate flare for the dramatic.

"My Lord," Miss Abigail breathed. "They're riding him on a rail." Both women left the tearoom, following the rebels' unruly parade, which ended at Long Wharf.

"Miss Abigail, what are they going to do?" Bethany asked. But already she knew. The unmistakable acrid burn of hot tar pervaded the wharf area. "Why Mr. Tweedy? He seems so harmless."

Miss Abigail's lips thinned into a line of concern. "Just this morning he admitted the *Eastern Star* into port, bringing three hundred crates of tea."

The customs official was hoisted high on a lading platform. Bethany stared in horror as his periwig was yanked from his head to reveal a bristly pate. His frock coat was stripped from him, then his waistcoat, stock, and shirt, the garments flung to the howling masses, who ripped them to shreds with evil glee.

"Can't something be done?" Bethany asked, her eyes riveted to the scene. She turned back in time to see Miss Abigail placing a shilling into the hand of a youth, who sprinted off in the direction of British headquarters.

"I've sent for help," she said briskly. "All we can do now is hope Mr. Tweedy endures the wait."

A vat of tar, steaming and wickedly black, was brought forth. Bug Willie leaped to the platform brandishing a tar brush, a lethal grin on his face. He plunged the brush into the tar and anointed Tweedy's shrinking flesh over and over again, until the victim's howls rose even higher than the curses and catcalls of the mob.

In an orgy of mischief, the rebels flung handfuls of

goose feathers at Tweedy, who soon resembled a macabre scarecrow. A lighted candle was held to the feathers.

Bethany looked away, expecting the worst, but the feathers failed to catch fire. Bug Willy put a halter around Tweedy's neck.

"Before we cart you the rounds, sir," Bug Willy mocked, doffing a rumpled hat, "we'd like to offer you a drink." Laughter rose from the crowd.

"Aye!" someone shouted. "Give him a taste of his own poison!"

Mr. Tweedy was given a large bowl of strong tea and told to drink to the king's health. With some confusion he complied, draining the bowl. Immediately the vessel was refilled and he was made to drink to Queen Charlotte, then to the Prince of Wales.

Having been forced to gulp three big bowls of tea, Tweedy staggered. "Please, no more," he begged.

But the bowl was thrust at him again. "Make haste, sir," Bug Willy said, laughing. "You've nine more healths to drink!" An unconscionable quantity of tea was forced down the victim's throat as he was made to toast nine others, beginning with the Bishop of Osnaburg and continuing until each of George III's offspring had been "honored."

At the last toast Tweedy went deathly pale beneath his coating of tar and feathers. Instantly he filled the bowl he'd just emptied.

"What!" Bug Willy boomed. "Are you sick of the royal family already?"

"N-no," Tweedy wheezed pathetically. " 'Tis the tea . . ."

"And yet," Bug Willy cracked, "you damned infernal rogue, you would drench us to the skin with this overtaxed poison!" Jeers rippled from the crowd.

"Hang him! Hang the scoundrel!"

Bethany was sure that, in this murderous frenzy, the deed would be done. But the rebels satisfied their vengeance by using the halter to "baste" the victim's neck until his ears bled. He was made to repeat various humiliating oaths until, weak, sick, and defeated, Mr. Tweedy resigned his royal commission.

He was seated on the rail once again in readiness to cart the rounds. But as the rail was shouldered by the jubilant rebels, three shots rang out, stilling the crowd.

Bethany watched, relieved, as the British militia appeared. Dorian Tanner was among them, barking orders. In minutes the crowd dispersed, the rebels scurrying to the anonymity of local taverns and private homes. Mr. Tweedy was carried off to his house.

Ashton came striding across the wharf. The fury of his pace touched off a shiver of apprehension in Bethany, but the concern on his face warmed her. He acknowledged Miss Abigail with a nod, then spoke to Bethany. "What are you doing here?"

"What does it look like I'm doing?"

"For God's sake, Bethany, you could've been hurt."

"I'm fine. Which is more than I can say for Mr. Tweedy."

"He'll be all right," Ashton said distractedly.

"If he lives, it'll be no thanks to the rebels. I hope every one of that mob is punished."

Miss Abigail intervened, her pale, shaken face devoid of hope. "A whole town cannot be punished."

"But they've committed a crime!"

"Miss Primrose is right," Ashton admitted. "The British are under orders to treat the rebels with moderation. Bug Willy will probably be pilloried for a time, if he doesn't light out in the bay somewhere." He took Bethany's elbow. "We're going home."

"I'm not ready to go home, Ashton," she retorted, feeling suddenly obstinate, and angry that her husband was in sympathy with the rebels.

But, as if to forestall an argument, Miss Abigail started walking away. "I've things to do," she said briskly. "We'll have tea again another time."

As soon as Ashton delivered Bethany safely to the cottage, he muttered something about going back into town. She was too proud and angry to ask him to stay.

"This afternoon's display didn't endear your cause to me," Ashton said darkly to Finley and Chapin Piper, who were priming their Franklin press in readiness to print up a bunch of handbills.

"We had nothing to do with Tweedy's tarring and feathering," Chapin said. His Adam's apple bobbed earnestly as he stifled a sneeze caused by a puff of dry ink.

"No, but people tend to lump all patriots together." Ashton turned to Finley. "You've got to do something to control them. That sort of energy could go a long way toward furthering your cause, but not if it's misdirected. People want liberty, not anarchy."

"I know, I know." Finley sighed in exasperation. He shot a treenail into the press's shank to secure it. "By the way, I ran into your wife this afternoon. Quite literally, I'm afraid. Dropped a sheaf of broadsides right at her companion's feet. Who was that dragon with her, anyway?"

"Miss Abigail Primrose, Bethany's teacher from New York."

"A teacher, eh? A redoubtable example of female independence and accomplishment, I'm sure." Finley's face soured. "She ought to go back to whatever lair she crawled out of. We don't need her breathing her Tory fire around Newport."

"Sounds like you got singed, Finley." Ashton chuckled. "Miss Primrose can have that effect on people. But Bethany regards her highly."

"Maybe your wife shouldn't make her Tory leanings so apparent," Chapin suggested. "After what happened to Tweedy today, I'm beginning to think things could get uncomfortable for Loyalists."

"It'll be the other way around," Ashton said. "I wouldn't be surprised if we were treated to full British occupation if the rebels keep this up."

Chapin looked glum. "We need a better organization. And we need to get rid of that infernal British sympathizer who's been reporting our every move."

"We'll catch him," Finley promised. His expression told Ashton exactly who "we" meant.

"How?" he asked reluctantly.

"We set a trap."

" 'Tis a spy we're after, not a lobster."

"Not that sort of trap." Finley chuckled. "But the same principle. The *Rose* is in the bay. Wallace sends longboats to the Purgatory Rocks to leave messages for his informants. If the water's calm, there should be an exchange tomorrow night." He rubbed an ink-stained finger over his chin. "Are you with us, Ashton?"

He looked away. "No."

"No violence, nothing like you saw today. You've my promise."

"Finley, I've things to do besides chase after a spy who's probably too smart to take your bait anyway."

"I don't understand, Ashton. You weren't so hesitant before."

"Someone I care about was involved, Finley."

"And you care less for liberty?"

"I care less for involving myself in something I'm not sure of."

"Will you at least think about it, Ashton?" Finley snapped his fingers in sudden inspiration. "I have something for you to read. Chapin, fetch one of those pamphlets from the shelf."

Ashton hesitated when he stepped into the cottage, standing quietly in the doorway to study his wife. It was uncanny, he reflected, her ability to move with such lithe grace despite her now cumbersome profile. As she turned to stir a pot of bubbling chowder, bending delicately forward, it struck him that her beauty had suffered nothing because of her pregnancy. Her hair was caught in a heavy coil at her nape, small wisps escaping to frame her sweet and earnest face.

She turned her head at the sound of his footsteps. Her spoon swirled nervously in the chowder.

"Hello, Ashton."

He reminded himself of the argument this afternoon. On the way home he had decided to inform Bethany that he didn't care to have his wife attending public mob scenes. But when he opened his mouth to speak, all he said was, "Come here, pet."

Her lack of hesitation told him that she, too, had lost her anger. She moved into his outstretched arms and laid her cheek against his chest, her hands creeping around his middle.

Ashton laid his lips on her forehead; her skin was warm from the fire, damp from exertion. He loved the taste of her, the spicy-sweet scent of her hair and skin. She was very much a woman now, and yet a child, too, evoking both passion and protectiveness that mingled together into a single heady emotion.

Life could be so good with Bethany, so good if only . . . He broke off the thought. There were a good many "if onlys" standing in their way.

His kisses made a slow path toward her mouth. "You shouldn't . . . have followed . . . that mob today," he murmured. " 'Twas dangerous, love." It was hardly the reproof he'd planned for her.

"I never felt I was in any danger," she whispered beneath his lips. "All the rage was directed at Mr. Tweedy. Capt—the soldiers weren't long in coming."

Ashton drew away from her. "How studiously you avoid speaking his name."

"We always seem to quarrel when Dorian comes up."

"Aye," he said roughly. "And we've better things to do than quarrel."

He captured her lips again, firmly, as if to wipe Tanner's name from them. Soon, though, he forgot the Englishman. He savored the soft openness of Bethany's lips and discovered, as if for the first time, the silk of her inner mouth with his tongue. A few months ago, if anyone had told him he could feel this raging desire for a heavily pregnant woman, he would have laughed at the notion. Yet she was so very, very soft, and her hands knew what course to take to cause him to burst into flames of wanting.

With a reluctant and concerted effort he set her away from him. "I'm hungry," he told her.

"So am I." He was certain she didn't mean the chowder. He moved toward the kitchen; she laid a hand on his arm and he saw a blush rise becomingly to her cheeks.

"Ashton, Goody Haas told me it was all right to—"

"Goody Haas is full of nonsense. If she'd lived a hundred years ago, she'd be tried for witchcraft." What he didn't say was that he was afraid of intimacy in her advanced stage of pregnancy. He was afraid of hurting her, of perhaps bringing on early labor, which was the last thing he wanted to do. Each day brought him closer to the truth of the child's paternity. Each day brought him closer to trust.

After supper, they shared, as always, the chores of cleaning up. Then they retired to the keeping room. Bethany had grown weary of knitting and mending weeks ago; lately she had preferred going over the Haas children's lessons in the evenings.

Ashton watched, feeling reluctant fondness as she twisted a tendril of hair by her cheek with an idle finger and smiled in amusement at a penciled drawing. Catching himself, he lent his attention to the slim pamphlet Finley had given him earlier—"Common Sense; Addressed to the Inhabitants of America," by an English immigrant named Thomas Paine.

At first his gaze meandered over the pages, remarking only that the text was unusually accessible; one needn't be law-trained or skilled in political economy to follow Paine's message. As for that message, the author's attacks on ministry and monarchy seemed high-pitched enough to set even a devout radical's teeth on edge.

And yet—Ashton slowed his perusal—and yet, there seemed to be much more to the treatise than hot tirade. Stark phrases stood out and thrummed through his mind: "Now is the seed-time of a continental union, faith, and honor. . . . Time hath found us! O! ye that love mankind, stand forth . . . and prepare . . . an asylum. . . ."

Ashton blinked as an unfamiliar feeling gripped him, a feeling of rightness, of devotion. The words and thoughts of "Common Sense" rolled out in a clamorous swing and sway of harmony.

Shaken, he stared at the final page. It carried a single line of stark black letters that spelled out with uncompromising daring: THE FREE AND INDEPENDENT STATES OF AMERICA.

The pamphlet slipped to the floor, its physical form forgotten but its message already burned into Ashton's memory. Numb in body yet curiously alive as never before in spirit, he walked to the window of the keeping room. From this point he could see beyond the bounds of Seastone, past gardens aflame with bushes of hot-glowing peonies and the purple eyes of mourning bride, past the stone-rimmed stable compound . . . to the meadows of swaying sea grass in the distance.

Freedom beckoned.

Bethany frowned when Ashton didn't answer her. He looked so odd, so self-possessed as he stood there by the window. He held himself in an expectant stance, knuckles pressed hard on the windowsill, eyes craning for something she sensed could not be seen, but only felt.

He seemed to be in the grip of some private awakening, an overwhelming thought, perhaps, intense but not angry, on the verge of discovery. Drawing a deep breath, she repeated his name more loudly.

This time he turned. His eyes had never looked so deep or clear. "Yes?" His voice was quiet and rich.

"I've invited Miss Abigail to supper tomorrow evening." She grinned. "My teacher refuses to believe I've finally learned to cook."

Regret and impatience showed on his face. "Sorry, pet, I won't be able to attend. I've an . . . engagement." His eyes begged her not to probe. She didn't. She left him alone with his thoughts; he turned back to the window.

Bracing her hands on the edge of the settle, she brought her cumbersome form to her feet. Quietly she crossed the room to Ashton's chair and picked up the pamphlet he'd negligently left on the floor.

She read swiftly, awed by the power of the prose, frightened by the effect it had had on her husband. Everything came suddenly into sharp focus: Ashton's strange mood of quict dcvotion, his claim that hc had an cngagement. . . .

She supposed this had been building for months, beginning, perhaps, with his disenchantment with the British army, revived by his erroneous arrest and farcical trial and indenture to her father. Now the transition from indifference to annoyance to commitment was complete.

Her husband had become a patriot.

* * *

Bethany jumped up at the sound of scratching. Although it was suppertime and she was expecting Miss Abigail, she knew her teacher would never scratch at the door. The lady was, of course, given to sharp, imperative raps. Gladstone whined and sniffed impatiently.

Her suppertime visitor was young Jimmy Milliken, whose mother ran the boardinghouse where Miss Abigail was staying. Bethany smiled at the eight-year-old, whose spiky nut-brown hair and endearing freckles gave him a look of irresistible appeal.

"Come in, Jimmy," she said, stepping aside. He hesitated; she pressed gently on his shoulder. "You're welcome here."

His face blossomed into a wide grin that was still lacking several permanent teeth.

The boy walked to the kitchen table and began digging in his pockets. "I've a message for you," he announced importantly. Bethany was amazed by the volume of his pockets. Those dusty brown homespun breeches seemed to hold more than Goody Haas's apron. She tried to keep from laughing aloud as she watched. His tongue stuck out and one eye was narrowed in concentration as he placed his treasures on the table, searching for the message.

There was a wrist rocket, a single copper for games of huzzlecap, a wooden top missing its spinning knob, the skeletal remains of some small animal, a blue jay feather, a half dozen seashells, and . . . last of all, crumpled by the weight of Jimmy's treasures and limp with boyish sweat, a small scrap of paper.

He held it up with a triumphant flourish. "There you go, missus. Just like the lady said."

Bethany thanked him and added another copper to the items he was scooping back into his pockets. Then she unfolded the message, recognizing Miss Abigail's script, so perfectly even it might have been a printer's set.

"To my dismay," Miss Abigail had written, "I shall be unable to visit this evening due to an unforeseen engagement. Do accept my sincere regrets. . . ."

Bethany put the note aside with a small sigh. So she'd be alone after all. Odd, how both Ashton and Miss Abigail had come up with engagements tonight. She glanced regretfully at the kitchen hearth, where a small feast of codfish, potatoes, and pudding was in preparation.

She noticed Jimmy Milliken was looking at the hearth, too, outright hunger in those wide brown eyes.

Impulsively Bethany invited him to supper and watched with gratification as he devoured his meal. She pretended not to notice when he slipped a crust of bread to Gladstone, who lolled at the boy's feet.

"You a friend of Miss Primrose?" Jimmy asked around a mouthful of potatoes.

"Yes, I am. She used to be my teacher."

He rolled his eyes. "Miss Primrose thinks she's everybody's teacher. Has me minding my manners even when I go out to fetch water. Lately I go to bed reading my letters off a battledore."

Bethany smiled. "That's just her way, Jimmy."

"You know what?" he asked, casting a furtive glance left and right. "I think she's a—an adventuress in disguise!"

Bethany laughed at his overactive imagination. "Is that so, Jimmy? Why do you say that?"

"You shouldn't laugh at me, missus. I do tell a good whopper, but not this time."

Something in his earnestness intrigued her. "Perhaps you should explain."

He dropped his voice lower still. "Well, just as I was leaving to come here, I heard this noise in the shed back of the house. Thought one of the chickens had gotten out, but then I saw it was Miss Primrose." The lad drew a deep breath and sipped his cider. "At first I didn't think it was her, 'cause she was all got up like a boy, but before she put her hat on I saw that hair of hers, all knottylike on top of her head. She covered up with an old hat and slipped right out of the yard!"

Bethany shook her head, bewildered. Either the boy spun an extremely plausible yarn, or he was telling the truth. "Where do you think she was going, Jimmy?"

"Don't know. But I'll bet my best huzzlecap copper she has a secret iden—identity. She headed off toward Purgatory Rocks!"

"Jimmy, how many others have you told this story to?"

"No one, missus. Honest."

"Good. Maybe we'd better keep it just between us."

The wag-on-the-wall clock chimed softly. Jimmy's lips moved silently as he counted the chimes. "Seven o'clock!" he cried, jumping up. "Mama'll have my skin where it counts if I don't get home."

He paused only to lay a fond scratch on Gladstone's head. Then, shouting his thanks over his shoulder, he ran out the door toward town.

Bemused, Bethany looked after him, unable to decide whether Jimmy's was a tale of boyish fancifulness or if it held a grain of truth. Absurd, she thought, shaking her head. Miss Abigail Primrose, disguised as a boy!

And yet, only yesterday she'd mentioned Harry, alluding to something few people could possibly know. Then there was tonight's engagement, sudden, unexplained . . . just like Ashton's.

Just like Ashton's. Bethany went cold inside, and the spoon she was holding slipped from her fingers and clattered to the floor. Her husband had become a patriot and Miss Abigail was a devout Tory.

A devout Tory who was suddenly in danger. Snatching her shawl from a hook, Bethany left the cottage and ran to the stables.

Chapter 12

Cloaked in darkness, three figures approached Purgatory by means of a dusty road that ran from Easton's Beach to Sachuest Beach. Soundless footfalls made small indentations on a broad stretch of sand. Keeping to the shadows of a high bluff, the men moved silently among a tumble of dark gray soft-slate rocks at the foot of the bluff. Thready salt grass and broom stirred in the night breeze.

A distant light winked on the waters of the Middle Passage. Finley gestured toward it. "The *Rose*. In rendezvous position."

"I don't see anyone," Ashton said dubiously.

"You will. Just be patient."

Above them rose a vast ledge of rock piled up in a most singular formation, remarkable for the size and position of the stones. At one point the escarpment reached out in a line, rising at the extreme outer edge on a bluff and then suddenly plunging down into the sea.

High upon a spur was a great boulder known as Negro Head, for the rock formation resembled an African profile. Fissures divided the rock as though tons upon tons of slate had been neatly cleaved by a knife.

Ashton, Finley, and Chapin climbed to a vantage point at the lip of the largest of the fissures, which plumbed fully one hundred sixty feet. Long ago the dangerous cleft had earned the name Purgatory and a reputation for swallowing drunken sailors. At the base of the forbidding chasm the sea broke ceaselessly in deep bass tones.

Ashton recalled playing games of nerve and bravado here with Chapin Piper and other childhood playmates.

But never, not even when as a youth convinced of his own invincibility, had he approached the huge, deadly cleft without giving heed to his footing.

Once, just once, he had leaped the chasm. Not willingly, not out of any sense of bravery, but at the bidding of a maiden.

He had been fifteen at the time and helplessly in love. Here at the sharp ledge of the cleft, on a day sweet with the smells of wild chickory and sorrel thorn, he and Peggy Lillibridge had pledged their hearts to each other.

But his pledge wasn't enough for Peggy. She demanded proof and believed firmly enough in her newly discovered feminine power to bend Ashton to her whimsy.

"Leap Purgatory for me, Ashton. As a test of your love for me. Jump, if you would claim me as yours, for on no other terms will I have you."

The words had been uttered years ago, but Ashton heard them now on the wind as if a soft female voice had just whispered them in his ear. He recalled the bitterness that had welled in him at Peggy's command: his first and startling discovery that love was not so much a matter of faith as a concept to be proven, like bravery.

He remembered Peggy's rapt face and felt again the thrum of taut nerves and senses heightened by danger. Then, bracing himself, he ran forward and with a wild spring reached the opposite bank.

He dusted off his hat and stood boldly erect, looking across the abyss at the face which showed supreme satisfaction and no anxiety at all. He raised his hat, bowed coldly, and turned and strode away, leaving Peggy Lillibridge alone, her pretty mouth agape in surprise.

Ashton's single lesson in the destructiveness of romantic love was one he had heeded well. Never again had he allowed himself to be goaded into foolishness by a woman. He found himself wondering if the cause of independence would be an equally demanding mistress.

Forcing his thoughts to the task at hand, Ashton peered at Finley and Chapin through the misty gloom of the spring night. Fog swirled in from the bay, rime-scented and pudding-thick. The moon was a haze of white light, casting shadows down into the depths of the chasm.

Chapin took out his pocketknife and began idly flipping the blade in and out with small, rhythmic clicks that set Ashton's teeth on edge.

Fog dampened and chilled his outer coat; his own sweat moistened his clothing from within. The phrases of Thomas Paine's pamphlet still lingered in his mind, although he had begun to wonder if this was what was meant by "Common Sense."

He wondered, too, about Bethany. The worried look she'd fixed on him when he last left the house told him she was aware of his new commitment.

His jaw tightened in annoyance. Couldn't she see what independence might mean to him? To them? Freedom from England meant freedom from Sinclair Winslow, for surely he couldn't hold Ashton to the indenture once a new nation had been forged.

A new nation . . . A year ago the idea had been tossed out by radicals, and ignored. Now the assembly of Rhode Island was about to formally declare itself an independent state. Surely others would follow until at last every one of Britain's thirteen unruly children had severed the umbilical cord of dependency.

Chapin suddenly stopped clicking his pocketknife. Finley's nudge sent Ashton's gaze downward to the breaking waves. At first he discerned nothing. Shadows within shadows, the whisper of the wind through birch trees. Then a moving shape, small and fleet and of a darker and more substantial quality than the shadows, flitted into view.

" 'Tis him," Finley whispered. "Not a very big man; could the Redcoats be using children?" Chapin started to edge toward the bluff, but Finley pulled him back by the sleeve. "Wait, lad," the older man cautioned. "We'd best make certain there are no others."

They waited and watched. The figure darted in and out of the shadows, then went to the foot of the bluff. A ship's boat slipped back out into the bay, toward the bobbing lights of the *Rose*. The figure gained the bluff and scrambled up to the road.

"Let's go," Finley said at length. "We don't want to lose him now." Moist salt grass cushioned their footfalls as they closed in on the spy. He was just a few yards ahead of them when his head snapped up.

The spy sprinted away. As Chapin gave chase, Ashton became aware of hoofbeats. Too late, he realized a rider was heading directly toward them from the beach road, sitting the speeding horse with curious clumsiness.

Chapin dove for the fleeing figure, catching an ankle and sending them both sprawling. At the same moment the horse jerked to a stop in front of the struggling pair.

"Leave her alone!"

Bethany's frightened command reached through the gloom, delivering a shock of recognition to Ashton's ears. Chapin seemed equally surprised; he held his quarry fast but gaped at the angry rider on the lathered, agitated horse.

"Let her go!" Bethany cried again.

Finley reached them first. "Here now, what's this?" he demanded, irritated that his plans had been hitched. He sent Ashton a look that promised a heated discussion later.

Ashton came to Bethany's side, his hand reaching to quiet the snorting mare. Calliope settled down immediately at his familiar scent. Looking up at Bethany's furious face, he knew his wife wouldn't prove so tractable.

"What are you doing here?" he asked quietly.

Before she could answer, Chapin uttered an oath of disbelief. His struggling prisoner's hat had dropped to the ground to reveal a perfectly neat, shining topknot and a small but livid—and distinctly feminine—face. Ashton's surprise gave way to a leaden feeling of disappointment tinged with deep chagrin.

"I know you," Finley exclaimed, staring dumbfounded. "You—you're—"

"Miss Abigail Primrose," came the clipped reply. She slid an offended glance at Chapin. "Unhand me, young man." Chapin dropped her wrist as if it had burned him.

Bethany slipped from the mare's back and went to Miss Abigail, walking a little unsteadily due to the bulk of her belly. "Are you all right, Miss Abigail?"

The lady was inspecting her wrist. "Quite," she said, then looked at Bethany. "But you, my dear. You shouldn't be out riding in your state. Whatever possessed you?"

Miss Abigail's eyes moved from Bethany to Ashton and then back again. "I see," she said. "You've guessed."

"It seems we all have, Miss Primrose," Finley said. "You've impeded the rebellion for the last time." He offered her his arm with exaggerated politeness. "Shall we go?"

"I'd sooner seek the company of the devil himself, Mr. Piper."

Finley chuckled. "You don't understand, Miss Primrose. You have no choice. Now, you can walk with me to my house like the lady you are, or I'll shoulder you like a sack of potatoes."

Bethany stepped forward, her fists clenched. "You're not taking her anywhere," she said fiercely.

Ashton turned to her. "Your friend won't be harmed, pet."

"Like Mr. Tweedy wasn't harmed yesterday?"

Ashton drew in his breath slowly, despising the position he was in. He was faced with an impossible choice. His loyalty to the cause he'd recently embraced ran at direct odds with his loyalty to his wife.

"You're awfully protective of the woman who betrayed your brother," Chapin muttered.

Her eyes blazed with bewilderment. "Betrayed . . . ?"

"Chapin—" Ashton began, wanting him to stop, wanting to protect Bethany from the truth of what had happened last Christmas.

"Aye," Chapin went on, heedless of Ashton's warning, " 'twas your dear lady friend here who sent the Redcoats to seize Harry Winslow in Providence."

Ashton watched Bethany's agonized gaze seek Miss Primrose's eyes. He saw deep disappointment in those wide, wondering depths. She wanted to disbelieve, yet Miss Primrose herself took things in hand.

"I'm afraid he's correct, Bethany," she admitted.

"Miss Abigail, when I spoke to you that morning in Bristol, I believed you would hold my confidence."

"I agonized over the information you gave me about your brother. If I'd left things to chance, Harry might have been caught by others and sentenced to death. So I struck a bargain with . . . my military contacts. I agreed to tell them where to find your brother in exchange for their promise he'd not be harmed, only traded in a prisoner exchange.'' Miss Primrose's voice quavered the slightest bit. ''I'm sorry, Bethany.'' The lady turned back to Finley. ''I shall not fight you, Mr. Piper.'' Docilely she held her hand out to him; reluctantly he led her away.

Finley and Chapin flanked the small form in boy's clothing as they started toward town. Ashton hung back, wishing there were some way to erase the hurt etched on Bethany's features.

''I'll walk you home,'' he offered. ''You look like you could do with a bit of a rest.''

''I'm going with Miss Abigail.''

''Bethany, there's nothing you can do—''

''I just want to be sure she isn't harmed.'' There was pure obstinance in that pertly angled chin and a sparkle of defiance in the deep, moonlit eyes. ''Not that *you* would care about her.''

Ashton drew a shuddering sigh. Far in a corner of his heart, feelings for Bethany waged a silent, relentless battle with reason, commitment, and honor.

''Very well,'' he said, and reached for her arm.

For the first time since he'd known Bethany, she pulled away from him.

The smells of Finley's darkened print shop tingled in Bethany's nose. The sweetish scent of ink mingled with stale tobacco to create a singularly nauseating aroma. As Chapin worked with flint from a tinderbox, she found herself swallowing bile.

''Bethany?'' Ashton was at her elbow, his breath warm in her ear. ''You don't look well.''

As she had back at the bluffs, she sidled away. ''Perhaps I'm not well, Ashton,'' she snapped. ''This whole incredible situation repulses me. What are you going to do to Miss Abigail, try her in some barbaric drumhead court?''

Scowling, he said, ''Would you rather we gave her a medal for arranging your brother's capture?''

''You heard Miss Abigail's explanation. I can forgive what *she* did.''

''But you won't forgive me.''

"You and the Pipers have mishandled a lady. *That* is unconscionable."

"She ought to count herself lucky *we* found her, rather than the mob that got George Tweedy."

Bethany turned away. Rubbing at a sharp twinge deep in her lower back, she stood in the shadows and waited for Chapin's spark to set fire to a candle. At last a long yellow flame appeared, casting mysterious patterns over the cumbersome shape of the printing press with its wooden frame braced against floor and ceiling, iron type forms stacked on a table, and a collection of stuffed leather ink daubers.

Bethany saw a shadow move in one of the corners. That shadow was joined by several other shapes. Human shapes. "Ashton . . ." she whispered, her anger forgotten as she clung to his arm.

Out of the gloom appeared the triumphantly grinning face of Bug Willie and eight of his cohorts, the same men who had brutalized Mr. Tweedy the day before.

Bethany brought her hand to her mouth. She saw Finley move in front of Miss Abigail. Turning to Ashton, she exclaimed, "You said she wouldn't be harmed!"

Bug Willie's evil snicker reached across the print shop with chilling glee. "So he might've," he growled, advancing. "You always were a bit too soft for my tastes, Finley."

"What are you doing here?" Ashton demanded.

"We're going to hold a trial," Bug Willie announced.

"A trial!" Anger exploded from Bethany. "What sort of justice will Miss Abigail get from you?"

"Don't worry, little mama," Bug Willie said. "We'll be sure our Tory meets with a proper punishment."

He was armed, as were his companions. The steel of knife blades and spontoons glinted dully in the candle glow. A wicked-looking spurlike instrument clanked against Bug Willie's paste belt buckle.

"This is no business of yours," Ashton said to the man in a low, careful voice.

"Come now, did you really think I'd not hear of your spy hunt tonight? I knew the *Rose* was skulking about the Middle Passage." The grizzled and scarred head moved from side to side. "Can't hide much from Bug Willie, can you now?" He fixed a small-eyed glare on Miss Abigail, who stared unflinchingly back.

"Bold little piece, eh?" he taunted. "Let's just see how bold."

Bethany's horrified eyes weren't quick enough to take in all that happened next. The intruders rushed forward, seizing Ashton, Chapin, and Finley, thrusting them against the wall. Two of the attackers howled, suffering the speed and anger of Ashton's resistance, but finally the point of a deadly honed spontoon, pressing into the exposed flesh of his throat, subdued him.

Bug Willie wasted no niceties with Miss Abigail. Whiplike, his arm shot out and grabbed her. Bethany moved forward with a cry of outrage, only to find herself detained by a thin and sniggering sailor. Ashton cursed loudly. She looked back to see the spontoon pressing into his neck, almost breaking the skin. As fear pounded through her, the odd pain in her back bit again, sharply.

"Let's see what the lady has for us tonight," Bug Willie sneered. He plunged his hand into her jacket pocket. Miss Abigail was quicker. Her fingers darted into the opposite pocket. She snatched out a silver bullet and popped it into her mouth, swallowing as calmly as if she'd just enjoyed a comfit.

Bug Willie's roar of outrage at the trick reverberated through the shop. "You goddamned high-and-mighty bitch! I ought to slit your belly and sift through your innards for that message." Appalled, Bethany realized that Miss Abigail had just destroyed a message encapsulated in the bullet. Her already roiling insides began to lurch with new wretchedness.

"No need to soil your hands," came a smooth voice from behind them. Bethany recognized Isaac Sewell, a young, bandy-legged apothecary's apprentice who had been guarding the door. He dropped a small cloth bag into Bug Willie's hand. "Tartar emetic," he explained. " 'Twill bring forth the ball—and anything else the lady's hiding in her Tory guts."

Bethany was nearly overcome by wave after wave of nausea as the purge was roughly administered to Miss Abigail. Never could she have imagined her teacher to suffer such humiliation, to be transformed by this wharf-side scum into the pathetic, retching creature who crouched miserably over the basin held by an exultant Bug Willie. Miss Abigail knelt on the floor, pale and mortified beyond speech. The bandy-legged apprentice covered his hand with a handkerchief and extracted the ball from the basin.

He opened the small silver object and painstakingly unfurled a tiny scrap of paper. Holding it to the light, he frowned at characters as tiny as flea tracks.

"What's this?" he demanded. "French?" He looked angrily about the room. "Can anyone read French?"

Bug Willie jerked Miss Abigail to her feet. "You! Tell us what that message says."

"I neither read nor speak French," Miss Abigail told him with remarkable steadiness. Bethany prayed Bug Willie wouldn't discern the lie; Miss Abigail was fluent in French as well as three other languages.

Apparently Bug Willie bought the ruse. He ground a keen look at Bethany. "What about you, little mama?"

"Leave her out of it," Ashton growled, still struggling against his assailants.

Bethany shook her head mutely and battled another sharp pain in her back, not trusting herself to speak. French had been one of her better subjects in school, but she would never betray England to a scoundrel like Bug Willie.

He took the message and pocketed it. "Doesn't matter a whit. We'll get someone to translate it later." With that he dragged Miss Abigail toward the door. "Hold the rest of them here," he ordered the others. "My lady friend and I are going out for a little sail on the bay."

As if aware that Ashton posed the greatest threat, his captors closed around him more aggressively. When he began to resist, the spontoon bit into the skin of his neck.

The sight of his blood, copiously soaking the opening of his shirt, caused something within Bethany to burst with sheer terror. She felt as if a great hand had wrapped around her and squeezed with breathtaking might.

Liquid warmth crept down her legs. She gasped, mortified, and struggled with the man guarding her. "Please," she said through gritted teeth. "The—the baby—"

Finley bellowed a furious oath. "Didn't you hear the lady, you damned bog-trotter?" he shouted. "Her time is near!"

The truth of Finley's statement slapped Bethany with stunning clarity. Goody Haas had told her of the water and the pain. . . . But the midwife had not given words to the clamp of agony that seized Bethany, sending her to the floor in a faint.

Warmth and pain . . . pain and warmth . . . The excruciating rhythm of Bethany's suffering melded with the surge and rise of the sea, with the rapid thudding of something firm and familiar close to her ear.

Dragging herself slowly from the comfortable stupor of her swoon, she cataloged what was happening.

Beyond the hot twinges clawing at her was her awareness of Ashton. The stubbly texture of his homespun shirt covered his chest; the unyielding corded strength in his arms circled her securely. His scent, that unique mingling of leather and sweat and salt air, enveloped her.

He was carrying her through the mist-shrouded night, cradling her like a child as he sat Calliope. Through a fog of anguish Bethany heard him admonish the mare to move slowly. She tried to speak, to give voice to her worries about Miss Abigail and to tell him of the awesome power of her own pain, but her voice failed her. All she could manage was a desperate strangled cry as she felt Ashton bring her down from the horse and take her into the stone-end cottage.

The familiarity of her bed did nothing to ease her pain. She couldn't appreciate the gentleness of Ashton's hand on her brow or the tenderness in his voice when he said, "Chapin's gone for Goody Haas, pet. Let me help you into bed."

She squinted at Ashton. His face, illumined by a flare from the betty lamp, was drawn and pale; beads of sweat stood out on his furrowed brow, and the blood was drying on his neck. She held weak arms out to him in supplication, aware that tonight she had lost faith in him, aware that this night what little trust he had in her would be destroyed.

But he was still Ashton, to whom she had run with her troubles since she was old enough to run. Buried deep inside her was a longing for the simple whimsy of the life they had led as children, gigging frogs in the millpond, staging mock battles with spear grass, eating warm sugar together when the maple trees ran in February. Her troubles then were trifling enough that Ashton could dispense with them by showing her a new card trick, or spending hours with her in lazy conversation as he worked his hands over a length of harness.

But now . . . there was nothing trifling about giving birth. The pain she felt was not so inconsequential that it could be soothed by kindness or softened by old memories. Fear sent sharp arrows through her body. She had little reason to suppose Ashton would even want to help her, not when he believed the imminent child was another man's bastard.

And yet his hands were gentle on her, grappling with the hooks of her dress and slipping off her shoes. "There you are, pet," he said in a soothing voice. "We'll get you comfortable." With shuddering relief, Bethany realized she'd underestimated her husband's compassion.

A huge contraction pressed giant fingers around her body and she stiffened, arching her back and clutching at Ashton's hand until she felt every detail of bone and sinew beneath his flesh.

"Comfortable," she whispered once the pain had subsided to throbbing dullness. "I'm afraid"—her tongue flicked out to moisten dry lips—"that I am dying, Ashton. And I'm not dying comfortably at all."

For a moment he held his breath, then he gave her a smile that looked only a little forced. "No, love," he assured her. "You only feel that way. Goody will be here soon; she'll know what to do."

But "soon" wasn't soon enough. Bethany endured endless moments of wracking shivers and harrowing pains. Each one came faster, gripped longer, and left her more breathless than the last. She found herself mesmerized by the wag-on-the-wall clock, visible through the bedroom door. The long pendulum measured the moments of her agony with such regularity that, oddly, she felt an inner quieting.

During a rare lull in the contractions she dragged her eyes from the swinging pendulum and focused on Ashton.

"M-Miss Abigail . . ."

"Hush, love, she'll be all right. Finley's gone after her."

"Why, Ashton? Why did you seize her tonight?"

A look of disgust crossed his face. "I had no idea she was who we were looking for. Believe me, I was as shocked as you were when I saw who we'd captured."

"And—and Bug Willie?"

"We didn't know he'd be waiting at the print shop."

But words could not erase what he'd done. The fact that, knowingly or not, Ashton had delivered Miss Abigail into the hands of dangerous radicals added a sharp edge of bitterness to the birth pains.

Further comment was impossible as a new convulsion roared through her. Her eyes sought the clock and her hands sought Ashton's. Deep beneath the pain was the knowledge of bitterness to come. Perhaps it was the baby's uncommon size, as Goody had said; perhaps it was the fast, heedless night ride and the shock of seeing Miss Abigail abused. . . . Reasons didn't matter. The cold fact that Bethany would soon have to face was that the child was early, coming too soon for Ashton to be convinced he'd sired it.

"Where're the women?" demanded a rasping voice. Bethany felt Ashton's grip slacken with relief at the arrival of Goody Haas. The contents of the midwife's apron stirred as she crossed to the bed.

"There's no one here but me," Ashton said.

"Can't very well have a birthin' without women," Goody grumbled. "Fetch the girl's mother. And didn't you say you had a sister?"

"N-no." Bethany's voice was firm despite her pain. She saw Goody's brows arc downward in disapproval. " 'Twould only m-make things worse."

"Her mother faints when she pricks her finger on a sewing needle,'' Ashton explained. ''And my sister is . . . she wouldn't be of any use.''

''An' y' suppose you will, eh?'' Goody asked speculatively. As she spoke, she moved her hands over Bethany, examining and gauging.

''I've attended countless foalings,'' Ashton supplied.

''Your wife's not so hardy as a mare,'' Goody snapped. ''But I'll let y' stay if y' can make yourself useful. Get me some basins of water an' . . . let's see . . . a goodly pile o' linens.''

''That's all?''

''Ain't much to a birthin'. Only a lot of pain an' sweat.''

Pain and sweat . . . sweat and pain. Seconds melted into minutes and into hours until even the relentlessly wagging pendulum failed to mark the passage of time for Bethany. She was in a stupor of agony and exhaustion.

Just when she was certain she couldn't go on any longer, she was tackled by an urge to give vent to a monstrous pressure building within her. Vaguely she saw Goody's face light up.

'' 'Tis time,'' the midwife announced. ''Now the real work begins.''

Bethany felt an inward deflation; hadn't she been laboring for hours with all her might? But the urge within her was strong, irresistible. She pushed.

''Y've the idea,'' Goody said. ''But it'll take more'n that to bring the child forth.''

Screwing up her face and clutching desperately at Ashton's arm, Bethany struggled, sure she would burst with the effort. Suddenly Goody gave an exclamation of satisfaction.

''Come here,'' she said to Ashton. ''Since y' insist on bein' present, y' might's well be the first to hold your babe.''

Bethany's focus changed for a brief moment from the mounting pressure within her to Ashton. Oh God, she thought, watching his indecision. Oh God, he's going to leave rather than witness the birth of the child he believes to be Dorian's.

But Ashton didn't leave. He squeezed her hand reassuringly, dropped it, and rounded the bed. And in moments found his trembling hands filled with what the midwife declared to be a good half stone of wet and squalling infant.

Thunderstruck, Ashton stared down at the baby in his arms. Emotions too fleeting and too intense to name pounded through his mind: awe at this tiny, perfect child that had been delivered into his hands; relief that Bethany's agony was over; and a deep pride that she had borne her nightlong labor so bravely.

Wasting neither time nor words, Goody Haas tied off the cord and severed it. She held a clean length of linen across her outstretched hands and Ashton gave her the child. "A boy," Goody said. "Near as fine as any I've ever seen."

Bethany was smiling as she received the squirming bundle. Ashton saw something in that smile he'd never seen before: a softness, a serenity, a supreme contentment that caused a tender stirring in some forgotten corner of his heart.

The baby quieted as Bethany held him to her. She moved a hand reverently over the tiny reddened brow, the tight fists that waved at her. Goody cleared her throat and Ashton noticed a suspicious gleam in her eye as she set about the business of tidying up.

Finally Bethany looked at Ashton. "We have a son," she told him quietly. In her eyes he recognized a silent supplication. She wanted him to claim the baby.

He wanted to. God's blood, but he wanted to make an everlasting bond with the child. But all he could bring himself to say was, "Congratulations, pet. You were braver than an entire army." He dropped a kiss on her damp brow. "What will you name him?"

She looked up at him tentatively. Her white teeth chewed a barely trembling lip, then she drew a deep breath. "I thought . . . we could name him for your father."

Ashton felt the breath leave him as if he'd just been sucked beneath a cold sea. Under different circumstances he would have been fiercely proud to name his son for the father he had loved. But now . . . his conscience would not allow him to give Roger's name to a child who might have been sired by Dorian Tanner.

Bethany was looking at him expectantly, waiting for an answer.

"I think not," he said, his voice quiet and full of regret. He made himself smile, made himself move the covers aside to peer at the wizened face, the tiny red mouth that worked silently like a little bird's maw. "Looks a mite like you and Harry, don't you think?"

That was true. The child had a fine nose and bow lips and a chin that promised the obstinance that was the hallmark of the Winslow twins.

"Henry Markham," Bethany said, not looking at Ashton. "I suppose 'tis fitting, since Felicia can have no more children."

"Your brother will be proud, love."

"And you, Ashton? Are you proud?"

Once again his lips were drawn to the fine, damp skin of her brow as he eyed the tiny bundle in her arms. The boy would be raised as his own no matter who had sired him. "Aye, love," he said sincerely. "I'm proud of you, and of this perfectly beautiful child."

He watched her exhale visibly with relief. And then, overcome with feelings he preferred not to explore, hc sat and stroked her temples until exhausted sleep claimed her. Carefully he extracted the baby from her arms. The child, too, seemed wearied by his travails, and the dark, slitlike eyes closed against the bright light of the world he'd just joined.

Ashton carried the bundle into the kitchen, where Goody Haas was working, pipe clamped between her yellowed teeth. "They're both asleep," he told her.

Goody eyed him through a thready haze of smoke. " 'Tis well," she declared.

"She named the boy Henry, for her brother."

The penetrating gaze never wavered. "I heard."

Ashton sucked in his breath. "I trust you'll say nothing. To anyone."

"Y' trust me right enough," Goody mused. She jerked her head toward the quiet bedroom. "But y' don't trust *her.*"

He swallowed. "We've been married but eight months." His eyes dropped to the sleeping bundle in his arms. "This fellow is as big and hale as a nine-month babe.'' He sought the midwife's eyes again. ''Goody, is there any way to be sure?''

She regarded him for a long moment, sucking on her pipe and scraping her hobnail boot idly on the puncheon floor. ''Aye,'' she said at last. ''Aye, there is.'' The bright eyes enfolded in aging flesh drilled into him. ''There's such a thing known as faith. Y' believe the child is yours because that woman in there loves y' enough to be truthful about it.''

He exhaled loudly. Was it enough that Bethany had said the baby belonged to him? Or was she sustaining a lie to protect the innocent life of her son?

Ashton didn't know. He didn't possess the faith Goody wanted him to have. All his life he'd believed only in that which could be proven either with his own eyes or by reasonable deduction. He wasn't the type to undergo sudden leaps of faith.

But when the baby turned to him and nestled more snugly against his chest, one thing became clear to Ashton. This was a child he intended to love.

Chapter 13

Bethany held court on the rope-frame bed all through the first day of her son's life, sitting with him in the sun-sprinkled bedroom that now bloomed with jars of Persian lilac and gillyflowers and blue-flushing grape hyacinth. The light scent of the flowers mingled with the unfamiliar and irresistible odor of baby. Not once did Bethany regret missing out on the formal, luxurious lying-in that would have been hers had she married according to her parents' wishes. There was no room to spare in her mind for such thoughts because her son's new presence filled her so completely.

The people who came to call were not the polite, murmuring highborn of Newport. They were Dudley, the cook, who bore the traditional fare of groaning cakes and caudle; Barnaby Ames, who shuffled his feet and gawked, promising that the newly foaled Indian pony would be ready for little Henry by the boy's third summer; and Finley and Chapin Piper, who brought a small printed card which read, "Welcome little stranger, tho' the Port is closed."

"Very witty," Bethany said wryly. She narrowed her eyes. "Where is Miss Abigail?"

The printer started to speak but was interrupted by a surge of stable hands and Moses Gibbs, the gardener.

"Congratulations," Gibbs boomed, pounding Ashton on the back. He lifted a mug of caudle. "To Ashton Markham's firstborn son!"

Bethany watched in uncomfortable silence as the others loudly bestowed their good wishes on her husband.

"How does it feel, having a boy of your own?" one man asked.

Bethany bit her lip as Ashton hesitated. She hoped the others wouldn't notice the strained edges of his smile when he said, "I'm . . . overwhelmed."

Apparently oblivious to Ashton's misgivings, Moses Gibbs began expounding on his views of child-rearing. Ashton, Finley, and Chapin slipped out of the cottage.

Then Carrie arrived, and for once the girl's hard cynicism was replaced by open admiration for her nephew. Bethany had to leave her query about Miss Abigail unanswered.

Henry bore up well under the scrutiny of the callers, waiting until they had gone before setting up a squall for his first meal. In her matter-of-fact way, Goody Haas showed Bethany how to suckle him. The baby's instincts made up for her ignorance, and soon both mother and son were content.

Some soft feeling too new to name eddied through Bethany as she stared at the baby nursing sweetly at her breast. "And to think," she mused, "that most women insist on engaging wet nurses."

Goody gave a satisfied grunt. "I'm pleased y' see it that way, girl. The bond y're formin' with that child is worth a hundred times the loss of a few vain inches on your figure."

"Did Ashton leave?" Bethany asked.

Goody nodded. "Off on some errand; he didn't say what. I told him you'd be in good hands all day."

Disappointment pushed through the brightness of the day like a thunderhead. Most men would have hurried to the nearest tavern to toast the arrival of a firstborn son. She knew better than to believe that was the case for Ashton. He was likely drinking as thirstily as any new papa, but not out of exultation. He would more probably be seeking forgetfulness in the bottom of his tankard.

Little Henry was sleeping in infantile fits and starts in his willow wicker cradle and Goody Haas was snoring on a truckle bed in the keeping room when Bethany heard Ashton return. He seemed unaware of her scrutiny as he entered the darkened bedroom and disrobed, shrugging into a clean nightshirt she hadn't even realized he owned. He normally slept somewhat less modestly clad.

There was something odd in Ashton's movements as he washed himself at the basin. Bethany peered hard at him. He didn't seem unsteady with drink, as she'd anticipated; rather he bore himself stiffly and moved almost gingerly. He hesitated over the wicker cradle, then supported himself with its hood as he bent to touch the sleeping baby.

The gratification Bethany felt over that gesture soon gave way to real concern. When Ashton slid carefully into the bed, she was certain she felt him wince.

"Ashton?"

"Hello, pet. I didn't realize you were awake." What was it she heard in his voice? Some rasping threadiness as if he fought pain. . . .

"What time is it?"

"I don't know. Past midnight."

"You were gone so long, Ashton."

"Goody said you'd be in good hands."

"I was." *But 'twas you I needed today.*

"Can I get you anything?

"No . . . yes. Kiss me, Ashton." She cringed at the childishness of her request, but she needed his touch, needed some confirmation that their relationship was not in ruins.

He complied with a haste that did nothing to allay her worries. The brief contact confirmed that something was amiss. The sheen of perspiration on his upper lip felt oddly cold. The scent that clung to him was alarming and unfamiliar, not the odor of stale beer and smoke from a taproom. Strangely, his hair was damp with seawater, and another smell mingled with the salt, sharp and distinctly unsettling.

Bethany shifted on the bed and saw Ashton stiffen. He drew his breath in. Sudden awareness dawned.

"You're bleeding," she said. "You've been hurt, haven't you?" He said nothing, and she knew she'd guessed the truth. *"What happened?"*

"Nothing, pet; don't worry about it. Just a bit of a scuffle with some rowdies . . . I took a nick or two."

"A scuffle? Ashton, you've never been a fighting man."

"And you've never been a prying wife." His hand crept to her chin, and this time he kissed her more tenderly. "We'd best get some rest while we can. Goody says babies entertain absolutely no regard for their parents' sleep."

"You—you *will* be a father to him, won't you, Ashton?"

"Aye. As best I know how to be. Now, go to sleep."

His abrupt dismissal rankled her and she was suddenly reminded that while they lay here in the security of their bed, Miss Abigail was still in the hands of Bug Willie because of what Ashton and the Pipers had done.

" 'Tis not so easy for me to drift off into peaceful sleep." Her voice was sharp with venom.

Ashton's voice, by contrast, was rough, as if he'd been on the edge of sleep. "What's that?"

"How quickly you've forgotten Miss Abigail," Bethany snapped. "While you were out drinking and fighting all night, she is still in the hands of that barbarian!"

"She . . ." Ashton coughed and winced with pain. "Bethany, listen—"

"I don't want to hear your excuses," she caustically returned. At that moment the baby began to cry and she flounced from the bed. Ashton muttered something about letting her temper sour her milk, but was asleep before she could deliver a suitable retort.

Morning's light, coming too soon after the baby's last awakening for a feeding, showed Bethany what a monstrous understatement Ashton had made about the "nicks" he'd sustained. His face was bruised and lacerated; his shoulder oozed ominously from beneath a crude gauze bandage.

Goody Haas clicked her tongue and dove a gnarled hand into her apron for a salve, then peeled the bandage away to reveal a deep and jagged cut.

"This promises a scar even more ugly than that one," the midwife said, indicating the depression in Ashton's side where he'd taken the patriot musket ball.

Bethany shivered as Goody deftly applied the herbal salve and rewrapped the wound. Ashton made no comment, but his face was visibly paler when he bent to kiss Bethany and then the brow of the infant she held.

"About last night, pet," he began.

"Never mind," she said quickly, trying to discount the exquisite warmth his kiss had left on her lips. She darted a glance at Goody. Ashton's eyes narrowed, but he merely shrugged and turned away.

After he departed, she sat wrapped in silence and confusion, wondering if the birth of the baby had left him so ill-tempered that he'd resorted to brawling. Confusion blossomed into elation when she heard the clipped, precise tones of Miss Abigail Primrose greeting Goody Haas.

Not a trace of her ordeal with the patriots marred Miss Abigail's meticulously groomed countenance. Beneath a neat little tippet every dark hair was in its proper place, and a gray cloak, perfectly clean and free of the slightest pucker or wrinkle, wrapped her poised figure.

Miss Abigail smiled a greeting at Bethany, but her eyes were entrapped by the sleeping child. The sharp gray of those eyes suddenly turned to the misty softness of pussy willows.

"It seems we've both been busy," Miss Abigail said, holding out her arms. "And who have we here?"

"Henry Markham," Bethany said as she put the baby into Miss Abigail's arms. "Now in his second day of life."

"He's lovely. . . . No, that's not the word I want." Miss Abigail spent a moment in grave contemplation of the small round face and the tiny balled fist that waved at her from the folds of a knitted shawl. "Superior in every way," she intoned. "Absolute perfection, my dear." She took out a rattle made of silver and sea coral and dangled it in front of Henry's face.

Then Miss Abigail did a strange thing. Her eyes never leaving the child, her disciplined face melted into a mask of foolish adoration.

"There now, here's our little man." The clipped voice dissolved into a string of the most outrageous, sugary baby talk Bethany had ever heard. "Come, nestling, a smile for Auntie Primrose. . . ."

Goody Haas's aptly timed entrance covered the giggle that burst from Bethany's lips. The sound of her hobnail boots and clanking apron seemed to bring Miss Abigail back to herself and she straightened, looking for all the world like a schoolgirl caught in the larder after hours.

''Fine little piece, ain't he?'' Goody remarked.

''He's divine,'' Miss Abigail agreed, gently laying the baby in the cradle and hanging the rattle on its hood.

Bethany smiled at the two women. It was impossible not to see the contrast they made. Goody's earthy, careless appearance struck oddly but not discordantly against Miss Abigail's stylish grooming. The two had nothing in common, yet they were united in their admiration of Henry and their concern for Bethany. For a moment an unpleasant feeling wriggled through her. There should be another woman here, offering love and congratulations along with the midwife and teacher, a woman who belonged here even more than the others—her mother.

But Lillian Winslow had been mortified by her daughter's crashing social descent and doubtless didn't want any connection with the grandson she would consider shockingly lowborn. Bethany toyed with the quilt to hide her hurt.

Goody hurried away to get tea; then, sensing Miss Abigail's desire for privacy, retired to the dooryard to sit among the lilacs and smoke her pipe.

''So you're the spy,'' Bethany said, peering at Miss Abigail, trying to reconcile the image of the tiny, proper little lady with that of a ruthless informer who committed acts of unprecedented bravery.

''Yes,'' came the prim reply.

''But *why,* Miss Abigail?''

The lady perched on the edge of a chair and sipped daintily from her teacup, wrinkling her nose at the ''Yankee brew'' Ashton insisted on. ''I really happened into it quite by accident,'' she explained. ''Last summer one of the girls at the academy became seriously ill. She had no kin other than her father, a lieutenant colonel in the army, who was defending Boston from the rebels. I was told there was no way to get word to him.''

Miss Abigail added a large dollop of honey to her tea. ''That should mask the taste. . . . So I decided to take matters into my own hands. People had been saying it was impossible to cross the Neck into Boston, but none of the rebel patrols thought to stop me."

Bethany had no trouble believing that. How could anyone suspect Miss Abigail Primrose of subterfuge? "When the girl's father learned how easily I'd slipped across the Neck," Miss Abigail continued, "he asked me to carry a letter to a gentleman in Bristol. After the success of that, there were a number of . . . requests." Slowly she stirred her tea, gazing out the window at a bobwhite perched on a pink-blooming branch of a cherry tree. "One thing led to another."

"To Harry. I admit I was shocked when I first heard you were the one responsible for his capture, but I realize you did the right thing. Harry's back with his family in Bristol. What about you, Miss Abigail? What will you do now?"

"I expect I'll be subjected to some sort of inquiry and asked to sign the Association."

"What's that?"

" 'Tis some document stating I've renounced my allegiance to the king, et cetera, et cetera."

"Will you sign it?"

Miss Abigail set her cup in its saucer with a loud clatter. "Certainly not."

"Will they punish you?"

She gave a thin smile that was taut about the edges. "Of course. It's become a point of honor with Mr. Finley Piper. Now, don't look at me like that; most probably I'll be required to remain in Newport under Mr. Piper's watchful eye. But enough about me, Bethany." Her eyes focused on the sleeping child and immediately softened. "Tell me of your son. Is Ashton as pleased about him as you are?"

Bethany glanced away. "He wouldn't let me name him for his father."

Miss Abigail's mouth tightened the slightest bit. "I see. So he still believes that nonsense you announced at his trial."

Bethany nodded. "He was so upset by the birth that he left me yesterday and didn't return until well past midnight. He—he'd been brawling. To vent his temper, I suppose."

The perfect arches of Miss Abigail's brows lifted high. "Brawling!"

Bethany cringed at her teacher's tone. She knew Miss Abigail had disapproved of Ashton from the start. Now, it seemed, he was bearing out the lady's image of him.

"Brawling!" Miss Abigail repeated. "Is that what he told you?"

"Aye," Bethany admitted softly.

Miss Abigail's hand reached for her, stroking her shoulder in maternal fashion. "My dear, your husband wasn't out brawling last night. He took a dory into the bay to get me away from Bug Willie. He wasn't brawling with the man; he was fighting for me!"

Bethany stared in shock. That explained the scent of seawater in Ashton's hair last night, the savagery of his wounds. "Oh, my God," she whispered. "I didn't know."

"I can't think why he didn't tell you."

"I—I never gave him a chance. Oh, Miss Abigail, the things I said to him . . ."

"I think you'd both best learn to listen to one another, my girl."

Bethany nodded miserably. And spent the remainder of the day wondering how on earth she and Ashton would ever find peace between them. When one was ready to trust, the other was ready to accuse, and she could see no end to the cycle.

Nearly six weeks passed before Miss Abigail was brought before the Committee of Safety in the house of Jarrod Kilburn on Broad Street. Bethany insisted on attending; Ashton demurred.

"There's no reason for you to be there, pet," he said with an excess of patience. "You'll only upset yourself."

"But I've taken such pains to arrange for the trip into town," she told him. "Carrie will look after little Henry. And this is my favorite gown." She folded her arms obstinately upon the sprigged lilac.

Ashton's eyes were drawn to her newly voluptuous bosom. "Aye, pet," he agreed, feeling a familiar heat in his loins. One of his favorite sights was watching Bethany nurse the baby, her breasts full, the child content. She had declared her recovery complete a week earlier. Since then,

Ashton, too, had enjoyed the bounty of her body, but in a different and supremely satisfying way.

"I'm going," she vowed, interrupting a thought so lusty that Ashton had begun to forget about the trial. "If you don't choose to accompany me, I'll go by myself."

"Damn it, Bethany, you should stay here with Henry. Carrie doesn't know the first thing about taking care of a baby."

"I don't understand you at all, Ashton Markham," she snapped. "While you loftily declare the rights of man, you demand absolute power over your wife."

Unexpectedly, Ashton's mood changed from annoyance to amusement. It had been some weeks since he'd glimpsed this side of Bethany, this pert and maddeningly adorable obstinance. She'd been so preoccupied with the baby that he'd forgotten the keenness of her mind, the depth of her thoughts.

He reminded himself that her interests went beyond this humble hearth and her charming son. His grin widened as her sweet nose rose still a notch higher and she brought her hands to her hips, assuming a challenging stance. He had a sudden urge to offer her the moon on a silver platter.

"You have me there . . . wife," he conceded, and offered her his arm instead.

The house in Broad Street was crowded with members of the Committee of Safety. With one sweeping glance, Bethany decided they resembled a company of tawdry town idlers rather than fierce warriors committed to the cause of independence.

Finley Piper arrived with Miss Abigail, who was dressed with uncharacteristic festivity in a gown of blue overlaid with a short jacket of red superfine, decorated with a white Mechlin lace fichu. Her choice of the Union Jack colors was not lost on Bethany.

Finley, too, seemed impressed. "You're rather grand today," he remarked as he held out a stick-backed chair for her.

"For good reason, sir. 'Tis the fourth of June, our king's birthday."

Finley rolled his eyes, and a murmur rose up from the assembly. "So. You've already set the tone for this hearing, eh?"

"In fine videbitur cuius toni," Miss Abigail intoned.

Again he rolled his eyes and translated for the assembly: "The end will show who played the right tune."

"Just dispense with matters quickly, Mr. Piper." She cast a disdainful eye about the room. Jarrod Kilburn looked away, clearly ill at ease. The rest, similarly chagrined, were a nervous, impotent-looking lot who wrung their hands and gaped in slack-jawed awe at the prisoner.

Miss Abigail sniffed. "If I must be devoured today, let it be by the jaws of a lion, not gnawed to death by rats and vermin."

Bethany swallowed her laughter at the pop-eyed astonishment the statement prompted. Stealing a glance at Ashton, she thought the slight tugging at the corners of his mouth looked suspiciously like a smile.

"Mr. Piper," Miss Abigail said in a patronizing tone, "this entire business is a mockery. Can't you gentlemen see that? Before long your rebellion will be put down by His Majesty's forces and you'll all be declared outlaws."

Finley glared at her. "Military power will never awe a patriot into surrendering his liberty."

"I see. So you intend to die slowly, by degrees."

"Let's get started, shall we?" He planted himself in front of her and lifted a sheaf of papers.

"What's this?" Miss Abigail said wonderingly. "*You* are to be my iron-jawed interrogator?"

That jaw, which resembled nothing like iron, tightened perceptibly. "Madam, I'm chairman of this committee."

"I see." She gave a sage nod. "The scum rises to the top in patriot circles." Her nostrils narrowed in a sniff as she reached out and selected a biscuit from a tray on the gateleg table at her side.

"What!" Finley snorted. "My God, does it eat biscuits? I thought it only ate raw meat."

Bethany barely managed to stifle a sharp intake of breath. Beside her, she felt tremors of silent mirth emanating from Ashton. Miss Abigail had been in Finley Piper's company for some weeks. Apparently during that time they'd sniped at each other ceaselessly. With a twinge of rueful admiration Bethany realized Finley was having moderate success in goading Miss Abigail; the lady appeared as rattled as Bethany had ever seen her.

Miss Abigail's look was a steel-gray dagger as Finley proceeded with the inquiry. He made much of her position as headmistress of the academy in New York, wondering aloud for the benefit of the committee how a woman born to no particular means or title had achieved a reputation that drew the very cream of Tory society.

Miss Abigail cleared her throat and faced the assembly with an elaborate flaring of her nostrils. "Gentlemen, I do not owe my position to a crooked spine and bruised knees brought about by groveling before nobility. Far from it. I have succeeded by the most conventional of means."

"And what, pray, would those means be?" Finley asked, emulating her formal, precise speech. Bethany realized he must be quite familiar with Miss Abigail's manner of speaking.

"Ways which are completely alien to you, Mr. Piper. Hard work, discipline, and intelligence."

Ashton made a slight choking sound when Finley's mouth worked like a codfish out of water. Although Bethany nudged him and slid an indignant look his way, she, too, was battling gales of laughter that threatened to erupt from her at any minute.

Finley set his face into a dark scowl. "How charmingly modest you are, madam."

"I am neither charming nor modest, Mr. Piper, but it doesn't really matter, does it? Unless those issues are at stake today—"

"Perhaps you'd like to tell the committee how it is you have a fortune amounting to"—he consulted his notes with a dramatic pause—"two thousand seven hundred pounds sterling."

"Sir, I would *not* like to tell your committee of hobbledehoys about my personal finances."

"Ah. Never mind; 'tis common knowledge General Gage keeps a fat purse to take care of his spies."

"I have never accepted money for performing my duty to the Empire."

Finley spent the better part of two hours trying to wring details of those duties out of Miss Abigail. Nail-hard, she refused to tell him anything he didn't already know. She sat like a small sparrow wrought of iron and denied knowing anything of the communications she carried, the people she contacted, the sources of her information.

Finley looked exhausted and the committee looked bored when at last he left off his line of questioning.

"Miss Primrose," he said in an elaborately patient voice, "we've given you every opportunity to exonerate yourself. There is but one thing left to offer you that might spare you a severe sentence." He laid a piece of paper in front of her with a flourish.

She recoiled from the document as if it were a hissing viper. "Never," she stated. "I will not sign the Association." Her eyes swept the dismayed faces of the committeemen. "I am an Englishwoman, and shall remain loyal. To my death, if need be." She picked up the paper by one corner, holding it at arm's length as if it were something unutterably foul, and let it drift to the floor.

Finley turned to the committee, clearly dismayed. "There you have it, gentlemen." He sighed. "We've no choice but to sentence her."

At last the committeemen stirred into animated discussion. Their suggestions ranged from a public ducking in the millpond to hanging, touching on all the various outrages in between. For the first time, Bethany felt real alarm. She braced her arms on the chair, rising in anger.

Ashton's touch was firm. "Don't, pet," he cautioned.

"There is no justice here," she exclaimed. "This arbitrary, petty drumhead tribunal is a sham!"

"Ah, yes," he replied smoothly. "And we're both well aware of the superiority of English justice."

That brought her back into her seat.

"Listen, pet," Ashton whispered, "I think Finley's arrived at a solution."

The printer had, and didn't bother pretending he wasn't proud of himself. Brushing back the lapels of his seldom-worn frock coat and hooking his thumbs into the plackets of his waistcoat, he rocked back and forth on his heels and sent Miss Abigail a self-satisfied look. "I've been a widower nigh on fifteen years," he said, feigning a bereft look. "Haven't had a lady about my humble abode in all that time. Might be nice to have a female touch here and there, have my socks darned properly and a decent meal now and then.''

His suggestion must have hit Miss Abigail like a blow from a siege engine, for her voice quavered when she spoke. ''Mr. Piper, I am a prisoner of war, not a bond servant.''

''You prefer the pillory to incarceration in my home?''

''I prefer being roasted alive by the devil himself to darning your socks, Mr. Piper.''

''Unfortunately, madam, that's not an alternative.''

Miss Abigail argued frantically; she did everything short of outright pleading, but Finley refused to relent. In the end she agreed to his custody, although Bethany suspected the lady fully intended to make Finley regret his sentence.

Jarrod Kilburn passed wine all around to toast the satisfactory conclusion of the inquiry. Bob Dutton, who had entered the meeting three sheets to the wind, stood and waved his glass, fixing a peevishly drunken stare on Miss Abigail.

''To King George on his royal birthday,'' he slurred. ''May the devil take him on his back and to hell with him straightaway.''

''Hear, hear,'' seconded the others.

Miss Abigail snatched a glass from Finley's hand and raised it gracefully. Her smile was cold and scathing. ''Damnation to the enemies of the king,'' she cheerfully pronounced.

''Amen.'' Bethany spoke quietly, but her voice sounded loud in the silent void that followed Miss Abigail's toast. Leaving Ashton's side, she rushed to her friend. ''Miss Abigail, will you be all right?''

The lady surveyed Finley with a curious mixture of distaste and rueful admiration. ''I shall be fine, Bethany. Little does Mr. Piper know what he's letting himself in for. I intend to serve England from that patriot scoundrel's own house!''

Chapter 14

Crouched between two brick warehouses in Bristol's wharf area, Ashton held Bethany until the cannonade ceased. The baby in her arms wailed in uncomprehending terror as the big guns of the HMS *Rose* belched a deadly threat on the town of Bristol.

In the cramped space, Bethany had her first taste of the acrid bite of sulphur, her first stinging smell of burning saltpeter. Ears accustomed to sounds no more threatening than the roar of the ocean crashing against rocks were now assaulted by the thunder of cannon fire. Her eyes smarted in a nefarious fog of black smoke and she closed them, snuggling herself and the baby closer to Ashton.

"There, love, hang on to me." His murmur rumbled comfortingly against her ear. "The shooting will be over soon. . . ."

Mercifully, the guns from the British fleet in Bristol harbor grew quiet. Little Henry's cries subsided to soft whimpers. The ensuing hush was eerie, uncertain, a nervous settling of smashed brickwork and plaster from the ruined facades of waterfront buildings.

Then the human sounds began: Voices rose into cries of agony; shouts escalated to bellows of rage. A mortified town greeted Captain James Wallace as he emerged from a ship's boat accompanied by red-frocked and gold-bedecked subalterns.

"Damn the bastard," Ashton muttered.

Bethany withdrew shakily from his arms and quieted the baby. Her eyes were wide with confusion and watery from the smoke. Her head throbbed and her legs felt weak, as if she herself had been a victim of the heartless assault on Bristol.

Slowly she shook her head, trying to make sense of the turn events had taken. What had begun as a family outing on a glorious summer day had turned into a nightmare. They'd gone to visit Harry and Felicia, to admire Margaret, their infant niece, and to show off little Henry. The day had been filled with congenial talk in the tiny parlor on Hope Street and games of piquet in the quiet garden.

They hadn't spoken of the war. Instead they had reminisced over childhood afternoons spent paddling and swimming in the bay, collecting mussel shells and turtles, digging clams. Summers were sweet freedom then, innocent irresponsibility, a time for riding horses and inviting the imagination to wander.

For a few hours Bethany had found affection and release in the cooing over the babies and the trading of nonsensical jokes. Spirits renewed, and feeling closer than they had in weeks, Ashton and Bethany had made their way back to the ferry.

Six British frigates had loomed like dark obscenities in the harbor.

Bethany would always remember that moment—Ashton's stone-hard face and the look of fury seething in his storm-tossed eyes. Harsh curses had issued from his lips as he hastened Bethany and the baby to shelter. From there they had witnessed the cannonade.

She looked at Ashton now and saw the anger still lingering in his eyes.

"Ashton, why would Captain Wallace do such a thing?"

His jaw worked as if he were fighting to prevent the emission of yet another string of oaths. "Would you believe he's hungry?"

"What?"

"Just listen."

They moved in among a loose ring of angry townspeople circling about the soldiers, who wielded evil-looking bayoneted muskets.

Captain James Wallace, the scourge of Narragansett Bay, flicked eyes ugly with anger over the citizenry and lifted his long, arrogant nose.

"Fifty sheep!" His voice belled out to touch every ear. "I demand fifty head of sheep from the town of Bristol. The King's Navy is in want of meat."

Amid grumbling both fearful and defiant, several farmers pledged sheep to forestall further bombardment.

Bethany hugged the baby closer and sagged against Ashton. "You were right," she mumbled. "He *is* hungry. Oh, Ashton, why did he have to bombard the town?"

As if he'd sensed her distress, Ashton let his fingers climb gently through the feathery honey-gold waves at her nape, beginning a tender rhythm designed to ease the tension from her knotted muscles.

"Civil war is the bitterest kind, love."

A month later Bethany found herself among another group of citizens. But shouts of joy rather than gunfire filled the air.

"This mob is no place for an infant," she said with a worried frown. Her eyes traveled over the throng gathered in the parade in front of the Colony House. All Newport, it seemed, had come to hear Major John Handy's announcement from the lime-washed balustrade of the impressive and curiously primitive-looking building. The people were hemmed against the edge of a park shaded by Dutch elms and poplars. A company of British regulars lounged indolently against hitch rails and gateposts. Their easy pose belied a readiness to subdue any mischief a gathering so large might produce.

Someone jostled Bethany from behind and the baby whimpered a protest. "Ashton," she said, "I think we'd best go back home."

"Hand the lad to me," he said, taking the shawl-wrapped bundle from her. He smiled down at the baby, who favored him with a wide, toothless grin. "I don't want you to miss this moment, little one."

Bethany instantly relented when she saw the look on Ashton's face. The hard, handsome lines of his profile became soft with the emotion that always seemed to touch him when he held the child. Relief played sweet melodies within her. A lesser man, doubting the parentage of the child, might have turned his back on little Henry. But not

Ashton. With tender pride he supported the small, gold-fluffed head to turn Henry's bewildered, blinking gaze on the scene at the Colony House.

"Your mother's not quite sure I won't drop you, lad." Ashton chuckled. "But we know better, don't we?" And truly, in the cradle of those big, gentle hands it appeared no harm could befall the child.

"Watch now, lad," Ashton said gravely to the baby. "A page of history is being written before our eyes. You'll tell your grandbabies about this day."

A lull of silence settled over the throng at the appearance of several men at the balustrade high above them. Major Handy, smartly clad in the blue and buff of the Continental Army, produced a large document with a ceremonial flourish.

" 'When in the course of human events it becomes necessary for one people to dissolve the political bonds . . .' " The voice rang clear, cutting through salt-tinged air and falling on ears rapt with astonished attention. On the reading went, dealing out hard, powerful words like cannon shot that shook the convictions of even the most radical of listeners.

Bethany felt herself begin to tremble. Independence! What else could the declaration mean but an all-out commitment to a war for which the new states were utterly unprepared and to which England had pledged the whole of her resources?

Long moments of silent reverence followed the reading. Then, with a rumble like a gathering storm, reaction began. People wept in jubilation. Hats were flung into the air and laughing ladies swung around in joyous salute to the Declaration. Bethany watched Ashton and her throat began to ache.

He celebrated quietly, clasping his son against him as the strong majesty of Mr. Jefferson's phrases washed over him like surf-beat on the rocks. He smiled down at Henry.

"There you have it, lad," he remarked. "You're no Englishman now, but an American." He seemed not to notice the coldness of Bethany's hand as he led her away from the parade.

They reached the end of the square, crossing directly in

front of a tight-knit group of Newport Loyalists. Bethany recognized angry outrage in the darkened brow of Keith Cranwick. On his arm, Mabel Pierce fluttered a silk fan emblazoned with the king's arms and declared in a high-pitched voice, "Imagine that! A ragtag mob challenging England!"

"They haven't enough guns or boats to sink a child's dory, much less the Royal Navy," Keith added smugly.

Bethany was aware Ashton had heard the comments; his grip on her hand tightened and his strides lengthened. At the end of Ann Street Miss Abigail Primrose and Finley Piper were locked in an argument so heated they didn't notice Ashton and Bethany. Miss Abigail flung dire warnings at the man who kept her as a "guest" in his house above the print shop.

But today the voices of Tory outrage were but feeble whimpers in the loud outpouring of patriot fervor.

On July 25, 1776, at the age of fifty-five, Sinclair Winslow fell in love.

He'd been in his library when a small sound disturbed him. A sound he hadn't heard in some nineteen years. The singularly stirring cry of a baby. Leaving his sheafs of bills and trading certificates scattered on his Goddard desk, he went to investigate.

At the top of the narrow back stairs he paused, covered the tightness in his chest with a hand gone suddenly cold, and frowned in annoyance at this evidence of physical frailty. Catching his breath, he lowered his head and walked to the maid's room at the end of the hallway.

The baby on the red-haired maid's bed was not merely crying. The child was in the throes of a full-blown, red-faced squall.

An imperious brow dropped to a scowl. "Miss . . . er, Markham!" Sinclair was pleased at his prompt retrieval of the girl's name. "What is the meaning of this?"

The maid's mouth worked codfishlike as she stared in horror at her employer. "Mr. Winslow! Sir, I—I'm sorry you were disturbed. . . ." Hastily she rose and dipped a deferent curtsey. "I offered to look after little Henry for

Bethany this afternoon," she explained agitatedly, "and I can't seem to get him quiet. Truly, sir, I—"

"Enough!" Sinclair stopped her short with the clipped imperative. "Miss Markham, I have looked the other way at all your various escapades over time, but *this*"—he cast a stern eye at the howling baby—"is inexcusable."

She swallowed nervously. "Yes. Yes, sir, I quite agree. I never should have brought the baby into the big house—"

"Pipe down," he snapped. "You're babbling, girl, and shirking your duties. Do you know nothing of caring for an infant?"

"I—n-no, sir."

Sinclair shook his head in disgust and crossed to the bed. "By God," he grumbled, "the child's soaking wet."

Carrie quickly drew a napkin from the supply Bethany had provided. Her hands fumbled uselessly as she tried to fold the square of cotton.

Sinclair snatched it from her. "Give me that. I can see the lad will stew in his own juices all afternoon if left to your questionable expertise." With a quick deftness that filled him with absurd pride, Sinclair folded the napkin and soon had the infant clad in soft dryness. Without looking at Carrie, he held out his hand. "The shawl." He spread the knitted garment at an angle, placed the baby on it, and wrapped the tiny body as securely as a parcel of herring from market. Still awash with pride at his own competence, he lifted the baby into his arms. The squalls dissipated to sobs, then tentative hiccups, then blissful silence.

Sending Carrie a smug look, he said, "And *that*, young lady, is how one cares for a baby. Don't forget it. And close your mouth. You look like a codfish."

"Uh, yes, sir."

Sinclair turned abruptly and walked to the end of the narrow room. A dormer window gave a view of the park-like gardens below and the vast reaches of meadows leading to the surf-battered coastline.

But Sinclair wasn't looking at the view. He was gaping with unabashed wonder at his grandson.

"Henry, is it?" he asked mildly. The baby gazed up at him with a steady blue stare. "Had one of those myself once,'' he mused, and fixed what he hoped was a properly severe expression on his face. ''Both my sons, alas, have proven useless: William's courting a dire case of the gout at his army post, and Harry's a popish rebel. I pray you'll become a better man than your namesake.''

The baby moved his head in an agreeable way and cuddled a flawless milky cheek against the worsted silk of Sinclair's frock coat. And then the miracle of a moist, toothless smile spread across the baby's face.

That was the moment Sinclair lost his heart. What he felt was not the responsibility-laden love he had for his own children, nor the dutiful regard in which he held his wife, nor the ambitious passion he showered on his properties and business.

Love for this tiny, beautiful child blossomed in his old man's heart. The feeling was as close to pure worship as Sinclair Winslow had ever come.

He brushed his lips over the smooth, downy head, tremulously inhaling the aroma of purity unique to babies. While Sinclair slowly gained control over his astonished emotions, Henry Markham tucked a tiny thumb into his mouth and fell asleep in his grandfather's arms.

Sinclair turned and laid the baby on the narrow bed, securing a corner of the shawl beneath the sweetly sleeping form.

''You see,'' he whispered to the dumbstruck maid, ''there is nothing to this business of babies.''

Leaving her to gape, Sinclair descended the back stairs and returned to the library. He bellowed for his day clerk, who came scurrying with ink salver, quill, and paper.

In a voice firm with conviction yet oddly thin with emotion, Sinclair Winslow dictated a new version of his last will and testament.

Bethany hid a smile behind her hand when Finley Piper, his apron dusted with flour instead of printer's ink, set a tray of scones on the table in his narrow parlor above the shop. Although at Miss Abigail's hearing he'd vowed she would serve him while living in his house, Miss Abigail had quickly taken the upper hand.

With singular and completely unfeigned incompetence,

she had created utter disaster in Finley's kitchen. After weeks of undercooked meat, charred toast, and slimy porridge, Finley had relented and taken over the cooking chores himself. Although Miss Abigail claimed her eyes were too poor to wield a darning needle, she appeared to have no trouble pouring over Finley's impressive library of books and pamphlets.

"Oh, my," she exclaimed in a too sweet voice, "you've outdone yourself with these scones, Mr. Piper. They're delicious." Making no pretense of a dainty appetite, she helped herself to three of them.

"Don't know where she puts all that food," Finley grumbled, casting a doleful eye on the tiny silk-clad figure. "Eats more than Chapin."

Miss Abigail sniffed and turned away, pretending to ignore him. Finley removed his apron and sat down beside Ashton, who held Henry, vigorous and inquisitive at seven months of age, in his lap.

Bethany loved the sight of her husband thus occupied. While many men would consider caring for a baby emasculating, the task suited Ashton perfectly. The diminutive and delicate child only made her husband's handsome largeness more striking.

Apparently Finley was not so appreciative. "Seems we're both doing women's work lately," he grumbled. "These two ladies are so spoiled, vinegar wouldn't save them."

Ashton only chuckled and rubbed his finger idly along the baby's soft cheek. He eyed Finley's apron. "You should know about vinegar, my friend, with as much time as you spend in the kitchen." Bethany no longer tried to hide her smile.

Abandoning his complaints with a grin, Finley replied, "And you should know about the political situation. I understand Sinclair Winslow has a distinguished guest."

Ashton nodded. "Governor Joseph Wanton."

"An excellent gentleman," Miss Abigail remarked, slathering another scone with butter.

"But a damned sorry excuse for a governor," Finley countered, watching her wield the knife. " 'Tis a good thing the General Assembly replaced him with Governor Cooke."

"Illegally," Bethany interjected, siding with Miss Abigail. "Governor Wanton still retains the colony charter."

"We'll see about that," Finley vowed. Chapin called up the stairs from the print shop, needing help with a fresh run of broadsides.

As Ashton handed the baby to Bethany, their hands met and gazes locked for an instant. She felt a familiar stab of frustrated longing and tore her eyes from his. Lately, most touches outside the bedchamber had been accidental. Ashton and Finley excused themselves and went to help Chapin.

"They're planning something," Miss Abigail said in quiet tones.

"Do you think they'll try to retrieve the charter?"

"Of course. The new governor can hardly run things without our set of laws."

Bethany slumped against the back of her chair with a dispirited sigh. "I hate Ashton's involvement with the patriots. We argue about politics endlessly." She shuddered. Often those arguments were so heated that they spent their nights with their backs peevishly turned to one another. The war was tearing them apart, and each was too stubborn to accede to the beliefs of the other.

Miss Abigail's pristine hand rested lightly on Bethany's arm. "Perhaps, my dear, you should think about moderating your political views."

Bethany's eyes narrowed. "Miss Abigail! I'm surprised to hear you speak so."

"My loyalty to England has cost me my personal freedom," the lady admitted. "But that is all. You, however, have lost something infinitely more precious: the bond with your husband. Such is too high a price."

Bethany shook her head. "I'll not pretend to embrace the patriot cause just to get Ashton back into my arms," she stubbornly declared.

If Miss Abigail was shocked by Bethany's frankness, she veiled her feelings completely. "But the two of you are suffering so."

"I try, Miss Abigail, really I do. But when Ashton starts

spouting things about self-government and individual liberty, I simply cannot keep myself from pointing out to him everything we stand to lose in this war. I cannot lie to him or myself. Besides, why should *I* be the one to concede my loyalty?''

''You've a point there. Both of you are too stubborn to give even a little.''

''Like you and Finley?'' Bethany couldn't resist the comparison, nor could she help smiling at the pair of pink spots that leaped immediately to her friend's cheeks. Although the two scrapped like quarreling terriers, they seemed to thrive on a constant state of adversity, trading insults that sometimes escalated to the sublime.

''Mr. Piper and I are sworn enemies,'' Miss Abigail insisted.

''I see.'' Bethany nodded, but she was still smiling. Henry began to fuss impatiently, clinging to the hem of her skirts. Scooping him up, she said, ''We must be going. This little one needs his nap.''

Miss Abigail dissipated into the ridiculous baby talk she reserved for Henry alone. ''Come back and see your Auntie Primrose soon,'' she said, placing kisses on the little face. ''And tell your grandpapa to let Governor Wanton hold fast to that charter.'' She looked up at Bethany. ''We'll make a proper Loyalist of the child yet.''

Bethany started down the stairs to the print shop. ''Not if Ashton has anything to say about it,'' she whispered. ''And he, unfortunately, will have plenty to say.''

Ashton experienced a ripple of displeasure at the task entrusted to him. Standing in the grand arched front hall of the manor house, he scowled down at an official commission from the Committee of Safety. The paper was poorly covered with hastily scratched writing, still gritty with blotting sand. He and Bethany had argued bitterly over what he was about to do; he could still hear the slam of the cottage door she had whipped closed after he'd left.

''What the devil are you doing here?'' Carrie's voice came from beneath the staircase.

''I'm here to see Mr. Winslow. And his guest. Where are they, Carrie?''

She stepped back, shaking her head. "No, Ashton. I know you; you'll only make trouble. Mr. Winslow hasn't been well lately."

"I'll only be a few minutes."

"Fool!" Carrie's voice became a sarcastic hiss. "Do you realize what you're throwing away by siding with the patriots? Good Lord, Ashton, Mr. Winslow is mad about your son; hasn't he made the lad his sole heir? He'd place all Seastone in your lap if only you'd give up this madness about independence."

Ashton fixed a hard look on his sister. What she said was true; taking everyone by surprise, Sinclair had recently willed the major part of his estate to little Henry, naming Ashton as trustee until the boy reached his majority. Ashton wondered if Sinclair appreciated the irony he'd created. As things stood, the possibility existed for Henry Markham to one day hold his own father's indenture.

He dismissed Carrie with a curt nod and climbed the wide staircase to the upper parlor. Sinclair and Joseph Wanton were smoking clay pipes and having their morning tea. As yet not wigged and dressed for the day, their heads were wrapped, turbanlike. Sinclair wore an India silk paduasoy gown, and Wanton sported a bright red Genoa robe.

Ashton's greeting was a perfunctory nod as he strode into the richly furnished room. "I'm here for the charter," he announced without preamble. He held out his commission. "I have orders here to deliver the document to Governor Cooke."

"Give me that," Sinclair snapped. Scowling, he snatched the paper and scanned it quickly before handing it to Wanton, who did the same. The ex-governor's jowls puffed out slightly in chagrin, but he remained stubbornly calm.

"Outrageous," he commented brusquely.

"Sadly, Mr. Markham here has become adept at committing outrages," Sinclair said. His scowl became a glower.

Wanton tossed the commission aside. "Tell the Committee I've refused to cede the charter."

Ashton was unruffled by this resistance. His activities

as an express rider served him well now, for he was privy to some rather useful tidbits of information.

With a rakish grin he said, "I'll tell the Committee. They might also be interested in passing on some facts about you to the General Assembly, Mr. Wanton."

The jowls worked agitatedly. "Intriguing, young man. Do go on."

"If you like," Ashton said pleasantly. "As things stand, most people are unaware of your part in the closing of the customs house, for example, and your rather questionable association with the Master of Rolls in England." He paused and watched with satisfaction as Wanton's face drained of color. "Shall I go on?" he asked. "Perhaps the Assembly would like to know the bounty you accepted from Captain Wallace's raids—"

"Enough!" Wanton cried, his fleshy chest heaving.

Sinclair's ruddy jowls worked up and down, and Ashton imagined his father-in-law was having any number of dark thoughts about the enemies such revelations would make the former governor.

Wanton turned his back pointedly on Ashton. "I'll not hand you the charter, young man," he announced. But he added, "However, were you to fetch the document from that coffer on the side table, I doubt we'd be able to stop you."

Ashton tried not to smile at the man's attempt to save face. He found the charter and slid it into his pocket.

"This will cost you dearly, Markham," Sinclair muttered.

"Dearly? In terms of what?"

" 'Twill cost you your son, damn you."

Fear sliced a cold blade through Ashton, although he made certain his face stayed impassive. "You've no hold on the boy, Mr. Winslow." He narrowed his eyes at the older man. Beneath a flush of outrage, Sinclair's face seemed oddly pale; there were taut lines about his mouth as if he were staving off pain.

"We'll see about that, Markham. Just take the damned charter and get the hell out of here."

* * *

Captain Dorian Tanner caught sight of himself in a gilt-framed Fauquiers mirror in the upstairs parlor of the manor house of Seastone. His obsidian eyes narrowed at the image, finding the brass gorget at his throat askew. A perfectly manicured hand straightened the ornament, then lightly patted the powdered tie-wig, which sprinkled a discreet puff of whiteness into the air. Dorian made a half turn, admiring the severe cut of his knee-length coat and the gleam of polished brightwork crisscrossing his profile.

Ten years ago even Dorian himself couldn't have imagined he'd ever cut so fine a figure. He'd dared to dream only after a certain member of the House of Lords had happened upon him as he performed horse tricks at a fair. Carnival life was preferable to spending his days up to his elbows in muck at his father's stinking tannery in St. Giles. But the titled gentleman had offered Dorian an even more appealing career.

Dorian made a delicate grimace, recalling the darker aspects of Lord Mawdsley's tutelage. The price of becoming a gentlemen had been dear, but worthwhile. Eventually the enamored nobleman had bought Dorian a commission, little suspecting his protégé would be shipped thousands of miles away.

Yet even this post was not enough for Dorian. The black eyes kindled like hot coals when he recalled how close he had come to marrying Bethany. She would have brought his fondest ambitions to full flower; she had beauty, wealth, and the one asset Dorian coveted above all else: respectability.

Finding her married to that great lout of a stable hand had been a staggering blow. Dorian meant to exact revenge against Bethany for the slight, and against Markham for putting him through the humiliation of the prisoner exchange. Markham *had* been involved in that affair; Dorian was sure of it. Unfortunately, months of investigation had given him not a scrap of evidence. Perhaps Dorian would need to resort to less conventional means of exacting vengeance.

A few minutes later he was shaking hands with Sinclair Winslow. They relaxed in Townsend chairs as a discreet servant poured Charente cognac into crystal snifters. Dorian enjoyed the elegance of his setting so much, he had to work at seeming nonchalant.

"I'm delighted to see you again, Mr. Winslow," he said carefully.

"Indeed. I hope you still feel that way when I tell you why I asked you here." Sinclair sipped his brandy, his eyes measuring the scarlet-clad figure shrewdly.

"Captain Tanner, I've an unusual request."

"As an officer of the Crown, sir, I am at your service."

"Yes, well, this is not a military matter. I'm not so old a man, Captain." His hand crept unconsciously to his chest. "But I know better than to assume immortality. My life has been a fruitful one." He waved a hand at the well-appointed room. "As you can see."

"Quite so, sir."

"I've become rather arrogant about my own achievements, I'm afraid. I have no wish to see what I've spent years building fall to ruin."

"Perfectly understandable, sir."

"I have two sons, as you know, Captain Tanner. To whom do you suggest I leave my estate? To Harry, who would doubtless turn Seastone into an outpost of rebel aggression, or to William, who was captured, stone-drunk, by patriots and is now mining copper in a prison camp in Connecticut?"

Dorian slid a probing look at the handsome but haggard older man. "If I'm not mistaken, sir," he said, "you've decided neither son is fit to care for your estate."

"Astute of you, Captain."

Dorian tried not to preen.

"Aside from the usual legacies to my wife, my daughter, my servants, and the church, I've decided to leave Seastone to my grandson, Henry."

Dorian studiously avoided showing the burning fury that seethed through him. Bethany's son! The child wouldn't be of an age to inherit for twenty years! Markham, that upstart, would have complete control over the entire estate.

"Henry's father," Sinclair continued, "is unfit to serve as the boy's trustee."

"I quite agree, sir," Dorian said, hoping he hadn't spoken too quickly in sudden relief.

"I need someone to do right by the boy, to hold Seastone safely in trust until he reaches his majority."

"You're wise in being so selective, Mr. Winslow," Dorian said calmly, although he longed to kick up his heels in jubilation.

Sinclair cleared his throat. "I know you to be a responsible man. You've shown good judgment in all your duties. As you know, I'd hoped to have you as a son-in-law."

"Your daughter's impetuous marriage to a commoner was a disappointment to me, too, sir."

Sinclair leaned forward. "Perhaps you can be associated with Seastone in another way. May I be so bold, Captain Tanner, as to ask you to be the boy's trustee?"

Dorian's every muscle tensed. Careful, he reminded himself. Go slowly. He schooled his face into a mask of sincerity. "Mr. Winslow," he said, with just the right amount of duty-bound gratitude, "I should be honored to serve in that capacity. Of course, my fondest wish is that the necessity never arises. That would be the most happy circumstance of all."

"Happy," Sinclair repeated, his hand straying again to his chest, "but alas, damnably unlikely."

"If, by agreeing to act as the boy's trustee, I can allay some of your concerns, then I'll gladly do so, sir."

"Very well," Sinclair announced, taking a many-paged document from a portfolio on a nearby gateleg table. " 'Tis done."

With that, Dorian realized, his fondest dream came suddenly within reach once again. Fortune was beaming down on Captain Dorian Tanner this day, and he intended to bask in the warmth.

As he rode back to town, he smiled at the dizzying paths his thoughts were taking. He smiled through a barely tolerable supper that would normally have caused him to roar at the cook. He even smiled when his favorite escort at Madame Juniper's complained about his lack of attention to her needs as he celebrated his good fortune.

By the time Dorian laid down to sleep in his quarters, he felt like a man who had seen a divine light. For within the twists and turns of his jubilant thoughts, he had discovered a means to achieve all he'd ever wanted.

Soon, he decided, before the year was out, he would have it all: Seastone, Bethany, and dark revenge against the hated Ashton Markham.

Bethany glared through midnight shadows at the wagging pendulum of the clock on the keeping room wall. The rhythmic ticking, usually so soothing in the night quiet of the cottage, irritated her now. Although she was staring at the clock, what she was seeing was Ashton when he'd returned from her father's house with the charter earlier that day.

A grimly satisfied smile had curled his lip as he entered the details of the day's activities in his journal. Lately that journal, which Bethany had hoped would become an outlet for Ashton's thoughts, had become a frighteningly long list of subversive acts, of espionage and sabotage, of things she didn't want to know about.

After finishing his writing, Ashton had at least had the decency to flinch when she'd fairly flung his supper at him. His conversation was calculatedly benign as he put the journal and charter away in his strongbox and retired for the night.

Bethany moved restlessly to the bedroom door, earning a disgruntled huff from Gladstone. An orange shaft of firelight illuminated two sleeping faces, so alike in form, so alike in dearness to her. Henry, on his railed truckle bed, poked a tiny thumb into his mouth and sighed contentedly. Ashton's sleep was equally untroubled, his face a disquieting vision of almost boyish innocence.

A strong urge welled up in her to brush a hand across a lock of hair curling endearingly toward the cleft in his chin. She clenched her hand against the impulse, turning away. How long had it been since she'd felt free to touch him, to give rein to the desire that clamored through her whenever he was near?

They were husband and wife, yet they lived more and more like strangers, always at odds, never completely in tune with one another.

Damn you, she told him silently. *Damn you and your bloody patriot cause and your high-sounding principles. Don't you see what you're doing to us? Don't you care?*

For months he had flouted her loyalty to England while

committing acts of treason before her very eyes, blithely certain she wouldn't betray him. For months she had resisted the urge to sabotage his efforts in the name of loyalty.

But until tonight the urge had been weaker than her need to turn a blind eye to her husband's activities.

His latest act caused her conviction to flare like a flame strengthened by a quickening breeze. She'd had enough of Ashton's subterfuge; it was time to act on her principles.

Bethany's fingers felt like ice as she stood on tiptoe at the corner shelf and groped for Ashton's strongbox. Her hand trembled as she raised the leather-hinged lid. She nearly dropped the charter in her nervousness. Forcing her hands to remain steady, she closed the box again and stowed it away.

The paper rustled like dead leaves as she slid the document into her pocket. Her mind worked at breakneck speed: the charter must be kept from the new patriot governor at all costs. There was only one person she could think of who had the intelligence and strength of will to safeguard the document from the rebels: Miss Abigail Primrose.

Bethany threw a shawl around her shoulders to stave off the chill of the November night and carefully laid her hand on the door latch. She depressed the lever with her thumb, eliciting a quiet metallic click. Apprehension pounded through her and she drew a deep, steadying breath.

The vaguest prickle on the back of her neck was her only warning. Dread thudded through her veins as she turned, slowly.

To face her husband's shadowed face.

''Going for a midnight stroll, love?'' he inquired.

Chapter 15

His easy pose in the bedroom doorway, the splendor of his masculine nudity, and the knifelike sharpness of his stare turned Bethany's insides to churning liquid.

"I . . ." Her mouth had gone dry. She moistened bloodless lips with her tongue and summoned conviction. "Yes, I am, Ashton. Do you object?" Despite her apprehension, the sight of his magnificent body as he crossed the room with a fluid motion made a traitorous part of her long to stay.

"Object, pet?" Long fingers, deceptively gentle, flicked at a stray tendril of hair at her temple and began a languorous descent. Bethany caught her breath as he traced a burning path over the leaping pulse in her throat, across her upthrust chin, rising to her trembling lower lip. "Why would I object?" he queried mildly. Slowly, very slowly, he closed the door against the cold. Then his hands returned to the tense contours of Bethany's body.

There was something taunting in the gentleness of his touch. Taunting, because he was aware of the compelling effect his unclad, aroused body had on her and no doubt aware she'd been hungering for him for weeks. Bethany pulled sharply away, only to find herself hauled against the fascinating expanse of his chest, her determined thoughts scattering like snow flurries.

The arm around her was gentle and Ashton's voice teased. "You cut me to the quick, wife, slipping off by yourself as if to escape my company." He gave a soft laugh. "And to think I fancied myself capable of keeping you home at night."

The scent and texture of him assailed her senses. Eyes heedless of the barrage of inner warnings she was sending herself remained fastened on the sensual curl of his lips and the lids of his glinting eyes, which played over her heaving bosom like a caress.

There was power in the touch that feathered across her cheekbone and dipped to the rounded neckline of her dress. Not the insistent power of a heavy-handed grasp, but a more insidious pull that drew her inexorably to him.

His smile was darkly sweet as his fingers left her bosom and traveled upward again, this time over her lips, expertly parting them. An inner voice warned her to flee, but she was hopelessly trapped by the arm that circled her waist and by her own undisciplined need.

Ashton's lips were a whisper against her own, gossamer-soft yet so explicitly suggestive that a slow burn of desire found a home deep within her, radiating out to limbs gone pliant with wanting.

"Ashton." His name trembled from her lips.

His tongue found hers and his teeth grazed her inner lip with cunning acuity. A slight motion of his hips sent her a frank message of temptation. As if she'd willed them there, his hands began to massage the tender ache of her breasts and then played over the supple column of her spine.

Even as she succumbed to his clever love play, Bethany felt small tingles like warning bells of alarm going off in her head. There was something different about Ashton, a sort of bloodless expertise in the movement of his hands and mouth. His touch was too studied, too emotionless. When he lifted his mouth from hers, she sought his eyes and saw chilling glints like ice crystals dancing in their blue depths.

He was angry. This was no bellowing rage, nor the petty annoyance he displayed when they argued; those emotions she could understand. The anger glaring down at her now was cold, as sharp and pure as a blast of arctic wind. The controlled gentleness of Ashton's rage terrified her.

She dragged herself up from the heavy fog of desire drenching her senses and forced her eyes to remain locked with Ashton's.

His hand, which had been curling tenderly through the waves of hair at her nape, kept up a soft, circular motion.

"Ashton, please." Bethany was shamed by the tremor in her voice.

"Please," he mocked softly. "Please what, darling?" Her response was an incoherent whimper. "What do you mean, Bethany?" he urged. "Please don't touch me . . ." His hand burned a trail over her heat-flushed cheek. "Or please do?"

With a swift motion he unfastened her apron and dress and skimmed the garments to the floor. Her shift and pantalettes met a similar fate. Bethany tried to protest and pull away, but her mouth would not form a denial; her limbs would not heed the warning of her mind. Apprehension mingled with rampant desire as he swept her into his arms and carried her to the rug before the hearth, wrapping her against his hard, sinewed form.

"You haven't answered me, pet," he murmured. His tongue curled wickedly into her ear. "Say you want me." His hands rode the ripe curves of her body, warming her flesh and raising a tempest of longing within her.

"I can't deny it. I hate it that we haven't been close these past weeks. I want you so much that I hurt."

His hand found a place of searing intimacy, and his touch left her breathless with wanting. "At least," he said, brushing his lips over hers, "you're honest about that."

Twisting, he laid her back on the rug, teasing her to readiness until tears sprang to her eyes. He took her swiftly, ungently, and thoroughly.

Riding a soaring crest of passion, Bethany was engulfed by a tumult of emotion. Their conflicting loyalties made them enemies, yet she adored him with a heart so full that it ached. His touch was angry, yet she found that anger wildly exciting. The task of delivering the charter was pressing, yet she forgot it in her ardor.

"Ashton . . ." Her feelings brimmed and overflowed. "Ashton . . . please . . ." She let her voice trail off, unable to say all that was in her heart.

He tumbled away from her, looking both replete and still dangerously angry. He cocked his head to one side.

"You repeat yourself. Please what? Perhaps you mean please let me go and hand the charter to my Tory friends."

Surging to his feet, he snatched up her apron and seized the document from its pocket.

Chilly gusts of reality chased away the warm afterglow of their love. Feeling suddenly vulnerable and afraid, she grabbed her shift and pulled it over her head. "Ashton, I—"

"Who were you taking this to, Bethany?" he demanded, shaking the charter at her. "Straight to Captain Tanner? My, my, you're getting as wily as your friend Miss Primrose."

Bethany went cold in every cell of her body when he disappeared into the bedroom, then emerged a few moments later fully dressed, the document protruding from an inner pocket of his jacket. He jammed on his hat and moved to the door.

In that instant her rage mounted to match her husband's. "How dare you," she seethed, planting herself in front of him. "How dare you condemn me for doing exactly as you've done all these months!"

"Move aside," he said wearily. "Obviously I can't trust the charter in the same house as you."

"I'm no more a thief than you are."

"But there's a difference, love," he asserted. "*You* steal from your husband. All these months you've talked of trusting one another, so convincingly that I saw no danger in being open with you about my convictions." Each word was a dagger thrust to her heart. "But it was all a lie, wasn't it? While you begged me to lay myself open to you, you planned on betraying me at the first opportunity."

"Do you think," she said, "that *I* never felt betrayed, Ashton? My God, every time you walk out that door to ride express or commit some act of sabotage, you betray everything I hold dear." She warmed to her topic. "I am an Englishwoman; I feel the same loyalty to my country as you do to this bloody new nation you call the Independent States of America. All this time I've said nothing; I kept my own counsel when you warned the farmers on Prudence Island about Wallace's raid. I sat and watched the *Sartoris* burn in dry dock, knowing one of your patriot friends had set it off. When the Brentons' barn was burned, I never let on that I knew the name of the person involved—your *good* friend, Chapin Piper! I've held my silence long enough, Ashton!"

His eyebrows rose in astonishment at the vehemence of her tirade. "So," he said, "the battle lines are drawn. What will you do now, Bethany? Match me blow for blow?"

"Don't be ridiculous," she spat. "But count on this, Ashton. I'll no longer keep my convictions to myself. I intend to help the British cause in any way I can."

"Do you think," he wondered, elaborately casual as he lounged against the door frame, "that we two will manage to live together under such conditions?"

Her head snapped up. "What are you saying?"

"That I'm through pretending, Bethany. This marriage was never meant to be in the first place; lately it's become insupportable."

"Are—are you leaving?"

His laughter lashed out, stinging her. "There's the irony in it, pet. I'm forbidden to leave. I belong to your father because of the indenture and to you because of Colonel Chason's mandate. Unless, of course, one of two things happens. I could simply steal off in the night like a runaway slave, or the Americans could win this war and your father would be forced to give me up along with everything else he's gained by exploiting the people of this city."

His statement found a region of her mind that such reasoning had never touched before. How was it that in all the hours she'd spent trying to understand Ashton's commitment, she'd never considered that his motives had to do with more than the independence of a new nation?

"Did you never think about that, Bethany?" He must have seen the transformation from anger to confusion in her face, for his voice had lost its harsh edge. "Did you never consider what independence from England would mean to *us?*"

"No." The faint whisper shuddered from her.

"You might consider it, then. You might consider your son, and his sons to come. And decide whether 'tis worth the price of your loyalty."

He left her leaning her forehead on the door, her teeth holding her bottom lip to stay its trembling.

The Liberty Tree ornament was a cold presence against Ashton's chest as he rode homeward. The Committee members, startled out of their sleep, had made much of his recovery of the charter. Ashton had accepted the silver amulet, which Samuel Ward of Westerly had promised to the man who recovered the document.

Ashton thrust the incident from his mind as he stabled Corsair and trudged up to the cottage. His reputation for subversive activities was growing, but he took no pride in that fact. Instead he thought of Bethany. And wondered anew at the murderous rage that had seized him on discovering her attempt to take back the charter.

That piece of paper had nothing to do with his reaction. No, his anger had sprung from the gut-twisting sensation of a trust betrayed. He'd been a fool to hope she might someday support his cause. Instead, she clung to her Loyalist ideals. Unwittingly or not, she was helping strengthen the ties that bound Ashton to her father.

Heaving a discontented sigh, he stepped inside the house, which smelled of wood smoke and the herbs and apple slices Bethany had hung to dry from the rafters. As he stood at the bedside and stared down at her beautiful face, the smooth cheeks marred by the salty ghosts of tears, he wondered how she always managed to appear so innocent, so guileless. Even when lying, she managed to sound earnest.

Despite all that had happened, the sight of her, softly sleeping, lips parted to invite the attention of his mouth in a way he found damnably hard to resist, made him long to pluck a single perfect star from the dawn sky and lay it at her feet.

Why? he wondered feverishly. Why did he feel this way about a woman who had maneuvered him into a marriage he did not want and fought his efforts to break free of the empire he did not support? Sifting through a confusion of disquieting emotions, he discovered one sentiment he could understand.

He respected Bethany. Respected her stubborn pride, her misplaced but dogged loyalty.

When he lowered himself beside her, cupping her body against his, she turned to him in sleep in a way that pride prevented her from doing when awake.

The flame of patriot fervor ignited by the Declaration of Independence burned unsteadily as the year drew to a close.

The fire of rebellion wavered when Pieter Haas, Goody's nephew, limped home to Newport to announce that the beaten Continental Army was evacuating Long Island. Admiral Richard "Black Dick" Howe's transport decks were thick with the blue uniforms and miterlike brass helmets of regiments hired by the Crown from the Duchy of Brunswick in Germany.

The candle glow of liberty weakened still further when Peggy Lillibridge had a letter from her brother in Fort Ticonderoga reporting that the American flotilla on Lake Champlain had been smashed down to the last bateau.

Slowly, inexorably, the British were pounding away at the brash American resistance, sending foraging parties out into the countryside, radiating like a deadly web, gobbling up American depots and supplies.

Although Bethany nurtured a quiet hope of the British getting matters in hand, she was chilled by the evidence of conflict trickling into Newport. Men returned wounded, sick, near to starving, with tales of wartime atrocities. Yet these ordinary-men-turned-soldiers remained steadfast in their commitment to independence.

For, despite the crushing defeats, the heartless marches, the endless discomfort of an army on the run, changes were taking place in America. Rhode Island's hero, Nathanael Greene, led a Virginia division into action. New Jersey troops responded to the commands of Anthony Wayne of Pennsylvania. Britain's "quarreling children" no longer balked at marching under the flag of a man from another town.

When he was not riding to some secret assignation or tending the horses, Ashton was a quiet, thoughtful presence in the cottage. The eyes behind his spectacles were expressionless as he wrote in his journal. Although he and Bethany reached a shaky truce over the matter of the charter, his silences grew longer, his smiles became less frequent. He ate less and worried more; tension filled every moment.

One evening in December Bethany had just finished boiling the best pudding she'd ever prepared. Henry, who moved at will in his two-wheeled standing stool, was by turns deviling the infinitely patient Gladstone and studying the fire screen as if weighing the possibilities of what might happen should he explore the forbidden wonder.

Using a pair of iron tongs, Bethany lifted the pudding from the Dutch oven, where it had been steaming for hours. Setting it on a tin plate, she carefully peeled away the gauze wrapping, inhaling curls of fragrant steam. A slow smile crept across her face. The pudding was a masterpiece of molasses and egg and flour and currants, redolent of gingerroot from Goody Haas's garden.

"Not a bad piece of work at all," she remarked cheerfully. Ashton, absorbed by his writing, seemed not to hear. Shrugging, Bethany crossed the keeping room and scooped up Henry, who began to wail at being interrupted in his gleeful tugging of Gladstone's ears.

The noise startled Ashton into crushing the point of his quill. "God's blood," he exclaimed, snatching the spectacles from his face, "must you make that child fret so, Bethany?"

She pursed her lips and began methodically securing the squirming, howling baby onto his mammy board and tucking a bib beneath his chin in readiness for feeding.

" 'Tis time for him to eat," she called over the wailing of the child.

Ashton glowered. "Doesn't appear to have much of an appetite."

She bit back a retort. "Come to the table, Ashton. The pudding's getting cold." Mercifully, the baby stopped crying.

Ashton stood, but he didn't come to the table. Instead he yanked his greatcoat from a peg by the door. "Suddenly I don't feel so hungry either. I'm going to check on the horses. Lately Barnaby Ames has made a habit of leaving stalls unlatched.''

He was gone in a swirl of wool and cold wind, his exit leaving a void of angry silence. Bethany glared at the door for a long moment, shivered in the lingering chill, and turned to the baby, who watched her with wide milk-blue eyes.

Seating herself in front of Henry, she took up a pewter porringer and began spooning rye cereal into the tiny red bud of a mouth.

''Papa doesn't know what he's missing,'' she told the uncomprehending child. ''I worked all day on that infernal pudding and he refuses even to taste it.''

Henry responded by puffing up his cheeks and ejecting the last mouthful of porridge. Bethany wiped it from his chin and poked in another bite.

''One would think each failure of the patriots was his personal defeat,'' she complained, ''for all he's been slogging around like Atlas beneath the weight of the world.'' A spoonful of porridge plopped onto the floor en route to Henry's mouth.

''Drat,'' she said. The baby made an impatient noise, so she didn't pause to clean it; Gladstone ambled over and gamely made short work of the spill.

''Honestly,'' she continued, offering another mouthful to Henry, ''your papa seems to have decided to take on the entire British Empire. . . .''

Outside the cottage, Ashton paused. Through the window, divided into four glowing and frosted squares, he could see Bethany feeding the baby. Her hands worked methodically, but her face was animated as she spoke heatedly. He doubted her conversation had anything to do with the merits of rye cereal. Unlike Carrie and that harpy Miss Primrose, Bethany didn't indulge in meaningless baby talk.

Tension, which had found a knotty home in Ashton's shoulders, suddenly seemed to flow away as he stood in the cold, surrounded by the sharp, barren smells of the dying year, and continued to watch as if mesmerized. He felt the unexpected tug of a grin at the corners of his mouth. Lately Bethany had made little Henry her confidant, heedless of the absurdity of pouring her heart out to the child. At the moment she was probably giving Ashton a verbal flaying on the matter of his shortness of temper.

A flaying richly deserved, he conceded ruefully. Little heartening news had sped to the Committee of late. And the last bit, like a frigid roar of wind, was the most chilling of all.

The British were coming to Newport. They were coming, and there were not enough fighting men in the area to mount even a puny resistance.

Ashton's sigh was a small drifting cloud against the window. The next few days would be trying. As hopeless as the situation seemed, he and the other patriots could not sit still and let Newport fall. In the morning he and Chapin were sailing to Point Judith to reconnoiter the occupying force. Bethany would ask all the usual questions; he'd have to tell her all the usual lies.

He went back inside, his spirits no higher than when he'd left, but all the anger gone from him. As he removed his greatcoat, he saw Bethany's narrow back stiffen and recalled how he'd stalked out on her as if she were the one responsible for all his troubles.

Remorse gripped him and held fast. Nothing could be further from the truth. Despite their political differences, Bethany worked hard to make life agreeable for him. The rich gingery smell of her pudding hung in the air, and he remembered how proud she was of her cooking.

He walked to the table and sat down, discerning pain and anger in her face. Gently he pried the baby's spoon from her hand.

"Let me, love."

Although her surprised gaze flew to him, she said nothing, only sat back and watched as Ashton spooned the last bites of porridge into Henry's mouth. Then he lifted the baby from the mammy board and cradled him in the crook of his arm, taking him to the settle in front of the hearth.

Ashton had put the baby to sleep countless times before. He enjoyed the quiet moments, enjoyed watching the child's eyes grow heavy-lidded. Yet tonight he studied Henry more closely than usual, gazing into the clear eyes, feeling emotion shudder through him. The bond between them was strong, their two souls knit in some forceful, mystic way. Sinclair Winslow's vague threat made Henry, blinking slowly with contentment, all the more precious to Ashton.

Something in that wide blue gaze stirred Ashton, knocking on a door of his mind until he could resist no more. He allowed the door to open, slightly at first and then cracking wide.

He felt himself begin to shake. He *knew* this child's blue eyes. He knew the soft shape of the mouth and the motion of the tiny fingers curling into a lock of wispy golden hair.

The eyes and mouth were Roger's, and the habit with the fingers had been Ashton's own way of soothing himself to sleep as a child.

Against everything he had heard and seen since the day he'd married Bethany, he finally admitted the truth. He sat pale and shaking with a hard lump of emotion in his throat until his son—*his son*—drifted into a secure cocoon of sleep. Gently he put the baby to bed.

His legs felt wooden as he came to stand before Bethany, laying his hand along her cheek and staring into eyes that searched his soul like a barber's probe.

"He's . . . mine." Ashton's voice cracked on the admission.

A smile trembled at the corners of her mouth as she stood up. "So I've said."

Ashton tried then to imagine the depths of the suffering he'd inflicted on her. She *had* said so; she'd sworn in anger and tears and frustration that she'd come to this marriage a virgin, only to encounter the cold wall of his disbelief. She'd lied, but to the military court, not to him.

"Bethany, can you forgive me for doubting you?"

"Forgive?" she echoed. "I'm not sure what you mean by that, Ashton. If you mean I should simply say, 'Of course I forgive you, darling, think nothing of it,' then the answer is no."

He drew in a breath that seared his aching throat. What he had put her though was not so trivial a thing as a forgotten birthday or tracking mud on her clean floor. He had doubted everything she'd ever said to him.

"But," she went on softly, breaking in on his thoughts,

"if you're asking me to give as before, to accept you, then the answer is yes."

Like a ripe fruit, relief burst within him, sending its healing juices to every cell of body and soul. He kissed her, injecting the kiss with every ounce of gratitude he felt.

She warmed to him, her lips softening beneath his, her hands gliding over his back. In a single grand sweep, Ashton lifted her, carried her to the bed, and made love to her. His every touch on her silken flesh was a reverence; his every kiss held the healing balm of understanding.

An act that had been sheer physical splendor now became a celebration of emotional release. Hands that formerly gave pleasure now gave something infinitely more precious, the tender understanding that had, until this moment, eluded their lovemaking.

Bethany was filled with a completeness she'd never felt with Ashton before. All he'd taught her of physical love over the months paled against the panorama of color and sensation she experienced in his arms now.

She didn't ask why he'd realized the truth now, long after she had ceased trying to convince him Henry was his son. That didn't matter. A new world opened up to her that night, a world that before had only existed in her imagination. It was a universe of texture and light and exquisite, scorching intimacy.

Only when she felt herself so full of him that she was on the brink of tears did Bethany realize how much bitterness she'd harbored. Now the bitterness was gone with a sigh, replaced by shuddering splendor.

Ashton smiled down at her astonished face as she lay recovering from a sensual assault that left her breathless. "I take it," he murmured, nuzzling her earlobe, "you've forgiven me, love."

She blinked slowly, dragging long lashes over her flushed cheeks. "You were so sure I was telling the truth at your trial."

"I was," he admitted. "Can you understand, Bethany? You rushed to me at the ferry, babbling your distress about Captain Tanner . . . and you were so ill."

"Seasick," she said. "If you'd given me half a chance,

I'd have told you the reason I was so upset that morning. Father had just informed me that I was to marry Dorian.''

A look of pain twisted his mouth. ''Then you should have run to him.''

She shook her head. ''I wanted nothing to do with him. I've always run to you, Ashton. Haven't you ever noticed that about me?''

''But you'd been keeping company with Tanner for weeks. A proposal was inevitable under those circumstances.''

The blush began to smart her cheeks. ''I never considered the possibility. The only reason I entertained Dorian at all was to get your attention, Ashton.'' She could barely meet his eyes. ''I never knew where my foolishness would lead.''

''Why the devil would you want to do a thing like that?'' he queried, sampling the tender flesh below her ear. ''Didn't you realize you were very much in my attention?''

''You made a point of avoiding me.''

''Aye. But 'twas easier to sidestep you in the stables than it was to drive you from my thoughts.''

She was astonished. She sat up, gripping the quilts to her bosom. ''Were you really thinking of me?''

''Aye. Day and night.'' His hand dipped inside the quilt. ''Especially at night.''

A smile of deep satisfaction curved her lips, and the sensation of feminine power rippling through her made her feel mature beyond her years. ''I see,'' she drawled, her voice low.

Laughter rumbled from him. ''Brat,'' he said, plucking the quilt away from her. ''Come here.'' Bethany sighed as she found her body enfolded into his arms, her soul enfolded into his safekeeping.

As the chill fingers of dawn slid into the dimness of the cottage through the frost-clouded window, Ashton smiled down at his sleeping son. Unbidden, Sinclair Winslow's cryptic, angry promise to take the boy crept into his thoughts. Winslow's influence was not to be scoffed at, but did he possess the power to wrest the boy from his own father? Or did Winslow mean a more insidious revenge, using his wealth and the indenture to one day seduce Henry into his influence?

Ashton didn't know, and he disliked the dark feeling of apprehension that gripped him.

Beside him Bethany stirred. She gave off a sweet, sleepy fragrance of jasmine and warmth and the less tangible scent of their love. Trying to shrug the black thoughts away, he leaned down and awakened her with a kiss.

"I have to go away for a few days, love." Although he spoke gently, he felt the jolt of her dismay like a physical pain. Hazel eyes that had gone soft at his kiss grew troubled.

"Where?" she whispered.

"Don't ask, pet. Please."

She looked away. "Last night I was so foolish as to think we'd reached an understanding, Ashton. Apparently I was wrong."

"We're closer now than we've ever been, love. But there are some things I can't share with you."

"Because you don't trust me."

He smoothed a lock of hair that had drifted over her brow. "You're wrong, love. If the British suspected you were privy to the things I do, both you and our son would be in danger."

She was troubled still, but when she lifted her arms and twined them sweetly around his neck, he felt her capitulation.

Their farewell was a brutal wrench after the new closeness they'd discovered. Ashton held his son, moving his cheek over the soft down of the baby's head and the milk-scented cheek.

Then he took Bethany in his arms, laying his mouth upon hers with a probing motion as if to memorize the sweet shape of her lips. Awash with regret at leaving them, he shouldered a well-provisioned knapsack and trudged down to the wharf to meet Chapin Piper and begin a desperate errand.

Chapter 16

Frigid dawn crept over the ice-capped rocks of Point Judith on the second day of the vigil. The jut of land, covered with dead salt grass and wild mulberry, was in the far southern corner of the mainland, affording a view of the roiling Atlantic. Ashton crouched in the frost-rimed grasses at the shore, set his back against a vertical upthrust of rock, and flexed his fingers to remind the blood to flow to their tips. Wordlessly he passed a flask of rum to Chapin, who took a long draw and passed it back.

"What's that?" Chapin asked, his breath puffing white as it mingled with the chill air.

Ashton squinted at the horizon, not really expecting to see anything. If nothing else, his experience as a patriot agent had schooled him in patience. Younger, and newer to the task, Chapin was given to restlessness.

But this time the young man's keen eyes had served him well. A line of ships, their dark hulls riding the swells beneath full sails, was approaching. As they watched the flotilla, Ashton and Chapin shared a few biscuits and a wedge of cheese and warmed themselves with more rum. The ships moved ever closer, but still not close enough to discern their colors. Hardy seabirds dove into the sinfully cold ocean after their prey, the winter wind soughed through the salt grass, and the moments wore tensely on.

Finally the first tall frigate swept close enough to see. British colors flew from the mainmast, snapping arrogantly in the wind. Behind the flagship glided the rest of the fleet, pushing relentlessly toward Aquidneck Island.

Betrayal and frustration engulfed Ashton, leaving him

breathless and furious. It was not enough that Wallace had choked off Newport's trade and stolen the better part of the town's wealth; now the British meant to make their perfidious possession of the city complete.

He jumped up and stretched the stiffness from his limbs. "Can we outrun them?"

"Must you ask?" Chapin said, leading the way to his sloop.

Ashton grinned at Chapin's pride in his sailsmanship. The pride was well founded; as a lifelong island resident, Chapin was an adept pilot. Yet as they cast off into the curling gray surf, the youth sent a troubled glance at the oncoming fleet.

"Plenty of Redcoats there," he remarked.

"If we make it back in time, there's a chance we can mount some sort of resistance."

"And if we don't . . . ?"

"The British will find Newport completely open to occupation."

Although Dorian Tanner's experienced eye wandered over the red-haired wench with lusty appreciation as they spoke together in the main hall of Seastone, he found her transparent admiration of his rank and figure almost laughable. The half-starved look she laid on him evoked pity more than preening. And the way she devoured the rare chocolates he plied her with told him she'd be as malleable as gold in his expert hand.

"So you are Ashton Markham's sister," he ventured. "Pity the man doesn't share your comeliness, my dear."

Carrie's blush wasn't genuine, but Dorian didn't care. "Neither does he share my good sense," she replied peevishly. "Can you imagine—he's married to one of the wealthiest girls in Newport and won't lift a finger to claim her portion. Instead he thinks to better his lot by fooling with codes and invisible ink and riding courier for the rebels. Why, only yesterday he sailed off with that no-account Chapin Piper. Said he was going fishing, but I know better."

God, Dorian thought, the chit was a veritable fountain of information. He smiled charmingly. Trapping the scoundrel who'd kidnapped him was going to be easy. Since no evidence could be brought against Markham for the crime, Dorian had begun a campaign to make the traitor pay.

"I wish there were some way to show him what a fool he's being, Captain." Carrie folded her lips into a peevish pout.

"Perhaps there is," Dorian suggested smoothly. "Miss Markham, I don't mean to pry, but I must have specific details of these activities. I can only help him if I learn the extent of his involvement."

She frowned and was silent for a time. Dorian fought the urge to curse her sluggish thinking. Instead he smiled and tipped her chin up with a gentle finger. "My dear," he said, "your loyalty will be well rewarded."

She returned the smile and sidled closer. "He keeps a journal."

Dorian deflated. "I don't imagine his wife would be amenable to showing the journal to me."

Carrie nodded glumly, then brightened. "Bethany's taken the baby to call on Miss Primrose," she said suddenly. She blushed for real this time. "Do you think, Captain Tanner, that we'd be terribly improper to . . ."

"Say no more, my dear. 'Tis for the greater good, you might say."

A half hour later he was swaggering back to Newport, his pockets bulging with the private journal of Ashton Markham, detailing every treasonous act he'd committed since August 1775. Every factor pointed to Markham's involvement with the rebels: a Liberty Tree amulet wedged between the pages, samples of patriot propaganda, letters from known outlaws. . . .

Ashton Markham had succeeded in the kidnapping, but he'd soon dangle from the gallows anyway, for serving the rebellion as spy, express rider, saboteur, and general informant.

"Your sails had wings," Ashton declared to Chapin Piper. "I'll wager we made the crossing from Point Judith in record time."

"We've plenty of time to carry the news to the Committee." Chapin laughed heartily. "The Redcoats won't find Newport such an easy mark after all."

They were standing on the dock, their backs turned from the harbor as they bent over the sloop, busily mooring the boat at a wharf that had been deserted due to Wallace's incessant pilfering.

Ashton lifted a dripping creel of fish. While sailing, he'd actually had a bit of luck. "Here's a bonus for our trouble, Chapin." He laughed, feeling confident and eager to get home to Bethany and Henry.

But when he turned, his smile faded. Before him stood Captain Dorian Tanner, flanked by six armed military guards.

"In the name of the king, I arrest you," Tanner announced triumphantly, his words a chilling echo of Colonel Chason's men in Bristol. "Come along, both of you." As he spoke, one of the guards deftly sliced through the sloop's mooring with a sword, setting the craft adrift.

Cursing, Chapin hurled himself at the soldiers, trying to break through the wall they'd formed. Steel flashed and Chapin's curse dissipated into a cry of pain.

His blood pounding with rage and frustration, Ashton swung the creel in a vicious arc at the officer, catching him on the side of the head. The force of the blow sent Tanner sprawling to the dock.

Ashton had little time to savor his satisfaction at the sight of the Redcoat's fish-slimed face. As Chapin sank, moaning and clutching at a blossom of blood below his ear, Ashton's consciousness splintered into a thousand bright lights of agony beneath the crushing blow of a rifle butt.

And on December seventh, in the folds of a dark gray dusk, the British fleet slid unresisted into Newport, and eight thousand red-frocked troops settled in for a long occupation.

William Bugston pulled closed the drapes of his room in the Newport town house and sent his manservant away. As he sat down to await his guest, his sharp eyes took in the new furnishings with satisfaction.

The antique French desk with its tooled leather top was a handsome addition, as was the delicate matching fruitwood chair. Over the mantel hung a whimsical Watteau painting, handily obtained from a failing Newport shipper. A tall wood and glass case from London boasted a priceless collection of Limoges china.

William smiled. People used to call Bug Willie a ne'er-do-well, a wharfside idler, but he'd proven them all wrong. Months ago he'd abandoned his leadership of the patriot mob, finding no profit in harassing the Tories. Now, with a complete absence of scruples, Willie straddled the fence between the two factions. Wartime shortages had made profiteering extremely lucrative.

A discreet knock stirred the silence of the illegally elegant room. Willie rose, crossed to the door, and drew his guest inside. In civilian clothes and a modest wig, Dorian Tanner hardly resembled a decorated British officer. The garb lent him anonymity; Willie knew well why he sought that trait.

Tanner shook hands briefly with Willie and accepted a crystal goblet of Madeira. They sat and Dorian inquired, "Are we quite alone?"

"Aye, Cap—er, Mr. Tanner. Just like you asked."

Tanner gave a satisfied nod. "Then let us get to the business at hand. You must be discreet, Mr. Bugston. I went through no little amount of searching to find someone who could provide me with the service I require."

"You got the right man. But I hope you know that if I hadn't wanted you to find me, you wouldn't have." Willie crossed his legs and laid his hands easily on the chair's armrests.

Tanner took a drink of his Madeira and narrowed his gaze at his host. They were two of a kind, Willie realized. Both ambitious, both more than willing to set aside personal and political scruples for the sake of advancing their own interests. Willie didn't much care for the Redcoat's disdainful manner, but he could stand for a lot of scorn for the right price.

Tanner said, "I want you to stage a profiteer raid."

"Christ, Mr. Tanner, the British are in complete authority here, as of yesterday. They're not buying from the profiteers now; they've no need."

"You don't understand," said Dorian. "I mean for this to look like a *patriot* raid."

Willie lifted a black eyebrow. "Smacks of treason, my friend."

"You object?"

"Not at all, Mr. Tanner. But I'm surprised to hear the request from a British officer."

"I have my reasons. And you needn't know them."

Willie rubbed a hand over his chin. "It's risky. And it'll cost you."

"I'm prepared to pay whatever it takes. If things go well, the adventure won't set me back too much."

Willie settled into the wings of his luxurious armchair. "Just what is it you want, Tanner?"

"A raid on the Winslow property called Seastone."

Willie's eyes narrowed, but he quickly concealed his surprise. "Go on," he prompted.

"Take the usual valuables and livestock, whatever else you can sell. And make it vicious, Mr. Bugston. Leave the main house intact, but burn some of the outbuildings. I want the rebels to look like the indiscriminate plunderers they are." He smiled coldly. "I've even arranged for a pair of culprits to take the blame."

Willie was burningly curious about the officer's motives, but the adventure promised such handsome rewards that he didn't question Tanner. "Anything else?" he inquired blandly.

"There is." Dorian lowered his voice to an intense whisper. "I want this raid to be the death of Sinclair Winslow."

Again Willie fought a reaction. He harbored no sentiment for the Winslow family, but Tanner's plan was singularly cold-blooded. "That'll take a mite more compensation."

"You'll get it," Dorian snapped.

In his mind's eye Willie envisioned amassing a small fortune for a night's work. "When shall I go to work on this?"

"I've thought that out carefully," Dorian said. "On Thursday next, General Clinton will reduce his forces by half. Newport's proven so docile, he's sending four thousand troops elsewhere."

"Aye," Willie murmured. "It'll be mighty convincing, the rebels feeling bold because of the reduced forces."

Dorian sketched out a detailed plan, then set a bulging coin purse on the desk. It was a dark irony that he'd wheedled the amount from Sinclair Winslow on pretense of needing money to entertain Clinton. Sinclair had been more than happy to oblige his favorite officer. "There's a deposit," Dorian said. "I'll pay you the balance when the job is done."

Bethany hummed as she worked in the kitchen, setting a pot of dried apples to stew beneath a sprinkling of cinnamon and maple sugar. Wiping her hands on her apron, she looked into the keeping room. Henry and Gladstone lay on the braided rug, a tangle of sweater-clad limbs and silky fur—fast asleep.

Smiling, she shook her head. "Fat lot of company you two are," she told them. "I'll be glad when your father gets home." Her smile softened and her eyes grew wistful. Ashton had been gone for four days. When had an eternity ever stretched so long?

She hugged herself, barely able to wait. Never had she looked forward to his return as she did now. Since they'd cleared up the matter of Henry's parentage, the future seemed brighter.

Everything would be different now. At last Ashton knew why she had lied at his trial. Soon, very soon, he would know that she loved him.

She loved him. The thought sang through her veins, and her feet traced a little dance of joy on the puncheon floor. Of course she had told him so, right from the start, on the very night of their ill-fated marriage. But he hadn't believed her.

In truth, what she had felt then had none of the depth and complexity of her emotions now. A year and a half ago she'd been an impossibly naive young girl, her head so full of romantic notions there hadn't been room for real thought.

Back then she'd seen Ashton as a storybook prince, the epitome of masculine perfection. In the darker moments of their marriage she'd realized her husband was stubborn and temperamental, a far cry from the girlish fantasy she'd created. Now she knew him as he was: human and fallible and endearingly flawed. And she loved him with the heart of a mature woman. She had drawn a mantle of love over his imperfections.

This new love burned like a bright star within her. It burned so brightly that Ashton could not fail to see it now.

She glanced out the window at the winter-white day. *Hurry, love,* she silently urged. *Hurry home to me. . . .*

As she looked out, a figure came into view on the path to the cottage. Bethany's smile became rueful. She didn't begrudge her father his visits to see Henry, but they never managed more than a few minutes together without arguing about Ashton.

As she opened the door for him, Sinclair placed a fatherly kiss on her brow. His eyes immediately sought Henry, hungry for a glimpse of the baby. Seeing the lad asleep, the man smiled indulgently.

"Worn himself out, has he?" He looked askance at Gladstone. "Must you let him loll about on the floor with that disreputable creature, Bethany?"

"They're the best of friends, Father."

"Aye, you're right. The lad's in more danger from his father than from the dog."

Bethany drew a cup of cider from the keg at the sideboard and handed the drink to Sinclair. "Father, don't start. I'll not listen to you criticize Ashton."

"By God, the man's in thick with the rebels! What are they, daughter, but a set of lawless pirates whose whole business is smuggling and defrauding the king of his duties?"

"Captain Wallace has chased every vessel from the bay, Father. If anyone is defrauding the king, 'tis he."

Sinclair looked startled. "Now he's got you spouting treason as well!"

She shook her head. "I'm only putting the blame where it belongs."

"Patriots," Sinclair spat, glowering into his cider mug. "A small, drabbing, contaminated knot of thieves, beggars, and transports collected from the four winds of the earth. What business have they in the loyal community of Newport?''

''We Loyalists are fewer than you imagine, Father.''

''Does that mean you must align yourself with traitors?''

''Ashton is my husband and the father of my child.''

''My dear, I was never aware that that was a cause of blindness. Yes, blindness, by God! Can you not see what he's made you?'' His hand encompassed the cottage in an annoyed gesture.

''He has made me happy.'' *As I never was with you, Father. ''You* have made me a bondsman's wife.''

''Because I couldn't stand to lose you, daughter.'' There was a curious catch in his voice.

''Let him go, Father,'' she pleaded. ''You know he was never meant to be a servant.''

''I cannot,'' he bleakly asserted. He glanced at the sleeping child on the rug. ''Don't you see, Bethany? Were he free to leave Seastone, he'd take you and Henry God knows where. Here, at least, I know you're safe.''

''Do you realize how selfish that sounds, Father?''

''I'm too old to pretend I'm not a selfish man.'' His hand sought his chest; Bethany frowned slightly at the massaging motion of his fingers. ''Old and stubborn,'' he maintained.

The baby awoke and crowed with delight at the sight of his grandfather. In moments the lad was being dandled on Sinclair's knee and toying with an array of brass buttons.

Watching them together, Bethany couldn't help softening. Her father remained immovable on the point of Ashton's indenture, but the love he showered unabashedly on little Henry bridged what before had been an unbreachable gap. For that reason, she indulged her father.

''Don't hate Ashton,'' she said as Sinclair made ready to leave. ''Would you think more of him if he had no ambition?''

''There is much to admire in your husband,'' Sinclair admitted. ''Unfortunately, there is even more to despise.''

''Father—''

''Damn it, girl, the man is a menace!''

''As are all opposing men in wartime.''

Sinclair shrugged into his greatcoat. "I can only hope the presence of General Clinton's forces will curtail Ashton's activities. I pray the fact that half of Clinton's troops just shipped out doesn't change things." He paused and, in a rare gesture of affection, touched Bethany's cheek.

"I can see one thing, daughter. I can see you love the man."

She moved her cheek against the warmth of his palm. There had been too few of such touches between them.

"Good-bye, father."

The dog's urgent whine brought Bethany awake to the chill gloom of the December night. She pushed herself up on her elbows, her eyes automatically seeking Henry. Finding him asleep, she scowled irritably at Gladstone. The spaniel crossed to the door, nails clicking over the puncheons, and whined again, sniffing loudly at a crack at the bottom of the door, pausing to look back at her, then pawing the floor.

With a longing glance at her warm bed, she slipped her arms into the sleeves of her wrapper and pushed her feet into her shoes. She moved the now frantic dog aside and opened the door.

And saw, high above the winter-bare tops of the Dutch elms surrounding the summerhouse, a faint orange glow shimmering with ghostly translucence against the night sky.

Gladstone let out a yelp and scampered outside. Seized by alarm, Bethany fled back to the bedroom and scooped little Henry up from his bed, tucking a shawl around him and gathering another around herself. The baby whimpered, then settled agreeably onto her shoulder. Outside, Gladstone's yelps had risen to agitated barking. Once again Bethany ran to the door.

This time she was greeted by four men smelling of rum, their faces concealed by scarves.

"Who . . . who are you?" Her voice faltered over the words, and the distant fire sounded like thunder.

"As if we'd tell you, you bleedin' Tory." One of the men thrust himself at her.

Her horrified scream streaked through the night air.

Hauling the baby closer, she hooked her foot around the edge of the door and tried to slam it shut. A vicious confusion of hands and feet assaulted her.

Bethany opened her mouth to scream again; a hand that reeked of pine tar choked off the sound. The baby, now wailing in fright, prevented her from fighting off her attackers; terror prevented her from thinking clearly. The world became a barrage of sound and movement: distant shouts, horses whinnying, the thud of running feet, the low rumble of the fire. In some unseen part of the dooryard Gladstone growled and snapped with unaccustomed viciousness, then was abruptly silenced.

Bethany flung her head from side to side in frantic denial, but the brutal hands held her secure. Amid a scuffle of laughing, cursing, rank-smelling men, she was dragged out into the dooryard.

"Comely little piece," one of the ruffians grunted as his hands traced the outline of her form beneath the wrapper. "Let's have a go at her before—"

"None of that, now," another said, shoving her down the path. "We've orders not to harm this one, nor the brat. Besides, some of the finest horseflesh ever bred is right down in those stables, ours for the taking."

Bethany twisted and struggled and wrenched her head around in time to see two dark shapes circling the cottage. A smoking torch touched the house's shingles, igniting a wicked flame. She made a desperate sound against her captor's hand, but the man only grinned.

"Shut that brat up," he ordered impatiently, "or I'll do it myself."

Bethany jiggled the baby and nestled him against her bosom. His screams dissipated to distressed sobs.

Ahead of her loomed the granary, its door yawning wide and dark. Rough hands pushed her inside.

"Please . . ." Bethany's voice was ragged, and her breath came in sharp, throat-searing gasps. But the door slammed mercilessly and she heard the latch rattling into place. Almost mindless with terror, she stumbled back against a hayrick, surrounded by unrelieved darkness and the pungent-sweet aroma of dry oats and hay.

Clutching Henry close until he quieted, she leaned,

dazed, against the hayrick and listened as the nightmare outside continued. Ugly curses, the squeals of panicked horses, the crackle of fire . . . and the scent of wood smoke.

Sinking to the packed-earth floor of the granary, Bethany cradled the baby, seeking comfort in the human warmth of her son. She tried to make sense of the nightmare, but there was no sense at all in the wanton destruction.

War was upon the colonies. Tonight war had touched her.

Chapter 17

With a chill of terror Bethany gathered the sleeping baby closer.

A loud thunk hit the door to the granary and she pressed herself against the far wall, wondering if the raiders, having despoiled the manor and stables, would now turn their attention to her.

The door swung open. The gray forebear of dawn outlined a large shape in cocked hat and jutting epaulets.

"Bethany?"

"Dorian!" her voice cracked; her throat was raw from the hours she'd spent calling desperately for help. "Thank God you've come. Is—is everyone all right at the house?"

He didn't answer, but took her by the shoulders and brought her to her feet. She wobbled unsteadily on legs that felt like calf's-foot jelly and leaned against Dorian. Although grateful for his strong, commanding presence, she wished fiercely Ashton had come instead.

Dorian cradled her hand in his. "You're as cold as ice," he murmured, leading her out of the granary.

"But the others . . ." Her heart froze at the sight that greeted her. To her right were the stables: every door ajar, every stall empty. And straight ahead was the stone-end cottage that had been her home.

Blackened stonework stood a bleak vigil over the charred remains of the cottage. Here and there, thready wisps of smoke reached to the dawn sky, climbing above the burned rubble of all she and Ashton had possessed.

Even more chilling was the sight of Gladstone's body, lying lifeless and blood-soaked in the dooryard. Bethany gave a horrified cry and tried to break away from Dorian, but he held her fast.

"Who did this monstrous thing?" she whispered.

"Patriots." His voice was hard with outrage. "I've sent a patrol out; already most of the livestock was found awaiting transport to Warwick Neck."

Bethany shuddered as a killing rage seized her. Patriots! No doubt the very scum responsible for Miss Abigail's drumhead trial.

As if he'd read the ire in her face, Dorian gave her shoulders a reassuring squeeze. "You'll have your retribution, dear; I promise you that."

"Who—"

"There now, I'll answer all your questions in due time."

Again she tried to move toward the spaniel's body, tears pricking hotly at her eyes.

"Please, Bethany," Dorian murmured. "There's nothing you can do for the poor little beast now. Come away, dear. Your mother needs you."

Careless, despoiling riffraff had ransacked the manor house. Dorian led her through a confusion of overturned furniture and shattered glass. In the main hall, the servants were crying and clutching at each other and wringing their hands.

"The damage looks worse than it actually is," Dorian explained quickly. "My men arrived in time to scare off the damned rebels before they had a chance to set fire to the main house." He glanced at Carrie Markham, who was blowing her nose loudly into a limp handkerchief. "Where's Mrs. Winslow?" Dorian asked.

"Taken to her bed, sir," Carrie said, sniffing. "Your surgeon gave her a dose of laudanum to help her sleep."

"Where is my father?" Bethany breathed.

Dorian turned her to face him, his features drawn taut with regret. "My dear, I'm afraid the greatest shock is yet to come." He swallowed and for a moment he didn't look quite so handsome—only human. "Bethany, my dearest girl, your father's heart failed him last night. The shock of the raid was too much for him."

Woodenly, Bethany placed Henry in Carrie's arms and trudged upstairs to her father's bedroom. Here, too, furniture had been overturned, drawers rifled. Dudley, the cook, was clearing debris from around the big four-poster bed. His thin, mustached face pale, he picked up a well-oiled fowling piece, which had been smashed beyond repair.

"He tried, ma'am," Dudley said. "But there were too many of the rascals. In the end your father broke his gun, declaring no damned rebel would ever burn powder in it."

She forced herself to look at her father. Death had erased the irascible lines of his aristocratic face. His stock hung open; the usual sapphire stud he wore there was gone.

Bethany sank to the bedside, her mind a turmoil of disjointed images and painful regrets. She and her father had never been close, but she'd loved him. Henry had loved him. She squeezed her eyes shut and groped for words to express her grief.

A hand touched her lightly on the shoulder. She turned to see Carrie. "You'd best go down," the girl said. "They—they've caught the culprits. I'll take little Henry here up to my room."

Bethany spared but a moment to wonder at Carrie's utterly serious, almost fearful manner. Then, dashing the tears from her cheeks, she walked to the stairs and paused to look at the men who had brought about her father's death.

In the dawn shadows below, Dorian and his three men struggled in the foyer with two rag-clad men. The reek of rum and unwashed bodies assaulted her senses as she descended. Curses filled the air. One of the captives wrenched away from the soldiers and lunged for freedom. Steel flashed; the man bellowed a final curse and fell against the door, his hands squeaking on its polished mahogany surfice.

Although the killing sickened her, Bethany forced herself to look at the man. Lank hair framed a thin, lantern-jawed face—the face of Chapin Piper.

"No!" The other rebel's bellow tore through the tension-thick atmosphere. Recognition exploded within Bethany. The furious denial hit her like an arrow aimed dead at her heart. Because the voice was Ashton's.

Gripping the banister, she swayed, then stumbled down

the stairs to her husband, her hands curling into claws of fury.

It took Dorian and two of his men to keep her from scratching the prisoner's eyes out.

The sound of boot heels clicking together in salute awakened Ashton.

"That will be all, private."

He sat up and automatically his eyes sought the damp surface of his cell wall. Squinting through the gloom, he silently counted the marks he'd dug on the brick with the edge of the manacle on his wrist: *One, two, three* . . . This was his fourth day in captivity.

Dorian Tanner entered the cell and closed the door behind him. Even the fact that he was manacled to the wall didn't prevent Ashton from lunging forth, filled with a rage so murderous it shook him to the depths of his hate-blackened soul.

The chains stopped him short, biting into the abraded flesh of his wrists. The force of his movement snapped him back; his breath left him with a hiss as his back smashed against the wall.

Tanner's chuckle was as smooth as rich cream. "Patience, my friend." With a grimace he plucked a silk handkerchief from his sleeve and breathed discreetly into the fabric, showing his distaste for the rank odor of the cell.

"You supercilious, bog-trotting son of a bitch," Ashton growled.

Tanner shook his elaborately wigged head. "My, my, I was hoping a few days in the cold and wet down here would dampen your temper. Apparently the heat of rage has been keeping you warm. I should have dispensed with you like I did your friend."

Ashton shivered and his mind shrank from the image of Chapin Piper, dead at the hands of the Redcoats. Dead, before his youth had flowered into manhood. Dead, before he could savor the taste of liberty for which he'd fought.

"So." Ashton expelled the word with disgusted loathing. "You can add murder to your list of credentials, Captain."

"Death to an enemy in wartime can hardly be called murder. He'd've hanged anyway. He was a dangerous spy."

The only dangerous thing about Chapin was the boy's devotion to the cause of independence. Ashton felt a tearing pain in his gut. Finley . . . Now, Finley was a different turn altogether. How would that extraordinarily ordinary man bear the death of his only son?

"Everything," Ashton vowed, his voice trembling with fury, "every single thing Chapin Piper suffered will be visited on you tenfold."

Dark laughter eddied from Tanner. "By whose hand, Markham? Certainly not by yours. You see, you're about to hang."

This was no revelation to Ashton. He'd never doubted the fate Tanner wished on him. "Even a British military court won't be taken in by your clumsy ploy to implicate me in the raid on Seastone," he muttered.

Dorian drew forth a small packet with a flourish. "I've no lack of evidence, my friend. Every single act of treason you've ever committed is documented right here by your own hand. Also the treasonous acts of . . . let's see . . . ah, Samuel Ward . . . Benjamin Tallmadge . . . other operatives. . . ."

Ashton felt the color leave his cheeks, and a chill crawled up his spine. "Where did you get that?"

Tanner's smile was a bright glitter of triumph in the gloom. "Where do you think, my friend?" He placed the journal and other materials back in the packet and patted it. "From your wife."

Ashton tried but couldn't quite manage to stifle the cry of betrayed outrage that escaped him. Doggedly he reeled in his wild fury and forced logic to take hold. Somehow his private papers had found their way into Tanner's hands. But Bethany hadn't placed them there. She couldn't have.

He almost smiled at the idea that Tanner, for whatever cruel purpose, wished him to believe Bethany had betrayed him. She'd never do that.

Because she loved him.

True, she'd nearly gone mad with fury on seeing him the morning after the raid. But doubtless she'd since realized that Ashton had been gudgeoned by Tanner. The thought had sustained Ashton through the days of inhuman cold and gnawing hunger. His recent discovery of the truth of Bethany's feelings had warmed him like fire glow.

She'd declared her love many times, but only on their last night together had the words penetrated his wall of distrust. She loved him, and now that he understood all she'd done for him, he was free to love her.

Almost. A rueful smile turned up the corners of his mouth. There was still the small matter of his impending execution. . . .

"Good God, man," Tanner said in annoyance. "I've just said your wife has informed on you. I see nothing at all amusing in that."

"No doubt you thought your lie would reduce me to an aggrieved mass of human suffering," Ashton said coolly, leaning against the wall.

" 'Tis no lie," Dorian hotly asserted. "Why wouldn't your wife—an avowed Loyalist—wish death on the man who caused her father's death?"

"I'm sure Bethany's realized the truth by now. Her first loyalty is to me." He smiled again, remembering how bravely—if misguidedly—she had come to his aid at the trial in Bristol.

"Not any longer, my friend," Tanner informed him. "Bethany is lost to you." He assumed a light, conversational tone. "You see, she hates you now. She's convinced you led the raid."

Ashton's insides grew as cold as the rest of him. "She'll know that for the goddamned lie it is," he returned hotly.

Tanner's pruned eyebrows drifted upward. "Oh, really now? Think about it, my friend. You've every motive to wish Sinclair Winslow dead. For God's sake, the man owned you! The two of you had a major run-in over the colony charter; Sinclair threatened you with the loss of your son. And no one knows about your little excursion to Point Judith. You have no possible alibi." The Redcoat laughed. "You look so surprised, my friend. Sinclair told me all about the charter business—just before he named me in his will as your son's trustee."

Every cell in Ashton's body froze. Tanner had worked

out his scheme down to the last evil detail. His manipulation had turned Bethany against Ashton, and Tanner would soon ensconce himself as lord of Seastone and guardian of little Henry.

The captain tossed a viciously exultant glance over his shoulder as he turned to leave. "Look at the bright side, my friend," he quipped. "At least you'll die a free man."

Two bodies were given up to their Maker at the Common Burying Ground at the end of Farewell Street. Bethany stood shivering with cold and grief and rage at the edge of her father's grave, her thoughts aswirl due to a liberal dose of laudanum. She was surrounded by only a scattering of people, for many had fled the increasingly dismal atmosphere of the war-ravaged city. Only days earlier, Newport's Loyalists had presented General Clinton with an oath of allegiance. Now they clustered around the gravesite, murmuring their outrage at what Bethany's husband had done to her father.

She wanted to scream at them, to hurl a demand that they leave her alone with her ravaged heart and broken dreams. But she stood quiet and dry-eyed and becalmed by the opiate as she accepted condolences from all those who had scorned her for marrying Ashton Markham.

The Pierces and the Malbones and the Cranwicks consoled her with empty words. Keith Cranwick, with a simpering and scandalized Mabel Pierce on his arm, paused to speak. "The scoundrel hasn't but a day left to make his lame denials before the royal commission; after that he'll be sent to the devil, where he belongs."

Bethany blinked, her drugged mind unable to dredge up a response. She drew her face further into her black mourning veil while her eyes sought her mother through its folds.

Lillian Winslow was, predictably, in her glory as the center of bereaved attention. She knew every subtle facet of funeral etiquette and played her role to perfection, her smile tremulous and beatific, her black-gloved hand daubing daintily at a tear.

Bethany turned away, scolding herself for her uncharitable thoughts. But she couldn't escape the realization that

Lillian mourned not so much the death of her husband as the loss of a secure and lavish way of life.

Backing away from the scene, Bethany nearly collided with a cloaked figure behind her. ''Careful there, sister,'' murmured a familiar voice.

She turned, awash with relief. ''Harry!''

''Hush. There're enough Redcoats around to rig out a man-of-war. I can't risk being recognized.'' He took her by the elbow and steered her away from the mourners toward the black-wreathed coaches and chaises lining Farewell Street. They stopped beneath the sodden and dripping branches of an elm tree. Bethany's laudanum-induced numbness began to give way to dull pain.

''Where's my little namesake?'' Harry inquired.

''I left him with Carrie. How did you know to come, Harry?''

''I had an urgent message from Miss Primrose. Where is our intrepid schoolmistress now?''

Bethany nodded at a group of mourners at the far end of the burying ground, this one even smaller and less grandly turned out. ''She's with Finley Piper.''

Harry made a sound of sympathy. ''Tell me, Bethany,'' he said, his eyes probing hers through the dark veil.

''Patriots raided Seastone,'' she told him in a whisper.

''That much I heard.''

''The raid was . . . led by Ashton.''

Harry laughed, startling her. ''Nonsense, Bethany; you can't possibly believe that. Ashton detests violence—''

''I saw him, Harry. Don't you see, it all fits. Ashton and Father were at loggerheads. Then Ashton left without explanation and was gone for several days. . . . And who but he would instruct the raiders to leave Henry and me unharmed?'' Finally the tears came, burning and bitter on the pale flesh of her cheeks. Harry held her briefly, then set her aside.

''I have to go, Bethany. We're attracting a few stares.'' He gave her hand a squeeze. She looked at him—really looked at him. He seemed tired; his hands were callused and rough in a way that told her he wasn't just keeping Mr. Hodgekiss's books in Bristol.

"Harry, are you well? And what of Felicia and little Margaret?"

"We're all fine, Bethany. Don't worry about us."

"Father's will has already been read." She looked away, unable to meet his eyes.

He seemed to know what her silence meant. "He's left me nothing." Harry's voice was cold, expressionless.

"If you need anything, I'll be at home. At Seastone."

He darted his eyes left and right. "Yes, well . . ." Again he squeezed her hand. "You'll be all right, Bethany. You always are."

She watched him go, wishing she had her brother's faith in her ability to deal with what was to come.

Bethany lingered at the burying ground after Sinclair's mourners had left. She approached the knot of silent, dark-clad people around Chapin's grave. In contrast to the gorgeous coffin Mr. Townsend had furnished for her father, Chapin Piper was buried in a pauper's box of knotty pine.

Finley stood watching, his face vacant, his eyes shot through with the redness of drink. Strands of graying hair whipped unheeded about his face. Miss Abigail was a discreet and sympathetic presence at his side, solemn and resplendent in black velvet. Her tiny gloved hand held Finley's. To Bethany the gesture seemed the very essence of comfort.

Spying Bethany, Miss Abigail murmured something to Finley, who nodded absently. She hurried to Bethany and embraced her. "Oh, my dear girl," she said. "I'm so very sorry."

Bethany swallowed. "I . . . find it hard to believe I'll bear this without losing my mind."

"I know, dear."

"Miss Abigail, how could he?"

"Are you so very sure the raid was Ashton's doing?"

Bethany nodded and, in a voice thready with pain, related all that had happened that night.

"He's certain to be hanged," she finished, shivering at her own words.

"And how do you feel about that, Bethany?"

"I don't know," she said miserably. "How can I live

with the man responsible for my father's death? Anyway, 'tis out of my hands. Ashton is to be tried tomorrow. Dorian says . . . the sentence won't be delayed long after that."

"Bethany—" Miss Abigail's voice rose as if a thought had occurred to her, but then she stopped herself. "My dear, I must go now. There is something I must do."

Dorian Tanner stood at the top of the range in front of Easton's Beach, armed with golf clubs and a supply of genuine Caledonian balls generously given him by one of General Clinton's officers. He wanted to laugh and shout and dance through the streets of Newport, proclaiming his triumph before all the town's miserable inhabitants. But he held the impulse in check, knowing better than to indulge in such an unseemly display.

Instead he indulged in the quiet, gentlemanly pursuit of golf, lining up his drives with studied precision. But, oh, how sweet was his private celebration. As he mulled over his triumphs, he applied his exultant energy to the leather-clad balls near his feet.

His first drive was short, but he couldn't stop smiling. He now held all Seastone in trust for a puling infant who wouldn't reach his majority for many years—if he did at all. True, Sinclair had surprised him by entrusting Bethany with a good portion of the horse interests. . . .

His second shot sliced to the right. But even that would soon cease to matter. In just days, the delectable Mrs. Markham would be a widow. . . .

The third drive hooked to the left. By implicating her husband in the raid, he'd left her vulnerable, searching for something stable in her life—Dorian's own compassionate, guiding hand. He'd already won her trust by returning the "stolen" livestock to the stables. Bugston had commanded exorbitant rates, but the money was trifling compared to what Dorian stood to reap from Seastone.

By summer he intended to win her hand in marriage. And then Seastone would be wholly and undisputedly his.

The final shot was perfect, straight and true, finding the very heart of the distant green, a tribute to Dorian Tanner's skill.

* * *

Miss Abigail Primrose smiled grimly as she heard the lock on Captain Tanner's desk succumb to her skillful probing with the middling pin she wielded. The drawer slid open. Beneath its false bottom she found what she was looking for: a stack of evidence against the prisoner Ashton Markham.

No qualms possessed the lady as, one by one, she tore the journal pages from the book and fed them to the fire. She hesitated at a particularly charming description of little Henry's first attempt at crawling, but doggedly burned that innocuous entry along with the rest. No trace of the journal must remain. She then burned the letters and pocketed the Liberty Tree medallion.

She checked the drawer again to see that she'd left nothing behind. Deep in one corner, a small object glinted at her, a stud such as gentlemen sported in their cravats. The stone was a good-sized sapphire.

She paused. Ashton owned nothing so dear. Yet in the back of her mind she recalled seeing the object somewhere. . . . Try as she might, Miss Abigail couldn't place it. Still, since Captain Tanner had seen fit to hide the jewel, there might be some significance to it. She dropped the stud into her pocket.

Miss Abigail frowned at the papers in the grate. The glowing embers burned the journal at a maddeningly sluggish rate. To stave off her nervousness, she mentally reviewed the steps she'd taken to ensure Ashton's safety. General Clinton, in her debt for quartering his junior officers at the academy in New York, had been only too happy to oblige her request to disallow the testimonies of Dorian Tanner and his men on grounds that they hadn't followed proper procedures in the arrest. Mortified by the violent murder of Chapin Piper, Clinton was preparing a stern reprimand for Tanner.

Ashton Markham would not be hanged now that no evidence remained. He would be released, and then it was up to him to prove to Bethany that he'd had nothing to do with the raid. Perhaps she would trust him, after the poor girl had sorted through all her grief and confusion.

Burning the documents was a crime against the empire

Miss Abigail had served faithfully, but what was at stake was far more important. Bethany and Ashton needed another chance, a chance to live and love and forgive.

Miss Abigail prayed her actions would give them that chance. She stepped from the office in Banister House, suddenly eager to get back to Finley. He might be comforted when he heard what she'd done for Ashton and for Chapin's memory. But when she reached the print shop, she found Finley too deep in his cups to appreciate her exploits.

"Oh, Finley," she said, going to him with outstretched arms. "Look at you. You're covered with ink."

"I . . . recruiting broadsides," he slurred, then fell against her. "Abigail. God, Abby, I hurt."

She didn't move away when he lurched against her, his hands soiling the bib and skirt of her apron with ink. She helped him up the stairs and into bed, then took off her ruined apron, forgetting the contents of its pockets as she added the garment to the rag pile.

Ashton spent a pain-filled moment surveying the charred rubble of the stone-end cottage that had been his home. Days in the frigid cell beneath the Colony House had reduced his clothing to mildewed tatters. A diet of stale beer and a gill of rice per day had robbed him of half a stone. Inactivity imposed by the chains shackling him to the wall had made his muscles slack from disuse. And the idea that Bethany had handed his letters and journals to Dorian Tanner had almost doused the tiny glimmer of hope within him that they might one day come to understand each other, to love each other.

That was the bitterest blow of all. No matter that the evidence against him had mysteriously disappeared, much to the foul rage of Dorian Tanner. No matter that Sinclair Winslow had willed Ashton his freedom. There was no heady triumph in having cheated the hangman, because the new life that had been granted Ashton stretched bleakly before him.

Turning his ragged collar against the bitter wind, he trudged to the main house to confront his wife.

Bethany looked fragile and unutterably lovely as she sat

in the downstairs parlor, her father's account ledgers lying forgotten in her lap. She was staring blankly at the fire in the grate, which winked at her from behind an iron embossed with the king's arms. Her head was bowed at a poignant angle. Neglected honey-gold hair spilled over her shoulders and caught the morning light glinting through the window.

Sweet Jesus, Ashton thought, had the devil really contrived such an adorable guise?

She looked up, startled, at the sound of his footsteps on the parquet floor. Her eyes sent him a message of loathing so clear that Ashton imagined he could taste hatred in the tense air that hung between them.

"So they've set you free," she said. Her voice was low and husky, much as it was when he inflamed her passion, but the hard edge of bitterness lent the sound a sharp bite.

"No thanks to you, pet." His answer was equally bitter. "Your captain managed to lose the evidence you gave him."

"I?" The ledgers fell as she surged to her feet with a rustle of black silk, stirring a maddeningly familiar scent of jasmine and a wealth of unwelcome emotions in Ashton. "I gave Dorian nothing!"

Ashton turned his filthy hands to her and applauded in a haughty imitation of an aristocratic theater patron. "Bravo, love," he told her smoothly. "A virtuoso performance. I've said it before: you're a superlative liar."

"I have no reason to lie to you, Ashton," she returned hotly, "because I no longer seek your favor." Her laugh sliced through the hatred-thick air. "Ah, I did squander a lot of tender emotion on you, trying to be a good wife even when you mistrusted me. That starry-eyed girl is no more. You taught me to love, yes, and then you taught me to hate."

He felt something inside him grow very cold. She was right, the bit about the girl she had been and was no more. Standing before him was a woman he no longer knew, a woman who'd been hurt, a woman who had learned to hate. An overwhelming sense of loss enveloped him and propelled him across the room to her.

Arms in rank-smelling tatters enclosed the elegant silk-clad shape; lips that had tasted nothing but prisoner's fare for days now sampled the clean essence of her lips. Ashton was compelled to search for what had existed between them, to probe until he found the sweet, sharp passion and that other deeper, sweeter thing he'd fought against during all the months of their marriage.

For a brief moment her mouth was soft openness, sending a spark of pure desire rocketing through him. Then she wrenched away, her face a pale oval in the curtain of her hair.

"Don't touch me," she seethed.

"Bethany, surely you can't believe I had anything to do with the raid."

She pivoted sharply, turning away from him. "The royal commission hasn't enough evidence to convict you," she choked, "but I know what I saw, Ashton. You may not have meant to do so much damage, but 'twas done. You may not have meant for my father to die, but he did."

"You would believe Tanner's lies over what I'm telling you now?" His voice was rough with astonishment.

She laughed humorlessly and turned back to level a bitter gaze at him. " 'Twas you who taught me to doubt, Ashton. You believe only that which can be proven. I am that way now. I no longer have the faith to accept your word."

Her speech was like a blow, leaving him breathless. "I take it," he choked, feeling bitterness pound through him, "that you intend to stay here."

"I have no other home. And you?"

"I'll be boarding with Mrs. Milliken in town."

"To carry out more of your treasonous schemes?"

He drilled a hard stare at her. "To be near my son. You can push me out of your life, Bethany, but not Henry's. I intend to be a father to the boy."

Chapter 18

In London the year began on a hopeful note. A betting-book was opened at Brooks Club; the first wager was penned by Handsome Jack Burgoyne and Mr. Charles Fox. General Burgoyne bet fifty guineas that he'd be home victorious from America by Christmas. Armchair strategists of the fashionable set envisioned the united forces of British, Hessians, and Tories setting themselves down as an anvil for the smashing sledgehammer blow Sir William Howe was to launch from New York.

In Newport the year began on a bleak note. Tory and patriot alike fled the besieged port city. Long Wharf, once the scene of frenzied commerce, became the site of boarded-up storefronts and empty warehouses. Citizens scuttled, heads down and feet hurrying, to avoid the domineering red-frocked occupying force.

Churches and public buildings became crowded barracks; private homes and riding academies were commandeered to garrison troops. The mansions at the Point were overrun by soldiers. Corrupt commissaries and barrack masters robbed drovers and bilked farmers on requisitions of wagons, teams, and livestock.

Some citizens lacked the means to flee. The city's poor remained—widows and their children, slaves manumitted because their owners could no longer afford to feed them, unemployed dockworkers, and their kin. These unfortunates huddled against the privations of war, burning furniture and even houses for fuel because the wood purveyors' boats had left the bay to seek less hostile marketplaces. Children took to begging in the streets and pandering to the swaggering and well-fed soldiers in hopes of garnering the small favor of a bread crust or a soup bone.

These were the children Bethany invited into her home, to warm themselves in front of the big library fire while she guided them in their lessons and filled their bellies with Dudley's cooking. The charity school was as much a product of the turmoil she'd suffered over losing Ashton to his patriot convictions as it was of her desire to succor the victims of war.

Her new endeavor sparked controversy in the household. Carrie Markham fussed and worried that the urchins would pilfer the valuables, most of which Captain Tanner had recovered. Lillian was appalled at the idea of opening her home to the city's poor, and wrung her hands, despairing of her reputation. Dorian, who as Henry's trustee had set himself up as master of the household, stopped just short of ordering Bethany to cease her tutelage.

But she would not be swayed, not by the scandalized gossip circulating about her and the husband she'd shut out of her life, nor by the wagging tongues wondering about her devotion to the children.

Teaching gave direction to her shattered life. When a child blessed her with a smile after reading a passage from the *New England Primer,* she forgot just for a moment her own unhappiness. When small, grubby fingers clasped her hand, she forgot just for a moment how much she missed Ashton's touch. Childish laughter chased away, if only for a moment, the mournful stillness of the household.

One bleak January day she was sending her small, ragtag class back to town, bending to tie Hittie Slocum's muffler more snugly, helping Jimmy Milliken to button his coat, giving them both a parcel of food to take home. Beaming, Jimmy clutched under his arm a brand-new edition of *Enteck's New Spelling Dictionary.* Miss Abigail had procured the book, and Bethany hadn't dared ask what the lady had gone through to get it. Aware only that new books were rare in these lean times, Jimmy impulsively threw his arms around Bethany's neck in a fierce hug.

"Thanks, Mrs. Markham," he piped. "I'll take good care of your book."

"Keep it for as long as you like, Jimmy."

He grinned and scampered off after his schoolmates.

Bethany looked up to see Ashton's broad form filling the doorway. Very briefly an indulgent light shone in his eyes as he watched the boy leave. But just as quickly indulgence gave way to searing anger.

Now what? Bethany wondered, trying to effect a calmness she did not feel. She stepped behind the desk and brought her hands to her bosom in an unconscious protective gesture. Ashton had been living at Mrs. Milliken's boardinghouse in town, but the hurt and anger flying between them were as fresh and sharp as if they'd never parted.

Despite the icy fury in Ashton's eyes, he exuded a powerful magic as he strode into the room and snatched off his hat, looking as lean and fit as a hungry wolf. He dug into his pocket and produced a newspaper, slamming it down on the Goddard desk so hard that Bethany jumped.

"No doubt you'll soon have your little charges reading *this,*" he snapped.

Frowning, and forcing her hands to remain steady, Bethany opened the paper. It was the first copy of the *Gazette,* a journal put out by thc loyal and royal John Howe. She should have been glad to see the seditious *Mercury* replaced by this Tory mouthpiece. But she wasn't.

" 'Tis well known," Ashton said, his voice dangerously low, "that the *Mercury* press was commandeered to crank out this self-serving propaganda." He circled Bethany like a cat about to spring upon a mouse. "But where did he get the type?" Ashton's smile was icy cold. "See the *n,* pet?" His finger jabbed at the character. "The letter is missing a serif. Finley Piper's type has the very same flaw."

Bethany swallowed a knot of fear in her throat. "What an extraordinary coincidence." But no one knew better than she that it was no happenstance.

"The extraordinary part, my love, is that there's no coincidence at all. Finley dismantled his press and buried his type. Only one person knew it had been buried behind Kilburn House. And that person is Miss Abigail Primrose."

Bethany's heart began to thud sickeningly against her

rib cage. Despite the nobility of her intentions, she simply wasn't made for subterfuge. "Ashton, Miss Abigail didn't—"

"Of course she didn't go digging up the type; Finley's been careful not to let her out of his sight. But she did receive you for tea not long ago."

"She did!" Bethany burst out, unwilling to cast more falsehoods on the heap of lies she'd already told. "And, yes—*I* was the one who showed Mr. Howe where the type was hidden!"

Ashton's curse made her ears smart. He snatched the newspaper from her hands and flung it savagely into the fire. " 'Tis not enough that you gave my journal to Tanner," he shouted. "Now you must take your petty revenge on Finley as well."

"The journals weren't my doing," Bethany told him in a low, shaking voice.

"So you've said. But why, pray, should I trust your word now?"

"Because it's the truth." She dropped her gaze to the blackened and curling pages of the *Gazette*. "But in the whole of our marriage you never trusted anything I said, so why should you start now?" She'd meant to sound angry, but a curiously wistful note had crept into her voice.

"Bethany—" His hand came up and for a wild moment she thought he was reaching for her. But he only picked up his hat from the desk. "I'd like to see Henry now."

Her first impulse was to deny him, but she checked herself. No matter what enmity existed between her and Ashton, Henry should not have to suffer the loss of a father's love.

"I'll see if he's up from his nap."

Ten minutes later she descended to the hall with the baby. Both were dressed warmly against the January chill. Henry's delighted crowing at the sight of Ashton tore at her heart. She turned away, hiding her pain as she gathered her brown cloak about her.

Ashton felt his anger ebb as he took the baby, holding him against his cheek, devouring the lad's sweet scent and the warmth of the squirming body. Nothing but the soft ache of yearning filled him now. "There now," he murmured, "off we go." He darted a look at Bethany, who was tying her cloak beneath her chin.

"You needn't worry, pet," he told her. "I'm not going to abscond with the child."

A maddeningly becoming flush rose in her cheeks. " 'Tis not that, Ashton. I—I just thought I'd join you on your walk."

Every moment in her presence was a hot needle of pain, but he couldn't bring himself to refuse her. "Come along, then," he said with a sigh, and held the door open for her. She passed close in front of him and left him dizzy with the jasmine scent that wafted softly from her hair.

Everything had changed, and yet everything was the same. Somewhere in the turmoil of betrayal and distrust was a tiny glimmer of some other feeling. Years ago, that feeling had made Ashton pause during a busy day in the stables to help an overprivileged and underloved little girl look for her lost kitten or to listen to some hilarious tale of a prank she and Harry had played on the dancing master. Buried deep beneath the drifts of bitterness lay the tenderness he had always felt for that vulnerable girl. She'd grown up indulged by him; he couldn't help himself—he indulged her still.

They walked through the winter silence of the gardens. Nearly all traces of the raiders' attack had been erased. Benches had been righted; hedges trodden by hobnail boots had been pruned to their usual geometric precision. But when they reached the summerhouse, Ashton saw that one ugly scar remained.

The structure loomed like a winter ghost on the precipice of gray slate overlooking the bay. Soot-blackened walls supported a charred roof, and the wind soughed through the unglazed windows. Although the sight gave Ashton pause, Henry seemed oblivious to the destruction. He was soon crawling happily about the frozen footpath, examining shells and twigs with babyish concentration.

Ashton slid a look at Bethany and found her staring at him with an expression of deep dismay. Anger prickled within him. "So you're still convinced the raid was my doing."

"Can you convince me otherwise?" she challenged.

He hesitated, then decided to tell her about the mission he and Chapin had set out on last December. No harm would come of an admission now; Chapin was well beyond needing protection, and the British were dug deeply into their occupation. Ashton drew a deep breath, feeling unutterably weary.

"Chapin Piper and I sailed to Point Judith to observe the British fleet. When we arrived back at the wharves, your good friend Dorian seized us."

"Did no one else see you?"

"Not anyone who'd admit to seeing us."

She lifted her chin and fixed a hazel-and-gold stare on him. "The British army doesn't simply arrest a man for mooring a boat."

He gave her a thin smile. "How conveniently you forget your own part in this. Tanner had my journals."

"He didn't get them from me, Ashton."

God, he thought, but she's a stubborn liar. "Oh, no? And who else, pray, knew where I kept my private papers?"

He watched her anger diffuse on a troubled sigh. "I can't answer that. You'll just have to—"

"Trust you?" His laugh was a bitter bark that startled the baby, who whimpered until Ashton stooped down and tickled him under the chin. "As you trust me, love? I'll admit we feel a wealth of emotions for each other, but trust is not one of them."

The clouds parted momentarily and a single shaft of sunlight found a glinting home in Bethany's eyes. There was a look of such profound sadness in those hazel depths that Ashton had to look away. He, too, felt that loss but was powerless to bridge the rift between them.

Discomfited, he turned his attention to the baby. The cold salt air nipped at the child's plump cheeks, causing them to blossom with healthy ruddiness.

Bethany, too, seemed eager to leave the subject of their estrangement. She walked to the steps of the summerhouse and peered at the gloom within.

"I'm going to have this place restored," she said over her shoulder. "I think it will make a perfect schoolroom."

In spite of everything that had just passed between them,

Ashton caught himself smiling. War had visited every corner of Aquidneck Island. Most people had no worries beyond wondering where their next meal was coming from or whether they would survive another freezing night without fuel. And yet, with a vision that was not quite so naive as it seemed on the surface, Bethany was planning on erecting a school.

She glared. "I see nothing amusing in trying to do a little good for the townspeople."

"Nor do I, love," he quickly agreed. "But I'm afraid these days most people are more concerned with keeping their bellies full."

"Still, I can't see the harm in nurturing the intellect. Stupidity is permanent; ignorance can be fixed. Just because a lot of unreasonable men keep trying to kill each other doesn't mean children shouldn't learn to read and write."

For reasons Ashton didn't quite understand, he found himself listening with unwavering attention to Bethany's plans for her school. Already she'd decided on a name: the Primrose Academy, in honor of the woman who had been first Bethany's teacher, then her friend, and now her mentor.

Miss Primrose had promised to acquire copies of *Bailey's English Dictionary* and *Blackstone's Commentaries* and paper through the black market. Ashton had to admit to a growing—if grudging—admiration for the hardheaded schoolmistress. Miss Primrose had taught Bethany well, had given her a set of convictions which, when combined with solid pedagogic principles and Bethany's own enthusiasm, had transformed the girl into a dedicated teacher. She could have idled in the protection of Dorian Tanner, yet instead she maintained her independence and dignity by pursuing a worthy calling.

"I like the idea," he remarked after she'd finished expounding on her intentions.

Her hazel eyes widened too becomingly. She seemed surprised at his confidence in her. "I intend to be a smashing success."

A maddening urge welled up in Ashton, an urge to take that earnest face between his hands and sample those moist lips. He hauled her against him swiftly, giving her no chance to protest. The sweetness of the kiss was deep and sharp—almost painful. Only after long moments had passed did she attempt to pull away.

"Ashton, we mustn't—"

"Damn it, Bethany, you are my wife!" Again his lips sought hers.

"But there's so much we—"

He laid his hungry mouth over her protesting one, filling his starved senses with the taste and smell and feel of her. The satisfaction of that preliminary hunger only gave her to a deeper, more disquieting appetite. One that could not be assuaged here in the cold winter garden with their son crawling about their feet.

When Bethany dragged herself away, he noticed tears sparkling like dewdrops on the ends of her lashes.

"Bethany." His voice was husky with desire. "Don't fight me, love, don't deny me." He lifted his finger to trace the trembling outline of her jaw and the pliant moistness of her lips. Desire roared through him with the force of a windhead on the bay. "Let me in, pet. . . ."

Fierce anger took the place of tearful uncertainty in her eyes. "Let you . . . ?" she stormed. "And what am I to do, forget all you've done and invite you to my bed, in my father's house?" She flounced away, rending him to pieces with a furious glare. "You weren't welcome there when he was alive, Ashton. Do you think you're welcome now that you and your raiders have brought about his death?"

Her scathing speech, uttered through the thickness of tears, sent sparks of pain straight to Ashton's heart. He was so stunned by her loathing that he made no move to stop her when she scooped up little Henry and hurried back to the house.

And as the weeks of the bleak, war-riddled year slid by, Ashton made no move to stop Bethany from shutting him out of her life.

Spring burst into full blossom over Aquidneck Island, bringing tidings from the mainland that Handsome Jack Burgoyne had arrived in Quebec, ready to smash down through New York and finish the rebels. Curled on the settee in the library one Saturday, Bethany read the news in the *Gazette*.

Feeling restive and at odds with the world, partly because Ashton was this moment in the garden with Henry, she put the journal aside and walked over to the paper-strewn desk where Dorian sat frowning at an account ledger. The frown disappeared when he looked up, giving way to a smile of frank appreciation. His dark eyes drifted over Bethany's dusky pink *robe à l'anglaise*.

"How fresh you look, my dear. I don't know how you manage when the rest of us are fairly melting in this unseasonable heat." He glanced at the paper she'd left on the settee. "Anything of interest in the *Gazette?*"

She shrugged. "Just the news of General Burgoyne's arrival."

"Ah. An excellent gentleman by all accounts. The rebels will be put down before the year is out. Can I get you some Madeira, Bethany?"

"Yes, please." She watched him move to the sideboard, handling the crystal decanter and Waterford goblets with studied precision. The term "excellent gentleman" could easily apply to Dorian as well. Since he'd taken over managing Henry's trust, he'd behaved with impeccable manners. Lillian Winslow couldn't speak highly enough of the captain. And Bethany . . . she could find nothing in him to fault, although it was not for lack of trying. Somehow he made her uneasy. And she couldn't help comparing him to Ashton. Dorian's smile was polite; Ashton's was genuine. And Dorian's touch—his hand at her waist when he escorted her to supper—was distant; Ashton's was . . .

Driving away the thought, she went around the desk and glanced idly at some of the papers. Her attention was drawn to a letter penned in Dorian's tight, painstaking script.

"What is this?" Bethany asked.

He set down the crystal goblets and snatched the paper away from her. "Merely some correspondence," he said quickly. "Here, drink your Madeira."

Bethany took a sip from the goblet. "That letter is to

the Bank of England, Dorian. Does Seastone have business with that institution?''

'' 'Tis rather personal, my dear.''

''I'm sorry, Dorian. I didn't mean to pry. So tell me, how are the finances getting on?''

His frown told her he didn't approve of a lady being interested in business matters. Her direct gaze made it equally clear that she intended to involve herself in anything having to do with her son's legacy.

Dorian sighed elaborately. ''I let Barnaby Ames go.''

Bethany's face fell. ''Dorian, no. Barnaby's worked here for years. He was so good with the horses, almost as good as—'' She stopped herself and raised the glass to her lips. Ashton was a sore point with Dorian; nothing would be served by mentioning her husband's name.

''I suspected Ames of consorting with rebel trash,'' Dorian maintained, scowling. ''I won't tolerate disloyalty on my—at Seastone.''

''I should think you'd hire a man for his skill, not for his political convictions.''

Dorian's smile was indulgent to the point of being patronizing. ''You are so charmingly naive, my dear. Never mind; 'tis done. I've already acquired another stockman down in Spring Street.''

''I see. And what is his name?''

''I suppose it shall be Winslow or Markham now that the man is Seastone property.''

Bethany's eyes flashed as comprehension dawned. A slave market was located at the corner of Mill and Spring Streets. She gripped the edge of the desk, leaning across stacks of paper and calf-bound ledgers. ''He's an African, isn't he?''

''Aye, and quite a good worker. The man was a runaway, caught skulking around Bristol some weeks ago. I'll keep him in line, my dear.'' Dorian buffed his nails on his sleeve. ''I intend to engage more Negro help around here.''

Bethany slammed her fist down on the desktop, scattering papers, sloshing the wine in her glass. ''You shall not,'' she said loudly. ''I forbid it. The Winslows have never owned slaves and we never will.''

Dorian's smile stiffened around the edges. "Bethany, dear, do be practical; figures don't lie. We'll save a fortune in wages. Your son's fortune."

"Figures don't lie, but liars figure," she retorted. "I will not have Henry grow up a slave owner. I want my boy to learn that a man has no right to hold another in bondage."

"Bethany—" Dorian's handsome features tensed.

"I will not have slaves at Seastone, Dorian. And furthermore, I shall give the man you purchased his free papers and pay him a regular wage."

"What about the money I spent on the man?"

"Consider it the price of learning the strength of my convictions, Dorian." She set down her wineglass and left the room.

Dorian glowered furiously in her jasmine-scented wake. Damn, but the woman was a meddler. She deserved a setdown . . . yet there was nothing he could do because of the terms of Sinclair Winslow's will. Until . . .

A smile curled his lips. Until she was his wife. At present Bethany was married in law if not in fact, but there was a remedy for that. A remedy that would have to be administered with utmost discretion.

Dorian idly picked up the *Gazette*. Before the year was out, the tabloid cried, Burgoyne and Clinton and Howe would have snuffed out the fires of rebellion. And before the year was out, Dorian Tanner would have Bethany as his wife.

Still in a rage later that afternoon, Bethany marched down to the stable offices to find the man Dorian had callously purchased. Freeing the bolt, she flung the door wide. Evening light poured over a slim, erect figure and a darkly handsome face. A face she knew.

"Justice Richmond!"

His hot brown eyes narrowed distrustfully at her. "So you be my new mistress," Justice said. Bethany frowned. His rich, musical West Indies accent was a thick drawl. Then she realized he was mocking her with a falsely subservient attitude.

"I am your mistress only if you choose to work for me,

Justice," she said hastily. "You *do* have a choice." Smiling, she handed him the certificate she'd had drawn up that afternoon. "I've manumitted you, Justice. You're a free man. If you stay here and work for me, I'll pay you exactly what we paid our other stockmen. Of course, if you decide to go back to Harry, I'll understand."

Astonishment lit his dark, angular features. "What sort of work?"

Bethany thought for a moment. "Didn't Felicia say you were a carpenter?"

"Aye. I've been known to wield a hammer and miter square a time or two."

"Justice, I'll pay you extra if you'll rebuild the summerhouse that was burned in the raid." Dorian had promptly fixed all the other damage from that December night, but his reluctance to tackle the summerhouse demonstrated his opinion of her continuing the charity school.

"Mrs. Markham, I don't think I've ever seen a summerhouse."

"That doesn't matter." She gestured at the charred building, which hugged a distant cliff. "I want it converted to a schoolroom. I've been holding classes for some of the children of Newport."

Justice Richmond glanced down at the manumission papers aswirl with a solicitor's artful script, then back at Bethany. "I won't build you a schoolhouse for money."

"Oh." She deflated a little. The British had employed all the carpenters in Newport building garrisons and earthworks. She'd never be able to find someone to—

Justice was grinning at her with uncanny warmth. "Not for money, Mrs. Markham," he amended. "But for something I want more."

"What, Justice? Name it."

"I want you to teach me to read."

Bethany felt a smile warm her from head to foot. "Done," she declared, setting her hands on her hips.

She was still smiling when she turned and saw Ashton standing in the doorway. Little Henry clung to his father's finger, chortling and toddling about his father's booted feet. Ashton nodded a greeting to Justice, who grinned and started up the path toward the summerhouse.

In the stables outside the office, Corsair blew a salute to Ashton, nodding his great black head. But Ashton wasn't looking at the horse. He stared intently at Bethany.

Feeling suddenly awkward, she blushed. "Hello, Ashton."

"Hello, pet." *Pet.* He hadn't given the endearment such a fond inflection in a long time. And he hadn't touched her as he was doing now in a long time, running a gentle, exploratory finger over the surface of her hand in a motion that never failed to set fire to her blood.

"I heard what you said to Richmond," he said.

"I . . ." What was it she saw in his eyes? Whatever the emotion, it was not the cool distrust she'd become accustomed to.

"You know, pet," he said softly, "there is much about you a man could love."

Could love. So conditional. So dependent on a trust neither of them could give.

Bethany took her hand from his and bent to pick up the baby. As if taking a cue from her retreating action, Ashton moved to the stables to look over Corsair, transferring his affectionate touch to his favorite stallion. He whistled a soft echo of the sound he'd trained Corsair to recognize as his own. The horse's ears pricked forward and Bethany heard his hoofs stamp eagerly. She glanced away, feeling suddenly guilty. Despite her protests, Dorian had commandeered the stallion in the name of supplying a king's man with a suitable mount.

Knowing how that fact galled Ashton, Bethany felt a softening. But her thoughts were interrupted by Dorian's arrival at the gate. Settling the baby on her hip, she walked across the stableyard to meet him.

"Hello, Dorian," she said distractedly.

Behind her, Ashton lounged in the doorway. "Tanner," he said curtly.

Dorian spared a brief scowl at Ashton, then put his hand gently on Bethany's shoulder. She stiffened, wondering what Ashton would think of the touch.

"My dear," Dorian murmured, "I'm afraid we've gotten some bad news."

She clutched the baby closer. "William?" she breathed.

He nodded. "Your brother died of the smallpox in that disease-infested Yankee prison in Connecticut." He moved to draw her closer, but she stumbled away, unthinkingly seeking Ashton as she always had in times of trouble. He covered the distance between them in three long strides.

Her husband's arms were warm and welcoming as he enfolded both her and the baby. "I'm sorry," he murmured against her hair. "So sorry."

"You lying bastard." Dorian's voice was a snarl of outrage. " 'Twas at the patriots' hands that William Winslow died. Is it not your objective to murder all those loyal to England?"

"William was my friend," Ashton returned, "and the brother of my wife."

"Yet the hatred you show toward all men of the Crown is the same hatred that killed the man."

"I was not the one who convinced William to enlist, knowing he wasn't suited to soldiering."

Bethany stepped away from the men, surveying them with tear-drenched eyes. "Stop it, both of you," she pleaded. "Can I not even grieve for my brother without being subjected to a political discussion?" Brushing past them, she clutched the baby and ran up to the house.

After that day a pattern developed in their relationship, a pattern of mutual avoidance. When Ashton came to visit Henry, he invariably chose a time when Bethany was busy in her new schoolroom. When she went to visit Miss Abigail, she went at the pub hour, when Ashton and Finley were sure to be swapping grievances with their cronies at the White Horse.

At times she ached to explore the possibilities of a reconciliation, for she longed for his touch, his smile, the warm things he used to whisper in her ear. Yet even if she could discount the raid, even if Ashton could believe she hadn't stolen his journal, the world itself seemed ready to tear them apart.

She saw him once in May, when Dorian took her to town for a victory celebration. Captain Esek Hopkins of the fledgling Continental Navy, a man distinguished for his flagrant and usually successful disregard of authority, had sailed into the bay to liberate Newport from the British. Royal vessels bottled the brash little fleet and then handily repulsed them, much to the delight of the Tory residents.

Amid the noise of artillery salutes in front of the Colony House the celebrants raised toasts of "Tory roosters," rousing quaffs of rum, rye, and fruit juice decorated with feathers. When Bethany spied Ashton walking toward her from the foot of the parade, she suddenly wished she hadn't imbibed so much of the potent drink. She would need all her faculties to face the blazing fury she saw in his forbiddingly handsome face.

As things turned out, she had no chance to respond to his temper. Their eyes held for a moment, exchanging a bitter message. Ashton swept off his hat and sketched an exaggerated bow, then pivoted and stalked away.

Late in the summer they met again. Major General Richard Prescott, the high-handed and bad-tempered commander of the British occupying force, had suddenly become a hero of sorts. While he was spending the night in Overing House on King's Highway, a party of rebels led by Colonel Barton had slipped across the bay from Warwick Neck and kidnapped Prescott. With typical patriot disregard of propriety, the raiders had forced the hapless officer to accompany them clad only in his nightshirt.

The humiliating act could only have been accomplished if the invaders were guided by someone intimately familiar with Prescott's comings and goings.

The day after the kidnapping Bethany saw Ashton at Hammersmith Farm, which the British were using for a military hospital. She was bringing quilts and bandages to the wounded. Ashton, no doubt, had contrived some pretext to circulate among the bedridden Redcoats. With a stab of resentment Bethany realized he was probably trying to extract secrets from the men. When he slipped out to the orchard, she followed him, intending to bring him down a peg for taking advantage of the helpless soldiers.

His dazzling smile nearly made her forget her purpose. "Hello, love," he called jovially. Snatching a greening apple from a tree, he tossed it to her. Unthinkingly, she caught it. "Hungry, pet?" he inquired mildly.

Scowling, Bethany thrust the apple into her pocket. "Hardly," she retorted. She couldn't help but notice he looked as if he had not slept. His jubilant grin told her exactly who Barton's Aquidneck connection had been.

Unable to stop herself, she approached him, hands on hips and chin upthrust. "You led Colonel Barton to General Prescott," she accused.

"Are you so certain of my guilt?" He spread his arms wide, and his blue eyes laughed at her.

She could tell Ashton's innocence was pretended. Her gaze moved meaningfully over his rumpled clothing, fastening on a tar-smudged pant leg. A smudge sustained, no doubt, when he'd shinnied down a wharf piling to help moor the contingent from Warwick Neck.

"I'm sure," she maintained.

He shrugged. "No harm done, pet. General Washington needed a bargaining chip, a man to exchange for Charles Lee."

"So you took it upon yourself to procure one."

"Let's speak no more of it, Bethany. The only wound Prescott sustained was to his pride. Such injuries are long in healing, but relatively painless, no?" He abandoned the subject with a blithe smile. "How is my son?"

"Henry is fine, of course."

"I've been wondering how Justice Richmond is coming along with that Indian pony. The boy'll be ready to sit a horse before too long. I was only two when my father started leading me about the training compound on a pony."

Bethany felt a prickle of discomfort. Ashton was determined that Henry would one day be as good a horseman as himself. But Dorian, it seemed, had other ambitions for the boy; already the captain had begun sending inquiries to England about tutors.

"The pony"—she swallowed—"has been sold, Ashton."

Anger kindled in his blue eyes. "By whose orders?" he demanded. "Never mind, I know. 'Twas Tanner, wasn't it?"

"Dorian felt it would be wise to wait several more years before allowing Henry to ride."

"Damn it, Bethany, who is raising the boy anyway?"

"You and I, of course, Ashton. But you must understand, as Henry's trustee, Dorian—"

"Can give him everything I cannot?"

She flinched. "I didn't say that."

"Not in so many words, no. But the message is clear to me each time you parade the lad about town in his Manchester velvet finery—purchased, no doubt, from a Tory profiteer. Or when you effuse to Miss Primrose about the shiny new lead soldiers Dorian bought. Henry is young now, but very soon you and the captain will lead him to understand that his father is a pauper."

She recoiled from his temper but refused to let him make her feel guilty about what had become of their lives. "You forfeited all, Ashton, when you became a rebel."

"Don't push me, Bethany," he warned. "I'm sure you try daily to forget, but let me remind you: You are my wife and Henry is my son. I've every right to take you away from your precious Seastone if I so choose."

"You won't. You may have stopped caring about me, Ashton, but I know you wouldn't force Henry to live in poverty."

His angry gaze held hers for a long, deliberating moment. She glanced down, saw his fist clenching and unclenching as if he battled against a storm of fury.

"Just don't push me too far," he repeated, and stalked away.

Bethany stared after him, fingering the apple in her pocket and casting about in her mind for the resentful anger she had every right to feel. But the only thought that came to her as she watched his broad shoulders disappearing among the branches sagging with abundance was an unbidden and completely illogical notion.

Oh God, I love him still.

Chapter 19

The summer of 1777 died on a wistful, lingering note. Petals fell from the wild roses tangled in fringes at the beachheads, leaving ugly bald rosehips to weather the cold season to come. More people fled the occupied island, yet a few returned. Goody Haas's nephew, Pieter, who had recovered from his first wounds only to reenlist and return to the fighting, limped home a second time with a wooden peg where a healthy limb used to be. Bleakly he reported that the British had trounced the rebels at the Battle of Brandywine Creek. Congress fled Philadelphia. York, Pennsylvania, became, to its uneasy surprise, the temporary capital of the United States.

October brought new hope to the rebels. Jimmy Milliken burst, breathless, into Bethany's schoolroom, puffed up with boyish importance as he handed her a crumpled newspaper.

"My Uncle Thad brung—brought this all the way from New York," he announced. "We beat the Redcoats! Smashed 'em all the way down the Hudson!"

Bethany rumpled the lad's sandy hair and smiled as Jimmy swiped the air with an imaginary sword. From the outset she'd kept politics out of her teaching, leaving that aspect of their training to their parents. Her smile took on an ironic quality. That very principle was closer to the tenets of patriot educators like Anthony Benezet and Thomas Jefferson than to British pedagogy.

She set the children to work in their copybooks and looked at the newspaper from Albany, New York. General John Burgoyne, Britian's golden hero, had been defeated.

Fleeing the rebels, his army dug in on the heights of Saratoga, only to find itself hemmed in from all sides by patriots, who slammed the door to the escape route to Fort Ticonderoga.

Bethany envisioned the humiliating scene: British men reduced to prisoners, marching past an American patchwork company of old men, young boys, and Negroes who bore arms as free men. Their faces would resemble the faces of men like Pieter Haas and Thaddeus Milliken: intense and rangy, hungry for victory.

Bethany closed her eyes, let a world-weary sigh escape her, and called the children to their arithmetic lesson.

By year's end the British had given up Fort Ticonderoga, Crown Point, and all hope of a Hudson-Champlain route. Their only strongholds were New York, Philadelphia . . . and Newport.

The occupation was wearing on the city. As winter swept in on salt-scented windheads across the island, still more residents fled. Making her way to Finley Piper's house to bring Miss Abigail a batch of Dudley's mince tarts, Bethany barely recognized the city whose golden age had abruptly died.

Much of the wharf area had been reduced to rubble by British guns and looters. The ruins had a sinister look because they were inhabited. People lived in barren rooms with rags stuffed in the windows. Girls younger than Bethany, who in better times would have been reading Scripture or doing needlework at the fireside, now received lusty soldiers at regular intervals to earn money for food. Children in rags clawed in the gutters for table scraps cast off by their British hosts. Bethany gave most of the tarts to a small waif and emptied the pennies in her reticule into the skeletal hand of an old man.

Revulsion threatened to erupt in her throat; she swallowed it back. Catching her cloak about her, she pressed on through the windswept squalor of the wharves.

She averted her gaze from the empty print shop below Finley's house. The few tools John Howe hadn't pilfered for his *Gazette* hung like dusty ghosts on the walls. When Miss Abigail invited Bethany to stay for a game of whist, she gladly accepted, to delay the return trip through the desolate scene she'd traversed on her way over.

Finley and Bethany were cordial, although threads of tension spun between them whenever they were together because of the incident at Seastone. Only Miss Abigail's skillful and relentlessly witty conversation drew Finley from his black thoughts and Bethany from her disconsolate mood.

"Are you ready to be thoroughly trounced at whist, Finley?" Miss Abigail chirped.

"Wishful thinking, Abby," he assured her, gallantly holding out chairs for the ladies. Miss Abigail's dainty hands deftly shuffled a well-worn deck of cards.

"Since we're only three, I shall have to deal a dummy hand. . . . Oh, I didn't mean you, Finley," she added impishly. "Ah, I feel lucky today."

"I feel rather cold," Bethany said, glancing at the meager glimmer of coals in the grate. "Shall we build up the fire a bit?"

Miss Abigail and Finley exchanged a glance. "Sorry, dear," Miss Abigail said too lightly. "Shortages, you know."

A blush burned Bethany's cheeks. She felt gauche and ill informed, living in luxury at Seastone while less fortunate people froze. She'd intended to point out also that the light from the single smelly tallow candle on the green baize table was too scant for cardplaying, but she'd already disgraced herself once. "I—I'm sorry," she said hastily. "I could bring some lamp oil and wood if you—"

"I can do without Tanner's charity," Finley grumbled.

Miss Abigail captured him with a hard stare. "Are you certain you're up to being humiliated today?" she inquired sweetly, turning the subject.

He snatched the cards from her. "Just be quiet. I'll deal."

But of course Miss Abigail kept up a steady stream of chatter, although her sharp eyes watched Finley's hands. Bethany hid a smile; Miss Abigail was sure to pounce at the first sign of cheating. Still watching, Miss Abigail nibbled daintily at a mince tart.

"Heaven," she proclaimed, her tongue flicking out at a crumb. "Finley, you really should learn to make mince tarts. Perhaps Dudley would share his secret with you."

"Tory fare," Finley grumbled, although he made short work of one of the tarts. "Too much cinnamon," he added.

"Why, Finley, I thought you liked everything highly spiced. Anyway, you seem to have overcome your aversion."

Bethany watched the two of them with a mixture of amusement and confusion. As always, the barbed remarks flew between them like shrapnel. And yet a subtle difference tinged their banter now. Pure rancor had mellowed to more genial taunts; the sour tang of their opposing political attitudes was sweetened like a drop of honey added to too tart lemonade.

Long ago Miss Abigail had ceased to be a prisoner in the scrupulously tidy chamber behind Finley's parlor. At first the schoolmistress had insisted on staying to keep her patriot host under close watch; Bethany realized a stronger tie bound them now.

They thrived on their daily sniping like hunters with a lust for the kill. Yet beneath the insults and backbiting lay a solid base of mutual respect. With a stab of pain, she admitted to herself that these two shared more than she and Ashton did.

As they played their cards and talked, her interest grew. The pairing was incongruous: Miss Abigail, the perfect lady, the epitome of English loyalism, and Finley, so crude and yet so sensitive, the most passionate of patriots. Unlikely as it seemed, the two had turned their fiery conflict into a mutual warm glow.

Suddenly Bethany saw her teacher in a different light. For the first time she regarded her as a woman, not a walking, talking paragon of etiquette and erudition. Clearly the lady didn't live by the intellectual food of Pope and Milton alone; she was a woman—with a woman's needs.

Needs Bethany understood all too well. She understood them because her own desires had gone so long unfulfilled. Her hand shook as she laid a trump card on the green baize table. Sweet Lord, but she missed Ashton.

A knock sounded at the door and Finley went to answer it. As if summoned by Bethany's ache of longing, Ashton entered the dimly lit parlor. The smell of cold salt air clung to him as he shook a mist of sleet from the shoulders of his greatcoat and hung the garment and his cocked hat on a hook. Tendrils of chestnut hair, damp with moisture, spilled over his brow. Bethany's fingers itched to comb through those wayward curls.

He was flashing that open, comradely smile as he said, "I've got it, Finley, my friend. At last—" He looked up and spied Bethany for the first time, squinting at her through the unsteady candle glow. His smile died along with his next words.

Bethany's heart sank with a resounding thud which sent tremors all through her body. She knew from the sudden dark veil of anger dropping over his face that her presence spoiled the visit he'd obviously been anticipating.

"We were just having a game of whist," Miss Abigail hastily explained. "Will you join us?"

Ashton's eyes flicked from Miss Abigail to Bethany and then to Finley. The older man nodded at an empty chair. His lips tautening with impatience, Ashton took a seat. Briefly his knee brushed Bethany's leg. Simultaneously they recoiled from the accidental touch.

"How is Henry?" he inquired.

"Our son is fine. Your sister is keeping him for the day." She didn't know what made her add, "I'm fine, too."

Ashton's look was long and measuring, touching her in places that ached for the caress of his hands. He seemed to be considering whether or not to rise to the bait she offered. "So I see," he said at last.

"How terribly neatly done," Miss Abigail said brightly. "You've managed to avoid apologizing for not asking after your wife's health and she hasn't even struck you yet."

Ashton's mouth struggled not to break into a grin. The sensual lips lost the battle; his teeth flashed whitely at Miss Abigail. "Bethany will have to practice for years if she's to achieve your . . . er, piquancy, Miss Primrose." He looked at Finley. "You seem to be holding up rather well as the lady's host."

Finley grinned. "Abby's a royal pain, but sometimes I find her zeal for British constitutional ways rather endearing."

"Is Finley always this annoying?" Bethany asked her friend pointedly.

"No . . . usually more so," Miss Abigail replied.

"Still, he's a passable cook. And he's rather handsome . . . in an elderly sort of way, don't you think?"

Oddly, the insults had a relaxing effect as the game started again. But even the cards were against Bethany. Every suit she led was promptly captured by Ashton's unending supply of high cards and low trumps.

He played with utter nonchalance, seeming more interested in discussing the war with Finley. He laid a packet of newspapers in foreign languages on the table. "News of our struggle has reached the ends of the earth," he remarked. He added a French journal to the pile. "It reached France first. The Comte de Vergennes is working with the American Commissioners in Paris."

Bethany started. His French pronunciation was flawless; she'd almost forgotten his education, which he'd ultimately paid for in bondage to her father.

Miss Abigail sniffed. "Meddling Frenchmen."

Finley laughed. "You're one to complain of meddling, Abby. You could write a book on the subject." He looked away from her prim outrage and addressed Ashton. "We'll have our alliance soon."

Bethany felt a prickle of alarm. If the French joined the rebels, the fighting could be drawn out endlessly. There would be no hope of a swift end to the hostilities. And no hope of a reconciliation with Ashton.

"I think we should look to Lord North's Conciliatory Propositions rather than putting our fate in the hands of a foreign power," she assessed.

"Conciliatory Propositions." Ashton's laugh was harsh and mirthless. "Lord North has suddenly become an indulgent injured mother proving affection to her unruly children."

"The proposal is fair, Ashton. All the original points of contention between England and the Colonies have been abolished. Including Parliament's right to tax."

Again came that harsh and mirthless laughter. Ashton had become so sarcastic. "Such things have been abolished on paper, to be sure. But do you think Congress so naive as to forget England's lust for domination and the fact that Parliament is not to be trusted?" Offhandedly he laid a trump over Bethany's queen of hearts, capturing her card.

She wilted inside. There it was again. Trust. Always the lack of it pushed them apart.

As Ashton proceeded to win the game, she noticed his restlessness and the way his eyes kept darting to the stairs leading down to the print shop. She did not mistake the looks he kept sending her, either. He wanted her gone. Stubbornly she laid down her cards, cupped her chin in her hands, and affected a leisurely pose, taking perverse delight in his discomfiture.

"Finley," he said at last, "do you think we could go down to the shop for a while?"

"Oh, la, gentlemen," Miss Abigail chided. "Are you so eager to leave our company?" The merry gleam of conspiracy in her eyes told Bethany that she, too, had noticed Ashton's impatience.

"Or better yet," Bethany suggested with sudden inspiration, "why don't we all go down to the shop?" She imagined she could see the steam of temper rising from her husband.

Miss Abigail rose from the table. "Come along, everyone," she chirped. "I, for one, am anxious to see how Dr. Jay's ink works."

Stunned silence reigned for a tension-filled moment, then Ashton's fist slammed down on the green baize table, scattering playing cards and pastry crumbs.

"Damn it, Finley," he growled, "how could you have let her know about the ink?"

"Nonsense, Ashton," Miss Abigail said. "Finley's been a perfect clam. Unfortuntely, some of your other associates are more talkative. I knew you'd be distributing Dr. Jay's ink a week ago." She wheeled in a flutter of velvet skirts and made her way down to the shop, followed by the others.

"Don't worry," Bethany heard Finley mutter to Ashton. "She's got enough evidence to hang us a dozen times, but she never seems to use what she knows."

Bethany felt Ashton's eyes on her like the touch of a knife point. She paused at the bottom of the steps and turned. "You needn't worry about me, either," she assured them coldly. "For some unknown reason I happen to value your lives."

Beneath the weak and wavering light of a betty lamp, Ashton laid out the contents of his parcel: a number of small vials, whittled quills, and some common paper-stuffs. Dr. James Jay, brother of the patriot statesman John Jay, had perfected an invisible ink and its developing agent.

Ashton tore the endpaper from an old almanac and was about to demonstrate the ink when sounds of a disturbance outside filtered into the print shop. Finley hurried to the window.

"Damn," he said, wiping the frosty glass with the side of his fist. "Looks like another lottery. I'd best go, since my name's in the hat."

Miss Abigail followed him. Bethany stared after them in confusion.

"A lottery?" she inquired.

Ashton shook his head, regarding her as if she were a spoiled child. "I guess you wouldn't know about such things," he mused, "ensconced with little Henry at Seastone, Dorian Tanner seeing to your every need and whim."

She bristled at his taunt. "I asked a simple question, Ashton."

"The answer's not agreeable, pet. In case you haven't noticed, there's a serious fuel shortage in Newport. The wood purveyors have been scared out of the bay by the British patrol. In order to keep from freezing, the people have been dismantling whole houses to use as fuel. They've agreed to draw lots to see whose house will be the next to burn."

Bethany felt a horrified flush climb to her cheeks. "I . . . I didn't know."

He drilled a hard sapphire gaze at her. "Tanner's kept you well insulated." His sigh came as a puff of frozen air. "I suppose I should thank him for that. Henry won't know the privation most people suffer." He studied her for a long, thoughtful moment, then scratched a quill across the paper in front of him. Bethany's attention was arrested by the large, firm hand gripping the quill, her senses snared by the warmth emanating from his body and the scent she recognized as uniquely Ashton's. His pen left no mark. He handed the page to her.

"Looks like an ordinary sheet of paper, doesn't it?" he asked.

She nodded. Then, following his instructions, Bethany treated the paper with the tangy-scented developing agent. Slowly the message appeared. At first she was too fascinated by the process to take in the words, but after a moment she read: *Love, why do we do this to each other?*

Slowly she raised her eyes to Ashton, his written question filling her with pain, regret, and longing. He stared at her intently, waiting for an answer. She forced her gaze not to waver.

"Because you're so committed to your damned cause that you've ceased to care about anything else. Because I'm still not convinced you weren't at Seastone the night my father died."

"God," he said, his voice gruff with anger and something else that made her go suddenly hot. "God. How can you look so beautiful even as you accuse me?"

As one, they moved together. Ashton's mouth was so close she could almost taste the warm honey of his kiss. His hands were but a hair's breadth from her own. But the distance might as well have been a furlong. For folded within physical desire were hurdles of distrust and misunderstanding, of stubborn pride and misplaced loyalty. The moment of hesitation stretched long, and then they moved apart.

"I'm going out to see how the lottery's coming," Ashton said.

Her stomach in knots, Bethany followed him. He paused in the dooryard, setting his hands on his hips and staring at Miss Abigail's laundry, which hung in geometric precision on a line stretched between two trees.

Bethany stopped and studied the ground, where crocuses had pushed through a patch of melting snow. Silently she prayed Ashton didn't know the significance of the laundry. Next to a black petticoat were pinned four handkerchiefs; Miss Abigail used it to tell her British associates at which bay inlet a patriot courier would arrive that night.

Ashton's muttered curse told her he was aware of Miss Abigail's code. He yanked two of the handkerchiefs from the line and cast them to the ground.

"Finley ought to be more careful," he grumbled, leaving the yard.

Bethany considered restoring the handkerchiefs, but held back. For some reason, she didn't want to give the British a chance to capture and sentence another spy.

Two blocks away they found a little group of people pressed around a barrel set on end. The drab garments of citizens contrasted with the bright scarlet coats of nearby soldiers. The Redcoats were leery of gatherings of any sort, ready to spring forth and subdue the first sign of an uprising.

Bethany stopped short behind Ashton. They didn't have to ask whose home was to be sacrificed for firewood. Goody Haas's rusty, distressed cry rose sharply above the babble of the crowd.

Incensed, Bethany pushed her way toward Goody, aware of disapproving eyes. Peggy Lillibridge pointedly swept her skirts aside to give Bethany a wide berth. The message was clear. Bethany was a Tory and not welcome here.

Feeling isolated yet still determined, she found Goody Haas surrounded by her nephew and his family. Bethany wrapped her arms around the frail, musty-smelling frame.

"Goody," she said, "you can't let them take your home. 'Tis not right!"

The woman looked old—old and lonely. Her eyes were bright with tears which runneled into the creases of her lined face.

"Right," she grated. "Who's t' say what's right anymore?" But the sharp, ancient eyes didn't accuse. "I was born in that little house in Spring Street. Raised my younger brothers and sisters and their young'uns after that. I guess that house is done servin' me. But Pieter and his wife . . ." Goody looked apologetically at her nephew.

"No . . ." Bethany felt a sudden crash of loss for Goody.

"I agreed t' the lottery, girl. This last year I've warmed myself at fires fueled by furniture and houses of others. Now I reckon I've a turn t' go."

"You can come to Seastone with me, Goody. All of you," Bethany said with sudden decision. "I've plenty of room."

Goody shook her head. "I can't do that, girl. Nothin' against y', of course, but . . ." The bright, tearful eyes darted to the lounging Redcoats. Bethany looked at Goody, then the soldiers, and then at Pieter Haas, who leaned on his good leg and held his wife tenderly while their three children clung to her skirts.

A hard lump formed in Bethany's throat. These people would sooner freeze than cast their lots with a Loyalist who housed a British officer.

Her pained gaze strayed to Ashton. She knew better than to expect any help from him, yet her eyes were drawn to his impassive face all the same. He regarded her steadily and she imagined he was thinking: *See? Do you see what your loyalty has cost you?*

Finley Piper moved his gangling form forward. Miss Abigail clung tenaciously to his arm, her face drawn.

"I've just spoken with the chairman of the lottery," he told Goody in a low voice. "They'll be taking my house and the print shop instead. Go on home, Goody." Already the relieved crowd was beginning to disperse.

"Now, Finley, y' can't do that—" Goody began.

" 'Tis done," he said wearily. "There's nothing here for me anymore. . . . I've a widowed brother in Tiverton who has a farm. He'll take me in." Finley effected a half grin. "Don't guess I'm too old to learn a new trade."

Goody and her family were effusive in their thanks; Finley colored visibly at their words of gratitude. Moments later, everyone was gone save Finley, Miss Abigail, Ashton and Bethany.

"You did a generous thing, Finley," Bethany told him.

He waved his hand dismissively. "I'm through with Newport. The town's spent and so am I. The press is shut down; I've not done a lick of honest work in months. 'Tis time I moved on." He glanced at Miss Abigail. "I imagine you'll want to move to Seastone to be among your own kind."

"Such nonsense, Finley," Miss Abigail said briskly. "I'll not let this be your excuse to unburden yourself of me. I demand that you take me to Tiverton with you."

Bethany watched as astonishment chased across Finley's face, followed by a look of pure pleasure. She glanced at Ashton, who stood aloof, grinning as if aware of a joke no one else understood.

Finley and Miss Abigail delved immediately into an animated, insult-laden argument, gesturing and talking even as they moved together down the street toward Finley's house. Before their voices faded, Bethany heard Finley grumble, "I don't know why you're so hell-bent on coming with me."

Miss Abigail pointed her nose high in the air. "I'll tell you on the way to Tiverton, beef-wit."

Bethany looked at Ashton, frowning at his amused and indulgent smile. "I don't understand it either," she said, setting her hands on her hips.

Ashton's laughter rippled to her ears. " 'Tis clear as sunshine, pet," he said. "She loves the man."

"She—" Bethany's mouth snapped shut. She'd been about to deny the preposterous suggestion, but suddenly all she'd observed between Finley and Miss Abigail fell into place like pieces of an interlocking puzzle. The many small, caring gestures sandwiched between cutting remarks, the glances of affection veiled behind challenging stares, the depth of true feeling hidden by stubborn pride.

She raised wonder-filled eyes to Ashton. "You're right," she breathed. "You're absolutely right." The idea of Finley and Miss Abigail going off together to forge a new life founded on love filled Bethany with happiness. Two such fine people deserved the bliss they were sure to find.

But beneath her happiness lurked an utterly disagreeable feeling, like the sensation of finding a worm in a ripe apple. Envy suffused her, seeping like poison through her happy thoughts. Finley and Miss Abigail faced a future bright with promise despite overwhelming hardship. She and Ashton had only bitter disagreements to look forward to.

"I expect," he said, cutting into her guilt-ridden thoughts, "they'll want to leave early tomorrow. Finley pretends to have no attachment to his house and print shop, but I doubt he'll want to stay around to watch the melancholy business of dismantling the place."

Bethany nodded. "I'll be around to see them off."

He started up the street. "Come on, pet. I'll see you home."

The send-off to Tiverton by way of a ferry across the Sakonnet River was a tribute to Finley Piper's popularity. Only as she stood holding the baby, Ashton silent and brooding at her side, did Bethany realize how many friends Finley had.

She'd known him for years, yet she'd never really known him at all. Mentally she flayed herself for having seen Finley as an ordinary man, no more deserving of her attention than a common sailor ambling about Long Wharf.

A sharp wind ruffled the winter-gray waters between Aquidneck's eastern shore and Tiverton on the mainland. Bethany caught Ashton watching her and knew he'd seen the guilty way she was looking at Finley. Lowering her eyes, she rubbed her chin thoughtfully over little Henry's forehead.

"I've been unfair to Finley," she admitted thickly.

She expected sarcastic and smug agreement from Ashton. Instead, astoundingly, he rested his arm across her shoulders. His touch felt warm and good and right, and she wondered how she'd managed so long without his affection. And then she wondered how she would survive without his touch through the weeks and months and—oh, God—the years to come.

Mentally recoiling from the painful thoughts, she directed her gaze again at Finley. "He was an important citizen of Newport," she commented.

"He's still an important friend to me," Ashton said.

The printer was doing his best to grin, accepting the backslapping of the townsmen and the funny-sad comments about learning to farm. But his eyes, the eyes of a man who had lost everything, kept straying to the white and brick spires of Newport.

Just when Bethany was certain Finley would break down and weep for all he'd lost, Miss Abigail placed her hand on his arm and murmured something. All mournfulness drained from his face and he smiled, lines of affection replacing those of sadness. The eyes lost years of age as they beheld the pretty, perfectly calm little woman in a gaze of open adoration.

Ashton's hand tightened on Bethany's shoulder. "See, love? They'll be fine."

She eyed the luggage at their feet. Two valises, a sack of rags, and Miss Abigail's books. "But they have so little, Ashton. How will they ever—"

He squeezed her shoulder again, and together they looked at the happy, frightened couple. "They've got the only thing they need," he reminded her.

She stiffened, wondering if Ashton meant for his comment and the unspoken part of it to hurt so much. The message was clear: Finley and Abigail knew what mattered in life, and she didn't. She lived in scandalous luxury, her every material need fulfilled by agreeable servants, yet she knew from recent disgruntled sessions in front of the looking glass that she lacked the glow she observed now in Miss Abigail's flawless cheeks. Bethany's eyes held none of the anticipatory sparkle of her former teacher's.

Ashton took the baby from her. "Come on. 'Tis time we said our good-byes."

Nothing could have prepared Bethany for the painful wrench she experienced as she was folded into Miss Abigail's slim, strong arms and engulfed by the lady's clean barley-water scent. At some point in the past two years Miss Abigail had been transformed from the teacher Bethany respected and admired to the friend she deeply loved.

"I thought," Bethany choked, "that when I left New York, all I had left of you was a scandalously excellent education. But since then you've given me so much more, Miss Abigail."

"Have I?" The sea-gray eyes narrowed in false severity. "Then why, pray, have I not charged you a *sou* of tuition? Tut, tut." The retort wasn't quite as crisp as usual. "You endow me with many more powers than I possess." She stepped back and regarded Bethany, her eyes blinking rapidly against a suspicious sheen of brightness.

" 'Tis you who have changed," she explained. "When I sent you off from New York, you were adept at declining Latin nouns and accepting invitations. But no formal schooling could have taught you to decline the stirrings of your heart or accept the reponsibility of your own life." The tiny gloved hands clasped Bethany's. "Look at you, my dear. See how you've changed, how you've grown. My awkward, outspoken student has become a woman, a wife—"

"A sometimes wife," Bethany said glumly. Her eyes shifted to Ashton, who was talking with Finley and jiggling the baby on his hip.

"—and a mother," Miss Abigail continued. "Just because you've chosen not to live with Ashton doesn't mean you're any less his wife."

"The choice was not my own to make. There's so much between us—"

"That you *will* settle," Miss Abigail said firmly.

"But he doesn't love me."

"He may not speak his love aloud, 'tis true. He keeps it safely locked within him like the very fragile and precious thing love is. 'Tis up to you to find your way into his heart. But beware, my friend. A man's heart is a dangerous place for a woman to dwell." She glanced meaningfully at Finley. "Now, kiss me quickly and let me go, or I shall never forgive you for causing me to disgrace myself by weeping in public."

Bethany had no such qualms about an open display of emotion. She cried as she embraced Miss Abigail and watched her teacher hug little Henry, jabbering as she always did in the baby talk that only the child seemed to understand. Finally, while Miss Abigail and Ashton exchanged a few words, Bethany hugged Finley Piper, the man she had once misunderstood, once disliked, and now respected. Over Finley's shoulder she watched Miss Abigail and Ashton. The lady said something that brought a thunderstruck look to Ashton's face. He responded—or protested—but Miss Abigail spoke again. Ashton looked as if the lady had driven an iron fist into his stomach. His expression did not change as he walked to Bethany. Henry yawned and rested his head on Ashton's chest.

Bethany sagged against Ashton as she watched the ferry push off for Tiverton.

Waves and good wishes sent the departing couple on their way. Breakers scooped the small craft out to sea, and the winter wind puffed the sails taut.

"Ready to go?" Ashton murmured, his breath stirring the hair very close to her ear.

She nodded and they drove southward in her chaise. The baby, lulled by the clip-clop of the horse's hoofs and the rhythmic creaking of the cart, slept comfortably on the board behind them.

"Ashton?"

He turned to her. "What is it?"

"What was it Miss Abigail said to you before they left? You looked so . . . so strange just after she spoke."

He darted his gaze quickly back to the rutted, muddy road. Miss Primrose's words were stamped on his brain: *Let yourself love her, Ashton. She needs you so.* He couldn't tell Bethany that. Couldn't tell her, because he dared not bare his feelings like that. And because it would be so easy, so damnably easy, to let himself love her.

He'd come close once, long ago, just after he'd discovered Henry was his child. But he'd returned to Seastone to find their house burned, to face Bethany, who accused him of having orchestrated the raid, all her faith in him gone.

"Ashton?" she prompted softly.

He leaned his wrists on his knees, holding the reins loosely. " 'Twas nothing," he said, chancing a quick look at her. God, how could that face manage to look so lovely and so hurt at the same time?

"Don't lie to me, Ashton," she pleaded. "If you don't wish to share what Miss Abigail said, just say so."

"I'm just trying to make sense of it, Bethany."

He watched her eyes fill with tears, and something cold twisted like a frigid gust of wind through his gut. "We always hurt each other, don't we?" he asked. "I wonder why that is."

She dashed her tears away and faced him levelly. "Think about it, Ashton. If we didn't care, it wouldn't hurt."

Chapter 20

On Henry Winslow Markham's second birthday, Bethany felt as nervous as a new bride. Surveying the east garden, with its springtime decor of Persian lilacs, freckled foxglove, and bright bursts of yellow forsythia, she shook her head, suddenly realizing the irony of the comparison.

There hadn't been time for nerves at her wedding. The ceremony, such as it was, had consisted of a hasty signing of papers at Bristol.

But she had had days to ponder the present celebration. She'd wanted to keep the party small, comprised only of little Henry's family and perhaps Goody Haas and some of the children from the school. But Dorian and her mother had insisted on a full-blown fete designed to impress the ranking British officers and socially prominent Tories rather than a two-year-old boy.

The thought of the placid garden overrun with brass-encrusted Redcoats and Tories was not the cause of her nervousness. Bethany had faced enough scorn and scandal to harden her sensibilities to the prying looks and finely honed remarks she was sure to garner from such company. Only one person's presence could ignite her nerves so that her hands shook and her throat went dry and her stomach disdained all save a sip of weak tea made from the stale leaves her mother insisted on hoarding.

Ashton would be at the party.

Dorian had thought of every excuse to keep her husband away, but to no avail. Patriot or not, Bethany had argued, Ashton was the boy's father and had a right to be present.

"You look," said a pleasant male voice, "like you're about to stand trial."

Startled, Bethany jumped, then turned as a broad grin spread across her face. She stretched out her arms. "Harry." They embraced warmly. Her own troubles fled as her hands encountered the worn fabric of her brother's coat and her eyes took in his thinness. He was her brother, yet she had the odd sensation of being in the company of a stranger, someone she used to know but no longer recognized.

"I wasn't sure you'd be able to come."

"Alas, I considered the crossing too dangerous for Felicia and Margaret, but I managed to find a ferryman willing to slip the British patrol and the *chevaux de frise* in the bay." He grinned ironically. "Imagine that—having to sneak through enemy lines just to attend a birthday party."

She laughed. In a nearby lilac bush a warbler raised its voice in trills of song. "Go on, Harry; the patrol isn't that bad. The ships are in the bay to protect, not to harass innocent people."

He clicked his tongue. "Still the tenacious little Tory, aren't you, Beth?"

She sighed, still bothered by her brother's world-weary look. "The war is almost three years old, Harry. I'm so tired of the killing I'm almost to the point where I no longer care who wins. But," she added stubbornly, "I should like to remain an Englishwoman."

Despite the changes in Harry, his eyes were still mirrors of her own. He regarded her with critical fondness. "I daresay there's little about you that resembles an Englishwoman. Here you are living independently, conducting a school for the common folk . . . I stopped in the stables to see Justice Richmond, and he told me all you've done."

She glanced away. "I've done only what circumstances have forced me to do. When the British quell your rebellion, I expect my life to be more normal."

"Not likely," Harry said cheerfully. "Not now that a French fleet is due to set sail any day. And 'tis a good bet they'll visit Newport first."

She took a moment to assimilate the news. Already the conflict involved Englishmen and Americans and Germans and Indians. The presence of French forces would blow the conflict into global proportions.

But at the moment Bethany had little time to ponder the implications of the French alliance. Carrie Markham came running into the garden, her ripe figure clad in a provocatively cut dress. No doubt the woman intended to exercise her considerable charms on some of the officers.

"You'd best get back up to the house, ma'am," Carrie said, sparing only a nod for Harry. "Little Henry is putting up a fuss about getting dressed, and the guests have begun arriving."

"Oh." Nervousness beat anew within Bethany like the relentless flicker of a bee's wings.

Harry chuckled. "Come, sister, 'tis only a birthday party."

"That's what I keep telling myself. But I can't help it, Harry." She twined her fingers together. "Ashton will be here."

Carrie's derisive snort spoke eloquently of her opinion of her brother. She went back to the house, patting her bright red ringlets and plucking at the lace of her décolletage.

"He's the lad's father, after all," Harry said.

"He and Dorian are not on the best of terms."

"The damned Redcoat's driven him away from his wife and child, after all."

Bethany shook her head. " 'Twas I who did not want to live with Ashton. That's as much my doing as Dorian's."

Harry leveled a sad look at her. "You still insist on believing he planned the raid and caused Father's death. The old man's heart failed him; 'twas none of Ashton's doing. Good God, the man's your husband."

Bethany stared at her brother. "We have different values, Harry. I cannot blindly accept what Ashton did just because he is my husband." With that, she hurried to the house.

And yet some errant, undisciplined sentiment seized her when, a short time later, Ashton strode into the garden. His unsmiling face was as rugged and elemental as Aquidneck's craggy shores. A light breeze tossed his chestnut hair into a mane that seemed to beg for her fingers to twine themselves into the gleaming strands. In spite of herself, Bethany let her eye caress the lean, strong body her arms longed to embrace.

Their gazes collided and held for a tense moment. Bethany managed to catch her gasp of yearning before the sound escaped her lips. Ashton turned away abruptly, as if eager to seek the less volatile company of his son.

Lillian's friends flitted here and there, their ears cocked and eyes darting for morsels of gossip to spread about the deliciously unorthodox situation at Seastone. British officers in dress uniform availed themselves freely of contraband Jamaica water. They raised toasts to the king and the Empire, making certain Ashton or Harry was in earshot. The schoolchildren worked havoc in the garden and attacked the array of delectable foods spread on tables on the verandah.

Henry Winslow Markham celebrated his second birthday with a typical mingling of childish jubilation and temper tantrums. Dressed like a fashion baby in figured blue Manchester velvet and at least half his weight in lace, he careened after the children on chubby legs and soiled his finery with berry stains and sticky sweetmeats.

When Bethany brought him to the verandah to receive his birthday presents, he protested volubly until he understood the purpose of leaving his play. As the toys piled up in front of him, he laughed and crowed for more.

Bethany was just about to explain that the supply of gifts was exhausted when Ashton approached. The handsome cut of his somewhat worn morning coat was muddy and fluffed with white fur. In his arms he held a perfectly adorable and utterly unruly puppy, a brown and white spaniel.

Ignoring the disdainful audience assembled on the verandah, Ashton hunkered down beside his son, allowing his squirming bundle to roam free. "I've been calling the dog Liberty," he told Henry gravely. As the boy shrieked with delight and scrambled after the dog, Bethany caught her breath and her eyes began to fill.

"Ashton," she said in a low voice, "he's just like Gladstone."

He grinned with pleasure at Henry's obvious delight. "Not quite," he amended. "He's a she."

The puppy was tearing the lace at Henry's sleeve with tiny white teeth. Henry giggled and allowed the dog to make off with a mouthful of the stuff.

"Bethany, can't you see the boy's clothes are going to be ruined?" Dorian's question held an unspoken command.

"Let him have a little fun, Tanner," Ashton said. Bethany heard a thread of anger in his voice and silently prayed the men would not indulge the suddenly interested audience with a scene.

"I don't begrudge the child his fun," Dorian responded tautly. "However, I don't think my guests are interested in seeing that—that disagreeable little beast destroy the child's garments." He stalked away and found Justice Richmond, who had been pressed into service serving up rum punch for the officers. "You! Take the dog down to the kennels."

Bethany saw Ashton start forward, fury on his face. She ran to him and placed her hand on his sleeve. "Please, Ashton," she said, "let him have his way—just for the moment."

"Pardon me," he snapped. "Far be it for me to make your guests uncomfortable."

Henry set up a resounding wail as Justice took the puppy away. Ashton stared at Bethany, and she saw the storm of temper in his eyes. She could understand that rage. He had just been publicly countermanded by a hated enemy. All Newport knew he'd been cast off by his wife and that his son's future was controlled by Dorian Tanner.

Glancing down at his clenched fists, she knew he longed to vent his fury on Dorian's too handsome face.

Desperately she said, "He'd love for you to hit him, Ashton, don't you see? Because then he'd have a perfect excuse to arrest you."

"She's right, my friend," Harry said, joining them. He grinned. "Why don't you best him in a way no one can fault—on the racing green? The contests are about to begin."

Relief dropped a thankful mantle around Bethany. Ashton's hands relaxed. With a final bitter look at her, he turned and led the way down to the racing green, a track bordered by a sandy beach. Bethany scooped up her howling son and followed the eager company.

No celebration in Newport was complete without a horse race. Even in these lean times, Seastone's stables remained populated with champion strains begun years ago by Roger Markham, nurtured years later by Ashton himself, and now sustained by Bethany and Justice Richmond.

Gentlemen who had been Sinclair Winslow's rivals during better days were eager to see if Sinclair's daughter and a manumitted slave had been able to keep the quality of the stables up to its former excellence.

The British officers were in their glory on the beach-edged racing green. Most were landed gentlemen disgruntled at having been uprooted to endure the barbaric conditions in the Colonies. Their buff-clad legs enclosed the flanks of their horses.

Captain Tanner began the festivities with a breathtaking display atop Corsair. The midnight stallion had become his favorite mount. Bethany hazarded a glance at Ashton. Predictably, his mouth was drawn into a taut line of repressed anger. She wished she hadn't bothered to look.

"The bastard's ruining Corsair's mouth," he gritted, his fingers curling around the rail at the edge of the green.

It was true; Dorian sawed forcibly on the reins in order to get the stallion to perform his flashy carnival tricks.

Bethany had a sudden image of Ashton as he'd been ten years ago: a golden, vibrant youth, awestruck as everyone at Seastone had been on the occasion of Corsair's birth. They'd hoped for a stallion; they'd hoped the Thoroughbred would be black like his sire and possessed of his dam's competitive spirit. Corsair's subsequent triumphs had surpassed their ambitions.

Much of the stallion's greatness was due to Ashton's gentle and patient handling. Now Corsair, at the end of his triumphant career, was being forced to perform like a circus pony, doing sly tricks far beneath his blooded dignity. Bethany ached for the man who had trained the stallion.

"He . . . Dorian doesn't do this often," she said.

"More's the pity," Ashton replied, scowling. "If I hadn't trained the beast to be so damned obedient, perhaps Tanner would break his fool neck." He sat down on a stone bench, taking little Henry into his lap.

Mercifully, Dorian's cocky display ended. He accepted the huzzahs of the onlookers and then the racing began. One of Justice Richmond's myriad talents happened to be riding. The applause became less appreciative and more polite each time he jockeyed one of Seastone's horses to victory.

Dorian surveyed the company with a glittering grin. "There we have it. Our stables reign supreme." The grin broadened. "But I've saved the best for last." He walked over to a beautiful sorrel stallion called Blunderbuss and took the reins from Justice Richmond. "I'll do the honors myself."

Dorian turned back and fixed an imperious gaze on Ashton, who met his eyes unflinchingly. "Care to race me, Markham? We could place a little wager on the outcome, eh?"

Bethany looked uncomfortably from one man to the other. When Ashton placed Henry in her arms, she knew her husband would accept the challenge. Too nervous to watch the baby, she handed him to Lillian, who looked in distress at the boy's soiled clothing, but said nothing.

Ashton approached Dorian. Together, the pair made a vivid contrast. The officer was resplendent in dress uniform, his wig perfectly sculptured, his face a falsely genial, handsome mask. Standing inches taller, Ashton looked raffish and unkempt in his simple garb. A spring breeze ruffled his careless hairstyle. No pretended civility dwelled in his features; animosity shone bright in his eyes.

"What sort of wager did you have in mind, Tanner?" he asked.

" 'Tis obvious you've not the means for a monetary bet," Dorian ventured. "Perhaps a forfeit, then?"

"I've little enough to forfeit."

"We'll see about that. You have, Markham, a rather annoying habit of coming 'round Seastone. I don't like that; I don't like you. Your visits upset Bethany and confuse the child. I propose that, should you lose, you'll agree to stay away from Bethany and the boy. Permanently."

Bethany saw her own tension mirrored in Ashton's stony face and in the sudden tautness of his shoulders. If Ashton lost the race, he'd forfeit his right to see Henry—and her. She pressed her fingers to her mouth, straining against the impulse to beg her husband not to be goaded into this cold-blooded proposal.

"And if I best you?" Ashton's voice was expressionless.

Dorian shrugged. "Name your price, Markham."

Bethany noticed a tiny, satisfied curl at the corners of Ashton's mouth. He began extracting his muscular arms from his morning coat. "If I win, Tanner, you give me the horse of my choice."

Dorian looked momentarily nonplussed. "The horses aren't mine to give. They belong to your son."

"Not Corsair. Bethany told me you'd commandeered the stallion for your own mount."

The Redcoat's head snapped up. "I . . ." He glanced over at Blunderbuss, whose coat gleamed like rich molasses in the afternoon sun. The stallion pawed the ground impatiently and arched his well-shaped neck toward the end of the green. Dorian smiled, suddenly exuding confidence. Bethany knew exactly what he was thinking. The swift four-year-old Blunderbuss was without equal on Aquidneck Island.

"Done!" Dorian said loudly, and clasped Ashton's hand briefly to seal the bargain. "Now, have you settled on a mount?"

"I'll ride Corsair," Ashton said without hesitation.

This brought Bethany to her feet and she hastened to his side. "Ashton," she pleaded, placing her hand on his arm. "Corsair is over ten years old; he can't possibly—"

He shot a bulletlike gaze at her. "Is it really the horse you doubt, Bethany? Or is it me?" His laugh was brittle. "Why should the outcome bother you? If I lose, you'll get what you've been wanting all along."

"Ashton, I don't want to lose you. I want you to be a part of Henry's life." *Oh, God, in spite of everything, I still want you in my life.*

The crowd buzzed madly as Ashton tossed his coat to the grass and approached Corsair. The stallion whickered softly as he stroked the muscled arch of his neck and murmured like a lover against the buffed-velvet muzzle. The crowd silenced as if aware of the solemnity of the communion.

Bethany saw with tides of relief that, despite the passage of time, the bond between Ashton and the stallion he'd raised was still strong. Then dismay pushed that feeling aside. While Corsair stood calmly at the starting line, Blunderbuss pawed the ground and strained at the bit.

Nervousness pounded like hoofbeats through Bethany as she went to the end of the green, stationing herself at the finish line.

One of the British officers set off the competition with a single thunderous pistol shot.

The two men sat low on their mounts, leaning over straining necks as the beasts ran. Bethany's eyes were fastened on Ashton. She thought she saw his lips moving and imagined him speaking to the stallion with gentle urging. A sudden memory assaulted her. During the early days of their marriage, Ashton's whispering voice had compelled her, many times, to do his bidding. Snatching her mind from the disquieting thought, she focused again on the race.

The horses ran abreast, heads and flattened ears even. Bethany nearly forgot to draw breath as she watched. The sorrel nosed ahead. Youth and a competitive spirit that nearly matched Corsair's gave Blunderbuss a distinct advantage. Bethany bit into her lower lip until it hurt. The sorrel's entire head was beyond the black's.

She crumpled inside with disappointment and started to turn away, loath to witness the defeat of Ashton and the magnificent stallion.

But as she turned, incredulous murmurs rose from the onlookers. Hope rose in her throat as she whirled back.

There were two things she had underestimated in this contest: Ashton's skill and Corsair's heart. This trait had characterized the stallion's career. Years ago Ashton had explained it to her. Racing hurts, he'd told her, but Corsair had always had the ability to get past pain and any temptation to slow down. He would win even if he must suffer in the process.

In a blur of movement horse and rider seemed to meld and become one awesome force of unearthly speed. Defying nature and logic, Corsair's hoofs appeared to leave the ground. The long, strong body with its skillful burden stretched to its limit, surging half a length in front of the sorrel, crossing the finish line with the grace of a mythical beast.

The cheering was sparse. Bethany's gleeful laughter mingled only with Harry's clapping and Justice Richmond's satisfied basso shout of approval.

"There be magic in that horse," the stockman stated.

"Either that or the rider's a wizard," Harry added, slapping Richmond on the back. Justice went to cool out the lathered, triumphant stallion.

The company of disgruntled officers and offended Tories gaped at the unplanned spectacle that would become fodder for the gossip mills for weeks to come.

Bethany Winslow Markham, long admired for favoring her Loyalist principles over sentiment for her patriot husband, ran like a girl across the end of the green. In a swirl of skirts, slim ankles, and musical laughter, she hurled herself headlong into her husband's arms.

Even the sternest cynic present could not fail to be moved by the sweet abandon with which the handsome young couple embraced in the shadow of the dark horse that had been a champion and was now a legend.

Ashton sat surrounded by June sunshine, swishing sea grasses, and hissing waves. The gulls were out in force, screaming and diving for prey amid the froth-topped blue waves. The cove had been a place of wonder and solitude for the boy he had been. Now it was a place of safety. The overinquisitive British patrol had not yet discovered the remote hideaway.

With relief and wistfulness, he reread a communiqúe in French from the subterfuge firm of Hortalez et Cie.

Now that the alliance was in place, he would no longer be involved in supplying the patriots with Lavoisier's powerful explosives. The company had been dissolved; the French would now supply the rebels openly.

He would miss dealing with his bright-eyed, cherubic French contact. Lamoral, as Ashton knew him, accepted requisitions for gunpowder with the ease and nonchalance of a banker taking an order for bread.

Now Ashton had another project to occupy him, one equally dangerous and challenging.

Since he'd won Corsair two months earlier, he'd decided to acquire and train horses for the Continental Cavalry. Preposterous, the committeemen had told him. Certain suicide. He'd be conducting his subversive business right under the noses of the Redcoats, stealing their horses and training farm nags and shipping the animals off on a dangerous crossing to rebel-held Providence.

But Ashton had the confidence to undertake the task. He also had this well-hidden cove. And he had Gaylord Parson's Middletown farm, so degenerated by neglect that the British hadn't bothered to occupy the place. Those three strokes of fortune promised tonight's success.

Behind him, corraled in a pen thrown together with driftwood, were the first four cavalry horses. He glanced at the beasts with a shake of his head.

A few years ago he would have snorted at the idea of placing soldiers on such beasts. One was an overfed country dobbin, the next a mongrel bay which, with its elongated muzzle and ears, could easily be mistaken for a mule. The third horse was a swaybacked nag with a sweet temper and a fondness for Russian thistle. The last illicit mount had been the most dangerous to acquire and showed the most promise. Ashton had stolen an officer's gelding from the yard behind Banister House. Corsair lorded over the motley herd, and Ashton felt a familiar thrill of pleasure as he regarded the beast.

There was more to his pleasure than the simple satisfaction of having bested Dorian Tanner. Because in the moment following the race, Ashton had held Bethany in his arms. His throat tightened as he recalled the feel of her pliant body against his, the musical trill of her laughter in his ears, the heady jasmine fragrance of her sun-warmed hair.

In that moment he had been stricken by a longing so intense it took his breath away. It was a moment of healing. The wall of animosity between them had developed a chink.

But then, as if by mutual agreement, they had broken the embrace. Reality became a stiff mortar in the wall. Bethany's guard went up and Ashton's spirits went down. He hadn't seen his wife since.

The wistful thought froze within him as he noticed a figure on a precipice high above the beach.

Bethany. Sitting beautifully on her dun-colored mare, she angled the horse down the narrow path to the cove. Watching her, Ashton felt a range of emotions that left him dizzy. The afternoon light streaked through her hair, gilding tresses worn loose, like a schoolgirl's. Longing leaped within him, as familiar as a nagging ache.

And yet the fact that she was here turned that feeling to a cold stone of bitterness. He had schooled his face into an expressionless mask by the time she reached him.

Or so he thought. There must have been a telling gleam of emotion in his eyes, for she said, "You look as if the world is chasing at your heels, Ashton."

He felt an unbidden smile tugging at the corners of his mouth.

"You said those very words to me," she continued. "Three years ago it was, on a summer day just like this." She slipped from the saddle and tossed the reins around a low bush. She plucked a wild rose and approached him, her hips swaying gently with unpracticed seductiveness. Ashton's fingers contracted, forming fists at his sides. Bethany touched him lightly on the chest with the rose.

"You were right, Ashton. The world *was* chasing at my heels that day. My parents were urging me to find a proper husband and I was fighting them." She sighed. He had never known a sigh could be so pretty. "I knew nothing back then; only that I did not want to live as my parents commanded."

"And now?" he inquired, barely recognizing his own voice in that rasping, emotion-laden query.

"Now I know much of life." She lifted her eyes to his.

Those sun-shot hazel depths couched a deep melancholy. "And of love . . . and betrayal," she added.

Her words tore at Ashton's heart. Suddenly he saw how much she'd changed. "I danced with you that day," he said, wishing he could peel back the years and the layers of hurt.

"I don't think our troubles can be danced away any longer, Ashton."

"I also kissed you."

"And I fell in love with you."

The next moment she was in his arms. He kissed her face and hair, reveling in her nearness. The delicate petals of the wild rose were crushed between their straining bodies. Then both the flower and their clothing fell to the sand, and in the next hour Ashton forgot his bitterness as he made love to his wife. He was amazed at how imperfect his memory was. He remembered her flesh was soft, but had forgotten its warmth, its heady fragrance. He remembered the glorious color of her hair, but had forgotten its silky texture. He remembered the feel of her arms and legs closed around him but had forgotten the tide of emotions the embrace evoked. Desperate hunger quickened within him when he felt her shudder. Her breath came in short gasps that almost sounded like sobs.

"God," he whispered, cradling her gently. "What happened to us, Bethany?"

A sudden heaviness seemed to engulf her. Trembling slightly, she extracted herself from his embrace and slowly dressed while he did likewise. She looked at the four horses, ignoring his question.

"Are they the ones bound for the Continental Cavalry, then?" she asked. "Not a very impressive lot, Ashton. Far beneath your usual standards."

"I had little time to—" He snapped his mouth shut. Was he actually going to discuss the matter with her? "How did you know?" he demanded.

She didn't flinch, but a flicker in her eyes sent guilt seeping through him. "Have you forgotten," she asked softly, "that I was schooled in subterfuge by Miss Abigail? I admit I'll never attain her finesse, but I have assimilated a few of her techniques. Is that Lieutenant Yarrow's gelding?"

He could only nod, and wonder where she'd gotten her damnably accurate information.

"Really, Ashton, did you have to take Michael Yarrow's horse? His poisonous temper has become legend. He nearly throttled a subaltern when he discovered the theft."

"As long as he attacks only his own."

She gazed out at the bay. "I expect you're waiting for dark so the transports can slip past the frigates. My guess is nine o'clock would be an opportune time. You *have* memorized the patrol's schedule, haven't you, Ashton?"

Before he could stop himself, he grabbed her by the arms and his fingers curled into her soft flesh. "Damn it, Bethany, what sort of game are you playing? Have you become a cat that toys with its prey before killing it? Why don't you just call for Tanner immediately and have done with your little amusement?"

"Is that what you think?" she asked, glancing pointedly at his hard-gripping fingers. "Ashton, Lieutenant Yarrow's horse isn't worth your life to me. I have no intention of informing on you."

His grip relaxed a little. "Then why have you come here?"

"I've been coming here every day since I learned you'd be supplying horses to the rebels. I knew you'd chose this cove because so few are aware of it."

"Tanner is," he reminded her unpleasantly. "You brought him here during your flirtation with him three years ago." He dropped his hands from her shoulders.

A stricken look flitted across her face. "I never brought Dorian here. I only told you that because you'd been ignoring me."

"You certainly snared my attention, then."

She walked a few steps away. "This is madness, Ashton. You're sure to be caught."

"It wouldn't be the first time."

"But if Dor—if Captain Tanner catches you again, he's not likely to let you get away."

"Your concern for my welfare is touching."

She caught her breath. "My main concern is for Henry.

What good will it do to leave him fatherless? With the things you do, he's likely to grow up never knowing you.''

''Would you rather he knew a father who was too weak to act on his convictions? A father who turned his back on the cause of freedom?''

''A father who mocks his king and turns against his neighbors?'' she shot back scathingly.

Anger jolted through him like a thunderclap. ''No doubt you and your captain will try to make Henry ashamed he was born an American. I don't know why we're arguing this anyway, Bethany. You're doing your best to shut me out of your life and Henry's.''

She stared at him for a long, searching moment, her eyes full of pain and regret. ''We cannot be a family, Ashton, until you abandon your dangerous and treasonous activities.''

''Or until you stop fooling yourself about the outcome of this war. The English cause was lost even before a few farmers took up arms against the Redcoats on Lexington Green. 'Tis only a matter of time.''

''Why must I be the one to change?'' she demanded hotly.

''Because I will not.''

Stubborn blue eyes locked with obstinate hazel ones. Ashton wanted to shake her lovely, delicate frame until her teeth rattled and she begged for mercy. Yet at the same time he longed to snatch her into his arms and plead with her to help him heal the hurt they'd done each other.

Instead he shook his head. ''There's no help for it, pet. You're determined to play hostess to Dorian Tanner. Or do you do more than play hostess to the dashing captain? I daresay he has the look of a well-satisfied man.''

His gaze dropped to her hand. Dainty fingers curled into a fist and he waited for her blow, almost wanting to feel the sting of her ire. But she merely stepped back.

''That is a filthy insinuation, Ashton.'' Her voice was rough and tremulous with outrage. He knew then that he was wrong, wrong to suspect her of a liaison with Tanner. And he'd been wrong to accuse her of such a thing. She might despise what he was doing for the cause of freedom, but she had too much honor to take solace in another man's arms.

"I shouldn't have said what I did," he told her in a low voice. "I'm sorry."

Her head came up sharply. "Do you know, Ashton, that is the first time I've ever heard you say you're sorry for anything?"

"Doubtless it will not be the last."

Chapter 21

Through the heavy, hot air of late July Ashton wended his way among the Seastone gardens to Bethany's schoolhouse. Unease crowded in on his feeling of exultation like an uninvited guest. Charles Hector Theodat, the Comte d'Estaing, was bringing his fleet northward from the Delaware capes to liberate Newport from the British. General John Sullivan headed a contingent of Continentals by land. By all rights and reckoning, the double-pronged assault should whisk the Redcoats from their island stronghold in a matter of hours.

And yet Ashton's unease persisted. The plan, formed by the Marquis de Lafayette and General Washington himself, seemed catch-proof on paper, but D'Estaing had a reputation for being overly cautious, and Sullivan's Gaelic temper and penchant for ill luck were legendary.

The retreating light of the late-afternoon sun gilded the schoolhouse in warm shades of summer. The ineffable fragrance of roses and Canterbury bells wafted to him, and a sentimental memory stole into his mind. He recalled sitting in the summerhouse with Bethany three years earlier, remarking in his practical way that the place ought to be put to better use than a mere garden ornament. He couldn't have known back then that she would find such a noble purpose for the folly.

And yet, while the building itself had been transformed by Justice Richmond's clever hands into a sound and useful structure, the outside bore signs of neglect. Unclipped grass and unpruned bushes of lad's love attested to Dorian

Tanner's disdain for Bethany's mission. In contrast, the stables and restored carriage house were immaculate.

Ashton hesitated at the door, squaring his shoulders and flexing his fingers as if in preparation for a fight. A tight smile curved his lips. He expected no less than a full-blown battle with his wife when she found out why he'd come.

Slapping at a lazy fly, he prepared to step into the schoolroom. He was about to make his presence known when Bethany's voice lifted in anger.

" 'Tis the most preposterous idea I've ever heard, Dorian!"

Intrigued, and not a little annoyed to find his wife alone with the Redcoat, Ashton paused.

Tanner's boots thumped on the planked floor as if he were pacing. "My plan is perfectly logical, Bethany. 'Tis never too soon to begin thinking about Henry's education. In just a few years he'll be old enough to enroll at Eton."

"I refuse to send my son to England for his schooling at any age." Her voice crackled like fire.

Ashton was familiar with that particular obstinacy. He remained beneath the window, curious as to how the Redcoat would bear up under Bethany's temper.

"You're being damned unreasonable about this," Tanner said. "All people of quality send their sons away to school. Both your brothers attended Eton."

"Aye," she stormed, "and Father spent a year trying to civilize Harry when he returned home. William was plagued by nightmares for months. I disagree with the forcing-house system of schooling that the English favor." In a more moderate tone she added, "Henry will receive a perfectly fine education . . . right here in this schoolroom."

Tanner's laugh was a dry bark that irritated Ashton like chalk scraping across a slate. "I see. So you'd have the future master of Seastone reciting treason alongside gypsy poor and former slaves?"

A long silence ensued. Ashton imagined a pair of hazel eyes shooting sparks at the imperious Redcoat. "Just because my students don't happen to be to the manor born," she said in a strong voice, "does not mean they don't deserve the finest education I can give them. A boy struggling over a difficult passage or a column of figures works just as hard whether he's a slave or a nobleman.''

Tanner made a choking sound. ''Listen to yourself, Bethany. You speak of equality and the rights of commoners like the most radical of patriots.''

''Do I? Then it seems the rebels and I agree on certain points.'' Indulging in a smile of satisfaction, Ashton leaned against the building and folded his arms.

''By God,'' Tanner said impatiently, ''I'll not have Henry lumped in with the displaced scum of a dying nation.''

''Ah, but who displaced the children, Dorian?''

He blew out his breath audibly. ''Bethany, please understand. I care deeply for the boy. Had you not impetuously surrendered yourself in marriage to Markham despite my respectful suit for your hand, Henry could have been mine.''

Ashton's smile disappeared beneath the thunderhead of a scowl. But for his mistaken arrest in Bristol, that unthinkable scenario could well have taken place.

''But he is not your son,'' Bethany asserted. ''Even if I were to consent to sending Henry off to England, Ashton would never give his approval. He is the boy's father; he has final say.''

A warm glow began as a slow burn within Ashton. For all her Tory convictions, Bethany had other loyalties as well. Loyalties that ran deeper than her commitment to England.

''You're constantly pointing that fact out to me,'' Tanner said irritably. ''I simply don't understand why. My solicitors tell me a divorcement is possible in your case. Think about it, Bethany. 'Tis clear you bear no love for the scoundrel who deserted you and brought about the death of your father.''

Suddenly Ashton wished he were anywhere but standing in the overgrown garden listening to this conversation. If Bethany confirmed Tanner's accusations, he wasn't sure he could stand what the blow would do to him. Yet, in spite of himself, he strained to hear her response.

"How I feel about my husband," she said in a low, angry voice, "is none of your affair."

"But you see, my dear," Dorian rejoined smoothly, "it is very much my affair. I should be delighted for you to rid yourself of that traitor Markham. I'm not satisfied with merely being Henry's guardian. My feelings for you have grown quite . . . tender."

Ashton heard Bethany's muffled sound of dismay and the scrape of a piece of furniture.

"Come here, Bethany." Tanner spoke quietly, but with an imperative tone.

Ashton chose that moment to step swiftly into the schoolroom. Bethany and Tanner stood facing each other. Ashton saw with grim satisfaction that she'd placed a wooden bench in front of her. The hunted look in her eyes spoke eloquently of her dislike for Tanner.

The Redcoat wheeled when he heard Ashton come in. The imperious face darkened to a mask of fury. "What the devil are you doing here, Markham?"

Ashton itched to embed his fists in Tanner's face. He'd never been of a violent nature, but the Redcoat's arrogance infuriated him.

"I'd like a word with my wife," he said. "In private."

Tanner hesitated, fixing his onyx glare on Bethany and then on Ashton. He emitted a single vivid oath, snatched his hat from a low table, and strode from the schoolroom.

Bethany was still angry. Her bosom heaved beneath the dimity bodice of her dress, and her fists were drawn taut against her sides.

"Yes?" she asked. "What is it, Ashton?" Her voice sounded weary. He noted with surprise that she looked fatigued as well. Dark crescents beneath her eyes bespoke a lack of sleep. Beneath a loose-fitting lavender dress her frame seemed thinner. Ashton realized with a jolt that Bethany was not only tired; she was desperately unhappy, a condition he knew intimately.

"Ashton?"

Her soft prompting brought him out of his troubled reverie. "I've brought you some copybooks," he said, handing them to her.

Her face lit in a smile that touched his heart like a shaft

of sunlight. "Ashton, thank you. Paper is so dear these days." She flipped through one of the pamphlets. " 'Queens and Kings, Are Gaudy Things,' " she read. She stopped smiling, but Ashton detected a glint of humor in her eyes.

Grinning, he shrugged. " 'Twas all I could find." Remembering his real purpose in coming, he said, "Sit down, Bethany. You're not going to like what I have to say."

She looked puzzled, but lowered herself to the bench. Ashton joined her, turning to face her. She looked haggard, yet somehow still vibrantly beautiful. But perhaps he only saw that because she was so dear to him.

"I assume you're aware d'Estaing's fleet is due to arrive any day now."

"Aye."

"I've arranged to have you, Henry, Carrie, and your mother transported to Bristol. You'll be safer there, with your brother and Felicia."

She surged to her feet. "No! I'll not abandon my home."

He took both her hands in his. Her fingers were curled stubbornly into her palms. "Listen to me. Seastone is a target for the Continentals, especially since Tanner has seen fit to store a good bit of ordnance in some of the buildings. I'd like to believe the patriots are incapable of harming women and children, but . . . atrocities have been committed on both sides."

"The only atrocity I've suffered in this war involved you."

He gritted his teeth. She just wouldn't leave that old wound alone. At the moment he had no time to dredge up yet another defense. "You're going to Bristol, Bethany."

"I'll not abandon my house like a coward."

"No, you'll seek a place of safety for the sake of our son."

Her shoulders slumped. "You're right." She listened to his plan for a secret bay crossing. Wearily she rose. "I'll get our things together."

He walked with her to the door, trying to hide his relief. "Bethany, 'tis best you tell no one you're leaving."

She nodded. "The British will be busy anyway. Dorian mentioned a meeting tonight at Banister House." She lifted troubled eyes to him. "I don't suppose there's any point in asking you what you'll be doing during the siege."

He smiled a little, wondering what she would do if he took her in his arms and kissed the lines of weariness from her pale face. Doubtless she'd push him away and remind him once again of the crime she was convinced he'd committed. Feeling bleak, he said, "I can't say, pet. But you can be sure I'll be busy." Nodding at a display of childish drawings on foolscap, he added, "I see your students have been busy, too."

A charming scene of a family standing in front of a boxlike house caught his eye. Looking closer, Ashton noticed a chilling touch of reality in the drawing. The man in the picture wore a wooden stick in place of one leg. Beneath the drawing was scrawled "Benstrom Haas." One of Goody's nephews. Slowly Ashton walked the length of the wall. He saw a stick-figure soldier standing duty beside an abandoned building, a headstone beneath a leafless tree, a bleak rendition of a family warming themselves around burning furniture. He muttered a curse.

"Sometimes," Bethany said softly, "the children's drawings speak more eloquently than political strategists. I hate it that they suffer from a war not of their making." She sighed wistfully. "When we were children, our most pressing worry was whether or not we'd be caught raiding the Pierces' melon patch or whether the millpond had frozen sufficiently for skating."

Ashton's heart lurched at the memory. "I'll send word round that you'll not be holding school for a few days."

"Will they be all right, Ashton?" she asked anxiously.

"Pieter Haas has made provisions for the families in town."

She nodded and started down the steps. Giving in to impulse, Ashton gripped her shoulders and brushed his lips over her brow. She smelled of sunshine and jasmine; she felt like love and forever. The dark shadow of a thought occurred to him. This could be the last time he ever held her in his arms. He thrust the unthinkable idea aside.

"Godspeed, love," he told her softly. "Harry will bring you home when the fighting is over."

She stared at him for a moment, her sun-shot eyes studying his face. She seemed about to speak, then closed her mouth and moved away. He watched her walk toward the house beneath an arching canopy of lilac and evergreen yew. As always, he was struck by her grace and beauty. And by the endearing vulnerability that warmed him to his soul.

Before leaving the schoolroom, he paused to look around. The room was tidy and inviting with its child-sized furniture and neat stacks of hornbooks and foolscap practice papers. Ink horns and Faber pencils stood in a row on a table. Glancing up at the big slate in the front of the room, he noticed a message in Bethany's artful script: "First say what you would be, then do what you have to do.—Epictetus." A smile glimmered about his lips. He was proud of Bethany, proud of the skilled and decisive teacher she had become.

"Good God Almighty!" Incredulity lent force to Harry Winslow's exclamation. Standing on the doorstep of the Tiverton farmhouse, he fixed a wondering look on a decidedly bulging midsection.

"Close your mouth, young man," Abigail intoned crisply. "We are not a flytrap. And mind the mud on your boots. Finley spent hours cleaning the floor." Abigail hid a smile as she stepped aside to let Harry into the house. The man well may gape; like most people, Harry Winslow thought of her has a spinsterish schoolmarm and not as a pregnant farm wife.

Harry removed the mud from his boots on the iron scraper outside the door. Then he entered the house, nearly falling over himself to help Abigail to a chair in the keeping room.

"See here, Harry Winslow," she scolded, "I'm a woman who happens to be with child, not some dangerous explosive."

"Sorry, Miss Primrose, I—"

"Miss Primrose?" she challenged. "Young man, I am *Mrs.* Finley Piper, but you, despite your ill manners, may

call me Abigail—or even Abby, if you feel the need." She wrinkled her nose slightly. "You Americans seem fond of overfamiliarity anyway."

The young man's hazel eyes widened even further. "You . . . you *married* Finley?"

Abigail felt humor tug at her lips. "Yes, indeed. Finley's a beef-wit and a card cheat, but"—she made an airy gesture with her hand—"there was no help for it. I lost my heart." Her eyes took in the perfectly tidy and charming keeping room of the farmhouse. "Anyway," she added impishly, "I would have been hard-pressed to find a man who cooks and keeps house as well as Finley."

"Wh . . . where is he anyway?" Harry asked, his mouth twitching suspiciously.

Abigail looked away, swallowing hard against the sudden knot of fear in her throat. "Finley has . . . gone to meet the French flotilla," she choked, unable to hide her trepidation. "He should be boarding the flagship *Languedoc* this evening."

Harry let loose with a low whistle. "Damn," he said softly. "I knew Finley'd never be content with farming. What about his brother?"

"Stephen has gone to town, where the patriots are mustering troops. His son, Douglas, is out finishing his chores." She fanned her face with a handkerchief, feeling restive and overwarm. "The boy's most unhappy that his father and uncle went off without him. Imagine," she scoffed, "being deprived of the privilege of being shot at." She glanced curiously at Harry. "What brings you here?"

He looked a bit sheepish. "I've come to enlist."

"Not you, too?"

He nodded.

Abigail felt inexpressibly sad. Harry was a man barely out of his youth. How many like him had died in this war? How many more would die? But she knew the pointlessness of trying to dissuade him from going. She'd had the same argument with Finley two days earlier.

"Have you been in contact with Bethany?" Abigail asked. "I've had only one letter in seven months—the post has been so sporadic."

"Ashton tried to send her to Bristol. He doesn't know she disobeyed him. At least she had the sense to let her son and Carrie Markham leave Newport. But Bethany's still housing Redcoats at Seastone, the stubborn chit."

"She's doing her patriotic duty, young man."

"I wish my sister would think of her wifely duties for once," Harry said, scowling.

Abigail nodded. Only recently had she discovered the joy of loving. Loyalty to a king three thousand miles away paled in comparison. Abigail had also discovered the pain of separation. "It seems you and I both believe Bethany and Ashton belong together," she told Harry. "Perhaps when the fighting is over—"

"She'll never forgive him. She still believes he caused our father's death. Damn!"

"Your swearing is unrefined and monotonous, Harry."

"Sorry, Abigail, but I'm so frustrated about this damn—unfortunate mix. I just know Ashton didn't organize that raid. But whoever did was damned thorough. Didn't leave a scrap of evidence."

Abigail sat thinking for a moment, going over the mournful events following the raid. A faint memory nagged at her, eluding her consciousness. Harry shifted on his chair, grumbling about the heat. He stuck his finger into his collar to loosen it and Abigail noticed a glint of silver. Harry was wearing a Liberty Tree.

The sight of the medallion opened a flood tide of memories, and Abigail shot to her feet. "My God," she said, "I found a good deal more than a mere scrap!" She hurried to a corner of the kitchen and searched through a sack of rags. She turned back to Harry, unfolding an ink-smudged apron.

"I was wearing this the night I went through Dorian Tanner's office. I'm afraid I completely forgot about it because Finley was in such a state over Chapin." She dropped two small objects into Harry's hand. "I know about the Liberty Tree—Lord, I was spying on the Committee when they gave it to Ashton. Do you recognize the other?"

Squinting, Harry held the sapphire stud to the light.

Abigail watched a curious array of emotions cross his face. Wistfulness, affection, then anger and resentment.

"This belonged to my father," he pronounced.

Then Abigail recalled where she had first seen the stud: nestled in Sinclair Winslow's stock as he hosted a reception two Christmases ago. "And to think that jewel has been in my possession all along. Damn!"

Harry cocked an impudent eyebrow at her. "Damn, Miss Abigail? Surely you can choose a more refined expletive."

"I'm furious with myself. I always took pride in my attention to detail. But in my concern for Finley, I forgot everything else."

Harry began to pace the room in agitation. "Tanner had this, you say? Then that can only mean . . ."

Abigail nodded, feeling suddenly cold all over. "It means Dorian Tanner was behind the raid." She laced nervous fingers together over her swelling middle. "Why didn't I guess? Who but Dorian Tanner benefited so handsomely from your father's death?" she said to Harry's hastily retreating back.

Over his shoulder he shouted, "I'm going to Seastone to get Bethany away from that double-dealing Redcoat."

Abigail followed, watching Harry as he leaped into his sail-rigged sloop and pushed off. The wind had risen, coaxing stiff peaks onto the water's surface. Harry turned and waved his hat at her, looking boyish and golden and impetuous . . . and heartachingly brave. Abigail turned and went back into the house.

The top deck of the flagship *Languedoc,* at the head of a fleet of eleven vessels, shifted restlessly beneath Ashton's feet. He'd never been aboard a vessel of such awesome size.

"She is a grand lady, eh?" asked Gaston, the helmsman. "With her ninety guns and a little luck, she will blow the English all the way to Canada." A gamin smile animated the aging face as Gaston shook hands with each American: Ashton, Finley, and five other members of the Committee of Safety. A few of the French sailors did likewise. As the Frenchmen greeted him, Ashton experienced a wave of trepidation. He hated the British, but did he hate them enough to participate in their extermination? Relief came on the heels of his uncertainty; at least Bethany and Henry were safe in Bristol.

Finley nudged Ashton and gestured astern. "Look at that, will you? Never saw so much brass in my life." His derisive snort suggested he was dubious about the new alliance.

"The conquering heroes," Ashton said wryly. "Why do we consider men about to kill other men heroes?"

Charles Hector Theodat, the Comte d'Estaing, arrived at the head of a gaggle of lesser officers. All were splendidly arrayed in white cloth coats and waistcoats studded with gilt buttons. Gorgets of silver flashed the royal arms at the American contingent. Goat-hair-adorned hats shadowed the men's eyes. The Americans, who had boarded the flagship at Point Judith to guide the fleet into battle position, gaped at the finery.

D'Estaing made a brief formal welcoming speech in heavily accented English, then greeted the Americans individually.

"Ashton Markham," he said, bowing a little. "I know you from Monsieur Talmadge's description. I was told to expect a huge, angry lion of a man, and I see that is precisely what you are."

Ashton grinned. "I'm not sure Ben meant that as a compliment."

"Eh, *bien,*" d'Estaing said. "Your associate also said you have an extraordinary talent with horses."

"I'm not sure that quality will serve me well on a sea invasion." In truth, he wasn't sure exactly what he was doing here.

D'Estaing and his guests retired to the admiral's stateroom to go over the details of the planned attack.

"I have instructed Admiral Suffren to open an east passage," d'Estaing said, indicating the location on his chart.

"That would be Sakonnet," Ashton said.

"Sakonnet," D'Estaing echoed. "Ah, *les peaux-rouges,* they give everything such impossible names."

Finley took large gulp of French wine. One of the officers sniffed a little and pointedly took a delicate sip from his own goblet. Finley countered by draining his cup and setting it on the sideboard with a resounding bang. He belched. "I agree with that move, Charles." Disapproving eyes widened even further at Finley's use of the admiral's given name. Ignoring them, Finley said, " 'Twill open the Middle Passage for an easy approach."

"We will be well protected," the count replied, his lips stiffening at Finley's manners. "Suffren has taken hostages."

"Is that necessary?" Ashton asked quickly.

"Assurément." D'Estaing nodded vigorously. "The hostages will be held on the *Languedoc* to discourage the English from bombarding us." The count scowled. "You think me cowardly, eh? But I have other reasons. If the flagship goes, the attack will fall apart—pouf!"

"I see," Ashton said uneasily. "But the Redcoats are on edge. Suffren will be hard-pressed to take any officers."

"That matters not, monsieur. The admiral has a list of Loyalists of some importance—civilians, *vous savez.* They will do just as well for our purposes."

Wise, Ashton thought. And shrewd. Support for the British was dissipating even in the Tory bastion of Newport. The Redcoats would be loath to jeopardize their standing with the Loyalists by allowing harm to come to the hostages. Ashton was glad he'd had the foresight to pack Bethany and Henry off to Bristol.

Despite his distaste for the hauteur of the French officer, Ashton had no argument with the plan. It was simple, direct, and brilliant. The French fleet would force passage on the west side of Aquidneck while the American faction would cross over and mount an assault from the east.

As the fleet waited off the point for word that the Middle Passage was clear, Ashton found himself enjoying life under sail. The French sailors were as friendly as the officers were stuffy. Once the men discovered Ashton understood their language, they regaled him with bawdy tales in their rapid-fire tongue, plied him with a seemingly endless supply of wine, and showed him how to climb high in the rigging for a breathtaking view of the bay.

Despite his anticipation of the battle, Ashton felt more at peace than he had in a long time. Bethany and Henry were safe on the mainland; Newport was soon to be liberated. And once that happened, he intended to liberate his feelings for Bethany.

For months—no, years—he'd denied his love for her, even to himself. His love was the only thing she'd ever wanted from him, and yet, like a miser protecting his fortune, he'd withheld it. But no more. Perhaps once she understood how he felt, she'd trust his word that he hadn't planned the raid on Seastone. Suddenly the future seemed as bright as the sparkling baywaters.

Gaston, the helmsman, proved an inveterate gossip. As they sat together one hot evening on the top deck, the equally talkative Finley told the Frenchman proudly of his conquest of Abigail Primrose, then launched into a tale of Bethany and Ashton's marriage.

"I am an expert in affairs of the heart," Gaston said smugly. "Tell me of your Tory wife, *copain.*"

Ashton, replete with the wine he'd drunk to drown the taste of weevilly ship's biscuit, obliged the Frenchman.

"I've known her since she was a girl," he said. "I remember her as a gawky little filly, leggy and clumsy and full of mischief. She went to New York for her schooling." His mind wandered back to the day she'd returned, hurling her newly curvaceous form into his arms. He grinned. "I practically had to peel myself off the rafters when I saw what she had become during her four years absence."

"She is *très belle?*" Gaston queried.

"Aye. More than that. She's spirited and brave and stubborn. And wiser than any woman has a right to be."

Gaston clicked his tongue sympathetically. "*Dommage, copain.* Such a woman is the worst kind. Enchanting and habit-forming, like good wine."

The next day a small boatload of enthusiastic aides approached the *Languecdoc* with good news. Admiral Suffren had left the wreckage of several British ships in the bay. The Middle Passage was clear. Troops under Sullivan and Lafayette had begun crossing to Aquidneck.

Suffren's hostages were brought aboard the flagship. One by one the unfortunate Tories were helped up the ladder:

Mr. Simon Pease, a slave trader; Mr. Evan Hunt, a distiller; and Mr. Keith Cranwick, whose curses sounded loud enough to carry clear across the bay.

Before the fourth hostage could be brought up, something happened to cast a pall on the entire expedition. Mr. Pease, looking ashen and thoroughly bewildered, suddenly clutched at his chest and fell over dead on the deck at d'Estaing's feet.

Letting loose with a vivid and articulate string of French oaths, Admiral d'Estaing shook his fist. Ashton wasn't surprised that anger rather than sorrow was the prevailing emotion. The last thing d'Estaing wanted was for any harm to befall the illustrious Newporters.

In the flurry of concern over Pease's death, the fourth hostage was momentarily forgotten. Ashton heard a sound behind him and looked back in time to see a small and decidedly feminine hand appear on the rail, followed by a bright mane of tousled curls, then an angel's face set in an expression far better suited to a harpy from the netherworld.

Ashton froze. "Oh, God," he said as hazel eyes aimed a lethal stare directly at him. "Bethany."

Chapter 22

"Pas de question," d'Estaing said to Ashton, straining the many fastenings of his coat. "What you ask is out of the question." Annoyingly, the officer buried his face in the broad mouth of a cone while a servant sent a great cloud of powder over his wig.

Ashton stifled a sneeze. "Admiral, she's a woman—"

The aristocratic face withdrew from the cone. D'Estaing coughed delicately. "One needn't be a Frenchman to discern that." The count sketched a curvaceous form in the air.

"You can't possibly keep my wife on this ship during a battle," Ashton said, his eyes narrowing. He experienced a distinctly unpleasant feeling at the idea that the ship was full of men who openly appreciated Bethany's beauty.

"But of course," d'Estaing replied casually. "She could not be safer than she is on the *Languedoc. Ecoutez, mon ami,* I realize taking a female hostage is a little irregular, but it is for the best. Besides, if Madame Markham were back in Newport, mightn't she be in greater danger?"

Ashton had a swift and vivid image of Aquidneck Island overrun by battling regiments. Suddenly he realized his quarrel was not with the diffident Frenchman but with his wife. The fool woman wouldn't be in any danger at all if she'd obeyed her husband and gone to Bristol with their son as he'd arranged.

"As you wish," he told the count. "My wife, however, will require a bit more convincing." In the few hours she'd been aboard the flagship, Bethany had had nothing to say to Ashton other than numerous scathing denunciations of the duplicity of his patriot friends.

D'Estaing clapped his highly polished heels together. "Dinner is formal tonight, Monsieur Markham. A proper welcome, if you will, for our American allies."

Ashton left the stateroom and followed the gangway to the common seamen's quarters. He found Finley Piper and the other Americans dressing as if this meal of glorified salt meat and beans aboard a warship were a grand society ball.

"Have you spoken to Bethany?" Finley asked Ashton quietly. Concern laced his voice and curiosity brightened his eyes.

"Only long enough to have my character raked over the coals. They've given her a private cabin."

"God's blood! Surely the girl's not blaming you for this. Why didn't she go to Bristol?"

"Lillian wouldn't hear of leaving Seastone. Bethany decided to stay with her, although she did send Carrie and little Henry to safety."

"Then this whole muddle is her own fault. Why's she blaming you?"

Ashton scowled. "Blaming me for things I haven't done has become habit with Bethany."

"Don't look so hopeless, friend. Just think of Abby and myself. A year ago she would have cheerfully set fire to me; now she's carrying my child." With a sheepish grin he added, "And I'm still doing her laundry."

Ashton blew out a disgruntled sigh and bent to rifle through the single valise he'd brought aboard. He owned one good set of clothing, an extravagance recently smuggled to Aquidneck in exchange for horses. He was less than fond of formal dress, but he'd brought the garments along in a spirit of optimism; General Washington himself would visit Newport once the city was liberated.

The white ruffled shirt was an annoying froth on his torso, spilling from the confines of an overdecorated winestone-fabric waistcoat. The too-tight buff knee breeches hugged his thighs. He grimaced at the delicacy of the silken hose, but he donned them and fumbled gamely with the garters. At least his tall ebony leather boots hid the stockings. A deep navy frock coat, embroidered with far too much gold needlework, sported miles of braid.

"Dashing," Finley commented wryly, preening like a popinjay in his own finery. "All you need now is a wig."

Ashton sent him a frown and tied his hair back in its usual inelegant tail. Then, along with the similarly garbed but less disgruntled Americans, he strode into the alleyway, heading astern for the captain's stateroom.

Bethany reluctantly followed a ship's boy across the darkened main deck of the *Languedoc*, stepping gingerly through a maze of low-beamed alleyways. They emerged onto the upper deck, where several seamen were finishing their chores for the evening.

When she appeared, a broad silence fell over the men, and she felt the sting of several pairs of lusty eyes trained on her with unconcealed longing.

A salacious whisper drifted across the deck. *"La belle . . . Mon dieu, ayez merci!"*

She turned away, hiding her scalding blush within the loose waves of her hair. It was not enough, she fumed, that she'd been seized from the Cranwicks' stables and deposited on this French ship like so much baggage. She was also forced to endure the leers of these foreign sailors. And Ashton, damn the man, seemed to think the entire episode was perfectly all right.

Admiral d'Estaing greeted her at the door to his stateroom. She looked past him but saw only a handful of silent servants moving around an elaborately appointed mahogany table. A knot of well-dressed men conferred in a corner of the stateroom. "Are you quite well, madame?" the admiral asked solicitously.

"I'm beginning to think the unfortunate Mr. Pease is better off than I," she replied tartly, directing a malevolent gaze at him. "He, at least, has escaped this prison you call a warship."

"Please, madame," d'Estaing said, smiling. "Do not be offended."

"Oh, but I am," Bethany retorted.

"Think of yourself as an honored guest."

"Then take heed, Admiral. You've a most unhappy guest on your hands."

"C'est la guerre, madame," d'Estaing said with alacrity. "Were this a time of peace, I am sure you and I would be the best of friends." He pressed close to emphasize his point.

Ashton was a sudden angry presence in the doorway. "I doubt my wife can appreciate your sentiments, Admiral."

Bethany could only stare at the striking figure her husband cut. From his neatly groomed hair to the gleaming tops of his boots, he looked every bit the gentleman. The elegant clothing gave him a distinct air of breeding, yet his blatant, broad-shouldered masculinity shone through the ornamentation of the costume.

He was staring at her with a look she'd never seen before. That softness, that gentle yearning, might have melted her heart had she been in a more sympathetic frame of mind.

"Hello, love," he said. Bowing low over her hand, he pressed his lips to the rapid pulse at her wrist. "You seem," he said smoothly, with a gentle pressure on her fluttering pulse, "quite excited to be here tonight."

Stunned by his formal greeting, Bethany felt her cheeks go hotly crimson. Damn him, she thought, snatching her hand away. Damn him for discerning her racing pulse with a surgeon's sensitivity.

"I hardly think 'excited' is the proper word," she countered with more bravado than she felt. "If I seem agitated, 'tis because I've just spent half the day being abducted and forced aboard an enemy ship."

"I hope," the count said genially, "that you will accept our hospitality in the spirit in which it is offered."

"Sir, I consider myself a prisoner of war."

Ashton propelled her to the long table, his hands deft and firm as he helped her into a chair.

Bethany refused to look at him during the meal. She gave her attention to Hunt and Cranwick, who ate too little and drank too much, both with churlish indignation.

Although Bethany barely knew Hunt and bore no liking for Keith, she blinked rapidly at her fellow Tories. "How terribly unfortunate,'' she said to Keith, ''that you chose to show me your new Narragansett pacers this afternoon. Had we stayed in your drawing room with Mabel and Mother, perhaps Admiral Suffren's lackeys would have passed us by.''

Keith nodded darkly. ''I was eager for someone knowledgeable to see my horses before the rebel bandits made off with them.'' He scowled at Ashton. ''Newport's been plagued by horse thieves all summer.''

Bethany felt an absurd and shameful urge to giggle. ''I believe your horse thief is well away from Newport at the moment, Keith,'' she replied. She stared at Ashton just long enough to watch him grow uncomfortable.

The Frenchmen seemed intrigued by her. Bethany guessed that the highborn officers didn't quite know what to make of her outspokenness. Yet they all vied for her attention, entertaining her in poor but flowery English with tales of their courtly life in France.

''You've a lot of admirers tonight,'' Ashton whispered as he pretended to listen to a long-winded account of a hunt in Chantilly. ''Myself included,'' he added. His finger trailed lightly over her upper arm. ''That's a lovely dress.''

Bethany sniffed and tried not to let his touch affect her. ''How fortunate Admiral Suffren's henchmen happened to seize me when I was dressed for tea at the Cranwicks'.'' She fixed an angry look on him. ''I care little about impressing anyone on this ship.''

She began to feel oppressed by the stares of the Frenchmen and the cloying odors of pomatum, perfume, and wine. She didn't bother to stifle a yawn before catching d'Estaing's eye.

''I'd like to retire now,'' she informed him, pushing back from the table. All around, chairs scraped in quick succession as the gentlemen rose. Lifting her chin, she went to the door, ignoring the chorus of good nights behind her.

Then Ashton was at her side, his grip firm on her elbow, as he propelled her into the alleyway. ''I'll escort you back to our cabin, pet,'' he offered. He looked so handsome in his formal attire that something inside her grew warm and weak.

She snatched her arm away. "You shouldn't refer to my prison cell as 'our' cabin, Ashton. I can find my own way."

"Sorry, love," he said lightly. "I've been waiting for months to get you alone."

"You can wait until the moon falls out of the sky, Ashton Markham," she retorted. "Or until you cease your patriot activities. And I'm sure the former is more likely to happen than the latter."

He hissed out a sigh as if battling a surge of temper. "Go ahead and get angry," she goaded. "I'm the prisoner here."

Ashton seemed not to hear her. He glanced out at the sky. "There's to be a moon tonight," he said.

Her gaze followed his and for a moment she forgot her anger. The night air was still and heavy with the tang of salt. The sky was velvety black and festooned with a brilliant array of stars that seemed very close and in constant motion due to the rocking of the ship.

"How long am I to be kept a prisoner?" she asked.

"Until Newport is ours."

"You sound very sure of yourself."

"Look about you, Bethany." Her gaze followed the sweeping motion of his arm, taking in the lights of the eleven other warships. "The Redcoats will never be able to repulse this force."

She was silent for a moment. Suddenly the prospect of a British-free Newport didn't seem so bad. She just wanted the fighting to be over. "You rebels have become adept at abduction," she observed.

"Of necessity." He studied her closely; his eyes touched her like a languid caress. "Even with your face set in a frown, you look lovely, Bethany." He brushed the underside of her jaw with his knuckles, his gaze oddly tender in the way it had been before dinner. She shivered. She would have better understood anger.

"I've something to tell you," he said gravely. "Something about myself—about us."

Confused by his tenderness, she sought refuge in spite. "There is no 'us.' Perhaps there never was."

At last she'd penetrated the mesmerizing fondness of his manner. His brow descended. "Will you not listen to what I have to say?" he demanded.

She glared at him. "No."

"Then perhaps you'll pay heed to this." A sharp gasp escaped her as he hauled her against him in a tight, uncompromising embrace.

"Let me be," she commanded through clenched teeth.

But his mouth closed over hers; his hands began a journey over the curves of her body. Bethany battled the heady feeling of his lips working compellingly over hers. Fighting the heated demands of his seeking tongue and the sensuous movement of his insistent hands, she nevertheless felt herself slipping into languorous submission. Until a nagging inner voice derided her: You are already a prisoner of war; will you let his touch make you a captive as well?

Her rage burned nearly as hot as her desire. She twisted her head away. "Stop," she said stridently, pressing her hands against the lace adorning his shirt. But he only tightened his embrace and his lips sought hers again. His nearness made her feel impotent yet curiously secure.

The sensation angered her further, for she disliked being at a disadvantage. Unable to combat his superior strength, she sought to punish him with her words.

"Those clothes may make you look the gentleman, Ashton Markham," she said, plucking disdainfully at a rumpled bit of lace on his chest, "but I know the man beneath. I know him for a traitor who must take what he wants by force. Force me, Ashton, for I'll not willingly give in to you."

He let her go so abruptly that she stumbled back against the rail. His mouth was a taut line of anger, yet in his eyes she saw . . . Was it a flicker of hurt? No, she told herself firmly. Surely 'twas a trick of the starlight glinting off the waters that made his eyes look, just for a moment, inexpressibly sad.

"Your cabin is this way, madam," he said gruffly, striding away. She followed him in contrite silence, dismayed that she found no satisfaction in her victory.

Bethany slept badly on the narrow bunk, awoke to a relatively cool August morning, then thumbed through a volume of *chansons de geste* with waning interest and growing agitation as the day wore on. The cabin became hot and airless. Through a single portal she could see the rolling blue waves as the deep-draft *Languedoc* cut a path into Narragansett Bay.

She couldn't tear her thoughts from the previous night. The guilt snapping at her consciousness was both unwelcome and unsettling. Why should she feel guilty about hurting the man who had destroyed her home and brought about the death of her father, the man who placed his patriotic ideals above his admittedly forced vows of marriage?

Because, she told herself with waves of remorse, Ashton Markham was not the villian she'd made him out to be. He meant so much more to her.

Anger and hatred cooled; self-reproof and hope found a bleak center within her. She was not ready to forgive Ashton, but she was ready to talk to him.

Closing the book of *chansons de geste,* she left the cabin and climbed a steep ladder, emerging into the light of a hot afternoon sun.

The bay islands were clearly in sight. Coloring uncomfortably under the stares of dozens of crewmen, Bethany walked along the rail. Behind the flagship the French fleet bobbed like wine corks instead of the deadly war machine they were. Ahead, through a web of shrouds and stout rigging, she saw their destination: Conanicut Island.

Buzzing and murmuring among the sailors alerted Ashton to Bethany's presence. She was easy to find in her soft dress of pale yellow silk, for she stood out like a primrose against the muted colors of ship and sea and sky.

Moving quickly, Ashton crossed the decks, jumping over coils of hemp rope and crates.

"You should stay below," he said curtly.

"Ashton, I . . ." Her voice trailed off as her eyes flicked

to the curious glances of the crewmen. "Why are we headed for Conanicut?"

He sighed heavily. "If I tell you, will you get below?"

"I might."

"D'Estaing is going to land about four thousand troops there. They'll be organized for a crossing to Aquidneck."

He watched her throat work beneath the pale covering of yellow silk. Her eyes were wide and fearful. "Up to this point," she said wonderingly, "it's all seemed so unreal. All the drills, the intricate plans, the rolling out of huge kegs of powder—it's all seemed like a complicated game."

" 'Tis no game, pet. 'Tis war." There was much about Bethany that Ashton didn't understand, but he knew what she was thinking now. Suddenly, with her native Newport in the distance and the wreckage of a few British vessels shifting in the bay, she'd become aware that a great battle was to take place. Hundreds would die, acres of land would be charred and trampled by advancing militia . . . He could well understand how daunting the thought must be to her.

Her quivering chin and wide-eyed terror touched him deeply. He moved to take her hand in his, then stopped himself. Her sharp words of the previous night stood between them.

"I can say nothing to allay your fears," he told her. "We've been fortunate to have escaped the ravages of war this long, but I fear 'twill make the battle seem all the more savage to you."

Standing close, they watched the debarkment of troops. Colonial regulars and their French allies poured out of the ships of the line. Each soldier looked fit and eager and ready for battle.

The *Languedoc* hove to and tacked eastward to oversee the harbor. Squinting, Ashton noted that the British had formed double lines across the island. Part of the front line was protected by a pond. The stronghold at Tomminy Hill seemed to take brooding command of the adjacent countryside.

"Who is this?" Bethany asked, pointing to a man who had just boarded from a ship's boat.

"The Chevalier de Pontgibaud," Ashton said. "He's aide-de-camp to the Marquis de Lafayette."

Looking agitated, the chevalier boarded and strode up and down. Short of stature and absurdly rotund, he breathed in impatient huffs. But his face, Ashton noticed, was something else again. Beneath a plumed hat and powdered wig the complexion was florid and the eyes were shrewd and intelligent. Despite his fussy mien, the chevalier was a professional soldier in every sense of the word.

And he was angry. "Nothing is working," he blistered, speaking English for the benefit of his Colonial aides. "The men behave like schoolboys at play."

"Calm yourself, Gui," d'Estaing said, striding across the deck.

The chevalier started to speak, but hesitated. He was staring over the count's shoulder. "Ah, *la belle,*" he breathed. *"Qu'est-ce que c'est?"*

Jealousy flared inside Ashton as his wife stepped forward like a grand lady. "I am Bethany Markham," she said in a silken voice, offering her hand to Pontgibaud. Her eyes flicked to Aquidneck, where an occasional brief flash and puffs of smoke could be seen. "God . . . it's started," she whispered, dropping her haughty facade.

"Merely a skirmish," Pontgibaud assured her.

"Sir, Newport is my home. Even a mere skirmish, as you term it, is more fighting than I care to see."

Ashton was irritated by the chevalier's rapt attention to Bethany. There was no power like a beautiful woman to make a man forget his purpose. "Sir, your report," he said.

With obvious effort the chevalier tore his gaze from Bethany. "Ah, yes, the foul news," he said. "The New England militia is quite a spectacle, let me tell you. Truly, the marquis has the patience of a saint. The cavalry looks like a flock of ducks in cross belts on bad nags—"

Ashton doubled his fists. He'd done his best to train those horses, making them into fighting animals.

Pontgibaud's eyes strayed to Ashton's hands. "Pardon me, Monsieur Markham; I know how hard you have worked. But even with the best of mounts a cavalry is only as good as the men who comprise it." He made a frustrated gesture. "And the infantry! They are deaf to the drumbeat and wear homespun clothing. I fear they are more anxious to eat up our supplies than engage the enemy."

Bethany wondered why she didn't feel heartened by the news that the brilliant coup was flawed after all. She knew she ought to feel smug, but instead she felt as worried as the patriots and Frenchmen looked. Suddenly, above the snapping of sails and the groaning of timbers, she heard a panicked shout. A party of Colonials scrambled aboard and raced across the upper decks to the officers.

"There's a squadron of His Majesty's ships approaching Point Judith," a man shouted. "Black Dick Howe's *Renown* and seven other vessels, complete with ketches and fire ships!"

A dreadful silence fell over the decks of the *Languedoc*. The waves lapped gently at her sides and a rising wind whistled through the rigging.

D'Estaing looked indecisive; his men looked fearful. After a long moment of deliberation the count issued a string of orders in French. Men raced to the sheets; others grabbed the halyards, and the sails were set and made fast.

Ashton began propelling Bethany toward a hatch. "Get below and stay there," he ordered. "Howe doesn't know about the hostages; they'll show no mercy to the flagship."

"I don't like that cabin," she said, balking. " 'Tis hot and airless."

He scowled at her. "Get down there, Bethany, or I'll be forced to carry you."

She regarded him for a moment as if wondering whether or not to test his promise. Apparently convinced of his earnestness, she lifted her skirts with dignity and disappeared through the hatch.

A roiling bank of coal-gray clouds rolled in, obscuring the heavy August sun. The high wind was completely useless to the French fleet. The crew tried desperately to win an advantageous position while at the Point the British were doing the same. The *Languedoc* headed south on the port tack, its crew hoping for a wind shift. The south-westerly breeze moved only two points to the east, and then settled.

The air was suddenly heavy, keeping the ships just out of range of each other. Ashton stalked the upper deck in agitation.

"Patience, *mon gars,*" said Gaston. "We are becalmed; there is nothing anyone can do. The sea is like a woman, is she not? She has the power to put many men at her mercy."

Ashton grinned and began absently knotting a length of rope.

"Why don't you go to your wife, *copain?* No doubt she has the same ennui as you."

Remembering Bethany's temper, Ashton shook his head.

"*Tiens,* are you afraid?" Gatson clucked his tongue. "A *grand homme* like you." He stood up slowly, making for the galley.

What an absurd little man, Ashton thought, slipping down the hatchway. I'm no more afraid of Bethany than I am a nervous filly. And yet even as he pushed open the door to the leaden-aired cabin, he dreaded feeling the sting of her ire. She was staring out the portal, her hair tumbling down her back. The look she gave him was as stormy as the weather outside.

"Why must I stay here?" she demanded peevishly. "I can barely stretch my legs in these cramped quarters."

Ashton couldn't help sending a meaningful look at the narrow bunk. "You could lie down."

"I want to go above. I'll die of the heat down here." His eyes took in the fascinating evidence of her discomfort. Perspiration had moistened the seams of her yellow gown, outlining a slim waist and the voluptuous rise of her breasts. Tendrils of topaz hair clung to her brow and neck. His mouth went dry as hemp as he imagined how her damp skin would taste and smell.

" 'Tis safer down here," he rasped.

"Safety be damned," she retorted. "All I want is to get home. I've half a mind to swim back to Aquidneck."

With fear he noted the defiant toss of her head. "Don't even try, pet. If you do, I'll see you're put under guard."

"Your cruelty fails to surprise me anymore."

"Bethany." Ashton swallowed. His arms ached for her; his heart and mind cried out for her to cast off her old accusations and allow him to say the words he should have spoken long ago. But her indignant gaze stabbed at him and stopped the words in his throat. He did love her, but revealing that truth now would only garner her scorn, for she would think the admission another one of his lies.

"Yes?" she prompted peevishly.

"Talk to me, love. You may as well; we're becalmed."

"Talk to you?" She laughed harshly. "What, indeed, shall I say to my husband? We've not had a civil conversation in months."

"Then perhaps 'tis time we tried." Grasping at an innocuous subject, he said, "Tell me of your school—the Primrose Academy."

Relaxing slightly, she gazed out the portal. "I think the routine of school is good for the children," she said. "For a few hours a day they behave like completely normal children, not the war refugees they are. When a child sits and recites from his absey book or Cocker's *Arithmetick*, he isn't thinking about the fact that his supper will probably consist of thin soup made from ingredients his mother had to steal." She glanced up at Ashton. "Does that sound terribly absurd to you? Dorian has always thought so. We practically came to blows over a set of letter dice I bought so the children could play Royal Oak."

"Tanner be damned," Ashton said hotly. "What business has he telling you how to spend your money anyway?"

"He's careful with Henry's inheritance," she said.

"God. You defend him still."

"No; only his way with money."

"Then what's his excuse for meddling in your school?"

Bethany looked weary. "I don't want to fight about Dorian. For the most part he's done a good job managing things at Seastone. But he has a rather strict code of propriety. Any deviation from that code appalls him."

"No doubt his sensibilities are under siege today."

A sudden adorably mischievous smile crept across Bethany's face. "Justice Richmond has become fond of baiting the captain. Dorian named the new colt after King George; Justice calls the animal Washington."

Ashton chuckled. "I'm surprised Tanner didn't have the man pilloried for sedition." Then he grew serious. " 'Tis a fine thing you did, teaching Richmond to read and write."

She smiled. "Teaching does have its rewards. But"—the smile fled—"it has its trials as well. I've not been as successful with all the children as I have been with Justice. Pamela Lillibridge, for instance. She's mean and sneaky and absolutely opposed to doing anything I ask. Some days I wonder why I bother." A delicate sigh rippled from her.

Suddenly Ashton began to see Bethany in a different light. She was not quite the dispassionate schoolmistress he'd thought her. Despite the noble calling of her profession, she was as lonely as he, searching desperately for someone she could trust. Like him, she had made her share of mistakes. Ashton realized how very hard it must be on her, battling with Tanner over the school, with her mother over the sorry state of her reputation. How many other battles had she fought?

He gave her a cup of fresh water, hoping the drink would soften some of the lines of fatigue etched on her face.

"You ought to sleep," he suggested, battling a fierce longing. She looked warm and languorous and artlessly sensuous.

With surprising obedience she lay back on the bunk, looking hardly comfortable.

"Shouldn't you take your slippers off?"

"I suppose that would be more comfortable."

"Here, I'll help you." With gentle hands Ashton removed first one shoe, then the other. He tried to ignore the powerful sensation the texture of her ankle ignited. Slowly, steeling himself against baser impulses, he peeled away the gossamer silk of her stockings, feeling the even smoother silk of her flesh.

"Thank you," she said almost shyly. She lay back and closed her eyes. Yet within a few moments she was shifting about in agitation. " 'Tis so damned hot in here."

Ashton smiled. "You ought to remove your gown," he

suggested. The prospect of seeing her in her dainty summer underthings was a disquieting one indeed.

She stared at him. For a moment Ashton feared she would ask him to leave. "Bethany," he said raggedly, "for God's sake, I'm your husband."

She said nothing, presented her back. He unfastened her gown and sucked in his breath. The filmy chemise and light petticoat were impossibly revealing.

Bethany sipped more water and relaxed onto the bunk. Ashton thought she looked perfectly comfortable, especially now that the heat she ignited in him had flared hotter than the heat of the day. But a pair of fat tears squeezed out from beneath her eyelids.

Ashton went to her side and put his arm around her. She accepted his touch, moving closer. Her tears dampened his shirtfront and, despite the warmth, sent shivers of emotion through his hungering body.

The years peeled back and suddenly she was a child again, seeking his comfort, needing him. "Don't cry, love," he whispered against the fragrant tangle of her hair. "Please don't cry anymore." Sweet gratification filled him as her sobs subsided.

Laying her cheek against him, Bethany felt a sudden urgent need for Ashton—not as a comforting friend, but as the husband she'd missed for so long. She turned in his embrace and, forgetting for a moment all the enmity that divided them, kissed him deeply. His response was swift, as if he'd been waiting for her compliance. He tightened his embrace and returned the kiss while one hand roved down the length of her warm body.

"Bethany—"

"No, don't talk. When we talk we only argue. Just hold me, Ashton. Hold me."

But he did much more than that. His fingers tugged gently at the ribbons of her chemise and petticoat, freeing warm flesh that ached for his touch. He seemed hesitant, as if unsure of her reaction. Bethany leaned forward and drank the sweetness from his surprised mouth, arching upward to invite the tender caresses of his hands. He had made love to her many times, but never with such care.

He cherished every inch of her, each kiss a reverence, each sigh a promise of fulfillment.

Stunned at the force of her reaction, Bethany caught her breath. Suddenly unable to endure the barrier of his clothing, she peeled the white linen shirt from him and applied her shaking fingers to the buttons of his breeches. She caressed him with the same tender eroticism he'd shown her.

"Sweet Christ, Bethany," he muttered, pulling sharply away.

She frowned in question and he smiled shakily. " 'Tis been a long time, love. Let's not make short work of our loving now."

Slowly, relishing each second, they made love in the airless cabin, the becalmed ship a gently shifting cradle. Long, lovesome moments quickened to burning urgency like tiny wavelets curling to huge, surging breakers.

Wordlessly, Ashton showed his wife all the love he felt in his heart. He took unbearable pleasure in bringing her sweet-scented body to life in his arms, all the while fighting to control the hot demand for release that pounded through him. At once certain he would die of want and determined to see to her pleasure, he held his longing in check. Then she cried his name aloud and clutched at him. Uttering an endearment, he moved over her welcoming body. The sudden rising surge of the waves outside the portal was insignificant compared to the tempest of their loving.

At last, at long last, Ashton felt his wife blossom beneath him with a silken burst of sound.

The ship's creaking was loud in the silence of their warm afterlove. For long moments Ashton held his wife and listened to the gentle neap and ebb of her breathing.

"Bethany." His voice sounded gravelly and somehow alien.

"Mmm?" By contrast, her musical query evoked volumes of sweet memories.

"Bethany. God, pet, the words seem so inane after what we've shared, but 'tis time I told you, I—"

A deafening crash drowned out his next words. "—love you."

"You what?" she mouthed, gripping the side of the bunk as the ship listed.

"I love you!" he bellowed. "I love you!" He yelled it again and again, knowing she must think he'd lost his wits, but knowing from the rapt look on her face that she understood. Wind and waves might drown his words, but not the fiery sentiment of his fierce embrace just before he left her to scramble into his clothing.

Bending, he kissed her one last time. And then a roar and a thunder seemed to rend the ship's timbers like an adze splitting wood. A wave rose high enough to spray the cabin portal.

The storm, which had been hovering on the horizon for hours, barreled into the bay.

Chapter 23

Ashton was half thrown from the cabin by a sudden lurch. The ship climbed a wall of waves only to drop with a bone-jarring thud on the other side. Bethany gasped and he looked back at her. Fear had chased away the love-warm look of her.

"Ashton!" Finley Piper's voice and the frantic pounding of his feet sounded in the alleyway. "Ashton, come quickly! They're calling for all hands—and if we don't do something to stop him, d'Estaing's going to reembark all his troops!"

"I've got to go above," Ashton told Bethany. "Stay here." She gazed at him mutinously as the cabin tilted. Grinning, he added, "Please." He ducked inside to kiss her swiftly, then hurried back out into the alleyway.

Shouts and running feet added to the cacophony of the hurricane. Ashton and Finley leaped to the top deck, where the Americans complained bitterly about the time lost because of d'Estaing's indecision.

Finley quickly added his own opinion. "The damned Frenchman's as inconsistent as a weathercock," he shouted over the wind and sea. "He could've bombarded Newport while Sullivan took over. But no, he thinks only of his own precious ships. And that stuffy little Pontgibaud; God, I've had enough—"

The howling tempest drowned out the rest of his tirade. Ashton had to agree with Finley's complaints. Despite a superficial air of cooperation—such as d'Estaing's sending barrels of fruit, and Sullivan's subsequent laudatory letter—the two factions were far from united.

All thought of battle fled. For now, the wind and the sea were more deadly enemies than a whole battalion of His Majesty's ships. The *Languedoc* heeled wildly, buffeted by fierce, soot-gray waves which gained steadily in height throughout the day.

Every beam and plank groaned and protested against the assault. Even after the crew had taken in the badly fished sails, the vessel continued to roll and pitch.

Having lived all his life on Aquidneck, Ashton had weathered years of storms, rescuing drowning livestock and dodging scattered debris. But here, on the churning crests of the waves, he felt himself in the very grasp of the storm.

He wanted desperately to go to Bethany, whom he'd left tousled by his love and probably doubting his sanity as well as his sentiments. He ought to have whispered his love on bended knee instead of bellowing it like a madman. But rather than retreating to their cabin, he found himself slipping along the treacherous topsides, clutching at the rigging as he helped clear the decks and batten openings.

"One hand for the ship and one hand for yourself," one of the crew cautioned. Ashton soon appreciated that wisdom. In reaching for some loose shrouds, he let up his grasp on the spars and nearly fell from the heaving decks. For a moment he clutched the spars, shaken by a vision of himself swept away on the crest of a yawning wave or blown aside by the awesome force of the wind. His new hope of regaining Bethany made him cautious.

Doggedly he moved down the decks, fastening canvas and stowing cargo. The day crept by, as dark as twilight. By evening Ashton's empty stomach whined for food and his fatigued muscles screamed for respite.

But the work was far from over. At the tiller Gaston and several others strained to steer the ship. The helmsmen called for help. Sweat mingled with rain and seawater, streaming down Ashton's face. The cords of his neck stood out as he gritted his teeth and braced himself alongside Gaston. It seemed he'd been struggling for hours when the steerage loosened suddenly.

A grinding of chains and a rending of wood deep in the

ship's belly reached his ears. The lever in Ashton's hands swung free, knocking him off his feet. Scrambling up, he recaptured the lever; it felt curiously slack in his grasp.

"Casse," Gaston shouted above the storm. "The rudder is broken. We are at the mercy of the waves now." The little Frenchman crossed himself and glanced fearfully to the west. Nothing was visible through the heavy squall, yet Ashton was aware of the dangerous stands of jagged rocks piercing the shoreline and the deadly *chevaux de frise* lurking in the bay.

Ashton relinquished his hold. He'd never felt more tired, more utterly drained and beaten. Not even the foulest-tempered horse had ever fought him like this vast, inky, churning ocean.

"Go and take some food to your wife, *copain,"* Gaston said. "The galley fires will have been put out, but there is plenty of beer and wine and biscuit."

"Come with me, Gaston. We can leave the broken rudder to the pilots."

Gaston grinned a little sheepishly. "My roots are in Provence, but my home has been a deck these thirty years. Yet I still suffer from the *mal de mer.* I cannot go below."

Ashton patted his shoulder sympathetically. *"Dommage,"* he said. "Hold tight, then. I'm going to see my wife."

Gaston nodded and turned to look at the sky. His tired eyes, squinted against the slanting rain, seemed to beseech the heavens to cease their downpour.

Poised above a ladder, Ashton heard the wind rise to a deafening howl. He glanced back, horrified to see that the mainmast was cracking. The huge beam gave way like a tall pine beneath a wood butcher's axe and crashed to the decks, bringing the mizzenmast with it.

Ashton reclosed the hatch and pounded across the deck. As he'd dreaded, Gaston's body lay crushed under the toppled mainmast. Bellowing for assistance, Ashton dragged the limp, bloody form free. A young and terrified crewman joined him.

"En bas!" the man cried, gesturing, and they shared the burden of Gaston's body.

Ashton nodded. He caught at the rail with one hand and

placed the other around Gaston, working his way down the decks. The *Languedoc* rolled abominably and the port side sank down to meet the huge curtain of water, inundating the three men. The wave was so deep and so slow to retreat that Ashton thought they would all drown. His tired, raw hand clung to the rail, and his grief-stricken mind clung to thoughts of Bethany . . . and survival.

At last the column of water rolled away and Ashton's lungs nearly exploded as he gulped for air. Gaston remained in his hold, but the young crewman was gone, snatched into the sea by the force of the wave. Cursing, Ashton struggled down to the main deck, battening the hatches behind him. Men clustered around Gaston, shaking their heads, some of them weeping openly because the little man with the gamin smile was dead. Ashton buried his face in his hands, cursed vividly, then went to find his wife.

Bethany sat on the bunk in the dim cabin, clutching at the sides to keep from being tossed to the planks. Her appearance was as tousled as when he'd last seen her, yet now she was pale and frightened, her hair disheveled as though she hadn't bothered to comb it since morning. Her chemise and petticoat were fastened about her in haphazard fashion.

She stared openmouthed at Ashton, and he realized what a spectacle he must appear. Soaked a hundred times over by rain and sea, his loose shirt was plastered against his chest and shoulders. Gaston's blood stained his clothing, and his boots bubbled and seethed with wetness.

Bethany noticed bruises on his arms and one on his cheekbone. She scrambled up, swaying precariously with the motion of the ship, and came toward him.

Somehow she understood he was suffering from something far more deadly than simple exhaustion. His weariness was of the mind as well as of the muscle. Ragged lines etched his weary face; a dull light of loss and hopelessness glimmered weakly in his eyes.

"An accident?" she asked.

"Aye. Gaston, the helmsman. He was crushed when the mast fell."

"You're shivering. Give me that wet shirt; you'll be warmer without it."

With slow, weary movements he peeled the shirt off. She sat him down on the bunk and removed his sodden boots and stockings. Without so much as a blush she demanded his trousers, handing him a blanket to wrap around his waist. She took up a towel and began to dry him, starting with his hair, then daubing his bruised face and brawny torso and back. Ashton sat passively, lulled by her touch and the relative quiet of the cabin's interior. "You're an angel," he murmured, then slid into exhausted slumber.

Bethany caught her breath at the sight of his legs. The shins and knees were horribly bruised. Bending, she kissed a swelling knot on his knee, then left him briefly to hang his dripping clothes on hooks beside the door.

The storm still raged with devilish vengeance, yet Bethany felt oddly at peace as she finished the task and sat on the edge of the bunk. Absently she smoothed a damp chestnut lock from Ashton's forehead, thinking, What an odd pair we are. We swing back and forth like this damnable ship, back and forth, never finding an even keel.

She lay down beside Ashton. Damn this flagship, she thought. Damn this war. Damn everything that came between a husband and wife and child who wanted desperately to be together, but were thwarted by events not of their making.

The storm's fury seemed to have abated somewhat, but the darkness to which Ashton awoke was meaningless. It could still be the middle of the night or well past dawn; clouds kept the sky perpetually obscured.

The warm presence at his side brought a smile to his lips. Bethany had been so frightened, and he so weak. Yet she had risen above her fear to see to his comfort. He climbed over her fragrant, sleeping form, careful not to awaken her, and reached for his still damp clothes. His flesh shrank from contact with the cold garments, but he braced himself against the chill and dressed quickly.

In the galley he found a lot of weary French seamen

and deathly quiet Americans. Finley managed a quavering, seasick greeting.

"*Salut,*" he said. His French accent was poor and the others laughed. "How do you like life under sail now, my friend?"

"What sails?" Ashton asked darkly.

"Ah," replied Rimbaud, a lieutenant, "but you must admit our life does offer a certain appeal, eh?"

"Appeal? Not for this landlubber." Ashton grasped a mug of small beer and took a sip. "I'm a horseman."

The others who understood made a few disparaging though good-natured remarks. "This one," Rimbaud said, "this big American, has more skills and fortitude than five men together. He proved that yesterday, working the tiller, then bringing our own Gaston to us."

Ashton sent Rimbaud a brief nod before going topside. Through a curtain of gray rain and in the occasional flashes of lightning, other ships were now visible, saved from the rocks by a timely wind shift. Those whose colors hadn't been struck still bore the fleur-de-lis. But the English were still about, he knew. Not even Black Dick Howe would have tried to navigate during the tempest.

The billowy white clouds of fair weather were piled against a sky of sharp azure. At dawn the storm had departed, leaving death and damage in its wake.

In the cabin where he'd passed a restless night, Ashton felt his leaden heart lift at the sight of his sleeping wife. In slumber her bright beauty was gently muted, though no less striking. He would have liked to stay and kiss her to wakefulness, but he had other pressing tasks.

His first was to convince d'Estaing to put Bethany and the other hostages ashore. But the count refused to spare an ear for him. He had a dismasted ship to deal with; the *Languedoc* would have to be towed into harbor.

The French fleet maneuvered back and forth, plagued by cannon fire from the British vessels. Working feverishly, for the broken flagship was an easy target, the crew managed to put two of the stern guns in working order.

They might have started working on the other eighty-eight, but toward evening a new threat appeared.

"The *Renown,*" came a shout from astern. Ashton stared at the approaching ship. The vessel belched iron balls at the *Languedoc,* ripping holes in her broadsides and thundering across her decks. Ashton helped man the pumps, wishing he were below, comforting Bethany.

D'Estaing shouted an order above the cannonade pouring from the *Renown.* The *Languedoc*'s proud colors were struck.

Realizing the meaning of that gesture, Ashton and the Americans tried to intervene.

"Not yet," Finley begged the count. "Look, some of our sister ships are moving to defend us. And night's coming on."

D'Estaing looked haughty and severe. "We are nothing but a wreck of splintered timber, with no steerage, nothing to steady us." He turned away from Finley and issued an order in French.

Lieutenant Rimbaud brought forth a sealed coffer of official papers.

The Americans looked on in frustration as d'Estaing unlocked the box and emptied its contents over the side. "At least the English will not find our secrets," he muttered.

Although the British fleet ceased firing at dusk, as beleaguered by the gale as the French, and limped home to New York, more bad news reached the *Languedoc* from a scouting vessel.

Vice Admiral John Byron's fleet had come to reinforce Howe. D'Estaing sent his hands into the air with a dramatic flourish and declared his flotilla incapable of any defense.

"Cowardly Frenchmen," Finley growled to Ashton. "Of course we can make a stand. Pray God General Sullivan can convince the count."

Bethany prayed that, in the purple twilight of the peaceful evening, no one had seen what she had seen from the tiny portal in her airless cabin. By the time she had donned her gown and raked order into her hair with her fingers, she was certain the tender bobbing in the dark waters about fifty yards distant had not been remarked upon by the French ships.

Dark was nearly full upon the bay as she squinted for a last glimpse of the tender. Then she left the cabin to find Ashton. The storm had been over for hours and she longed to see that he was safe and to beg him to escape with her. Surely he would agree.

Resolute and no longer afraid of the leering Frenchmen, she climbed to the top deck and wove her way along the stern side, searching for Ashton in the shadows of the broken masts. As she passed by the door to the captain's stateroom, she heard voices, and froze.

The door was slightly ajar. "You must understand my position, General Sullivan," d'Estaing was saying. "My first obligation is to the fleet."

" 'Twould take so little time," replied a gruff voice, which Bethany attributed to the patriot John Sullivan. Apparently he'd boarded after the storm. "Just give us twenty-four hours—"

"You do not need my broken fleet," d'Estaing said with conviction. "Take Newport on your own."

"With what?" Sullivan bellowed. "Listen, Admiral, the storm wasn't much kinder to us than it was to you. The wind blew down every tent. Our powder got wet; 'tis completely useless. Dozens of General Greene's and my men drowned, lying under fences, covered with water."

"Surely the British are no better off."

"I say they are, damn you! If you desert me now, I'll be forced to retreat."

Bethany heard a heavy and overdramatic sigh followed by the loud crash of a fist hitting a table. "*Alors,*" d'Estaing barked, "what you angry Americans fail to understand is that France is fighting a global war. Your thirteen states are but one theater and not necessarily the most important one. France has possessions in the West Indies which need watching far more than this defeated port city."

"What of the alliance?" Sullivan demanded bitterly.

"I must put into Boston for refitting and then go on to the West Indies, according to my orders. And I must waste no time; Byron is at our very heels."

"Orders be damned!" Ashton's voice was a sudden and unexpected roar that set Bethany's teeth to chattering. "Newport is ours for the taking, Admiral, if you'd just render us the support you've promised."

Bethany heard d'Estaing clear his throat. "You Americans are a brash, insubordinate lot. Leave me now. We sail for Boston at midnight. And as to your request on behalf of the hostages, Monsieur Markham, I must say no. Some of my men have been taken prisoner on the island. I shall need the Tories to exchange for them. The hostages will come to Boston."

Ashton burst from the stateroom, cursing bitterly. He stopped short when he saw Bethany. "Pet, you shouldn't—"

"I will not go to Boston," she interrupted. "I'd sooner swim to Aquidneck!"

"D'Estaing's just sulking because his ship's been wrecked," Ashton said, visibly trying to control his anger. "He'll come around. General Sullivan will convince him to stay in Newport."

A curse exploded from the stateroom. "The General sounds the very essence of diplomacy," Bethany said wryly.

"Just give us a few more hours." He took her by the shoulders and his lips skimmed her forehead. "Please."

"No." Bethany looked up at him beseechingly. "Ashton, we've been on this French wreck long enough. I want to see Henry again. I want to go home." She took his hand and drew him to the rail. "Look, Ashton, at that abandoned tender out there. We could swim for it and be home by daylight."

He glanced at the small craft, then shook his head. "I can't leave now. We're so close to winning Newport back. Besides, that tender looks none too sturdy, and these waters are full of dangers. Go below to the cabin, love, and I'll return and talk to d'Estaing again."

Her shoulders slumped. Ashton and his damned cause. He wouldn't put it aside even this once for her. Extracting her hand from his, she left him standing outside the stateroom.

Ashton watched her go, feeling torn. He understood her

longing for Henry and home; he prayed she understood the commitment that kept him from doing her bidding.

"Bethany looks none too pleased with you," Finley observed, mounting to the stern.

Ashton nodded. "With good reason."

"Don't look so glum, my friend. Do you realize Newport will be ours as soon as we convince d'Estaing to stay? 'Tis the fulfillment of our dream, Ashton!"

He shook his head. "I don't know, Finley. Maybe I'm following the wrong dream. Maybe the right dream just walked away from me."

Her eyes fastened on the barely discernible shape of the tender, Bethany stole across the deck and found the cap, a rope ladder, swinging gently down to the waterline. Twenty-four hours indeed, she thought, grasping the cap. She wasn't about to remain on this wreck and risk being taken to Boston. Swallowing a surge of trepidation and hoping Ashton would understand, she climbed down and slipped into the water.

Her gown immediately became a too heavy weight. Hooking her leg around the cap, she stripped down to her shift and set her gown and petticoat adrift. The idea of going ashore in her shift was daunting indeed, but over the course of the war she had acquired enough aplomb to cope with all manner of disapproval.

Striking out with the sure strokes Ashton had taught her years ago, she approached the tender. Concentrating on the muted sounds of the ocean and her own rhythmic gasps for air, she tried not to think about the sharks she knew frequented these waters. According to sailors' lore, the beasts could strip a body of flesh in a matter of minutes. Instead she focused on a distinct feeling of satisfaction, for she had gained freedom all on her own.

The tender was more distant than she'd reckoned. To preserve her strength, she floated on her back for a few moments. A southerly current from the dozens of rivers emptying into the bay began to tug her back toward the French flotilla. Her defying muscles screaming out for mercy, she began to swim again.

She collided with the sodden wood of the supply boat.

Tears of gratitude streamed from her eyes as she heaved herself up and over the side.

And found herself sprawled across two dead bodies.

She would have screamed had she not been so breathless. Instead she recoiled in horror and scrambled off the lifeless forms of a man and woman. Huddling as far from them as possible, she peered through the gloom. Cannon fire had shattered the woman's face; the man's chest was a dark hole from which an unspeakable stench emanated. His eyes were open and staring. And his face . . . was one she recognized.

Bug Willie. Suddenly Bethany realized what had happened. Bug Willie had undoubtedly been smuggling supplies and had brought a female companion along, probably a starving refugee from the wharves. His greed had cost two lives.

Aware that she would soon be missed, and unwilling to row ashore with the corpses, Bethany gritted her teeth and set to work. She surprised herself with her presence of mind. The stench and the feel of slack limbs and formless flesh should by rights have brought her to her knees with revulsion, yet her mind worked with clarity. The woman's dress was of cheap stuff, but it would serve Bethany well enough. The fabric tore slightly as she removed it. The hair, stiff with spindrift, had a texture so like Bethany's own that she shivered. Although it was too dark to tell, she imagined its color matched her own.

Having completed the gruesome task, Bethany choked out a disjointed prayer and heaved the bodies over the side, to become fodder for the scavengers of the bay. A large piece of the boat's stern came away, but she meant to reach shore before the vessel sank.

She took up the oars and began rowing. The sensation of freedom had lost its sweet taste, but she had not lost her purpose.

Finley understood all too well the awe and fear he observed on the faces of the sailors of the *Languedoc.*

Ashton Markham was a man not of this earth.

On the top deck, beneath the splintered shafts of the

masts and amid the tangled coils of useless rigging and shrouds, the men stepped back to give him a wide berth.

He was a fearsome sight: hair wild and plastered to his pale cheeks, eyes alight with beastlike rage, his entire frame shaking from hours of swimming the bay in a desperate search for his wife.

A search that had yielded flotsam from the tender and the gruesome remains of his wife. Finley shuddered. The cover of night could not disguise the fact that marine scavengers had transformed Bethany's body into fragments of flesh and bone. Not a trace remained of her lovely face; only a few strands of dark blond hair were left. The hand that had worn a wedding ring was missing.

When he could not stand the fearsome pain any longer, Finley snatched up a sodden sailcloth bag and emptied its contents heedlessly on the deck. Hurrying to Ashton, he moved to take the hideous burden.

"No," Ashton whispered in a voice Finley had never heard before. "Don't take her from me—"

At a gesture from Finley some of the sailors stepped forward, their faces pale and horrified in the moonlight. They had to wrest the body from Ashton, thrusting it into the bag.

"Let her go, Ashton," Finley instructed hoarsely. "Let her go, so she can be at peace." He fastened the bag securely and, leading Ashton like a child, brought him to the rail. Placing the bag in his arms, Finley urged his friend to send Bethany to her grave. He experienced a moment of trepidation as Ashton clutched the dark, wet bundle to his chest. Finley worried that his friend would attempt to follow his wife in death.

"Think of your son, Ashton," he urged. "Think of Henry. He'll need you now more than ever."

His words seemed to penetrate the chilling mask of grief. With sudden resolution Ashton murmured some incoherent phrase and slipped the bag into the dark bay waters.

Taking his friend by the shoulders, Finley led him away from the rail. The older man's heart ached at the sight of his shattered and devastated friend, but no words of comfort came to mind.

A nearby sailor murmured something in French and pushed a flask into Finley's hand. He uncapped it and his nostrils were filled with the smell of good brandy. He placed the flask in Ashton's hand.

"Drink," he said.

Ashton stared numbly at the flask. His hands twitched convulsively, but he made no move to drink.

"Did I swill ten like that," he said in an alien, rasping voice, " 'twould hardly numb my pain."

Finley sucked in his breath and felt a rending sensation in his heart. "God. I don't know what to say."

Ashton turned away. He heard Finley's pained words as if from a great distance, as if the message were shouted from a world Ashton no longer belonged to. He dropped the flask, certain no mortal potion could dull his grief. With slow, shaking steps he trod the length of the deck, stopping only when he reached the rail at the bowsprit.

"Bethany." He whispered her name to the night sky and heard the faint sound like another's voice die on the gentle soughing of the wind.

Dissatisfied at his attempt to send her name to the heavens, Ashton muttered a curse. Slowly, like a man awakening from a nightmare, he became aware of an unfamiliar wetness on his cheeks. He raised a trembling finger to his face, feeling his own tears for the first time in his memory.

He recalled that Bethany had urged him to cry, those three years ago when he'd lost his father. You've made me cry now, love, he told her silently. But look what you had to do to bring me to tears.

Ashton spoke his beloved's name again, this time with a scream that poured from his throat like an onrushing tide of agony.

Chapter 24

Bethany sat, aching and dry-mouthed, beneath an overhanging bank on the mainland side of the Sakonnet. A stiff northerly wind and the strong surge of an incoming tide, combined with hours of dogged rowing, had delivered her safely from the bay.

She was proud of herself for escaping a humiliating and unnecessary trip to Boston. But, her fatigue-battered brain reminded her, the cost of freedom was dear. In fleeing the *Languedoc* she'd also fled Ashton, doubtless destroying the healing that had taken place between them. Maybe, she told herself despondently, maybe he would understand her desperate need to rejoin her son. She considered that hope with a sigh.

Aquidneck lay at the opposite bank, a mile to the west, so she couldn't consider her nightlong journey a complete success—not yet. But with her feet planted solidly on the mainland, nothing could compel her to get into the tender again. The leaky craft rode dangerously close to the waterline, and hours of rowing had left her muscles as soft as pudding.

Weary to the marrow, hunger pangs gnawing at her belly, she eyed her surroundings. The bank gave way to a thick wood which wore an early-morning shroud of fog. Though unfamiliar with the area, she knew Tiverton lay to the north and Little Compton to the south.

Her grip was weak on the dew-slick grasses at the water's edge, her hands numb and blistered from wielding the oars. Muddying the gaudy cherry lutestring dress she'd pilfered from Bug Willie's woman, she gained the top of the bank and paused, gulping the mist-thick air of dawn. Upriver, barely visible through the haze, she noticed an ominously endless flotilla of boats slipping silently across the river from Aquidneck. Unable to tell whether the transports were American or British, she scrambled to the shelter of the woods.

She glanced northward, wondering how far Tiverton was. Tiverton . . . Sudden realization rang clarion-clear in her exhausted mind. Miss Abigail lived near that town, in the house belonging to Finley's widowed brother.

Bethany struck northward, hope quickening her pace and a breeze drying her hair and clothes. Scaring up sweet-voiced larks and scolding chipmunks, she trekked through bracken and wild sorrel thorn. Her bare feet crushed tender and pungent leaves of spearmint.

Glancing up, she discerned fog threading skyward. Or was that smoke? Realizing she must be nearing the town, she felt her heart lift. She began to run, her feet slipping and sliding. She emerged from the woods and caught her breath at the devastating sight.

Tiverton, if indeed she had found it, had become a fire-gutted place of outcasts. Mildewed sailcloth battened across cellar holes provided scant shelter. Board shacks and brush lean-tos, some of them burned, all of them gutted, lined the muddy track.

For a moment Bethany was so stunned by the destruction that she didn't realize the town was nearly deserted. Ragtag bits of humanity miserably clothed in homespun scurried northward, women burdened by crying children, old and crippled men carrying pitchforks and spades.

Beyond the rubble she spied a number of soldiers, most of them Negroes. Although the men were clad in the buff and blue of the patriots, she felt no fear. They were shouting at the townsfolk, urging them to evacuate their crude shelters.

Hesitantly, clutching the immodest bodice of her red dress, Bethany approached a man crouched beside a blackened cellar hole. "Please," she said softly. "What's happened here?"

At first she thought the man hadn't head her and began to repeat her question, then realized his body was convulsed by eerie, voiceless laughter. The man raised a face so marred by smallpox that she had to school herself not to glance away, reminded of the disease that had killed William. She waited in trepidation for his silent, spasmodic laughter to abate.

"You don't know?" the man asked.

She shook her head. "I—I've only just arrived."

"Have you not eyes to see?" he demanded. "War!" The word was a bitter burst of sound. "That's what's happened, missy. If you know what's good for you, you'll take to the woods. The Negro regiment's come to warn us the British and Hessians are chasing in from the river."

The British army and their hired German killers no longer meant sanity and security to Bethany. Somehow she felt safer in the company of the Americans. She plunged after the fleeing townsfolk and didn't stop until a sight even more appalling than the devastated village arrested her.

An ill-clad woman, her blunt-featured face twisted with agony, unwashed children clinging to her skirts, stood in a clearing, aiming a rusty flintlock pistol at a horse.

Bethany ran forward and seized the woman's arm. "Are you mad?" she demanded. "Would you shoot this poor beast in the sight of your children?"

The woman wrenched free, pulling her lips back in a bitter, gap-toothed sneer. "Better I kill the mare than leave her for the Redcoats to take."

"One horse," Bethany exclaimed in horror. "What would the soldiers want with one horse?"

" 'Tis all they need to tote one of their big guns. Christ." The woman looked pained. "I don't like doing away with Bridie any more than you do, but—"

"Perhaps you could outrun the soldiers."

"With this brood of mine?" The woman's eyes flicked back to the river road. "For God's sake, they're the enemy! 'Pon my faith, how can I give them this horse?" Hands that should have been grinding corn with a quern now cocked the pistol. The barrel wavered slightly, then the woman fitted it against the horse's broad brow.

"Hab," she commanded in a ragged but determined voice, "take the little ones off into the woods and wait for me.'' The oldest child shepherded his terror-stricken siblings away.

The finger, its nail chewed to the quick, tightened on the trigger.

''No!'' The scream ripped from Bethany's throat.

''Wait!'' A basso bellow mingled with her voice.

Bethany and Justice Richmond reached the horse at the same time. Although questions furrowed Richmond's dark brow, he turned away to address the woman.

''I'll see to the horse, ma'am,'' he said, taking the bridle. ''The Redcoats won't get her.'' He jerked his head toward the north. ''Take yourself and your children to safety.''

''But you can't—''

''Let him try,'' Bethany pleaded. ''I know this man well, and he knows horses. Please.''

The woman nodded briefly and followed her children.

In seconds Justice was on the mare's back. He gripped Bethany's arm and swung her up behind him. The mare grunted and started off in a reluctant trot.

''Justice, what—''

''I'm takin' you to the Piper farm. 'Tis safer there.''

Under Justice Richmond's expert guidance the mare showed more heart than Bethany could have credited a farm plug with. The trot quickened to an unschooled but brisk canter.

''What's happening, Justice?'' she asked over his shoulder, alarmed by the scent of burned powder that clung to his woolen coat. ''What are you doing here?''

''Reckon I'm a soldier. Joined up with Chris Greene's regiment. We're trying to protect General Sullivan's command as he withdraws.'' He flashed a quick look behind. ''What about you, Mrs. Markham?''

Briefly, trying not to think about Ashton, she sketched out her kidnapping and subsequent escape from the *Languedoc.*

''You were with the French?'' Justice asked incredulously. ''Why didn't you stay? We're allies, for God's sake.''

''But they're the—'' Bethany broke off and closed her mouth. The enemy? After all the years of the war, she wasn't sure anymore. She'd been harmed by Americans and British alike. "I just wanted to get away," she finished weakly. "I wanted to get to Henry."

They emerged from the woods into a clearing planted with tassel-topped corn. In the distance Bethany saw a few outbuildings and a small house. Primroses, their yellow heads closed against the morning light, grew in clumps in the dooryard.

"The Piper place." Justice helped her down. "Be careful," he admonished her. "Take care of that boy."

"Won't you stay, Justice?"

He shook his head, looking grave. "I've fightin' to do." He turned the horse and disappeared into the woods.

As she approached the house, Bethany heard a vague rumble, like distant thunder. Dear God, was she hearing cannon fire? Shuddering, she went to the Dutch door, the top half of which was open to the foggy morning air.

She caught a glimpse of a woman sitting at the kitchen table, her face obscured by dark hair tumbling neglectedly down her back; a shapeless sacque dress was draped over a belly big with child. In her hands the woman held an iron instrument. Scissors? No, nothing so homey and familiar as that. The tool was a bullet mold, of all things. A decidedly curious way for a woman to wait out her confinement.

Bethany frowned. Stephen Piper was a widower, so who was this woman? Suddenly self-conscious, she knocked softly.

The woman turned. Bethany felt her eyes widen in wonderment. "You—"

"Close your mouth, girl. We are not a flytrap."

Butterflies scattered through the grass-sweet air around Ashton. The air was alive with bird song. Leaves, tickled by the summer wind, sang a soft, restless song.

But Ashton noticed little of the beauty around him. His eyes were riveted on the scene below the knoll where he and Finley stood. A hundred yards distant, against a relief of verdant woods and misty sky, a battle raged.

"Damn," said Finley, puffing with exertion from their hike inland. "I thought when d'Estaing put us ashore we'd find the Americans victorious, but it seems everything's gone wrong. Sullivan must've had to beat a retreat from Aquidneck."

Ashton nodded. At first the Americans had approached the British lines with confidence, even mocking the enemy's formal fighting style. But then a six-pounder had been pulled in on a field carriage. All joking ceased when the big gun began to score.

Finley's weary eyes scoured the battlefield. "That cannon'll blow them to Little Compton, for God's sake. Why don't the patriots retreat?"

Ashton blinked as he watched the British cannon recoil, spitting iron into the American ranks. He glanced dispassionately away. The man he had been before losing Bethany would have been appalled at the carnage. The man he was now felt a strange, joyless pride in the brash Americans who stood their ground against the determined Redcoats. Even in defeat the patriots were superb, refusing to yield even as they faced the deadly cannonade. His glance caught a movement off to the right.

"There's your answer, Finley," he said. "That's why the Americans aren't retreating. The cavalry—such as it is—has arrived."

Finley watched the approaching mounted company with a dubious look on his grizzled face. "Now I see what Pontgibaud meant. A flock of ducks in cross belts—and this flock seems leaderless."

It was true, Ashton saw. The company rode up the knoll in haphazard fashion, some allowing their horses to stray and graze. One of the men spurred his mount to a gallop, calling Ashton's name.

Beneath an oozing bandage, Ashton saw a pair of familiar hazel eyes and felt a shock of pain so intense it took his breath away. Bethany's ghost haunted her twin brother's broad grin. Sliding a glance at Finley, he realized the older man's thoughts mirrored his. Neither of them wanted to tell Harry Winslow of his sister's death.

As it turned out, neither had a chance to speak of Bethany. The company all began talking at once. From snippets of conversation Ashton learned no officer was among them.

"Aye," Harry explained, looking pale and grim beneath the bandage around his head, "Captain Tarnover was killed by snipers, and his second-in-command took to the woods." Harry drove a fist into the palm of his hand. "Damn. We were going to charge the cannon."

Ashton eyed the cavalry unit dubiously. The disorganized company of callow farm boys and worsted-stocking knaves looked incapable of treeing a squirrel, much less charging a cannon. With a leader, perhaps they might mount an assault. But, injured and confused, none of them appeared capable or inclined to spearhead the charge.

Scowling, Ashton looked back at the battlefield. Things were worse than ever; British reinforcements were closing in on the right flank. At the head of the new contingent was a red-frocked officer on a prancing midnight stallion.

Ashton took a step forward. "Tanner," he exclaimed softly. "By God, he's on Corsair."

"The bastard must've stolen your horse from the Middletown farm," Finley said darkly.

The Thoroughbred danced wildly and Tanner sawed cruelly on the reins. "By God," Ashton swore, "Corsair isn't battle-trained."

But the mount was trained to obey—by Ashton's own hand.

"Let's go," Finley said wearily. "I don't want to stay and watch this. My brother's farm is three miles to the south. If we skirt the fighting, we'll get there safely enough." He started down the hill. In Finley's shoulders Ashton recognized the weary look of a homing man. He paused, looking back. "Are you coming, Ashton?"

Slowly Ashton shook his head. "I'm staying, Finley," he said dully. "I'm going to lead the charge on the cannon."

Incredulous, Finley spread his hands. "You? Lead a charge? Good God, Ashton, you swore you'd never take up arms against another man."

"That was . . . when I still cared."

"Don't you care about your son?"

"Aye," Ashton admitted. "But Bethany has left me to the wreckage of myself. Henry has no need of the person I've become. I took care of his future before we boarded the flagship, although I thought I, not Bethany, was at risk of not returning. Harry will raise the boy."

"God, Ashton, you'll be sliced to ribbons." He looked down at the Redcoats, who formed a bristling wall of bayoneted Brown Bess muskets around the cannon. Then his eyes returned to Ashton. ''I don't like that look on your face, my friend. You're not afraid, are you?''

''No,'' he replied with total honesty. It was true; it was easy to be brave when there was nothing left to live for.

''But you haven't got a horse,'' Finley maintained.

Ashton's smile was a humorless ghost about his lips. ''Oh, I've a horse,'' he assured his friend. Turning, he placed his fingers to his lips and gave a single high-pitched whistle.

On the battlefield below, he saw Corsair grow still for a moment, ears pricked. Encouraged, Ashton tried again. This time Corsair tried to break Tanner's restraining hold. Tanner jerked back on the reins. Furiously Ashton repeated the whistle again and again. Finally, as if drawn by some irresistible force, Corsair rose, pawing the air with his forelegs, jerking his head back in the sly old trick Ashton had never been able to school completely out of him.

Tanner, encumbered by full battle regalia, was unable to evade the swift back-arching motion of the stallion's head. He lost his grip on the reins and fell to the ground.

Ashton felt a dark surge of victory as Corsair trampled the Redcoat, broke free of the confusion around the cannon, and thundered up the hill toward his master.

Bethany sat sipping a mug of strong chicory brew, trying not to sway with exhaustion. She was unable to talk about her ordeal on the *Languedoc,* even to her dearest friend, Abigail. Her feelings were still too raw, too unformed. She couldn't probe the open wound of her emotions, not so soon and not in her overtired state. Abigail seemed, understandably, most interested in the fact that Finley had survived the storm at sea.

As she calmly continued molding bullets from melted lead, Abigail seemed to sense Bethany's reluctance to talk. And so Abigail spoke, of her marriage to Finley, her elation over the babe, her utter contentment to live in simplicity on the farm. Even the constant thunder of distant cannon fire didn't seem to disturb her.

''Are you truly happy?'' Bethany asked.

Abigail's smile was soft and womanly. ''Supremely. Oh,

we have our little differences. I, of course, sleep neatly, while Finley thrashes unforgivably all the night through. Still, such complaints are minor."

Watching the small hands deftly wielding the bullet mold, Bethany realized how much Abigail had changed—from an impoverished and overeducated gentlewoman to a person whose hands were no longer perfectly manicured but rough from doing daily chores.

Bethany frowned as she stared with glazed eyes at the growing pile of bullets.

"I had no idea the Royal Army needed bullets."

Abigail looked genuinely surprised. "The Royal Army? Of course not! Bethany, dear, these bullets are for the Americans." She took up a jackknife and began trimming the sprues off the new bullets.

Bethany drew herself to immediate wakefulness. "You mean—"

"Yes." Abigail smiled. "My husband has finally shown me that we are no longer English, but Americans. Me . . . and you, Bethany." Regret mingled with hope in the pussy willow gray of her eyes. "I used to think of the war as a bitter family quarrel, a clash of brother against brother, but I was wrong. Perhaps it all began long before our time, in the minds and hearts of the very first people who settled here. This conflict involves another breed of men entirely . . . who no longer think of themselves as Englishmen."

Images crowded, unbidden, into Bethany's mind: Finley, changing from ordinary printer to extraordinary patriot; mobs surging through the streets of Newport demanding no more than what they considered their natural-born rights; Goody Haas, righteously indignant that English law allowed her to grow and spin flax into linen, but forced her to ship it to England to be woven into cloth; the poor, fleeing woman in the woods who would have killed the family horse before ceding it to the enemy. . . .

Her swirling thoughts turned inevitably to Ashton. Ashton, bursting with pride as he held his infant son to hear the reading of the Declaration of Independence. Ashton, riding missions so dangerous, even the Committee of Safety had begged him to stop.

Her husband, Bethany realized with wonder and even

pride, was no more an Englishman than a draft horse was a Thoroughbred.

Bethany looked across the table at Abigail, who had once served England at great risk to herself. Bullet molding was repetitive and boring, but the softness in her eyes told Bethany the mundane chore was a labor of devotion . . . of new commitment.

Teetering on the precipice of a great leap of allegiance, Bethany asked, "What if the reb—the Americans are defeated?"

"We won't be," Abigail said with certainty, scraping the sprues back into the melting pan. "If it takes a hundred years, we'll fight to be free." A sweet-sad smile curved her lips. "I'm not trying to make you change your mind, Bethany. But look what you've become in the past four years. Is there anything about you that even vaguely resembles an Englishwoman?"

"A proper English lady," Bethany said dully, "would be scandalized at the things I've done. Dorian has said so many times."

Abigail set the knife on the table with a clatter. Her eyes hardened to the cool gray of steel. "Do you still credit that scoundrel's opinion after what you know of him?"

Bethany shrugged. "Not really. In truth, Dorian and I often clash. And as for what I know of him, that's little enough."

"Little enough?" The gray eyes narrowed. "Is it not enough to know Captain Tanner staged the raid on Seastone and tried to have your husband hanged for the deed?"

Bethany went completely still and felt the color drop from her face. Her stomach turned to a cold fist of dread.

"What did you say?" she whispered.

Abigail blinked. "Oh, dear God," she said. "Harry didn't find you, did he?"

"I haven't seen Harry since my son's birthday in April."

"He was coming to show you proof that Dorian Tanner planned the raid." Quickly Abigail related the bits of information she and Harry had discovered.

Bethany nearly stopped breathing. Her tears had the sting of Dorian's betrayal, the burn of humiliation that she'd allowed herself to be duped by his smooth wiles, and the searing heat of remorse, for she'd blamed Ashton for a crime he hadn't committed.

As she mentally reeled like a ship heeling in a storm, Abigail spoke on. "I know some other things about Tanner as well. It seems he's not the well-born gentleman he'd like the world to believe. He is the son of a London tanner. At a young age he joined a traveling carnival. He excelled at horse tricks and caught the notice of an English lord, who bought his commission."

"How could I have been so wrong?" Bethany wondered aloud through a painful haze of regret. "Ashton must hate me for not believing him."

"When he had his doubts about you, did you hate him?" Abigail countered.

Bethany shook her head. Loving Ashton had always been as natural and necessary to her as breathing. She thought of their time together on the *Languedoc,* and hope sprang like a bud bursting to flower within her. Perhaps, just perhaps, he would forgive her. But her spirits descended again.

"I don't even know where he is," she said. "He may have gone to Boston with the French."

"He did not," came an angry voice from the doorway. "Although I'm beginning to wish he had."

"Finley!" Abigail jumped up and hurried to embrace her husband.

He held her affectionately for a moment, but anger snapped in his eyes as he regarded Bethany. "What the hell are you doing here?"

Bethany was confused by his temper and far too weary for explanations. She stood up. "Please. What of Ashton?"

"What of Ashton?" he mimicked. "A fine time to show concern for your husband. You should have thought of him when you faked your own death. Did you never consider what that would do to the man?"

Bethany scowled. "What a bizarre accusation, Finley. I did no such thing."

Anger left him for a moment. "All right, maybe it wasn't intentional, but he believes you dead. Right after you disappeared, a body was found—a woman's body. Too eaten away by scavengers to distinguish, yet we could only conclude . . .'''

"Oh, God." Bethany's stomach did a sickening lurch as she recalled Bug Willie's woman. But her thoughts returned immediately to Ashton. "Finley, what of my husband?"

"You've turned a principled pacifist into a cold-blooded killer. He means to lead a charge on the British cannon."

Her heart stopped, then started a wild tattoo of terror in her chest.

"He has enough rage in him to command an entire army. Ashton has become dangerous. He fears nothing, because he believes he has lost everything."

Horrified, she started for the door. "I must go to him."

"Bethany, no—" Finley began, concerned.

Abigail took his hand. "Do you think you can stop her now, my love? Would I do any less for you?"

Finley still looked worried but stepped aside. "Have a care, Bethany," he said gruffly. "And God speed your way."

Abigail embraced Bethany, soaking the shoulder of the red dress with tears. "Look at me," she said, smiling as she wept. "At one time I thought it disgraceful to weep so openly. Now I know feelings are to be shared—even the sad ones."

Bethany battled the urge to join Abigail's sobbing. At the moment tears would hardly serve her purpose. "You must visit us at Seastone," she forced out, as if concluding a social call. "I think you'll both be pleased at some of the changes I intend to make."

"Changes?" Abigail hiccuped. "What changes?"

"I've heard our Continental Cavalry is in need of good horses. What better place to raise them than at Seastone?"

She left Abigail gaping and Finley grinning, not sparing a moment for tears or fears as she plunged through the woods to her husband.

Seated on Corsair at the head of the small company that had adopted him as its commander, Ashton felt a primal surge of power. He was empty of softer sentiments, as if Bethany's death had drained the humanity from him.

That lack of tender emotion would serve him well, he reflected darkly. Feelings had no place in a battle.

The sword given him by one of the cavalrymen was an unfamiliar encumbrance on his thigh. He glanced down at the gleaming metal peeping from the hilt. Would he be able to slice through human flesh with that blade?

He considered the plan they'd concocted. The two flanks of the foot-soldiers, beleaguered by cannon fire, would part at a signal from Ashton. He and the cavalry would then descend, hacking a path toward the cannon. If they managed to take the big gun, the Redcoats and Hessians would surely disperse, since the Americans were superior in number.

Ashton drank deep gulps of the hot summer air. He considered, with odd clarity, the very real possibility that he'd be dead in the next few moments. And he didn't care.

His hand was steady as he unsheathed his sword, raised the blade high, and barked an order. On the field below, the American ranks parted.

The bright green leaves of summer and the blood-red heads of poppies became a swirl of color as the horses galloped down the slope to the Aceldama. Ashton's heart rose to his throat; his blood pounded with a dark, awful joy.

They thundered past the American ranks and plunged into the British defense. Coming up from the side was a soldier brandishing a bayonet. Ashton's sword whistled as it sliced the air, meeting cloth and flesh and blood. A fierce cry of victory ripped from his throat.

He became aware of the burn of powder and the flashes of gunfire all around him. A musket ball buzzed past his ear like a deadly wasp. The sounds and smells and danger made him feel furiously alive.

Soldiers were all around him now, cursing yet fleeing him. Vaguely he realized he looked every bit as fierce and purposeful as he felt. Self-hatred, he reflected, must be very frightening to watch. He gained another of the scattering soldiers and swung his sword. The blow reverberated to his shoulder. When he drew his sword, it dripped crimson. Blood spattered the ground like the poppies of summer.

The area around the cannon was a scene of panic. The horsemen cantered to and fro, bellowing, brandishing swords and pistols. The Redcoats dispersed.

The smell of gunpowder seethed over the area. Ashton's head throbbed and his heart hammered.

"By God!" bellowed Harry Winslow, his young face powder-smeared, pale, and jubilant. "The devils're retreating!" A cacophony of yips and whoops rose from the rebel ranks.

Ashton's gaze swept the trampled field. Butterflies flitted over the lifeless body of a fallen Englishman.

The elemental pounding in his head subsided and he was ashamed of the violence that had possessed him during the charge. While around him the Americans tossed their hats in the air and celebrated their victory, Ashton felt himself go completely hollow. Not even the sharp sense of exhilaration animated him now.

In the past few minutes, he'd learned what war could be and what it could make a man become. Somehow, he couldn't share in their jubilation. He took Corsair off to the side, into a sheltered copse of linden trees.

Victory was as meaningless as everything else in his life now that Bethany was gone. Still, when he heard the cold, sharp click of a pistol being cocked and looked up to see the equally cold and sharp eyes of Dorian Tanner, he had no desire to die.

Yet now, it seemed, he had no choice. Although bruised by the tumble Corsair had given him, the Redcoat held the pistol steady and pointed at Ashton's head. Ashton sent a glance over his shoulder.

"You'll get no help there, you bastard," Tanner said. "I was watching and waiting for you. None of the Americans marked your exit." Laughter flowed in silky mirthlessness from the angrily curling lips. "I've waited long for this day, my friend. Your death will be the final culmination of all I've worked for. Now Bethany will be mine and I'll have complete control of Seastone—and your son."

A hideous rage built within Ashton, but all he could say was, "Bethany's dead."

The dark eyebrows cocked in brief surprise, nothing more. "I'll spare no tears for her then. The woman was comely as a spring flower but unbiddable as choke-weed. Lillian Winslow will be only too glad to hand the boy's estate to me."

In the woods behind Dorian, Ashton detected a brief

flash of red. Good God, how many others were lurking in the trees?

"Aye!" Dorian barked. "The boy will forget you before you're cold in your grave." Slowly his finger curled and tautened on the trigger.

Ashton awaited death, not with squeezed-shut eyes and sudden prayers for repentance, but with an angry glare at his executioner. Again from the corner of his eye he saw the glimmer of red and, by some trick of the light, imagined a tawny gold mane streaming out behind. God, was he dead already and in heaven with Bethany?

Tanner's laughter brought him back to earth. A final sneer of farewell slithered over the Redcoat's lips as he prepared to discharge the pistol. A blur of red flung itself on Tanner's firing arm. The pistol exploded with a streak of white light and sulphurous yellow smoke.

Ashton sprang forward to the two figures struggling on the ground. Unthinkingly he subdued Tanner with a kick to the temple. The Redcoat went slack.

Big, blunt-fingered hands closed around small, trembling ones. Eyes of unbelieving blue locked with tear-wet, sun-spangled eyes of hazel. And then yearning, thankful lips melted together in a brief, fierce kiss.

"Bethany. Oh God, I thought you—"

"I know, Ashton. 'Twas all a terrible mistake." Her palm was a warm and welcome presence on his cheek. "I've made so many mistakes, my darling. Abigail told me Dorian was responsible for the raid on Seastone. How could I ever have believed you'd do such a thing? I'll spend a lifetime earning your forgiveness . . . if you'll only let me."

"Let you?" He hauled her against him and filled his arms with her beloved, trembling warmth. "God. What a question."

"Ashton!" Harry's voice bellowed from the battlefield. "Let's go—we're giving chase!"

"No." Bethany stumbled back. "Ashton, don't go."

Coldness touched his heart. "Still the Loyalist, Bethany?"

She rushed back into his arms. "Of course not, you silly man. Do you think after all I've learned I still favor capitulation?" She looked proud and weary as she faced him. "I'm as American as you are, Ashton." She smiled. "Lately."

"Ashton?" Harry's voice reached them again. "Where the devil are you? We're leaving now. . . ."

"Don't go," Bethany said again, her eyes pleading. "Don't go to war, Ashton. You're no soldier; your skill is with horses. You can help win this war without killing. We'll train horses for the cavalry at Seastone . . . if you'll agree to live with me there," she added hesitantly.

He gathered her against him. "I'll agree on one condition, love."

"Anything."

A shower of pride and adoration burst within his chest. "You must do me the honor of letting me spend the rest of my life showing you how much I love you."

Her eyes danced with a happiness that might have driven the gods mad with envy. "You do love me, don't you, Ashton?" she said wonderingly.

"Aye, my sweet. You can't know how much."

"Oh, but I can," came the soft reply. Her smile grew slightly playful. "Still, I don't mind letting you prove your love."

Their next kiss was long and all-enveloping, healing them in a way words could not, their souls fused, bonded by love and trust and a sudden oneness of purpose.

Ashton glanced down at the defeated Redcoat. "Leave him to defend his treason on his own," he muttered, taking Bethany's hand in his and reaching for Corsair's reins. "Let's go get our son, love."

Epilogue

Newport, Rhode Island
11 July 1781

On the steps of the schoolhouse Bethany sat with her husband and tilted her eyes to the evening sky. Fireworks burst overhead, saluting the arrival of the Comte de Rochambeau's fleet. The force had come to liberate the war-ravaged city and to drop the final curtain on the war that had dragged on far too long. Distant bells tolled a welcome, and the guns in Newport's earthworks and batteries fired a welcome to the French.

Bethany's eyes returned to the garden, wandering contentedly over the slowly opening petals of the pale yellow evening primroses Ashton had planted three summers ago as a testament of his love.

She was reminded of an even more distant time, that summer in 1775 when Roger Markham had died and she had felt the first stirrings of love for his handsome son.

"You look pensive," Ashton observed, closing his warm hand over hers.

"I was just thinking," she mused, "how we used to sit together in this very spot years ago."

"Back then the summerhouse was a place to spend idle hours and not the place of learning it is now. The reputation of the Primrose Academy is growing, pet; perhaps in years to come you'll tell your students about what we've lived through these past six years . . . about Miss Abigail, the intrepid schoolmistress who was a spy; about your brother's exploits with the cavalry. . . ." His eyes darkened a shade. "Dorian Tanner's hanging for high treason may even appear in the history books."

She clutched his hand. "What about my own husband's heroism?" she asked. "Surely the historians won't ignore your charge on the British cannon in the Battle of Rhode Island!"

"I'd rather we made our own private history, Bethany. Right here at Seastone."

She nodded in agreement. In front of them, five-year-old Henry gamboled in the grass with his toddling sister, Abby, and the spaniel dog called Liberty, who somehow managed to keep a watchful eye on both children as well as her squirming litter of pups. Abigail and Finley, over from Tiverton for the celebration, strolled on the path beneath the lilacs, their daughter, Sally, swinging between them.

A distant whicker from the stables brought a smile to Bethany's lips. The horses of Seastone, once fabled for their domination of the racing green, now were destined to bear the patriots to victory. A victory Bethany wanted as much as any American. Her heart rose as a new shower of fireworks colored the sky.

"Like it?" Ashton's deep whisper stirred silky tendrils about her ear and she shivered deliciously. She'd never grow tired of his nearness, the taste of him and the sound of his voice, the splendor of his gentle touch. If anything, she loved and wanted him more with each passing day.

"Mmm . . . yes," she murmured, fitting her hand around the curve of his thigh and, wickedly, letting her touch stray upward.

"Lusty wench," he teased with a rich chuckle. "I was talking about the *feu de joie.*"

Glancing up, she said, "Lovely. A proper fuss for our liberating force—like flowers suddenly blooming. But the fireworks are so quickly gone." She snuggled against him, fitting her head into the hollow of his neck.

"I much prefer our own garden," she confessed. Her eyes moved lovingly over the soft, starlike primroses drenched in dew. As a host of encircling moon-colored moths came to sample the faint, ineffable fragrance of the flowers, Bethany leaned up in the evening light to kiss her husband.

SUSAN WIGGS

While living in Europe, SUSAN WIGGS made frequent imaginary pilgrimages into the past, sitting up all night in the fog on the boat train to England. She loved to climb the ruins of remote, crumbling keeps to smell the mustiness of the dank walls and wonder about the heroes who haunted the time-worn castles of the northern fells. ''Stories leaped out at me from every echoing hall,'' she says. ''I try to make my characters breathe life into the cobwebbed events of old. They lived and died and loved and hated as people have always done. It's fascinating to place them in their fabulous settings and test their grit.''

She continues, ''I've been asked how I can write after a day of teaching and caring for my four-year-old, Elizabeth. The truth is, writing isn't a chore for me. My husband Jay doesn't mind that I'd rather have my nose buried in a history book than in a cookbook. He's not even startled anymore when, after a long, dreamy silence, I suddenly shout, 'God's blood!' and begin scribbling furiously in a notebook as a new story springs to mind.''

Susan Wiggs is the author of the Avon Romance *Briar Rose*.